PENGUIN B

A BROTHER'S BLOOD

Michael C. White is a professor of English and creative writing at Springfield College, Massachusetts, and he is founding editor of the annual fiction anthology *American Fiction*. His own short fiction has been nominated for a Pushcart Prize and a National Magazine Award and has been published widely in national magazines and literary quarterlies. He lives in Wibraham, Massachusetts, with his wife and two children.

MICHAEL C. WHITE

A BROTHER'S BLOOD

A NOVEL

PENGUIN BOOKS

PENGUIN BOOKS

Published by the Penguin Group
Penguin Books Ltd, 27 Wrights Lane, London W8 5TZ, England
Penguin Books USA Inc., 375 Hudson Street, New York, New York 10014, USA
Penguin Books Australia Ltd, Ringwood, Victoria, Australia
Penguin Books Canada Ltd, 10 Alcorn Avenue, Toronto, Ontario, Canada M4V 3B2
Penguin Books (NZ) Ltd, 182–190 Wairau Road, Auckland 10, New Zealand

Penguin Books Ltd, Registered Offices: Harmondsworth, Middlesex, England

First published in the USA by HarperCollins 1996
Published in Penguin Books 1997
1 3 5 7 9 10 8 6 4 2

Printed in England by Clays Ltd, St Ives plc

For Karen, Caitlin, and Wesley

ACKNOWLEDGMENTS

I WOULD LIKE to thank Springfield College for its unsparing support during the writing of this book; the library staff at the University of Maine; the late Miklos Ats, a former POW, for his generous translations of German documents and for his invaluable insights into the prisoner of war experience. I would also like to acknowledge my debt to the following sources: Austin Wilkens' book *Ten Million Acres of Timber*, which included information about and pictures of the POW Camp in Seboomook, Maine, upon which the camp of this book is loosely based; to Robert Pike's wonderful and lively history of logging in New England, *Tall Trees, Tough Men*. I'd like to thank Diane Reverand and Jennifer Griffin for their support and advice. Finally, I'd like to offer a special note of gratitude to Nat Sobel for his unswerving faith and ceaseless efforts in seeing this book into print.

> "The voice of thy brother's blood crieth unto me from the ground."

—Genesis

PROLOGUE

2 JULY 44: IN CAMP two weeks already but so exhausted have not been much inclined to record thoughts. At night, crawl into bed and sleep like a rock. Close my eyes and next thing they are herding us into trucks and taking us into the woods again. All in all, should not complain. Must remind myself of horrid conditions in Mateur. Poor sanitation, cramped quarters, the freezing nights and blistering hot days. Not to mention the scorpions and sand storms. And that, of course, nothing compared to what it must be like for my dear old friend Bruno Ruppe, taken with von Paulus. We hear the most terrible rumors of what goes on in the East.

Arrived here after a long train ride from Boston, Massachusetts, U.S.A., where our ship put in. Last seventy-five kilometers rode by army truck over logging roads to what must be the most remote spot on earth. America! A place as vast as the deserts of North Africa. But instead of sand and camelthorn, endless mountains and lakes and forests stretch to the horizon. Skies the most delicate blue, perfect as Dresden china, and no planes fly overhead. Before leaving camp in Africa, some Luftwaffe fellows said States had been heavily bombed and only a matter of time before the Amis sued for peace. Utter nonsense! Quiet and peaceful here as if there were no war going on at all. Reminds one of the Oberhof, only mountains are more wooded and desolate. Nights quiet, like they could be in the desert. Hear mosquitoes buzzing over our heads and the metallic drumming of crickets in the night. Men snoring or talking in their sleep, or relieving their loneliness in the close, stuffy darkness of our barracks.

5 July 44: Last night heard explosions. Sounded like small arms fire coming from just beyond fence. Several men hit the deck, and a rumor (we live by rumors here!) quickly spread through camp the Amis were executing some of us. Supposedly in retaliation for something that had happened in the war. Only later did we learn it was their Freedom Day—just the fireworks of the village children.

Amis treat us firmly but fairly, not at all as we had feared. In fact, some are quite friendly. One guard shared a box of homemade cookies sent to him from his family. CO a Major Ryker. Slight man with large ears and wire-rim spectacles. Looks more like a bookkeeper than an officer. First day in camp gave us a lecture on hygiene. Seemed more concerned about an outbreak of lice than an outbreak of men. As camp showers are not in working order yet, has allowed us to bathe in nearby lake. A Strandbad only three hundred meters down the road where we go for a swim. Water frigid. Five minutes in and your body turns numb. But good to bathe after the many weeks it took getting here.

Camp an old logging supply farm. A large barn has been converted into barracks which house about 200 of us, as well as a few Czechs. Can still smell the sharp animal odor, though not really unpleasant. Makes me think of Grandfather's, where Wolfie and I used to visit as children. Next door is the kitchen and mess hall. Beyond that the maintenance shop and garage, the infirmary, then double rows of barbed wire. In each corner are guard towers manned by soldiers with submachine guns. Most of the time, however, they are sitting with their noses in magazines and couldn't care less about us. Ami enlisted men housed in barracks near canteen, while officers live in separate building towards the lake. At night we sometimes hear their Victrolas playing music. American Negro music, this fast, brassy sort that shakes the night. Makes me think of the Blue Swan, that cabaret Mariam and I used to go to in Leipzig before the war.

Food trucked in each day and not bad at all. Several times a week we have meat—real meat, not the Alter Mann beef tins we had in Africa. Lagerführer Heydt and Obergefreiter Badsteubner, a cook before the war, went to CO to ask if we could prepare our own meals and were granted request. Young Gunter Schessl, a gunner from my tank crew, helps Badsteubner over in the kitchen. Now we have Bauernseufzer and Klösse and Pfannkuchen. Even fatback sandwiches on dark bread for lunch in the woods.

Lights in our barracks have gone off again, fourth time tonight. Camp generator still not working correctly. So am finishing this by candlelight. Have just heard the sad cry of a bird somewhere out on the lake. Like a human voice really. Poor thing sounds as lonely as I feel. Makes me think of lines from Goethe:

> *Who never spent the darksome hours*
> *Weeping and watching for the morrow . . .*

8 July 44: Take our noon meal right in the woods, sitting beside the Amis. Quite a sight—captors and captives breaking bread. Sometimes hard to imagine under different circumstances they could stick a bayonet in your gut. Woods have made us brothers of sorts. One guard named Lazzari, from New York City. Friendly, always joking with prisoners and forever trying to barter cigarettes for German souvenirs. Today, Wattenberg working next to me in the woods. He's career Wehrmacht, from an old Prussian family, but not a bad egg. Been a POW since Agedabia in '41 and has had time to mellow. He pointed at Lazzari, who was urinating against a tree, and said, "Dieter, do you think the American girls like such a puny schwanz?" We laughed out loud and Lazzari asked me what was so funny. After I translated for him he said, "You know what the problem with you damn krauts is?" "No," I said, playing straight man. "You're too goddamn worried about size—big guns, big bombs, big cocks. I never had any complaints from my old lady." Without missing a beat, Wattenberg joked, "Nor I." We all had a good laugh, most especially Lazzari. Everyone, that is, except for Feldwebel K, who had overheard us. He comes around checking to make sure we only make quota, don't give the Amis a drop of sweat more than we're obliged to. Red-faced swine thinks we shouldn't have anything to do with our captors. "We are still fighting for the Fatherland, Kallick," he has told me on several occasions. He makes out the work assignments. Cross him and you'll find yourself shoveling shit in the latrines. Or worse. A bloody nose or a few broken ribs. Or like that fellow in the camp in Mateur. Found the poor bastard hanging from the rafters, his hands tied behind his back. Called it suicide! He had gotten too friendly with the Tommies and paid the price.

9 July 44: Cutting wood is very hard work. Up at six for breakfast and in woods by seven-thirty. Blisters on both hands. Aching muscles. Worst thing a tiny insect called a black fly. Gott im Himmel! As bad as the flies in Benghazi. Have tried kerosene and pine pitch—even cologne! Yet the fresh air and vigorous work have done wonders, and being busy helps pass the time.

Am keeping this record of my captivity in my Tagebuch. For posterity—if there is one. Have decided to write in English both for the practice and to deter those I'd rather not have see it. Spies everywhere, looking for traitors to the Reich.

10 July 44: They have made me an interpreter for one of the American foremen, a rough-hewn woodsman if I ever saw one. Drives prisoners hard and doesn't hide fact he doubts he can turn us into good workers. Can't tell if he hates us or just our inability to learn forestry. Uses one of our own, Oswald Grutzmacher, to get us to do his bidding. Grutzmacher had some previous logging experience on his family's farm in Bavaria. Like the American foreman, he abuses the men and treats them with contempt. Grumbling in camp about his being so cooperative with the Amis. One thing to follow orders, quite another to do it so willingly.

Have to admit, some of our men, especially those from the cities, were quite unfamiliar with axes and saws. A few were even afraid of Indians hiding in the woods. One youth, a former Jugend member with peach fuzz still on his chin, who'd been captured after only a week in the Korps, said that is what he'd learned about America from Karl May's books. Indians! Did we believe they had only horses and six-guns with which to fight our Panzers? Like those brave and foolhardy Poles who used cavalry charges against our Mark III tanks. Of course to say such a thing here is unwise. Wattenberg is always warning me, "Dieter, you have to be more careful." Even here it's the Lagergestapo, that pig K and his bunch of thugs, that's really in charge. Yet if all are too timid to speak out, what will it all have been for?

16 July 44: After breakfast went to church service this morning. Chaplain an Ami officer. Tall man with a high bony forehead. Speaks only a little German so has me translating for him. Directs all his words to me, not to the congregation. Gave a sermon on vengeance. From Judges, told the story of Samson avenging himself on the Philistines. "And he found a new jawbone of an ass and put forth his hand, and took it, and slew a thousand men therewith." Pointed his finger at me and said this was what was happening to Germany now. "You are the Philistines and the invading Allies the Samsons wielding a mighty jawbone." Said we still had a chance to repent, to cast off the sins of the Fatherland and become righteous. Right in the middle of his sermon, D, one of K's bunch, farted loudly. Everyone laughed and the chaplain became enraged. Called us—me—Satan's ministers and said God would wreak a terrible vengeance on us.

After church took a walk along the barbed-wire fence. Day sunny and warm, with the sweet smell of pine in the air. Some people from the village came in cars to stand on the other side of the fence and stare in at us. They speak and point at us as if we are animals at a zoo. One woman stood there and cursed us, throwing rotten fruit over the fence. Had the eyes of someone insane. Sometimes feel I am little more than a caged animal, a beast prowling back and forth in a pen. Like Rilke's panther.

> From the prison diary of Corporal Dieter Kallick
> Fifteenth Panzer Division
> Afrika Korps
> Captured in Bizerta, May 1943
> 81G–77–462
> German POW at Unternebenlager
> Sheshuncook, Maine, U.S.A.

Part 1

Part I

1

SATURDAY MORNING, EARLY. The road up ahead is quiet and dark. The headlights slice through the darkness like a sharp fillet knife gutting fish. But what spills out isn't the gleaming entrails of morning but only more darkness. In the rearview mirror it closes seamlessly together again and goes on forever. Luckily I was never one afraid of the night, even as a kid. Darkness was just another kind of skin, cooler than your own but more forgiving, too. On summer evenings, when I was a girl I'd walk the dirt road from Abbey's store where I'd gone to buy something, heading past the old village graveyard in Sheshuncook on my way around Daggett Cove toward home. I never thought twice about it. Not about imaginary dangers, like ghosts. Nor even real ones, like in spring when the bears would come down out of the woods to root around in Asa Shaw's dump. Shaw ran a chicken farm, and out behind his trailer he had a pit where he tossed out broken washing machines and engine parts, garbage and kitchen scraps, and the carcasses of diseased chickens. Most nights you could hear the bears out there. And smell them, too, a smell as hard as axle grease. Once I passed so close to one in the road I could've stuck out my hand and touched him. Even then I wasn't afraid—they don't do anything if you mind your own business.

Not so for Leon. He always imagined darkness held secrets that could do harm: ghosts from the graveyard, hands that would grab his ankles when he got out of bed at night and ran to my room. *They almost got me, Lib*, he'd cry. Always *they*, as if there were not one but a pack of demons after him. His little heart thumping wildly in his chest like a small trapped bird, his bony feet like icicles against my thighs. His feet were always so cold. Sometimes I would lift my nightgown and put them right against my stomach. I would hold him until he fell asleep, but always bring him back to his own bed before daylight so Ambroise wouldn't get mad. *He's too goddamned big to be sleeping with you, Lib. Want the kid to grow up to be a pansy?*

This morning around five, I turned the Closed sign face out in the store, got in the truck, and started driving the three hours south. Going to pick Leon up. Going to bring him home at last. I picture the regulars, Al Royce and Hoppy McCray and Roland St. James, men who haul for Great American Paper, pulling in in their rigs and wondering where I am. "What the hell's up with Libby?" I can just hear them saying, before they drive on into Piscataquis for their coffee and eggs.

My mind's been everywhere except on the road, like it will when you're behind the wheel this early. The last twenty miles are a blur: dirty snow flickering in the pale cone of headlight along the roadside, and just beyond, the hulking greasy black shapes of spruce and fir. Once in a while a rig heading up to Millinocket will blow by me, its wake shivering the truck, telling me I'd better pay attention. And just outside of Corinna this young bull moose came sauntering down out of the woods and just froze in my headlights. Wouldn't budge, eyes glowing red in the glare, head lowered in defiance. I thought I was going to hit him, I really did. But last minute he thought better of it, turned, and hightailed it up into the woods, his gangly legs bounding over the deep snow. It looked almost as if the darkness had sucked him in.

I haven't slept much tonight, and the lack of sleep finally begins to hit me—makes me feel my age like a heavy woolen coat that smells of rain. I roll down the window and the cold night air grabs me by the throat, shakes me awake. From the thermos on the front seat I pour myself a cup of coffee, strong and bitter. I turn the radio on, trying to get that talk show out of Portland, the one where people call in to this woman psychologist, a Dr. Paula, about their lives—how they can't sleep, how they stay up worrying about something they did a long time ago. Or the war wives, their husbands over in the Gulf, lonely young women just wanting somebody to talk to. Early mornings sometimes when I can't sleep I'll tune in myself. It always amazes me what people will tell about themselves at three in the morning. As if the darkness, that cool, forgiving skin, covers up their hungers and their fears, their sins, too. Just covers it all up. Dr. Paula's answers are always the same: keep busy, look on the positive side, change what you can, accept what you can't. One woman a few days ago talked about her husband who was paralyzed. She said they hadn't touched each other in years. She said she was still young, still had needs. She wanted to be told it was all right to take on a lover, I guess. Dr. Paula told her to do crafts, go bowling with her girlfriends. I kept wondering where the husband was. Downstairs in his wheelchair, listening all the time?

I fool around with the knob but all I get are loud pops of static. The radio in the old Ford hasn't worked right in years. So I turn it off and ride in silence. I slam headlong into that darkness, hoping that if I go fast enough I'll shatter it like a piece of smoked glass. And on the other side?

Maybe morning.

After the dream last night—the second time in three nights—I lay in bed for a long time, unable to sleep but not wanting to get out of bed. I kept staring at the solemn red face of the alarm clock, waiting for first light. Outside, I could hear the wind sweeping down over the lake, scratchy as silk under a man's rough hands, thumping a loose piece of tin up on the roof. Now and then a loud boom out in the night as the ice heaved and cracked. But when the wind died down it was quiet, like it can get up here. So quiet you can hear the blood moving in your brain. And those small night noises you never usually hear. Things that make your heart pause before you say, *It's only the sign out front,* or *Just the barn door. That's all.* Like the mice up in the attic insulation, scratching around. If it's quiet enough and you listen real close in the middle of a cold winter night, you can actually hear what I call mice talk. It's like what you hear sometimes on the other end of the phone, those scratchy little voices that don't sound like people at all, that sound more like the burrowings of tiny animals. The mice say things that sound like *When garbage sits long enough it'll begin to stink.* Strange things, things you wouldn't expect mice to say.

And when I start hearing the mice talk, I know I've got a good case of cabin fever and I'd better get out. So I got dressed in the blue cold of the bedroom without the lights on. I didn't want anybody passing by out on the road to know I was up, as if anybody would be at three o'clock, or if they were, much less care what I was doing. Yet I didn't need a light. I knew exactly what to wear, what I always wear to visit Leon: the black cotton dress gathered at the waist, the one I got at the Sears catalog store in town, and the pink sweater my niece Stephanie, Leon's kid, sent me last Christmas. As I ran the brush quickly through my short hair, I glanced out the bedroom window, out at the dark, frozen driveway.

What's there to tell? My name is Irene Libby Pelletier—Libby to most people. French Canadian on my father's side, Irish on my mother's. I run a small general store and diner—Libby's Country Kitchen, the sign says out front—twenty miles north of Piscataquis, on Moosehead Lake, Maine. Great American Paper country—logging, pulp mills, lumberjacks. Rigs loaded with pulpwood headed for the mills gear down as they pull in for coffee in the morning, spewing acrid puffs of diesel and the sweet odor of fresh-cut spruce. In the fall I get the hunters, men with Rugers in the gun racks of their pickups, men wearing fluorescent orange vests or mackinaws with bandoliers slung over their shoulders, men with the smell of gun oil heavy on them and a certain wildness of the blood in their eyes. Winter it's snowmobilers. They zip across the lake in great long caravans, or head for the trails that snake all the way up into Canada. Spring and summer bring the fishermen, and the tourists on their way up to Baxter. My store is the last stop before you hit the logging roads, and they pull in in their Airstreams and Winnies for gas or bait, maybe some lunch, a few last-minute canned goods, or authentic Maine souvenirs, carved wooden ducks or loons—things I buy from the Indian reservation in Cherokee, North Carolina. What do they know?

I've owned the store for the past twenty-six years. Bought it from a man named McDonough with the insurance money my father, Ambroise, a logger himself, left me when he died. I fixed it up, put in a lunch counter and some tables. I sell bait and fishing tackle, even rent out videos to tourists whose bored teenagers couldn't stand this much nature for two straight minutes. The place has a two-room apartment over it, which is just enough for me and Mitzi, my Doberman bitch, and a room behind the store where Leon puts up when he stays with me.

I don't mind chewing the fat with loggers or summer tourists. What I like is being my own boss, not having to punch a clock like those women over in the mills, women like Margie Tatro who has carpal tunnel because she's worked the same machine for thirty years. That's not for me. When I feel like going fishing I just stick the Closed sign in the window, head across the road to the dock, jump in my Starcraft, and go trolling out in Lily Bay. It's pretty up here: I got the lake right out my front door, sunsets people would kill for, and about a two-million-acre woodlot out back that stretches north to the Saint John. So it's plenty quiet. Though sometimes, like in the middle of the night when I can't sleep, when I stay up listening to the mice, too quiet. Funny how that can get on your nerves, too. Then I get antsy and wonder why I ever bought a place so far out of town, so far away from people. And why, at my age, I stay.

I'll be sixty-one this May. I have short reddish blond hair, which only in the sunlight gives away its gray, and good working hands—I can still swing an ax or use a chain saw, or manage the Case backhoe out in the barn when my septic tank needs work. I'm not tall, but I've always felt substantial, with solid calves and wide hips that would've come in handy if kids had been in the cards. I've more health than a person my age has need for or a reason to expect. "You're as healthy as an ox, Libby," Doc Proulx tells me when I come in for my once-every-ten-years checkup. In that, I take after Ambroise, who, except for the drinking, was never sick a day in his life. I've his features, too, same long, broad nose, olive-colored eyes, prominent brows. Though I'm not dark like him. I'm more fair-skinned, like my mother—at least from what I recall of her.

The other thing about me, what you might remember after you'd forgotten my other features, is my mouth. I was born with a harelip that was badly repaired by a shaky-handed GP over in Millinocket. He turned it into a thick, knotted scar I've carried all my life. When I was a kid it seemed to matter, the way things always do when you're young. The names the kids at school used to call me stung like yellow jackets: Libby Lips or Sucker Mouth or Cunt Face. I was always self-conscious about it, even when I pretended not to care. I never had a boyfriend growing up, didn't even kiss a boy till I was seventeen, though then I quickly made up for lost time. I remember my mother telling me, "Libby, you're going to have to work twice as hard with the boys. To overcome your handicap." When I was nine she handed me a tube of Lady Esther Passion Plum lipstick she'd bought in Pavel's Pharmacy in town and showed me how to make the best of what I had. She used to make me practice walking with a straight back, a book describing feminine grace balanced on my head, all the while pushing out my brand-new breasts and taking these small, rigid steps—all intended to direct the boys' stares away from my "handicap." She was good at knowing what drew men's stares, all right.

The lessons didn't change anything. I was always more of a tomboy, liked to fish with Ambroise and go logging into the woods with him. My mother used to tell me I'd never get a man, as if a man were a fish you needed the right sort of bait to hook and then you had to know just how to play him. She said if I wasn't careful I'd wind up a dried-up old maid like Aunt Eunice, my father's sister. She made it sound like ending up alone was the worst thing that could happen to you, worse than getting sick or dying or even going to hell. I guess I pictured hell as this group of old maids sitting around playing rummy and thinking about all the men who'd slipped through their bony fingers. So she gave up on me, thinking I was a hopeless case, even beyond the miracles of Saint Jude or Passion Plum lipstick. That was before she gave up on all of us and left. Before she ran off with the scrap-metal man. Funny thing is, she was right about my ending up alone.

Lately I've begun to think about her, and I don't even know why. I'll wake up at night and find myself trying to conjure up her face. What her hands were like, the shape of her ears. Her smell. I wonder whatever happened to her. I try to form a picture in my mind of how she spent the last half century. Did she stay with that man? Or did she leave him eventually, too? Did she die all alone or is she still alive somewhere? Was she happy in the life she had chosen apart from us?

It's her—not Leon, not any of the other business—that's on my mind when I become aware, gradually, of the noise. *Ca-tunk, ca-tunk.* Finally I realize it's the engine. The old '65 Ford has been pushing oil like crazy, and like a fool I forgot to check it before I left. Billy Hanson at the Mobil station in town says the engine's tired. He says it needs new rings and bearings, maybe more once he gets inside and begins poking around. He says this like a surgeon looking for cancer, getting you ready for the worst. I start looking for a gas station, but this early I probably won't find a thing until I hit the turnpike. I don't like the idea of getting stuck out here. On the bank sign back in Piscataquis it said eight below—that's without the wind chill. Up in these woods you make a dumb mistake and you pay for it. It's an unforgiving sort of place. Last year a snowmobiler ran out of gas up near the dam in Ripogenus and tried to hike out. In the spring they found him, what was left anyway, after the coyotes and crows had gotten through with him.

Just after I pick up the turnpike in Newport, the oil light starts blinking on and off, then comes on for good—a red demon eye staring back at me. I know I'm in trouble. Usually I keep a quart of oil under the seat, but I used that the other day and forgot to replace it. Lately, that's the way it's been going—forgetting things I should remember, and remembering those I'd be better off forgetting. I'm wondering what I should do. Turn back? Pull off and say a prayer to Saint Christopher? Or keep going and hope I make it to Augusta? Luckily, I spot a tall, brightly lit Shell sign and pull off the highway. A young kid in orange coveralls comes out to wait on me. He has long blond hair hanging out from beneath his wool cap, and the slow, fussy movements of a raccoon.

"Yeah?" he asks, blowing into his fist and shifting from one foot to the other in the cold. "How much?"

"No gas. Could you check the oil?" I ask.

"*This* is self-serve," he says, pointing to the sign over the pumps. "Over *there*, that's full service."

"You want me to move it?" I ask.

"Never mind," he snorts, annoyed. He lifts the hood and checks the oil. In a minute he comes back and shoves the dipstick in the window at me, like a matador aiming a sword at a bull. I smell burnt oil and see that the stick is bone dry.

"You trying to blow a rod, lady?"

"I guess I need some oil," I say.

"I guess you *do*," he replies. "What kind you want?"

"How about straight thirty?" I reply, thinking a heavier weight will keep it from slipping by the rings. Something Ambroise taught me. He also taught me how to notch a tree so it fell in whatever direction you wanted. How to tie flies or field dress a deer. Things you needed to do with your hands, things to survive up here.

"In this weather!" the kid says. "Your engine won't turn over."

"Ten-thirty, then. You got that?"

He nods, goes back inside, and comes out with several quarts. He grumbles as he puts them in, then leans around the hood and says, "It's not such a hot idea to drive without no oil."

"I usually check it." I roll up the window because of the cold.

"Your engine'll seize on you," the little shit lectures me. With one hand he makes a circle that is supposed to be the cylinder, and with the other he makes a fist that's caught in the circle and won't budge. "Like this." I catch him mouthing the words, "Then you're fucked good, lady."

While the oil drains, slowly in the cold, he comes back around to my window. He stands there, lifting his shoulders up and down. I open the window a crack. "Where you headed this early?"

"I have to pick up my brother. He's being discharged down at the VA hospital."

"The VA?" he says, as if he's going to say more but doesn't. He checks the oil again, then slams the hood down, harder than necessary. When he comes around I hand him an old twenty that's been taped together. The halves of Jackson's face aren't straight: They look like one of those optometrist's exams where you have to make the two dots line up. It was left by a heavyset man who came in the store the other day asking for information. He only had a coffee but he left a twenty. The kid looks at it for a while.

"It's still good," I say.

He pulls out a wad of money from his coverall pocket and starts counting out greasy bills. When he finishes he just stands there. Up close I see his eyes are light gray in the overhead lights, pupils dilated as if he's stoned. Like the eyes of a cat hunting at night, needing all the light it can get. Finally, he asks, "Your brother's at Togus. Down in Augusta?"

"Yeah."

"My old man was there."

"What's his name?" I ask. "Maybe my brother knows him."

"I said *was*. He died about five, six years ago."

"Sorry to hear that," I offer.

"Cancer. Primary of the stomach. With mets to the brain," the boy says, cocky with his handle on the language of death. "He had all these operations. Christ, they kept cutting things out of him. First the stomach. Then intestine. Then more intestine. After that it showed up in his brain. Plus they kept blasting him with chemo and radiation. He looked about eighty years old before he died. At the end he didn't even know who we were anymore. He was a grunt in Nam, and got sprayed with that Agent Orange crap."

"Really?"

"That's what we think. A bunch of his old army buddies are getting cancer, too. But the government doesn't want to admit they screwed up. It'll cost them too much."

"I suppose not."

"Ain't the money so much, though my mom sure could use it. We're just looking for the bastards to tell us the truth. They done all these tests on Agent Orange. It's supposed to cause all sorts of problems—down the road. I read someplace I got like ten times the chance of thyroid cancer. Just because my old man was exposed twenty years ago. Hell, I don't even know what my thyroid is."

"Those are just odds," I say. "Doesn't mean it's going to happen."

"Could. He's dead but *I'm* the one still paying for that fuckin' war. Pardon my French."

"You ought to see yourself a lawyer."

"Hell, we seen plenty of those assholes. They're just out to make a buck. I tell you one thing."

"What's that?"

"They ask me to go fight Saddam, I'm gone. What do I got against him? How many A-rabs you see in Maine? My brother's in the reserves, he just got called up. Still buys that flag and country crap. Me, I know this place up north where they'd never find me. Take my thirty-aught-six and a box of shells. Head for this cabin way up near Jackman. You know that country?"

"Yeah," I reply. My father had run a logging camp up there on the Moose River, before the war. He'd taken me and Leon with him a few times. Sometimes during school vacation he'd bring one or both of us with him if he was logging way back in the woods. I sort of liked going with him, but Leon hated it. It was pretty desolate country. The kid's right—nobody could find you if you didn't want them to.

"I could get by," the kid says. "Hunt and fish. They feed you all this crap about patriotism. It's just a snow job. What'd it ever get my old man? I only fight for number one now."

He smiles, fingering that thought like a warm penny in his pocket. Then he leans toward the truck and raps the door with his knuckles. "Just remember to check the oil, lady," he says. "You can't kill these old small-block Fords. Long's you keep them in oil."

"Thanks," I say and pull out. In the rearview mirror, I see him standing there with his hands on his hips, blue smoke in his face.

The engine's quieter now, but I know I'm looking at an overhaul or another truck even. I've been trying to put aside a little money, just in case Leon needs something. Like an operation or a private-duty nurse. Or maybe one of those hospital beds for home use, if it comes to that. I could set it up in the room out back. I'd take care of him. It'll be like the old days, just him and me. I've always told him if he ever needed a place he's got one. Except for Stephanie, I'm the only family he's got. And I know she won't take him in. He's been in and out of the VA for months now; a couple of times he was pretty bad, but I don't think she's been to see him twice. She only lives down in Portsmouth, too. Don't get me wrong, I'm not blaming her. Leon hasn't exactly won any medals as a father. I'm just saying I'm his sister. I've always watched out for him and I guess I always will.

I pull over at a rest area just before I reach the city. Behind me, the sun's a weak sliver of pink bleeding through the slate gray sky, like the side of a rainbow trout. I'm way early. They won't even let visitors in yet. So I decide to wait for a while and then drive in later. I pull behind a rig with a full load of spruce logs and shut the engine off. Up ahead is a convoy of reserve units, probably just called up to head over to the Gulf. Young boys in fatigues and newly shaved heads walk from the rest rooms back to their camouflaged jeeps. They laugh and joke easily in the early-morning cold, as if they were doing nothing more than going duck hunting. Not off to kill and die.

I lay my head against the cool window, just trying to rest for a few minutes. *We're just looking for the bastards to tell us the truth*, the boy back there had said. I think of radiation and chemo. I can hear the engine cooling down, going *tick . . . tick . . . tick*, like a bomb just before it goes off.

I close my eyes and what I see are soldiers. Not ours. I see those other soldiers, the young German prisoners, the ones at the camp up in Sheshuncook. It's been forty-six years, but I see them so clearly, as if a thick fog has suddenly burned off. I see them standing behind the barbed wire, the *P* and *W* painted in white letters on their sleeves. Those tan, baggy Afrika Korps uniforms. And the way they'd stare at you when you'd walk by on the road to the lake, their eyes the sad, frightened eyes of lost children. Not warriors, not conquerors or killers, but children. Children afraid they'll never find their way back home again. Children who've learned the terrible secret of slaughter and *know* they can never go home again.

The trucks drive past the camp, around Daggett Cove, their head-lights spraying the night. They park in the snow-covered driveway and the men get out and stand there. From the kitchen window where I've been waiting, it seems for years, I watch them. Their cigarettes glow in the darkness like fireflies. The only other light is that from the truck's headlights, backlighting the figures in the driveway and distorting their features. Their smoky breaths mingle with the exhaust of the idling trucks. Dark shapes, in heavy coats and hats. Some carry things in their hands, long heavy objects, axes and peaveys. A pair of hunting dogs stand in the bed of one truck, yapping occasionally, their snouts hitting the air for a scent, though no noise reaches me. The men might be talking, but from the kitchen it's hard to tell. They just stand there in the cold dark night, waiting for something. Finally, two figures break apart from the group and walk slowly up to the house. Their footsteps over the packed snow make a noise that sounds like a file being pulled between a saw's teeth: grrr, grrr. I watch Ambroise and Leon approach. I run to the door, turn the latch, throw it open. The cold dark air comes whooshing in, filling the room and making me shudder. But instead of my father and brother, an ashen-faced boy is standing there, a hand wrapped in a bloody rag extended toward me.

"No!" I cry. "Please, no!"

"You all right?" a voice asks.

Startled, I open my eyes to see a man's face on the other side of the glass, not a foot from mine. He has a full red beard, and he's rapping on the window with his knuckles. His breath flies at me in billowing clouds, and I think of the dark cold air in the dream. A dream that started after that man came in the store the other day asking questions. That's when it started.

"Hey, lady," the bearded man repeats. "You okay?"

"Yeah," I mumble.

"You looked like something was wrong."

"No. Nothing's wrong."

He stands there for another second, then scratches his beard and walks away, his jeans loose in the rear. I look at my watch. I've only been asleep for fifteen minutes, yet it seems like much longer—hours, days, maybe even years. As if I'd fallen asleep during those war years and just woke up. That's how it's been lately. Time seems to have lost its texture, is able to expand or contract, to take on new shapes like a cloud on a windy day.

2

MY BROTHER'S ROOM. I stand at the foot of his bed for a moment, watching him sleep, startled by the sudden change in him. Leon's curled up tight, like a fetus, and an image of him as a child—those times I'd stayed up at night watching over him when he had a fever—comes to me. Yet the figure I see now isn't a boy anymore. It's an old man, a sick old man. The sharp bones of his cheeks and nose strain against the papery, jaundiced skin. Except for the painfully swollen belly, he's gaunt as a corpse in the bed. His liver is shot from the years of drinking, but it's in the last few months that he's really gone downhill fast. Throwing up blood, the bloated belly, his being confused at times. It's finally catching up with him. His doctor, Dr. Bedrosian, has told me that if he doesn't give up the booze it'll kill him. They bring him to the VA, dry him out, get him back to where he's feeling a little better. But as soon as he's discharged he goes on a binge again and winds up back in the hospital. It's only been a week or so since I've been down to see him, yet now he suddenly looks so old. Like a leaf that could be blown away in the wind. It scares me.

It's a four-bed room, but there's only one other patient now—a man with tattoos and a black T-shirt that says "Harleys R Us."

"Lee's still pounding his ear," the tattoo man says to me. "You his old lady?"

"Sister," I reply.

"Sure, that's right. Lee talks about you all the time. What's your name?"

"Libby."

"Libby, yeah. Listen, Libby. I wouldn't normally ask. But you wouldn't have a coupla bucks you could spare? For a friend of Lee's."

While I ought to know better, I open my purse and hand him two dollars.

"You're an angel," he says. "You'll be in my prayers."

On the chair, I set the bag of clothes I brought and pull the curtain around my brother's bed. It's a poor excuse for privacy but it's something. On the nightstand are Leon's dentures, the upper plate half resting on the lower in a sort of lopsided smile. The room smells, of urine and excrement and the sickly-sweet odor of flesh having gone bad. The bedpan, as usual, is full. I pick it up and head down to the bathroom. Then I go and find one of the aides, a heavy, young girl with braces still on her teeth, and ask her for some soap and a towel.

"My brother's being discharged today," I say. "I want to clean him up a little."

"The other aide called in sick," she says defensively.

"I don't mind doing it," I offer.

"I got the whole ward to myself. I can't do everything."

When I get back to Leon's room, the tattoo man says, "Lee don't sleep too good at night. He has these nightmares."

"Nightmares?" I say, thinking about my own dream.

"Yeah. He's yelling all this crazy stuff you'd think he had the DTs. But he's been off the sauce for a coupla weeks now."

I begin to take the soiled johnny off Leon. He wakes with this, startled and confused. Staring right at me, his hands raised protectively in front of his face, he cries, "No. Ge'out. Ge'away from me." The words are distorted because he doesn't have his teeth in. The whites of his eyes are the dull yellow of chicken fat, and he doesn't seem able to get me in focus. His eyes blink rapidly, the pupils narrowing to sharp points like those of a hawk.

"You need a bath, Leon," I say, pulling his johnny off. "You smell."

"You smell, you dirty bitch. I tol' you, get the hell out."

"We're leaving today. Don't you want to look nice?"

"I wanna be leff alone," he says, shaking a bony fist in my face. "UNNERSTAND!"

"It's just me, Leon."

He eyes me suspiciously, searching for familiar territory, a crevice his mind can get a foothold in. "Ma?" he asks finally. "Is that you?"

"No, it's not *her*, for heaven's sakes. It's me. Libby, your sister."

His expression changes, and he waves me off with his hand. "Who you shittin'? She's long gone, that one."

"I didn't go anywhere. I'm right here."

He stares at me, then shakes his head. "Ran off with the junk man."

Leon has his good days and his bad. On his bad days he's hounded by old demons, pursued by a childhood bully named Lars Gundersen, cries out against some meanness of Ambroise's. Sometimes he won't even recognize me. Calls me Claire, his ex-wife's name. Other times he thinks I'm our mother, begins to cry and asks why I left. It almost breaks my heart to hear him go on like that. Dr. Bedrosian says that besides the cirrhosis, he has something called organic brain syndrome, which means all those years of drinking and sleeping in alleys and not eating right have damaged his brain. I picture his brain like a scratched record, one of those old 78s we used to play on the phonograph. Sometimes it gets stuck and keeps playing the same lines, over and over again. It's amazing how he'll remember a small thing that happened fifty years before and not even know Bush is president or that I'm his sister. Trick is to get him past the scratches. Sometimes, then, he's almost the same old Leon. Sometimes.

"See. Libby," I say, taking hold of his hand and pressing it against my shoulder: Flesh is its own reality, makes its own past and present. But he pulls his hand back, almost as if the sweater his daughter gave me were on fire.

"Where you taking me?" he asks.

"Don't you remember?" I reply. "We're going home today."

"I don't wanna go anyplace. I wanna stay right here."

"Don't you want to come and stay with me? Up on the lake. I got your room all fixed up."

"My room?" he asks.

"Yeah, remember? Out behind the kitchen. You always liked staying there. In the summer we can go fishing on the lake. Like we used to as kids."

"They still got togue up there?"

"Plenty of togue. And landlocked salmon, too. Remember what we used to use for bait, Leon?"

His eyes light up as his mind grasps something in the dark attic of his memory. "Dough balls fried in bacon grease."

"That's right, Leon! You do remember. It'll be just like the old days. Let me get you cleaned up and we'll get going. Everything'll be all right once we get home."

He becomes distracted, maybe sees us out on the lake in Ambroise's boat, hooking a big lake trout. I begin to bathe him, the way I used to in the kitchen sink at home, boiling water on the cookstove. I scrub his face, then move down to his chest and the painfully swollen belly. I quickly soap up his penis, which looks like a small dried egg sitting in a black nest. Modesty is something we have both left behind us. I roll him over and wash the shit that is caked between his cheeks. I do his legs last, then wash his feet and trim his long yellow toenails. I'm surprised he lets me. Usually he fights me, doesn't like his nails done. When I finish, I get out the shaving cream and the blue plastic razor from his nightstand, and go to work on his gray stubble. His skin rips easily, like that on an overripe pear, and though I try to be careful I soon draw blood.

"Jesus," he moans. "Tak'it easy, would you."

"Just a little nick," I tell him. "Hold still."

"Fatasswhore," he cries, the words spilling out as one.

"You watch your mouth, Leon Edward Pelletier, or I'll get a

bar of soap and wash it out good for you. You're not too big for that."

I don't know if it's saying his full name out loud or the old threat about washing his mouth out with soap, but something jogs his brain, gives that stuck needle a shove. A smile carves his face in two. He looks up at me as I finish shaving him.

"What's the matter?" I ask. "You know who I am now?"

"I know."

"Who?" I ask, testing to see if he really does.

"A hard bitch," he says. "Always were, too." So he does recognize me after all.

"Hard enough for us to get by," I say, grabbing the bag of clothes I brought along. At Mercier's in town, I bought him some things: a pair of pants, a flannel shirt, a new pair of shoes and some socks, underwear, a new winter coat. Even a plaid hunting cap with earflaps, though I doubt Leon will be doing much hunting anymore. "Here," I say, handing him the bag. "You needed some new clothes."

"I got clothes."

"Yours were pretty ragged. Put these on."

Leon takes the hat out of the bag and sets it on his head. "Remember the time I got head lice?" he says.

"I remember."

"You scrubbed my head with that damn horse brush."

"It wasn't a horse brush. It was a regular brush."

"It still hurt like hell. You were always so rough. Like Aunt Eunice."

"Stop jabbering and get dressed. I have to get back to the store and we got a long drive ahead of us."

While he gets dressed I go around and pack his things. When he's finished I see that the shirt and pants are way too baggy, that he's lost even more weight than I'd imagined. I wet and comb his still dark, still thick hair. Then I take his dentures over to the sink and rinse them under the water. After he has his teeth back in he doesn't look half bad. In fact, he's still a good-looking man, with soft, fine features, these long lashes framing what are my mother's striking green eyes. He looks just like her. I take the compact mirror from my pocketbook and hold it up for him.

"There. Isn't that better?" I ask.

He gazes at himself for a moment, his head tilted at a sharp, haughty angle. The way I remember my mother looking at herself in the mirror, checking for gray hairs, crow's-feet, the slow erosion of her fragile beauty in an inhospitable place like northern Maine.

As if he's been reading my thoughts—it's scary how we can read each other's minds sometimes—he says, "Was I asking for her?"

I see the confusion in his eyes as he struggles to distinguish now from that warm June day in 1943 when she left.

"Yes, Leon," I say, zipping up his new coat and turning up the collar against the cold. "But that's all right. It's the booze, Leon. We'll get you straightened out."

"I must've been dreaming. I thought she came back."

"No, Leon," I say. "Never did, never will. Listen, I have to go and sign the discharge papers. You wait here. I'll be right back."

Going down in the elevator, I think of her again—a woman capable of running off and leaving two young kids behind, during a war, without so much as batting an eyelash. I can picture her: the way she held her head, high and haughty, though Ambroise said she was nothing but shanty Irish by way of Beantown, just another bogtrotter putting on airs, looking down her nose on the Canuck Pelletiers and our stinking backwoods logging village of Sheshuncook; I remember the aroma of the baby powder she sprinkled between her breasts on sweltering August afternoons; the blue-checked two-piece bathing suit she wore to go swimming in the lake, and the way the men in the village, standing on the porch of Abbey's store, would rub their eyes like liniment all over her as she walked past, unused to someone who flaunted her body that way; her ordering a gin and orange juice when we'd go to a bar down in Piscataquis and the caressing way she held her glass, as if it were a microphone and she was singing into it; and, of course, her full, pouty, red-lipped mouth, which seemed to mock my own twisted one. I remember all that. And I remember that summer during the war, when I was thirteen and Leon just ten.

Of course, she'd taken off before, headed back down to Boston to stay with family—at least that's what she said. Sometimes for a few days, sometimes longer. But she always came back. We'd come home from school and she'd be sitting at the table smoking a cigarette and drinking a gin and orange juice, and staring dreamily off over the lake. This time was different. I remember the scrap-metal man came through town in a flatbed truck buying scrap metal for the war. The truck was filled with castoffs: old rusted bikes, car bumpers, iron bedposts, bathtubs, the iron plumbing from the Tohays' place that burned down across the cove—metal that would be turned into tanks and rifle barrels and shell casings to kill Japs and descend on German cities. I remember he came to our house several times. Ambroise was away, off at some logging camp. I don't even recall the scrap-metal man's name or what his face looked like. Only that he was short and wore faded blue coveralls, and had these enormous forearms covered with coarse black hair. From us he bought an old six-cylinder flathead engine block that had sat out on the side of the barn for ages. It amazed me how he just grabbed ahold of the engine by the empty cylinders, hoisted it up, and then tossed it on his truck bed as if he were lifting a child's bike. I remember my mother inviting him in for a beer, the way she had other men who'd come sniffing around when Ambroise was away, and the two of them sitting in the parlor, he drinking his beer, she her gin and orange juice. I remember her laughter, high and delicate as morning sunlight. She seemed another person then, someone other than the somber, grim woman she was around my father.

The scrap-metal man came back several times to buy things—ax blades and broken saws and rusted tools. He kept coming even when there was no scrap metal left to buy. My mother would shoo us out of the house, give us a nickel to spend at Abbey's store in the village. I guess I suspected even then that her laughter had a hidden meaning. Once when I came home I found a nub of a cigar in the ashtray in their bedroom, though Ambroise never smoked cigars. When the scrap-metal man left town a few weeks later, he took our mother, too, as if she were just another piece of scrap that he'd lifted effortlessly onto his truck with those strong, sure arms of his. We assumed that after a while she'd come back, just like those other times. But she didn't. That was the last we ever saw of her.

After she left, Ambroise sometimes would drop us off at the house of a friend of his in town. Tom Weston, who worked as a logger with my father, and his wife Peg never had any kids, but they didn't mind our staying there, sometimes for weeks at a time. Peg was nice. She would take us to the Strand to see war movies or buy us ice creams at Pavel's in town. We liked staying there. But sometimes Ambroise would have his old-maid sister Eunice come down from Madawaska near the Canadian border to watch us. Aunt Eunice used to have stringy gray hair she never washed and these long nails she'd sink into the soft flesh in back of your arm, to get you to mind. She reminded me of a witch. If we so much as smiled in church, she would lean over to you and dig her claws into your arm. "Don't embarrass me, you little bastards, or you'll pay when we get home." Once when she called our mother a *putain* and Leon called Aunt Eunice the same thing, she took his pants down and beat him with a piece of garden hose.

But through much of the war, at least, Ambroise was logging close enough to Sheshuncook—Pittston Farm over to Northeast Carry—that he came home most nights. And after the war, when he'd go off to run a camp up north, we were big enough to fend for ourselves. I was sixteen then and Leon thirteen. Just him and me. After a while I even preferred it that way. Ambroise would send us money once a month and I would take care of groceries and things, pay the bills. When I was seventeen I quit school and got a job in a shoe factory to help us get by.

Though we never again saw her, she did write a couple of letters. In one she sent along a picture of her standing in front of this waterfall. She was smiling at the camera, as if to show how right her decision to leave us had turned out, how happy being away from us made her. I used to think the waterfall was Niagara and she was going on a second honeymoon, only with someone besides Ambroise. Leon kept it and a few other pictures of her, as if he expected her to come back and wanted it to make sure he would remember what she looked like. It's the only way I remember her. Thin-boned like my brother, still young and pretty, bareheaded, her cinnamon blond hair bobbed in the fashion of the early forties. But she had the sort of looks that wouldn't hold up. Overnight she'd turn hard looking and old, she'd lose her teeth and her cheeks would collapse—you could tell that from the picture. The way pretty, delicate-featured women in those backwoods always turned out: one minute ablaze with youth, the next a shrunken hag. I kept hoping this wrinkled old woman would show up someday in the store, saying she was my mother. Some old woman I'd mistake as a tourist at first but who would later turn out to be her. I pictured her begging forgiveness, for having left Leon and me. I wouldn't have forgiven her, of course. Not so much for what her leaving did to me as for what it did to Leon.

He cried every night for months after she left. Even years later he was still missing her, still thinking she'd return some day to plug the hole her leaving had ripped in his life. I did what I could, tried to take her place. I became more mother to him than sister, though I'd never asked to take on that responsibility. I made sure that he ate right and had clean clothes for school. Ambroise thought Leon would be better off if he quit school after sixth grade and learned to be a logger like himself. All the Pelletiers were loggers: Ambroise, his twin younger brothers, Uncles Robert and Ronald, who had moved back up to New Brunswick before the war to cut wood, and their father before them, Pepé Pelletier. But Leon could've been more than a Canuck shantyboy. He was sharp, did well in school. I saw to it that he did his homework, practiced his arithmetic and spelling. When he had a problem in school, I was the one who went to see his teacher. I made sure he had a bath every week. I used to boil water on the stove and wash him in the kitchen sink. We didn't have an indoor bathroom, not even in the forties when most people in our small village already had at least an indoor privy. He was small enough to fit in the sink even at ten. A pretty child, with green eyes and the small bones of a dove.

At night he would have bad dreams, dreams that got even worse when he was twelve or thirteen. I'd let him come into my bed, even when he was too big anymore for that sort of thing. Sometimes I would wake up and feel his hands on me. On my thighs, my belly, my breasts. Urgent little hands exploring me, as if searching a field for something important he'd lost. I'd pretend I was asleep and turn over onto my stomach. Though I knew it was wrong, I never said anything. Not to him, nor to Father Julian in the confessional. I figured it was his desperate loneliness. I figured he would grow out of it. When he didn't, I started locking my door at night. I would hear him outside my room, his voice just beginning to change, to deepen with the sadness of the world, saying, "I'm scared, Lib. Can I come in? Please." And often I'd relent, unlock the door, and fall asleep cursing her for leaving us.

Leon always seemed frail, in need of mothering. He got colds and sore throats and fevers. He got rickets when he was eight, and when he was nine he almost died from the influenza that came through the village and took the lives of several people. I remember staying up all night with him, putting mustard packs on his chest. At school the other kids used to pick on him. On the playground once, a burly Swede named Lars Gundersen had called our mother a whore, which she was, of course, but Leon came to her defense. The boy had my brother on the ground and was punching him in the face when I came up. I jumped on the kid's back and bit him on the ear until I tasted blood. I got sent to the principal's office for that. But I could handle myself, even as a girl. And when Ambroise was drunk and looking to hit somebody, I shielded Leon. Ambroise always thought twice about hitting me. Maybe because I was a girl or maybe because he knew who made his meals and washed his clothes and kept his house. But I could be hard on Leon, too, would box his ears if he needed it, wash his mouth out with soap, make him say his prayers at night, do his chores, toe the mark. Somebody had to. After she left, Ambroise spent more and more of his time in the bottle. He hardly paid any attention to us. We grew up like wildflowers. But we did all right.

In the truck, heading north. A light snow falling but one that's picking up a head of steam, driving out of the northwest with some punch. It's collecting along the shoulders, beginning to cover the treetops. Skiers in BMWs and Audis zip past us, heading for the mountains—a late-March bonanza. Leon sits silently, hunched over, on his lap a brown grocery bag containing all his worldly possessions. He hasn't said two words since we left the hospital. His mouth hangs open.

"I bought a used TV in town," I say, trying to make conversation. "I set it up in your room."

"Yeah?" he says.

"It gets pretty good reception. And I put a space heater out there, too. In case it gets cold."

Leon nods absently, picks at the scab on his jaw where I cut him shaving. He stares out the window, his gaze angled back toward the way we came. He looks at the passing countryside—the stands of fir and spruce, the broken pastureland, the frozen bogs—the way you'd look at woods you were lost in: searching for something you'd passed earlier, that link between where you are now and where you hope to get back to. I can recall Ambroise, an experienced woodsman, warning us that when we walked in the woods we had to pay attention. He said to look over your shoulder every once in a while, so when you were coming back some things would look familiar. Find a marker, he'd advise, a tree struck by lightning maybe, or a rock formation, the bend in a stream. It might keep you from getting lost.

"Spotty was asking after you," I say, trying to plant a marker for him.

"Spotty?" he says.

"You remember Spotty Haines, don't you?"

"Of course I remember him," he snaps at me. "Just that I haven't seen him in years. How is he anyway?"

"Same old Spotty. Just gets older and crankier."

"He still running that guide service?"

"Yep. His son and daughter-in-law help him out. Didn't you go to school with Warren?"

"I don't remember him. He must've been younger than me. Where'd you run into Spotty?"

"He dropped by the store the other day." We drive in silence for a few miles, just the wipers making their *squeegit, squeegit* noise. After a while I say, "You'll never guess what we talked about. Remember when we were kids, Leon, living up in Sheshuncook? Where they had the camp?"

"Camp?" he repeats, without looking away from the window.

"You know, the POW camp. During the war. It was down the road from Abbey's, toward the lake. Other side of Daggett Cove from us." I can't tell if he remembers or not, if any of this is sinking in, so I go on. "The paper company was using the Germans to cut wood. Ambroise had them working for him. He called them Hitler's whores. Remember how he called them that, Leon? Hitler's whores. We worked up there for a while, too? Me and you. Helping Ambroise out. Remember?"

Leon finally glances over at me, but his eyes are flat, all cloudy surface, like the scum on the top of a stagnant bog. You can't even guess what's underneath. "Yeah, I remember," he says. "So what?"

"We were just talking about it. That's all." That's not all, of course, but it doesn't make much difference, I suppose. I decide to drop it.

"You hungry?" I ask, trying to change the subject.

Leon shrugs. "Naw. What was it you and Spotty was talking about?"

"I don't know about you," I say, "but if I don't have a coffee pretty quick I'm gonna fall asleep behind the wheel."

I pull off the turnpike, look for a restaurant. I settle on a small green shack of a diner called Gwen's Eats. Inside, a huge woman—Gwen?—who must go three hundred pounds with a pile of flaming red hair perched on top of her head, seats us in a booth. She wears a filthy apron and satiny white uniform that holds her in like a dam. "What can I get yous?" she asks.

"I'll just have a coffee," Leon says. "Where's the head?"

"To the left of the cigarette machines," says the woman. "Gotta really pull on the handle, hon. It sticks."

"Two coffees," I order. "One with extra cream." I remember how Leon likes his coffee. In the mornings when he'd go to work in the woods with Ambroise I used to put half a can of condensed milk in his thermos. I sit at a table looking out the window, watching it snow. The woman comes back over with the coffees, her legs making a swishing noise like a paddle cutting the water.

"We're gonna get a good one, it looks like," she says, staring outside.

"Looks like."

"They were only talking flurries. What're you gonna do?"

She sets the coffees down and heads back to the kitchen. I sip my coffee. When he comes out, Leon sits opposite me. He picks his cup up and holds it with two hands. Even then his hands aren't so steady, though. I can see the tan-colored coffee vibrating in the cup. "So what?" he asks.

"What do you mean?"

"You was talking with Spotty about the camp. So what?"

"So nothing. We just were, is all."

"Why'd you tell me, then?"

"I don't know. I thought you'd be interested."

"Why?"

"I told you, I don't know. Let's just drop it."

But instead of dropping it, Leon, who's always had this stubborn streak in him, one that used to get him in trouble with Ambroise, says, "Why the fuck would I be interested in the goddamn camp?" His hands now are really shaking. The hot coffee splashes over the edge, down onto his fingers, pools on the table. He doesn't even seem to notice, however.

"I can see you got a bug up your ass today." I reach for some kleenex in my pocketbook, to clean up the mess. That's when he grabs me by the wrist. He grabs me hard, with more strength than I'd have thought possible, and when I try to pull away he squeezes harder, sinking his long fingernails into the skin.

"Leon, let go," I say.

"What did you and Spotty talk about?"

"Leon! You're hurting me. Let go. What's gotten into you?"

"Tell me! What did you and him talk about you thought I'd be so damn interested in?"

"Nothing."

"Nothing?"

His bony hand tightens even more around my wrist, so the pulse in my fingers begins to throb. His face is only inches from mine. I can smell his breath, like a bushel of rotting apples. His eyes no longer have that glaze covering them. They're wild now, the eyes of a gut-shot deer, and he frightens me. Really frightens me. I wonder who this person is—certainly not my brother.

"This man . . . ," I say, just so he'll let go. "This man was in town. He came to see me the other day."

"What man? Who?"

"This German fellow. His brother was at the camp. He was asking questions."

"What kind of questions?"

"I don't know. Different things. It's not important."

"Why from you? What the hell would you remember about the camp?"

"It was a mistake. He was really looking for Ambroise. I think his brother may have worked for him. He thought maybe Ambroise might remember him."

"Ambroise is dead," he says.

Just then, from behind the counter, Gwen calls over to us. "You folks all right there?"

I look at Leon and he lets go of my wrist finally.

"The coffee's fine," I reply. Then to Leon, whispering, I say, "That's what I told him." As I try to rub the feeling back into my wrist, I notice that my fingers are smeared with blood. It's all over my wrist. I'm covered with blood. "Just look what you've done. Are you crazy? Am I bringing a crazy man home? What's the matter with you, anyway?"

"Sorry," he says.

"Just sorry? You act like a maniac and that's all you can say?"

He tries to touch me. "Lib," he says. "I'm—"

"Get away from me. I go out of my way for you and this is how you thank me. Who else would take you in? All my life I've stuck my neck out for you." I pause for a moment. I'm not even sure why, what makes me say what I say next. "His brother was the one who escaped, you know."

Leon stares at me, his eyes wide, his lower jaw dropped open like a fish five minutes out of water. For several seconds he doesn't say a thing, and I wish I hadn't told him. Wish I hadn't brought any of it up. Finally he asks, "What?"

"Never mind. Forget it," I say.

"His brother was who?"

"The one who escaped. The one they found dead. Don't you remember anything? Or is your brain so soaked with booze you can't even remember that?"

He gets up so quickly that the coffee cup slips from his hand, splatters on the table, rolls off and explodes on the floor like a gunshot. "Leon," I call after him. "Leon. What's the matter?"

But he leaves the restaurant and heads out to the truck. I get my kleenex and begin trying to clean up the mess. The fat woman comes over then, a mop in her hand.

"I got it, hon. Don't worry," she says. "You okay?"

"Yes," I reply, fumbling in my pocketbook for some money.

"I got some Band-Aids in the back. You oughtn't to let him do that."

"I'm all right."

"My first husband was that way. Used to raise his hand to me. I thought that was normal. Then I wised up real quick. I packed his bags and told him not to let the door hit him in the ass on the way out. That's the only way to deal with those kind."

I drop several bills on the table and hurry out to the truck, my wrist throbbing.

3

EVERYTHING STARTED THIS past Tuesday when Spotty Haines came in the store. He'd ridden across the lake on his Yamaha. Most of the tote roads north of here had been closed from the last storm, and snowmobile is about the only way in or out. Spotty and his son Warren and Warren's wife Alice run a guide service over in Northeast Carry, and he stops in now and then to pick up supplies or grab a bite to eat, or just to shoot the breeze. He's an old friend of my father's. Sometimes on winter nights he and I'll play a couple of hands of setback in the store and talk about the old days. Once in a while he'll tell me something about Ambroise I'd never known, things from when my father was a young man. Like how he had almost killed a man once down in Bangor, in a fight over a woman.

"Jesus. Freeze your balls off out there, Lib," Spotty said to me, rubbing his hands over the stove. On the Bardahl thermometer near the gas pumps it said thirty below, but that hadn't worked right in a long time. It was pretty cold. Earlier, Harve Michaud, the Fish and Game agent, said he'd had to take an ice fisherman down to Doc Proulx's. The guy had a couple of frostbitten toes.

"I wouldn't have to worry about that," I told him.

"Don't suppose that you would," Spotty said, laughing. He sat down next to me at the counter, puddles of dark water circling his boots. "Hey, Harve," he called to Harve, who was sitting a few stools away sipping a coffee.

"What are you up to, Spotty?" asked Harve.

"Not much. How's about some coffee, Lib?"

"You ain't crippled."

He got up and went around the counter and poured himself a cup. He sat down again and dropped in about four teaspoons of sugar.

"Why don't you have a little coffee with your sugar," I said.

"I always did have a sweet tooth," he kidded, smiling to show the three blackened teeth he had left in his head. "I like it *real* sweet," he said, winking at Harve.

"You old fart, you wouldn't know what to do with it anymore," I said.

"Maybe not. But Christalmighty, I'd have a ball trying to remember." Spotty laughed. His face was windburned, the bluish red of an undercooked lobster. He still had the marks where his goggles cut into his nose. He's a small, leathery old man, must be seventy-five, but he still takes hunters into the woods every fall and fishermen in the spring. He knows these woods better than anybody, even better than Ambroise used to, and that's saying plenty. Knows all the best fishing spots, the coves where the landlocked will be spawning. The sportsmen he takes out always bag the biggest moose and bear. Spotty sat there smoking, his index finger strangling a cigarette.

"So what'd you come all the way over here for?" I asked. "Getting cabin fever up there?"

"Alice is in one of her moods," Spotty said, rolling his eyes. "Figure I'd better get out while the gettin' was good. By the way, Lib, some fellow called yesterday. He's staying at Frannie's Cabins over in Rockwood. He wanted to go across the lake."

I said, "Ice fishing's lousy I heard."

"Yeah, nobody's catching shit," Harve tossed in.

"He wasn't interested in fishing," Spotty continued. "He wanted I should take him out to the old POW camp."

"Oh, yeah? One of those reporters from Boston?" I asked. Every once in a while some newspaperman gets the bright idea of coming up here and trying to milk another story out of the camp. Nazis make good reading. Most people don't even know we had German prisoners in the States. It takes them by surprise. When a tourist stops in and he hears we had a POW camp, not fifteen miles from here, he'll say, "In Maine? Germans? You're kidding." But we had nearly four hundred thousand prisoners in the States, and about three thousand up here in Maine alone. What most people know about POW camps is *Hogan's Heroes* or that movie with William Holden, *Stalag* something or other.

"No," Spotty said. "This fellow was all the way from Germany."

I hoped it was just another one of those German fellows wanting to come back and see the camp, see where he'd spent the war. A few years ago we'd had one come for a visit. Helmutt Posner. Arrived for the fortieth anniversary of V-E Day. They made a big deal out of it in town. They had this big celebration and gave him the key to the city, whatever that meant. He was on the front page of the *Piscataquis Herald*, even made some of the big downstate papers. In the newspaper photo somebody like Vernon Fuller from the Piscataquis Chamber of Commerce and Elton Bishop, the old police chief from back then, were grinning from ear to ear and shaking the guy's hand. Like there'd never even been a camp. Like they were just long-lost war buddies who'd fought on the same side. Of course that wasn't the feeling back then. Then they were just those "lousy krauts." Our *enemy*. For most people stateside during the war, the word *enemy* meant only what they saw in newsreels and in the papers, something without a face or a voice or a smell, but for us it was real. You could jump in your car and drive out to the camp and see them standing just on the other side of the barbed wire. Occasionally you might even see them in trucks being driven through town to other logging sites. They were here, among us. Our enemies.

"You didn't catch his name, did you?" I asked.

"Some damn kraut name. Dolf. Or Rolf. Something like that."

"Wolf?" I said without thinking.

"You know, it might've been. Anyways he's over here seeing if anybody remembers his brother."

"His brother?" I asked. "His brother was over here?"

"Yeah. He was that one tried to ex-cape," Spotty said. "They fished him out of the lake after ice-out. You remember that, don't you, Lib?"

As soon as Spotty said that, I could feel a sour, burning sensation inching up from the pit of my stomach, making toward my throat. It tasted like a piece of fish.

"I vaguely remember," I said.

"Christ," Spotty added, "after he took off everybody in town was locking their doors and keeping a gun by their bed. You'd have thought Rommel himself had landed in Portland. Remember that, Harve?"

Harve, who's in his early forties and so too young to remember, said, "Hell, I wasn't even born yet, Spotty. But I do recall my old man talking about the camp. He told me those Germans lived the life of Riley."

"That they did. They had it easy, those boys," replied Spotty, blowing a ring of smoke into the air. He picked something out of his ear and inspected it, like he had half a mind to put it back. "They were offering a hundred-dollar reward for the one ex-caped. Big money in those days. Remember that, Lib?"

"Forty-six years ago, Spotty. Hell, I got a hard job remembering what happened yesterday," I said, forcing a laugh. But I did remember. Of course I did. I hadn't thought about it in a long, long time but I remembered the escape all right. I was just a girl of fifteen then, yet it was the sort of thing you didn't forget easily. An escaped German POW in a little pissant town like this. I remembered my father and brother and the other paper-company men out late looking with the soldiers for him that night. And the big stink the escape caused around here afterwards. I remembered all that.

I picked up my cup and went behind the counter. I washed it in the sink and set it in the drainer. I looked out the window toward the lake. It was sunny out but windy. The wind was blowing hard, sweeping the snow like mad. In some spots the wind had cleared the snow down to bare, gray ice. It looked like galvanized metal. The ice would be a couple of feet thick. That's what the fishermen who had to bore through it with augers said. Thick enough to drive a truck across. Yet as I looked out on the lake I thought how nearly every spring you heard of some crazy kid going through it with his old man's car or somebody from downstate getting careless with a snowmobile and driving over black ice. Just last year they lost a caravan of snowmobiles over near Rockwood. Lucky nobody died. But that sort of thing happened all the time around here.

"I remember the escape like it was yesterday," Spotty said. "One thing I got is a good memory."

"Except when it comes to your bill." Spotty had a tab he hadn't paid in months. I really didn't lose any sleep over it. He'd done me plenty of favors over the years, brings me cuts of venison and salmon fillets. But I liked to get on him for it.

Ignoring me, Spotty said, "That fellow, the dead one's brother, was asking questions."

"I'd heard somebody was asking around about the camp," Harve said. "Bert Osgood at the post office told me that."

I poured Spotty and Harve some more coffee, then broke down and got out an apple pie I'd just baked that morning. Spotty would talk all day if you kept him in food or butts. Harve didn't want a piece, said his cholesterol level was out of sight.

"You wouldn't have any ice cream to go with that?" Spotty asked.

"Don't push your luck," I said. "What's he want? The German fellow."

"Wanted to know if anybody was still around from the camp. Some of the old-timers."

"What's he want with them?"

"I don't know. I said one of the guards used to live over in Brownville Junction. Didn't recall his name. And there's still a few of the paper-company boys around. Tom Weston's right here in town. He worked for Great American at Sheshuncook back then. You know Tom, don't you?"

"Sure, I know him."

Spotty didn't use a fork with his pie. He just lifted it up to his mouth and shoved it in. He mangled the pie with his gums, then slurped down some coffee, burning his mouth. "Holy Jesus," he cried.

"What's he looking to find out?" I asked.

"Who knows? Oh, yeah. He asked about your old man. Somehow he knew Ambroise had been a foreman up there and worked with the POWs."

"What'd you tell him?"

"I told him he was out of luck. That Ambroise's been dead for, what, twenty years?"

"Twenty-six," I corrected.

Spotty neatly snuffed out his cigarette without bending it, then put the butt in his shirt pocket. He crammed the rest of the pie in his mouth so his cheeks puffed out like a squirrel's stuffed with acorns. He wiped his mouth on his sleeve and stood up to go, still chewing the pie.

"I took that fellow up to see the camp," he said, tying his scarf around his neck.

"I thought the road in is closed," I said.

"It is," Harve added.

"Went by snowmobile," Spotty explained. "I picked him up and we rode out over Daggett Cove."

"That's a long ride for nothing. There's nothing there to see," Harve said.

"That's what I tried to tell him. But it was his money. He wanted to see where his brother spent his last days. Afterwards we visited the old graveyard out there."

"He came all the way over here just for *that*?" I said.

"Guess he was looking to say something over his brother's grave. But Christ, the snow was too deep. Couldn't even find any of the Germans' stones."

"There aren't any," I said.

"What do you mean?" Spotty asked. "I thought some of those krauts were buried out there."

"They were. But the stones were all stolen years ago. Souvenirs, I guess."

"Well, we only stayed a few minutes and then rode back," Spotty said. "The damn fool didn't even have any boots on. If he got frostbit, Alice'd have my ass in a sling. Insurance rates are already killing us."

I'd driven up there once myself, eight, ten years ago. Along the Golden Road, then over the dam to Sheshuncook. I don't know why. Curiosity, I guess. About where I'd grown up. About my past, the way you get to be curious at a certain age about things you have no power to change, like the weather. Or like a mother who'd run off on you. I hadn't been up there in ages. I'd had no reason to after I'd sold the house and moved over here. Didn't have any close friends over there, none that I would miss anyway. I visited the old place across the cove. The people who had bought it from me, a couple named the Dwyers, had fixed it over and now it was a summer place. New paint and shutters, a screened-in porch. It looked real nice. The small village itself hadn't changed much: It still clung to the north side of the lake like a piece of moss. The dirt road that ran through the middle and down to the lake still wasn't paved. The Sheshuncook Inn was gone, of course, had burned down right after the war, but Riley's boat rental was still there, as was Tohay's small-engine repair place, Asa Shaw's chicken farm, which was being run by his son Bobby, and the half-dozen run-down shacks of logging families who'd lived there for generations, families with names like Crimmins and Gagnon and Klatka and Bouchard. The general store was still there, too, though this young couple from New York, back-to-nature types, were running it now. The wife with a long Indian print dress, the husband with wire-rims and a bushy mustache. They were selling dried herbs and homemade ice cream. Used to be owned by an old man named Charlie Abbey.

Abbey's General Store. I remember he had one glass eye. You could never tell if he was looking at you or not. Leon and I'd go in and buy licorice and Shakespeare fishing line, cans of Prince Albert tobacco for Ambroise. And under the table he used to sell moonshine whiskey.

Just past the store toward the lake is where the camp used to be. It was all grown over when I was there, some white birch and spruce, a few summer cottages. There was no sign at all that the place was once a prison, that it'd held in check the lives of young boys caught up in the war. Back down the dirt road the other way, the old graveyard was still there, of course, right on the river. They weren't going anywhere. It used to be the village graveyard, but it was where they'd buried the handful of Germans who had died in the camp. I thought of stopping and looking at the place. I hadn't been there since I was a kid. The stones, which used to say *Soldat*, were long gone, but I remembered about where the Germans were buried. Set off by themselves, down by the river near a big willow tree, as if even in death they were still the enemy, still needed to be isolated. But it was getting dark. I don't believe in ghosts, but sometimes it's not such a good idea to flaunt what you don't believe in. So I turned around and headed home.

"Say, how'd you know his name was Wolf?" Spotty asked, zipping up his parka.

I thought of telling him about the letter. But then Spotty would've wanted to know why I hadn't told him about it in the first place, and for that I didn't have an answer.

"It's a pretty common German name," I said. "Like Fritz."

"Lib, whyn't you throw a pack of Camels on my tab, too," Spotty said. He pulled on his goggles and this leather aviator hat of his, so he looked like one of those World War I flying aces.

"You going to square up one of these years?" I said.

"You know I'm good for it."

"Good for nothing, you mean."

He stopped at the door to pull on his mittens. "You know, there was something else I was gonna tell you."

"What?" I asked.

"Slipped my mind now."

"I thought you had such a good memory, too."

"I don't forget things. I just misplace them," he said. "See you later, Harve."

"See you, Spotty," called Harve.

I watched Spotty get on his snowmobile and take off across the lake, the tread kicking up little packets of snow.

About a year and a half ago I received the letter. It was from overseas, with those strange stamps—Erfurt, DDR, the return address said. It had been addressed to Ambroise Pelletier, care of the Great American Paper Company, Millinocket, Maine. Somebody over at the mill must have known he was my father and forwarded the letter to me. I held it in my hands for a long time. Ambroise didn't know anybody in Germany, so I wondered what it could be about. Whatever it was inside the envelope, I knew it wasn't good news.

July 23, 1989

Ambroise Pelletier
c/o Great American Paper Company
Millinocket, Maine 04462
United States of America

Dear Herr Pelletier:

It is my understanding that you were a logging
supervisor during the years 1944–45, for the Great
American Paper Company. German prisoners were
employed by your company to harvest timber at the
Sheshuncook prisoner of war camp in Maine. My
brother, Dieter Kallick, was one. He was part of
Rommel's Afrika Korps and captured in North Africa
in 1943. He was sent to the U.S. during the summer
of 1944, and spent the duration of the war in Maine.

My brother never returned home, however. According to information I received from your government shortly after the war, he drowned during an escape attempt.

Herr Pelletier, I am writing to persons who were at the camp and might have had contact with Dieter. In fact, I have reason to believe my brother worked for you; therefore I am writing this in the sincere hope that you may remember him. Any information you might have of him or the camp itself, however slight, would be most helpful. I realize that many years have passed since then, so I am enclosing a picture of Dieter. I have also enclosed a self-addressed envelope with sufficient postage for your reply.

Thanking you in advance for your kind consideration, I remain sincerely yours,

Wolfgang Kallick

I wondered how he'd managed to get ahold of Ambroise's name, but then realized it actually would have been pretty easy. There were probably records over at the paper company, and most people in town knew my father had been a foreman up at the camp. That was no secret.

I looked at the photo. It was a reproduction of an old photograph. The surface was slick and glossy, but the picture itself was faded and blurry, the edges of the objects in it blending into each other the way things do at nightfall. It showed this young boy (fifteen? sixteen?) on skis, a background of grayish snow and bare trees. He had regular features, ones that could have been anybody's. A high forehead, the faintest hint of a smile, the cocky sort boys have, as if they own some precious secret. On the back was written, "*Dieter Kallick, Februar, 1938, Oberhof.*" Just some boy. Could have been any one of the dozens they had up at the camp, I told myself. It was a long time ago, and I'd been just a girl then.

Yet, the more I stared at the picture, the more familiar he looked. Especially the eyes—hooded, narrow—and the wide, full mouth. I could almost see his lips parting, hear that exotic language of the enemy slipping out. Even now I can recall some words, a few German expressions, scattered phrases. They're stuck there in my mind like dead insects in a cobweb.

You see, I'd worked up there at the camp for a little while, as a cookee, a sort of cook's helper. During that first summer they arrived and a few times after that whenever my father needed me. Despite the Germans' presence, we'd had a labor shortage, and the paper company took any warm body they could get, even fifteen-year-old girls. I'd help bring the Germans their noon meal in the woods and carry tools back from the maintenance shop, so I got to see some of those boys up close, closer than a lot of people in town came to them. Close enough to hear them talk and rub shoulders with them, even smell that peculiar German smell they had. I don't know why, but they smelled like hot grease and metal, like a machine shop.

I continued to stare at the photograph. Though I kept trying to convince myself I didn't recognize him, after a while I came slowly around to the view that I did. I *had* to. After all, even if I didn't recognize *this* boy in *this* picture, I knew it *had* to be him: There was only one German who had escaped and drowned. The name Dieter didn't mean a thing to me. It could have been Klaus or Werner or Hans or Peter, or one of a dozen other names from the camp and it wouldn't have meant anything to me. The one I'd remembered I knew only as "the interpreter," the one on my father's logging crew. The one I'd sat next to in the truck a few times, who'd cut his hand on a power saw. The one who had escaped. The one they'd found in the lake. I remembered *him,* and this picture, I was being told, was *his* picture.

I thought about writing. I could understand this man's need to know about his brother. After all, I knew something about the strong pull of blood, how powerful it could be even after many years, how sometimes it even got stronger with time. But he wasn't blood and I had to think about my own. I didn't want him coming here stirring up trouble, dragging Ambroise's name into whatever it was he was looking to find out. Besides, what did I know? How could I—just a girl when the interpreter had escaped—help this Kallick fellow? A few memories about that boy, his brother—how would that help him out? And then somehow the letter got misplaced and I didn't have his address anymore and couldn't write even if I wanted to. He'd written, *Any information you might have of him or the camp itself, however slight, would be most helpful.* And helpful for what? And why now, after all these years? I never told Leon about the letter, never saw any point. I did keep the picture though, hidden in my purse, beneath a picture of an old lover named Frank Cobb. I'm not even sure why I kept it. Maybe to remind me of those days, the war, when I was a girl. Yet when I didn't hear from Wolfgang Kallick again, I put it out of my mind. It was finished business.

But one night a year ago last November, I was at the bar in the Spruce Goose, a tavern down in Piscataquis. I was having a couple of drinks with Roland St. James, this man I see from time to time. The late-night news came on the TV behind the bar. It showed all these people standing on this wall. They were shouting and holding up banners, and some of them were banging away at the wall. They had sledgehammers and picks, anything they could get their hands on. Earl Teed, the bartender, was about to turn the channel when I said, "Wait, Earl. Who are those people? What are they doing?"

"Where you been, Lib? That there's the goddamn Berlin Wall," he said. "They're finally getting back together, those krauts."

"We better watch out," Roland joked.

"You ain't shitting," Earl replied. "The goddamn Fourth Reich."

I watched the TV with curiosity. Behind the wall it looked like there were hundreds, thousands of people, waiting in cars, in lines, carrying suitcases, finally being released. And then it hit me: The war for them hadn't ended in 1945, it was ending only now. It was as if they'd been POWs all this time, too. I remember one young girl being interviewed. Through an interpreter she said she was going to see her grandfather in the West, who she'd never laid eyes on before. And I wondered how many people would be seeing loved ones the war had separated, and how many more would be looking for the ones they'd lost.

"I had a letter from some German fellow over there," I said to Roland, pointing at the TV. I don't know why I told him. I hadn't told anybody else. Maybe it was the booze talking.

"Yeah. What about?" he asked, already getting jealous. Roland's a jealous man. If he sees me talking with somebody else he gets mad.

"He had a brother who died in the POW camp over here."

"So what? What's that got to do with you?"

"Nothing," I replied. "He was looking for Ambroise."

"Why?"

"Ambroise had been a foreman up there. Somebody forwarded the letter to me. It's got nothing to do with me, really. Or Ambroise, for that matter."

Roland finished his drink. "You want to go back to my place? It's closer."

On the drive over to Roland's place—he lives over near Indian Pond—I kept thinking about that German girl, waiting to meet a grandfather the war kept her from. And the other German, too, the one who'd written to Ambroise about his brother. Maybe, alive or dead, they just wanted to reclaim what was theirs.

4

THE DAY AFTER Spotty came in and told me about the German, I was frying up some liver and onions, the special of the day. Roland, Hoppy McCray, Jack Duchene, and some guy named Karl I'd never laid eyes on had stopped in for lunch. Their rigs were idling outside, full loads of pulpwood waiting to be turned into paper at the mills. They were sitting over in a booth near the window. Every once in a while, when they thought I wasn't looking they'd pass a pint bottle around. I don't have a liquor license, and I could get shut down if that got around. But normally I figure way out here, what I don't see won't hurt me. That's my attitude about a lot of things, and most of the time it makes a lot of sense.

"You hear that woman's husband is pressing charges?" Hoppy said. "He's trying for manslaughter."

"No way it'll happen," Duchene said. "Ain't a hunter's fault she didn't have brains enough not to go in the woods in season."

They were talking about something in the *Maine Telegram*. A woman was killed by a hunter who thought she was a deer. He shot her in her own backyard while she was hanging clothes, right in front of her kids. Now the husband was trying to have the hunter brought up on manslaughter charges. It was a big deal up here, even made the national news. I got nothing against hunting, mind you, but all those hunters' groups were digging in, saying that if a man didn't have a constitutional right to go shooting a woman hanging clothes, then the country was in sorry shape. It made me sick to my stomach.

"Well, it says right here he's trying for first-degree manslaughter. What do you think, Lib?" Hoppy yelled over to me.

"Humph," was all I said, without turning around.

"I feel sorry for her kids," Roland said.

"Me, too," Duchene added. "But any way you slice it, Rollie, it's still a goddamn accident."

"Some accident," I tossed in.

"Sure it was," Duchene said.

"She was in her own backyard, for heaven's sakes," I said. Bite your tongue, Lib, I warned myself.

"We ain't saying he shouldn't have been more careful, Lib," Roland said. "It's just that she should've known better. Hunting season and she wasn't even wearing orange."

"I suppose if he came in her house and shot her in bed you'd want her wearing orange."

"An orange nightie," Duchene said. The others laughed like fools.

"These downstaters got to learn they can't come up here and play by *their* rules, Lib," said Hoppy, a short, stocky man with big ears. He wore a plaid hunting cap and had a nub of a cigar stuck in the corner of his mouth like a fishing plug. He's Roland's brother-in-law, married Roland's sister Trudy. Sometimes the four of us get together, go bowling over to the Moosehead Lanes or snowmobiling up north.

"Rules?" I said. "The damn fool shot her in cold blood. What kind of rules you talking about, Hop?"

"They got to learn what's what," the other one named Karl threw in. He was a large man, with a full beard streaked with gray and a red nose that looked like it'd been hit with buckshot. An old-fashioned woodcutter's toque sat on the back of his head. "Give you ten to one whose idea it was to prosecute, too."

"Some downstate shyster," Hoppy added.

Duchene said, "Count on that." With a finger he bent his nose sideways. The others laughed again.

"What really burns me," said the big guy, "is them coming up here, buying up *our* land, and then telling us we got to play everything by *their* goddamn rules."

"You got that right, Karl," said Duchene. He always rubbed me the wrong way. He had these small, glossy black rodent eyes and a head no bigger than a grapefruit. He was one of a tribe of Duchenes who lived way back in the woods north of the dam. All of them had heads the size of grapefruits and those same rat eyes. Ambroise had never liked them, said he wouldn't trust a Duchene as far as you could throw one.

"We oughta pass a law," Duchene said. "Keep all those sons a bitches the fuck out. We don't need no circumcised shysters telling us how to run things up here."

I knew I should've shut up, just chalked it up to the booze. But it wasn't just the booze. It was the way they thought. The way people in these small backwoods places think, places where the men sit around drinking from the same bottle and smelling of sweat and sawdust and gun oil, and deciding who should stay and who should go. Who's American enough and who's not. They get half-cocked and go off and do something, get in a fight or beat up their old lady. Or maybe go down to the draft board and sign up for Desert Storm. I think it's something genetic or in the water maybe, something that starts early and gets worse the older and dumber they get. I don't know. I've seen it plenty. A few years back this nice older man named Howie Green moved in up on Lily Bay Mountain. Retired postal worker, came up here with his wife. Used to stop in to fill up his Blazer and we'd talk about the Red Sox. He'd come from Boston and was a big Sox fan. He wasn't here six months when some damn fool painted a swastika on his mailbox. When he told me about it, I felt ashamed, I really did. Because I've lived here all my life and I know the sort who'd do such a thing.

Normally when they start talking like this, I let it slide off me, but today I didn't feel like it.

"Duchene, your grandfather was nothing more than a stinking Canuck woodcutter, just like mine. Who're you shitting?"

"My grandfather was born right here in Millinocket. He was American."

"Then his father. Ambroise used to say all those shitkicking Duchenes never had a pot to piss in or a window to throw it out. Lived back in the bush like wild dogs."

"Huh! Ambroise should talk," he said, leaning back in his chair and hooking his thumbs inside his belt loops. "Three sheets to the wind and the stupid bastard walks in front of a tractor."

"He slipped."

"He was shit-faced. Everybody knows it. And while we're at it, how about that alky brother of yours? He drink himself into the grave yet?"

"Watch your big mouth, Duchene. I'm warning you."

"*You* got the mouth to watch," he said, smiling.

"That's enough, Jack," Roland warned.

I was used to jokes about my mouth. It didn't matter. But I wasn't going to let him get away with that crack about Leon.

"You watch it, Duchene. You'll be out of here on your ear," I said.

"Who's gonna do it?" he said, laughing.

"You just keep it up, and you'll find out."

"Jack, knock it off," Roland said again, pointing a finger at him. "And I *mean* it."

"Sorry, Rollie," Duchene said.

Roland got up and came over to where I stood in front of the grill. He poured himself a cup of coffee. "Take it easy, Lib," he said under his breath. "Jack didn't mean anything about Ambroise."

"Yeah, sure. Jack's a moron. And tell them to put that bottle away," I said. "You want to get me closed down."

"What's the matter?" he asked.

"Nothing's the matter. I don't have a liquor license, remember?"

"Put the bottle away, fellows," Roland called over to them. "Lib, I was thinking."

"When did you start that?"

"You got anything on for Saturday night?"

"I don't know. I'll have to check my social calendar."

"Maybe we could go down to the Goose and do some dancing."

"Leon might be getting out of the VA this weekend. I'll have to see."

Roland's wife died of breast cancer about five years ago, and he and I go out now and then. It's no big thing, nothing serious. He's a couple of years younger than me, a heavyset man with thick lips and the chocolate brown eyes of a Chesapeake Bay retriever. He's worked for the paper company for years, first as a logger, then after he'd hurt his knee, as a driver. We have some fun together. We'll go to a movie in town or do some ice fishing. Sometimes, if I'm in the mood I'll ask him back to my place. Lately, though, Roland's started to get some ideas. He's looking for a place to park his boots. A few weeks back he asked me what I thought about him moving in. I said I didn't think it was such a hot idea. He said we could share expenses, and he could help out with the store. I told him I didn't need any help. I told him maybe Leon was going to come and stay with me for a while.

"How's our order coming?" Hoppy called over to me. "We got to get back to work, Lib."

"It's coming."

"So's ice-out."

"What do you say about Saturday, Lib?" Roland insisted.

"I told you, I'll have to see," I snapped at him.

I went into the kitchen to get some rolls and butter, a can of creamed corn. When I came out this man was standing there talking to the others. I saw Roland point over to me. The man looked to be in his mid-sixties. He was short and solid, thick through the middle. He wore one of those little hats, what I think of as yodeling hats, with a small grouse feather in it. He even looked like a grouse, with a small beak of a nose. The hair on the sides of his head was silver, curly. The other thing I noticed right off was that he wasn't dressed for winter up here. It was twenty below and here he was with only a sports coat on, a turtleneck sweater, no gloves or boots. He stuck out like a sore thumb. I could see Roland and the others giving him the eye. We don't get that many strangers here in March, and not dressed like some professor from UMaine. I should've known right then who he was. I just didn't put two and two together.

"I'll be right with you," I said. With the spatula I moved the liver and onions around on the grill. I put some rolls and butter in a basket and took them over to Roland and the others. Then I opened the creamed corn and put it on the stove. Finally I came back over and said to the stranger, "So what can I get you? You want a menu? The special's liver and onions."

"No, thank you," he said. I caught the accent. "I am looking for Herr Ambroise Pelletier's daughter," he said. "I was told I might find her here."

"I'm Libby Pelletier," I replied.

"My name is Wolfgang Kallick."

"What can I do for you?" I said, wiping my hands on my apron. I picked up a rag and started to mop up the counter, as if he were just another tourist asking directions. I told myself I had no reason to be nervous, that whatever he wanted it had nothing to do with me. But for some reason I was nervous.

"I wrote a letter to your father, Frau Pelletier. Over a year ago."

"How's our lunch coming, *Frau* Pelletier?" Duchene asked, elbowing Hoppy. The two started giggling like schoolboys.

"Hold your horses," I told them. Then to Wolfgang Kallick I said, "Sorry. Now what was it you were saying?"

"I said I'd written to your father. It was about my brother. He was a POW at the camp in Sheshuncook." His mouth tightened as he said this, these fine white cracks forming above the upper lip. He spoke slowly and carefully in precise English, occasionally putting a thumb and forefinger to his mouth as if he were actually picking out the exact word he wanted.

I thought of telling him I'd received the letter, but then I didn't know how I'd explain about not writing back. So I said,

"My father's been dead for twenty-six years." Which was the truth, after all.

"Yes, I have since learned as much," Kallick replied. Though he had to be around my age, his skin was as smooth and supple as a child's, and pale, too, as if he didn't get out much. His eyes were blue, the bluest I'd ever seen. A soft powdery blue, the color of carpenter's chalk. If you touched them you could imagine the color coming off on your fingers. "Frau Pelletier—" he began but then stopped abruptly. He looked over at the other men, who were staring at us, whispering.

"I guess we could sit down," I offered.

I led him to a booth toward the back of the store, near the rest rooms. I thought we'd have a little more privacy there. Though I wasn't sure what he wanted from me, I didn't like the idea of Roland and the others hearing it and blabbing all over town. I asked him, "Can I get you some coffee?"

"*Bitte,*" he said. "That would be nice."

I poured us both a cup and then sat down.

"Do you mind if I smoke, Frau Pelletier?" he asked politely.

"Go right ahead." He took out a tobacco pouch from his coat pocket. He filled the pipe's bowl, tamping the tobacco down with his thick thumb. He lit it, puffed hard several times, his cheeks sinking, pulling the skin taut over the sharp bones of his face. The tobacco smelled sweet, like blueberries. His hands were fleshy and soft, but the nails were embedded with what looked like a narrow rim of grease. He had a thin, silver wedding band that cut deeply into his fat finger. He didn't seem to be in a hurry to say anything. I got the sense he was catching his breath after a long journey. He glanced around the room. I noticed him staring at an old crosscut saw on the wall above us. I'd hung a lot of old logger's tools—pulp hooks and peaveys, double-bit axes and bucksaws. Things Ambroise had left after he died. It had been Leon's idea to put them on the walls. He thought the tourists would like it. Give the place some atmosphere.

"*Die Schrotsäge,*" Kallick said, not so much to me as he was just thinking out loud. I knew he didn't expect me to understand, but I did. The Germans at the camp had used that word a lot. From the woods they'd call "*die Schrotsäge*" and I'd have to fetch them a sharpened saw from the truck. Even after all these years I still remembered it. Kallick explained. "A crosscut saw. We used them on my grandfather's farm to cut timber."

Kallick's eyes were slightly hooded, giving him a vaguely Oriental look. That was the only similarity I could see to the thin, young boy in the picture he'd sent me, the only connection between this fat old man and the young interpreter.

"Frau Pelletier," he began, "my brother never made it home. He died over here in the camp. After the war your government reported that he had drowned."

"Yes," I said. "I remember that. But it was a long time ago, Mr. Kallick."

"You are right, it has been a long time. You see, only recently could we in the East travel freely. It was not impossible before but it was quite difficult. I have always wanted to see where Dieter was buried. To say something over his grave."

"That's a long way to come for a prayer."

He took a long puff on his pipe, seeming to gather his thoughts.

"Some time ago, Frau Pelletier, a man came into my place of employment. He said he had been at the camp with Dieter. It was he who told me Dieter had worked for your father. Herr Wattenberg was his name. I could not believe it. He just showed up one day. After forty-four years, out of the blue. So much was happening in our country, so many changes. Everything was being stirred up, I suppose something like this was bound to happen. Many old wounds were reopened. In Erfurt I knew a woman whose husband had died in the war and she remarried. She had a family, started a new life. Then one year ago her first husband knocked on her door and said, 'Here I am,' as if he could pick up where they had left off. You see, Frau Pelletier, after the war many Germans never had a chance to let those old wounds heal. We had to get on with the business of living."

"And?" I asked, my patience running thin.

"Forgive me, I'm getting away from my point. This friend of Dieter's, Herr Wattenberg, said he had tried unsuccessfully to contact us after the war. Everything was so chaotic then. After a while he gave up. Then recently—I don't know, through a mutual acquaintance, one of those things that happen—he learned I was alive and he came to visit me."

Kallick placed his thumbnail to his lips and pressed. When he took his hand away his upper lip was white. "You know what is odd, Frau Pelletier?"

"What?"

"I had not thought about Dieter in so long. I had mourned him. I even had a stone made for him and placed in the cemetery in Erfurt where our parents are buried. But you cannot mourn forever. Dieter was just a small photograph on a mantel for me."

"What did Wattenberg tell you?" I asked.

"He said Dieter had disappeared."

"You mean escaped?"

"Perhaps."

"Why perhaps? You don't believe what they told you? That he drowned in his escape?"

"Let's just say that I have my doubts now."

"Why? What did that man tell you?"

But just then Hoppy called over. "Christ, Lib, we got to hit the road."

"Excuse me," I said, getting up quickly. I'd forgotten about their orders. I hurried over to find that the liver had burned and that the onions had turned black. I had to scrape it off the grill. I put the food on plates with some more rolls and slices of tomato and bowls of creamed corn, and went over and set them in front of the men. Duchene said, "Crissakes, you expect us to eat this shit?"

"It's just well done," I said.

"She's yakking with goddamn Fritz while our food is burning."

"If you don't like it, don't eat it."

"What's he want?" Roland asked.

"I don't know," I replied. "He's interested in the old POW camp."

"You know him?"

"I've never seen him before in my life."

The big guy named Karl said, "Esther Pavel, at the drugstore, said she heard somebody was in town asking questions about the camp."

I left them and walked back over to the German and sat down.

"What does all this have to do with my father, Mr. Kallick? Or with me?"

"Your father was a supervisor. Dieter worked for him."

"So? A lot of Germans worked for my father." I suddenly felt very protective of Ambroise.

"I just thought . . . ," he said, his voice trailing off into smoke. The words seemed to hang there for a moment, waiting for me to pick them up. With his thumb he rubbed the wedding band hard, almost as if he were trying to rub completely through the thin metal. I chanced looking up from his hands and saw that he was staring at me. At my mouth, the way people do sometimes. "Is it possible your father mentioned something?" he asked.

"To me? Like what?"

"Perhaps about my brother?"

"You're talking forty-six years ago. Besides, my father was pretty quiet. Kept things to himself."

"Did he ever say anything about what went on at the camp?"

"What do you mean, 'what went on'?"

"Any problems."

"Mr. Kallick, those boys were just cord cutters to him. That's all. What went on at the camp wasn't his concern. You want to know that, you ought to talk to somebody in the military. The camp guards. They might know." Finally I said, "I should be getting back to work."

He took one last puff on his pipe, then stood up. "Thank you for your time," he said, bowing slightly as he offered me his pudgy hand. Nobody had ever bowed to me before. Wolfgang Kallick's hand was moist and warm, hot almost, as if its owner had a fever. He held my hand a moment longer than necessary. I had to pull it back finally.

Before I turned away, I said, "Can I ask you a question?"

"Certainly," replied Kallick.

I should have just dropped it. Should have kept my mouth shut. After all it wasn't any of my concern. But I was curious. "What do you hope to find out after all these years?" I asked.

He extended one hand, palm up, the way someone feeling for rain would. What flashed through my mind, however, was his brother's bloody hand, cut by a power saw. The image made me shiver. Finally Kallick said, "*Was ist passiert.*" He tapped his thumb against his lips. At last he said, "What happened."

"'What happened'?"

"Yes. I want to know what happened to my brother."

I was going to ask what that meant, but I decided not to. He took out his wallet like he was going to pay for the coffee, but I said, "That's all right. It's on the house." I just wanted him to go, wanted to be rid of him.

"*Danke*, Frau Pelletier," he said. "You are very kind."

"Just a coffee," I said. Then I added, "Good-bye. And good luck with whatever it is you're after." I picked up the cups and carried them back to the kitchen. I stood at the sink for a moment, looking out the window. After a while, I saw this red car, a late-model Buick with Massachusetts plates, pull out of the parking lot and drive off, heading for town. I tried to light a cigarette and saw that my hands couldn't hold the match steady. I hoped that was the end of it.

As I was cleaning the table off, I saw he'd left a twenty-dollar bill, one that had been taped together. Also on the table was a business card. I was a little annoyed with the money, since I'd told him the coffee was free. But I slipped both the card and the bill into my apron pocket.

"*Frau* Pelletier," Hoppy said, as he paid his bill. "Jesus Christ. Ain't we getting hoity-toity."

"Why did Fritz want to know about the camp?" Roland asked again.

"Just curious, I guess."

"Was he one of them Nazis?" Hoppy wanted to know.

"No," I said. "And anyways, they weren't *all* Nazis. Most were just soldiers."

"Hell, I didn't know there was a difference," said Hoppy. "I was stationed over in Germany in the fifties. What I could never figure out was where the hell all the Nazis went to. You couldn't find one to save your ass."

The guy named Karl handed me a ten and said, "Take out for Jack's, too. I remember one time my old man took me up there. To the camp. Have a look at them krauts. I must've been about twelve. This was right after we got the news about my uncle Ansel. He died in Normandy. When my old man heard he broke down and cried like a baby. It was after that he took me up to the camp. He had his three-oh-eight in the truck, and I swear to God he had some ideas about evening up the score. We waited in the truck watching those sons a bitches for the longest time. It was summertime and we sat there in the dark just outside the barbed wire. I remember my old man saying, 'Be like shooting fish in a goddamned barrel, Karl.' True story. Lucky for those krauts he didn't go through with it."

When the others moved off toward the door, Roland whispered to me, "You ain't mad anymore, are you, Lib?"

"What?" I said, my mind still on Wolfgang Kallick.

"Mad about before."

"Why should I be?" I could smell ginger brandy on his breath. He had a quarter-moon-shaped scab on his chin where he'd cut himself shaving. He was leaning over, close enough so I could see the black hairs in his nose.

"I don't know. Just seems like you're mad."

"I'm not mad."

"Good. Listen, I got a couple venison steaks in the freezer. I was thinking on Saturday we could fry them up and then later go out to the Goose with Hop and Trudy. Paul Dixon and the Rainmakers are playing. How's that grab you?"

"I might be busy."

"What's the matter?"

"I told you, nothing's the matter."

"You got something going on the side, Lib?" He said this loud, so the others could hear. "You sure that guy was only ask-ing questions?"

"Don't be a jerk, Roland," I said. "I told you I never met him before."

"He seemed like he knew you. What the hell's going on?"

"Nothing's *going on*, for heaven's sakes."

"Well, don't act so high and mighty. I thought we had . . . I thought it was me and you."

"You got it wrong. We ain't anything."

"What about them steaks?"

"You leave your meat in the freezer, Roland," I told him, also loud. "It'll stay hard that way." Over near the door the other three started laughing.

"She got you there, Rollie," Hoppy said. "She got you real good. Attagirl, Lib."

They climbed into their rigs and headed toward Millinocket, puffs of smoke shooting out their smokestacks as they shifted gears. I walked over to the window and watched until they were out of sight. I took the card out of my apron pocket. It said "Wolfgang Kallick," and then below that, "Uhrmacher" and below that, "Erfurt, Wahringerstrasse 176, DDR." I wondered what *"Uhrmacher"* meant. What he did with those soft, fleshy hands. I flipped the card over. On the back was written "Frannie's Cabins" and a phone number. It was over in Rockwood, on the west side of the lake, where the Moose River flows in. It was a long drive, a good sixty miles around. If you drew a line from Frannie's Cabins to my place, then up to Sheshuncook where his brother was buried and finally back down to where he was staying, you'd have a perfect triangle. Well, almost.

As I was looking out across that frozen triangle, I told myself I hadn't lied to Wolfgang Kallick. Not really. He'd wanted to know if Ambroise knew anything about his brother or the camp, and *that* I couldn't say. Ambroise hardly ever spoke about the camp. In fact, in the twenty years after the end of the war, I couldn't recall him once speaking of it or the Germans. It was like those years had never existed for him, like they'd been cleared from his memory the way the bulldozers had cleared the camp away.

Yet I knew that if I hadn't actually lied, I hadn't told him everything I knew, either. I did remember, some things anyway— the place and the Germans, what it was like back then. And his brother, too. I remembered him a little. Why hadn't I told him? Why was I afraid? People like that Karl fellow, people who had wanted to make the Germans pay for what they'd done. Maybe it was because I thought it would just stir up all those bad feelings. Maybe that was it, after all.

5

By THE TIME we get home, it's almost dark and snowing hard. Must be six inches on the ground. Before I pull into my unplowed driveway, I have to stop and get out, lock the front wheels, then shift into four-wheel drive. Roland usually plows it and the parking lot out front for me, but after the words we had the other day I guess he decided not to. I park the truck in the barn and get out.

"Take my arm," I say to Leon, who's not said a word the rest of the way home. "It's slippery."

"I ain't crippled," he replies.

"Suit yourself."

The snow, with tiny pieces of ice in it, rakes my face as we walk up the outside stairs to my apartment. From the light at the top, I notice the footprints on the steps right away—the broad, deep prints of someone both heavy and older, the flat-footed, cautious walk of someone who's worried about falling. It takes me a second, though, to catch sight of the envelope shoved in the crack of the door. As I'm putting my key in, I see it. FRAU PELLETIER, it says. Leon's behind me and I'm sure he doesn't see me slide it into my coat pocket.

Mitzi, alone all day, jumps all over me and pees on the floor, a habit I've not broken her of in the nearly eight years we've been together. I got her as a pup from a tourist passing through, who didn't want his camper smelling of dog piss. I called her Mitzi, after

Mitzi Gaynor, the movie star. The dog is spoiled rotten, like an only child, and I'm to blame. She chews the woodwork, begs from the dinner table, sometimes even sleeps up on the bed with me.

"How's my girl?" Leon says, petting her. Mitzi makes these whimpering noises as my brother scratches her along the throat. Though he hasn't been up here in more than a year, she still remembers him.

"She must be hungry," I say. I head downstairs into the store, and from the fridge in the kitchen I get half a dozen hamburger patties that were starting to go bad.

"Give her these," I tell Leon.

He sits at the kitchen table, peels the paper backing off the hamburgers, and makes Mitzi get up on her hind legs and beg. She looks so silly.

"Attagirl," he says. "You miss me?"

When she finishes the hamburgers, she heads over to the door, puts her muzzle to the knob.

"Wanna go out, Mitzi?" Leon asks.

"Better tie her on the chain. Otherwise she'll run deer all night."

If I let her go free she meets up with Connie West's Lab from down the road and a couple of ragged-looking strays and they run winter-weakened deer. About a week ago I came across a doe carcass in the woods behind the barn. It was a mess. Blood all over the snow. They'd torn out the bowels and left the rest for crows and coyotes. They don't even do it out of hunger, just bloodlust. Destructive as a carful of teenage boys tanked up with booze and nothing to do. Up here people'll shoot a dog that runs deer. They figure once a dog gets a taste of venison, there's no breaking him of it. So I keep Mitzi chained up now.

But when Leon opens the doors, she hesitates before going out, sniffs the air cautiously, then growls once. A gust of cold, snow-filled air sneaks into the kitchen, making me shiver.

"What's the matter, girl?" Leon asks. "Smell a coon?"

After Leon comes back inside, he stomps off the snow on his

shoes. I ask him if he wants something to eat, but he says he's not hungry.

"I could make you a sandwich."

"I don't want a sandwich."

"How about some bacon and eggs?" I ask.

"I don't want anything. Jesus."

"You have to eat, Leon, you want to put on some weight."

"Leave me alone, would you, for crissakes," he snaps at me. He hangs up his coat on one of the pegs near the door. Then he turns and looks at me. "I 'preciate you taking me in, Lib. I do. But I just don't want you hounding me every five seconds. I'm a big boy now. I can take care of myself. I don't want anything to eat, I just want to hit the hay."

"All right, let me get the stove going first. It's pretty chilly in the store."

Downstairs, I stoke up the woodstove, which had all but burned out. I open the door, throw in some old *Piscataquis Heralds*, then some birch kindling, and begin to blow on it. Next I throw on some pieces of pine two-by-fours. When it's going good, I shove in a few oak slabs. I get my wood free, from loggers who'll drop off a load of hardwood now and then as a favor. Then I shut the door and open the damper. Soon the stove's ticking with warmth: *tick . . . tick . . . tick*, driving out the cold.

I go into Leon's room, out back off the kitchen. I fluff up his pillows and put an extra quilt, one I'd made for him a long time ago, on his bed. I turn on the space heater. I even go and get the hot-water bottle, fill it, and put it under the sheets, like I used to do when he was little and had the chills. I want everything to be nice, want Leon to feel this is his home. I hope maybe things will work out and he'll stay this time around.

When Claire kicked him out years ago, he bummed around for a while. He'd shack up with some woman until she got fed up with him, then he'd stay in rooming houses and Ys. Sometimes he even ended up on the street like some skid-row bum. He wandered around aimlessly, windblown, in an alcoholic stupor most of the time. I'd get sporadic postcards from him, from places like Baltimore and Cleveland. Or phone calls asking for money, saying he owed somebody or needed bail, or wanting me to come and pick him up at some bus station. But only when he got desperate would he swallow his pride and ask me for help. I kept telling him he could come and live with me up on the lake if he wanted. But no booze, I said. He was going to play it straight.

Finally he showed up one day, his hands shaking, white as a ghost, asking if he could stay with me. He was on the wagon for months that time. He worked around the place—painting the barn, fixing things that needed fixing. He hooked up an old bathtub for live bait. We sold smelt and minnows, and he even tied flies that were good enough to fool the tourists, if not the locals. He'd go into town for supplies, or mind the store when I had something to do. In the navy he'd studied electronics, so he'd pick up some small jobs on the side—fixing somebody's TV or putting in the wiring for an addition—to bring in some extra money. Things were working out. Sometimes his daughter, Stephanie, would come up for a visit. It was nice, the three of us, like a regular little family. Leon was different then. He hadn't touched a drop in months, not even beer. I was making his meals and he was starting to put on some weight. His hands were steadier now and his color was coming back. Our nights were long and quiet, just the wind sweeping down over the lake. We'd sit there beside the stove and watch TV, play some cards. I might sew while Leon read. He always liked to read, about faraway places— the Taj Mahal and Tahiti, places he'd always wanted to see as a kid. I was starting to let myself believe it could go on like this— just me and Leon and this place—and that nothing could touch us. Not the past and not the future. There was just now, and that was plenty. I pictured us getting old together, sitting out on the dock across the road on summer nights, throwing a line in the water and watching the sun melt like a slab of butter over Mount Kineo.

But then something happened. I'm not even sure what. It could've been anything, I know. Leon wasn't one to stick with something very long—whether it was a job, a woman, a place to live. He'd never really had to search hard to find an excuse to screw up his life. Pretty soon he started hitting the bottle. It was Ambroise all over again, only worse. He'd drink up all the booze in the house, the cooking sherry, even the rubbing alcohol from the medicine cabinet. He'd take money from my pocketbook, a five or a ten mostly, and go into town and get drunk. Sometimes Earl Teed, the bartender down at the Spruce Goose, would call me to come and pick Leon up, that he was in no shape to drive home. Once the police called to say Leon had been arrested for drunk driving. But I let all that slide. As long as we were together, I figured.

Then one morning, I woke up and he was gone. No word, not a note, nothing. And over two hundred dollars was missing from the strongbox I keep in my closet. I figured Leon had flagged down a rig heading over to Millinocket, caught a bus south. I didn't see him again, didn't even know where he was, until he showed up on my doorstep almost a year later, filthy and broke, his hands quaking with the DTs, looking about ten years older. I should've washed my hands of him, worrying me sick to death like that. But he looked at me with those sad green eyes of his, gave me a sheepish grin, and said, "Sorry about the money, Lib. I'll pay you back. I promise." So I relented and took him in again. He'd stay around for days, sometimes a few weeks, but then one day without warning he'd just take off again. It became a pattern, his coming and going. Whenever things seemed too good I'd begin to worry. It was like he never wanted me—or anyone for that matter—to get too close to him. There was always this part of him, a protected, closed space inside him, he kept from you, never let you see. Ever since he was a kid he was like that.

I hope this time, though, it'll be different.

"You should be all set," I say to him as he comes into his

room. He glances around. "Oh, in the top bureau drawer you'll find some new thermals. A belated birthday present." His birthday was two weeks ago.

"Thanks," he replies. "Listen, Lib. About before . . ."

"Forget it," I say. "That's behind us. I'm just glad you're here. What do you want for breakfast?"

Instead of answering, he gives me a hug, hard enough so I can feel his ribs through his shirt.

"You need anything, you just give a yell," I say, turning and heading out.

After Leon's asleep, I go upstairs and from under the sink I get out the fifth of Fleishmann's I'd hidden with his coming. I pour myself a glassful, add a little water. I've never been much of a drinker. Having a father and a brother who were alcoholics I've had to be careful. Two drinks and I'm on my ass. But tonight I need a good stiff one. Then I hunt around in the cupboard and settle on a box of Ritz crackers, a tin of Norwegian sardines packed in oil. I'm not even that hungry, though I haven't eaten all day and think I'd better if I'm going to drink.

I don't like eating alone in my cramped apartment, never have, even at night with the store closed. So I let Mitzi in and I take my supper and my coat, and I head downstairs. The dog follows me, her nails clicking on the wooden stairs. I pull the shades in case somebody going by on the road thinks I'm open. It's only eight o'clock, and I might get somebody coming back late from the mills, wanting to pick up bread or milk in case the storm keeps up. Outside, under the single light near the gas pumps, I watch the snow fall. It's so quiet out. The snow drops steadily, like a white net catching all noise and pulling it down into the ground.

Then I go around and check the doors: the front one, the one off the kitchen, the cellar door. I even check the rest rooms. I've lived way out here, alone, for twenty-six years and have never been the spooky sort. Never even bothered locking the doors, never had reason to. But lately I've taken to locking them, jumping when I hear a noise. About a year ago there was a break-in; nothing important was taken so I figured it was just some kids high on something. Yet since then I've begun to keep Ambroise's old Luger, loaded, in the strongbox in my closet. It helps me sleep, just knowing it's there. Maybe a sign I'm getting old. As if my life has suddenly become valuable with age, like some antique, and I'd do anything to hold on to it, even kill.

I head into the kitchen. I can hear Leon snoring out back, a thin, raspy sound. I try not to make much noise as I fill up the big kettle with water, put it on the burner, light the propane stove. I grab a ten-pound bag of Aroostock County potatoes they grow not twenty miles up the road and empty it in for tomorrow's home fries. I try to forget about before, about how angry Leon got, but as I lift the potatoes my wrist throbs painfully where his nails broke the skin.

I go back out and sit in a booth near the stove and open the can of sardines. I lay them one at a time on the crackers. The fish oil glistens purple and blue and yellow, like the sheen of oil in the bilge of a boat. I sip my whiskey and feel the booze-warmth fanning out through me like smoke, pushing the cold away. I try not to think, not about Leon, not about anything. I try to let my thoughts flatten out, become smooth, the way the lake is on summer mornings when you can see the clouds reflected in it and a quarter mile out you can see fish hitting the surface. That's how I'd like my mind to get.

By the time I finish my drink, my neck is loose and the potatoes are done. I drain the water, steam rushing up around me, making me light-headed. I run cold water over the potatoes, and begin to peel and slice them. When I'm done, I sprinkle paprika and pepper on them and put them in the fridge. Then I load the filters with coffee and go around refilling salt and pepper shakers so I'm all set for tomorrow's breakfast crew. The safety of routines.

That done, I sit down again and take out the envelope finally. I hold it in front of me for a moment, staring at my name, which looks so odd written that way: FRAU PELLETIER. The last time, all those years ago, it had been "Fräulein"—that's what the German POWs had called me. "*Guten Morgen, Fräulein,*" they would say. Or, "*Danke, Fräulein.*" As I look at the envelope a tiny voice in my head says, *Just throw it out, Libby. Don't even read it.* But I end up opening it. Inside, I find a note written on motel stationery: BEST WESTERN, PORTLAND, MAINE. The note is in a careful, school-teacher's hand, with each *t* crossed and *i* dotted, and all the letters lined up like troops in formation. It says, *Dear Frau Pelletier: I would like to talk to you again about my brother. Would it be possible for us to meet? I ask only a few moments of your time.* What more does he want? It's not my business.

The phone rings upstairs. I take my sweet time heading up, figuring it'll stop before I get it. Probably some family way back in the woods calling to see if they can come down and get some aspirin for a sick kid. Or some eggs for breakfast.

"Hello," I say into the receiver.

Silence on the other end. But it's not really silence, not still-ness, I hear. *Breathing*—that's what I pick up from the other end. The hoarse, hollow-lunged breathing of a two-pack-a-dayer.

"Hello?" I repeat.

After a few more seconds a voice—an older man's, hoarse, scratchy as number forty sandpaper—asks, "Where's Leon?"

Whoever it is I wonder how he knows Leon's staying here. Stephanie knew. And the people down at the VA. But I don't think I told anybody else. I didn't want all his drinking cronies coming around, helping him to slip up.

"He's sleeping," I tell the person on the other end.

"I need to talk to him."

"I'd rather not wake him. He needs his rest. Who is this?"

I hear the breathing again.

"I could have him call you," I offer.

"That's all right."

I hear a click and then a dial tone. I hang up the phone and go back downstairs. I pack the stove tightly with wood for the cold night. While I have the door open I take the German's letter from my pocket, hesitate for a moment, then toss it in. I watch it until it explodes with fire, the writing turning white like a negative, the paper curling gray like old skin. It isn't my business, I tell myself again. I got Leon to worry about now.

6

WHAT I REMEMBER is Leon shouting, "Look!" He was seated in the bow of the boat and pointing off over my shoulder, toward shore. He was wearing the blue-checked shirt he'd had his school picture taken in that year: Mrs. Levesque's fifth-grade class, 1944. "Is that them?" he asked.

I remember we were fishing. It was a summer day, hot and clear, and the few clouds were shoved against the horizon like caulking, making water and woods, mountains and sky a seamless thing. The sort of childhood summer day that would have blended into a thousand others, if it hadn't been for what I saw when I turned. There was this group of tired- and dirty-looking men making their way slowly down the dusty road to the lake. It was the first time I'd laid eyes on them, but I knew right away who they were. The thought sliced through me like a grass cut, leaving a shiver of pain in its wake.

For months before that rumors had been flying around that German POWs were coming. Nazis, right here in Maine. In our town, almost in our backyard. To a child the war was a fuzzy idea half a world away. We knew there was a war because of the shortages—you couldn't get meat or cigarettes or gasoline easily, and sometimes not at all. And, of course, there were those images of the bombed-out cities and marching armies we saw in the papers or on newsreels in the Strand Theater in town. And Roosevelt, who we heard on the radio at night, talking of sacrifice and hardships. And there was something else, too, something I could only think of as a smell, floating vaguely in the air, most of the time hidden under the overpowering odor of Asa Shaw's chicken coops, a smell you were never really conscious of but one that was always with you nonetheless, hanging over everything, *on* everything like a film, getting in your mouth and your nostrils when you breathed, making everything you ate taste funny. A faint, distant, bitter smell I would always later associate with the war.

Once in a while the war did strike closer to home, when someone's cousin or uncle, or now and then a brother or son, was killed: Claude Bellanger and Moxie Phipps, Duncan Nourse and Vance Tohay's son Charlie, who grew up right down the road from us. Then it might seem more real. But not for long, and not in any tangible way. We still went on with our lives and the war was just an inconvenience. But it was coming here. Now it was real. The men who started it all, who were responsible for thousands, hundreds of thousands, even millions of deaths, who were the *enemy*—these men were going to come here.

There were a lot of wild stories going around. We heard they were all going to be top SS men, Hitler's elite. That they'd escaped from other camps. That they were troublemakers and hard-core Nazis, and the government wanted these dangerous men as far away from civilization as possible so they couldn't sabotage anything. We imagined blond giants, built like Johnny Weissmuller or Max Schmeling, wearing swastikas and jackboots. We pictured the impressive columns of soldiers we saw in the newsreels, in those crisp uniforms, doing the goose step as they marched through Prague or Warsaw or some other city halfway around the world. What did we know? We were kids, isolated from the war. And though most people didn't exactly like the idea of Germans right in our backyard, if we had to have them then I think we secretly wanted something to get excited about. Something large and filled with at least the possibility of danger.

I remember Bobby Shaw always carried on him the smell of

chicken shit from working in his father's coops. Once on the school bus, he said he'd heard Rommel himself was among the Germans coming. Others talked of the murderous Huns. Of the unspeakable acts of cruelty and barbarism they'd committed against the Poles and the Russians. I guess we all wanted something to relieve the boredom that had come over our lives with the war.

One day, not long after the rumors began about the Germans coming, the three of us—Ambroise, my brother, and I—were in Abbey's store. It was before ice-out, and the snow was still on the ground. Abbey's was the center of the village of Sheshuncook, the only store unless you wanted to drive the rough logging roads— all we had back then—the thirty miles into Piscataquis. The store was a place where the locals hung out, bought canned goods and fishing line and ammo, and where they sat on an old car seat at the back near a blazing woodstove and swapped stories. Abbey, who spoke with authority, said the krauts had something up their sleeves. He said he wouldn't be surprised if they were all Göring's boys planted here, with the plan of breaking out, getting ahold of some planes over at the air base in Houlton, and raising all sorts of holy hell on our own soil. He spoke as if he knew this for a fact. Occasionally he'd open the stove door and spit tobacco juice into the fire, which made a hissing noise. Abbey seemed a very old man even then, with white hair turning the color of straw, and that glass eye. The eye was all black pupil, big and flat and lifeless, like the eye of a fish after you'd whacked it on the back of the head. Frightening. Leon was afraid of that eye. As kids we always used to wonder if he left it in at night, and if so, did he close his eyelid over it or did the thing stare into the darkness all night, like a sentry.

"I'm keeping my Mossberg right next to the bed," the old man said to my father and the other men there. "Loaded with double-aught buckshot. Those kraut bastards come sniffing around they'll find themselves a new arsehole."

The men sitting on the car seat laughed.

"You think I'm kidding?" Charlie said, spitting into the stove. "You still got that Luger, Ambroise?"

"Yeah," my father replied. It was a heavy, black gun that he kept in the truck and took with him when he went hunting with Spotty Haines or Tom Weston. For moose or bear, he said, though I'd never seen him shoot it. It was a 9mm Parabellum with fat little bullets that looked like grubs. The gun had been left to Ambroise by his uncle Henry, who'd fought in the First World War. We'd heard the story many times about how his uncle, who we'd seen only once or twice, a dour-looking man who lived up in the Gaspé Peninsula, had taken it off the body of a dead German. And when Ambroise would die he'd leave it to me.

As Charlie rang up our order, he said, "You ask me, they oughta put all those sons a bitches in a boat, bring it out in the middle of the Atlantic, and use it for target practice. That's what them U-boat fellows do to ours."

Out in the truck Leon asked if it was true about the Germans coming. My father, a logging foremen, said he'd heard the paper company had pulled some strings down in Washington, with Senator Brewster, and they were getting some able bodies to cut pulpwood. The company had been short on labor through most of the war.

"Where they gonna put 'em?" Leon asked.

"The supply farm down the road," Ambroise said. "The old Sheshuncook Farm."

"There's no fence," Leon countered.

"They'll have to put one up. And make some other changes, too," Ambroise said. "Ain't enough water for the number of men they're talking."

"How many Germans?" I asked.

"Coupla hundred, I hear."

"Will they have chains on?" asked Leon. "Like a chain gang?"

"Won't be much good cutting wood with chains on. Lib, honey, reach me under the seat and grab me my bottle."

That summer they converted the company supply farm at

Sheshuncook into a camp for the POWs. The workmen came every day with lumber and rolls of tar paper and great big spools of barbed wire. Leon and I watched as the carpenters turned the old potato barn into a barracks, erected spotlights here and there, built latrines and several outbuildings, and around the perimeter of the compound stretched double rows of barbed wire with four guard towers at the corners, like turrets in a castle.

"Will they have machine guns up there?" Leon had asked me one day as we were walking home from fishing down at the dock near the Sheshuncook Inn. We had to pass by the compound. It was late spring now, and the white flowers of the mountain ashes were in bloom in the woods behind the camp. The smell of lilac and pine was sweet in the air.

"I guess so," I said.

"You think they'll fire warning shots if they try to escape? Or will they just mow 'em down?"

"You ask the dumbest questions, Leon."

For several weeks after they finished the camp, there were still no Germans. The American servicemen arrived and took up residence in two houses just outside the fence. We sometimes ran into them at Abbey's store or swimming down at the lake. Mostly young boys, some with odd southern accents, though a few older ones, too, the officers and NCOs. If asked when the krauts were coming, they'd just shrug and say, "Purdy soon, I reckon," or "Who knows?" Ambroise got to be friendly with one and was able to get cigarettes and evaporated milk and some other items, which the soldier bought at the PX at the base over in Houlton, and later from the canteen store right here. In return Ambroise showed him where to fish, where to get moonshine whiskey, where to go in Bangor for some fun.

This day, the day we first laid eyes on them, Leon and I were out in my father's boat in Daggett Cove, fishing in close to shore. We'd fished all along the northwest shore, from the Toe of the Boot off Socatean Bay all the way up past Ogontz to Daggett

Cove. We trolled with smelt or cast bread-dough balls fried in bacon grease. We were casting just over the drop-off that started thirty feet from shore, where the water was deep and very cold even in the summer. It was almost two months past ice-out and the fishing wasn't very good, even deep down. Mostly pumpkin seeds and dace in close to shore, though once in a while if we trolled deep, out in the middle of the cove, we might land a small togue on a smelt or a gray ghost. I was about to cast when Leon cried, "Look!"

I thought he was talking about a fish. But then I turned to where he was pointing. They were maybe fifty yards away, yet the lake was calm in close and their voices carried over the water. You could hear them laughing, some at least, and talking in what I knew was German, the German I'd heard in movies and on the radio some nights, harsh and guttural, and yet silky at the same time. Like the sweet rip of a chain saw going through softwood. I stared at them. "Must be," I said finally. "See those guards."

"They don't look like krauts."

"And just how are they supposed to look?" I laughed, but I knew what he meant.

They came down the road to the lake, shuffling tiredly in pairs. Most naked from the chest up, these slender men who looked more like high school boys being marched down to the principal's office than captured soldiers. They could have been a baseball team after losing a game. They were dressed in baggy trousers and heavy boots. A few wore shorts. It was hot and they moved slowly, the dust making tiny explosions around their boots. A few guards walked on either side of them, their guns slung casually over their shoulders. One or two had their helmets dangling from bayonets.

"They're not even blond most of them," Leon said. "And look at that big fat one." He pointed at a heavy German near the end of the line. He was large and pink skinned, and his face was this screaming red. His belly flowed over his belt like dough rising over the sides of a pan.

"You think krauts can't be fat?"

"I never saw a fat one."

"You never saw one *period*."

"Those guards don't even have their guns ready!"

Leon was edgy ever since he'd heard the Germans were coming. He was always reading these comic books that showed Germans chewing on the bones of children and shooting old ladies. I told him they weren't going to just let them run loose, that they'd be behind the barbed wire at the camp, on the other side of the cove from where we lived. They had gun towers and searchlights, too. Besides, just where would they run to? They were out in the middle of nowhere, with miles and miles of nothing but woods. We didn't have anything to worry about. Yet after they arrived Leon was always careful. He'd do things like tie a couple of empty beer cans to his bedroom door at night. Just in case, he said. And he wouldn't walk past the camp by himself, and never after dark.

We watched the Germans move down to the water in the shimmery afternoon heat. Some sat on the rocky shore, while others took off their boots, rolled their pant legs up, and waded in up to their knees. Some had towels and bars of soap to wash themselves. A few sat in the shade along the shore and rested. One guy had a red kerchief tied around his head like a pirate. Several were splashing each other, horsing around like regular boys at a beach. One German, who had waded so far out the front of his pants were soaked, even waved to Leon and me. He was young, with short, light brown hair, and he reminded me of a boy in school who played on the basketball team. I started to wave back, but a shrill whistle stopped me.

"That's far enough, Fritz," one of the guards called to the brown-haired German. Like a child who had been reprimanded, he hung his head and moved back toward shore.

I found myself thinking, *My God! They're just boys!* This master race that was going to take over the world. That had done all those terrible things. That had bombed cities and killed children.

Boys! It seemed funny and odd and incredible all at once. After all, how could these boys do more than play some innocent pranks, I thought.

As we watched, the fat German, who was standing on shore with his hands low on his hips, shouted something to one of the men in the water. The man in the water at first just ignored him. Yet the fat man continued to shout, even wagged a finger at him. Soon the two were shouting back and forth. For several minutes they carried on like this, with some of the men joining in on one side or the other. They were arguing about something, but what, I had no idea. After a while the fat man gave up and went over to sit in the shade.

"What were they saying?" Leon asked.

"How should I know?"

"Maybe they were making plans to escape."

"You're such a jerk, Leon."

"And you think you know everything, sucker lips," he said.

If we hadn't been in the boat I'd have smacked him for saying that. Though Leon was getting bigger, I could still handle him. But he knew I wouldn't do anything to him in the boat. I wasn't a good swimmer and Leon was. He smiled teasingly at me.

"If you don't watch it," I said, "I'll tell the big one what you called him."

"You don't even know how to speak kraut."

"He might speak English. You ever think of that?" This took Leon by surprise, that they might speak English, too. "Maybe he'll sneak out at night and come into your room and slit your throat. Want me to tell him?" I asked, cupping my hand as if I would yell out to the Germans on shore.

"Just shut up," Leon said. But I could see the threat worked—he was scared.

After a while, the guards rounded them up and headed them back up the road toward the POW camp. One guard yelled at the fat prisoner who dawdled behind, "C'mon, Fritz. Let's get your fat ass in gear. *Schnell, schnell.*" I watched them until they disappeared up the road.

That was the first we saw of the Germans. I was fourteen then. I remember that day very clearly, even though I haven't thought about it in a long time. The water was smooth in Daggett Cove, choppier out in the middle of the lake. The sky was a polished blue, and somewhere off in the distance a loon cried, the sort of sound that makes your throat tighten with sadness. And I remember thinking, *These men—these boys!—would kill us if they had the chance.* I don't know why I thought that but I did. I wasn't afraid, not like Leon anyway. Not in any tangible way. But knowing there were people in the world who wanted you dead, people living just down the road, people who, if they had it in their power, would kill you—this made you see things differently.

Later, I started the small Merc outboard and we headed across the cove for home.

"How long you think they'll be here?" Leon asked when we got in the house. He was lying on the couch in the parlor, reading one of his comic books. I could see him from the sink. He had his shoes up on the couch, something our mother would never have let him do. But now that she was gone he was trying to get away with murder.

"Get your feet off there," I said. "Till the war's over, I guess." I put the dace we'd caught in the sink and got the fillet knife from the silverware drawer. I cut their ugly heads off and then began cleaning them, cutting from the anal fin right up to the gills. The guts spilled out into the sink: bright reds and blues and yellows, the blood greasy as olive oil. Ambroise, I thought, would appreciate fish, even dace, for supper. Instead of potato pancakes and eggs again.

"Then what'll happen to them?" he asked.

"I guess they'll let them go home."

"Maybe they'll shoot them."

"No, they won't."

"How do you know?" he challenged. "That's what they do to our prisoners. Just line them up and shoot 'em."

"Where'd you hear that?"

"In school. Harry Klatka told me that. And his brother's over there."

"Well, we don't do that."

I took out one of the Chesterfields I'd stolen from Ambroise's pants pocket. He got them from the guard at the camp. Regular cigarettes, like Pall Malls or Camels or Lucky Strikes. Normally he had to roll his own because of the war rations. The rolled ones had no taste. I'd wait till my father hung up his pants in the hall closet at night and then I'd hunt through his pockets, taking a few cigarettes, maybe a quarter or a buck. I lit the cigarette and took a drag, then placed it in the ashtray on the counter. My hands smelled of fish. I picked up the slippery offal in the sink, went to the back door, and tossed them out for the cats. We had three or four mousers that lived under the porch. They loved the fish heads. They would battle over them, with one big tom, who had half an ear gone, usually coming out on top. When I came back, Leon was seated at the small kitchen table. He had my cigarette in his mouth.

"Give that back," I said. "It'll stunt your growth." I put the fish fillets in the icebox and then washed my hands.

"I'll tell Dad you stole 'em," he threatened.

"You better not. And did you split that wood he brought home?"

"Yeah. C'mon, just one more drag. Please, Lib." I let him take another and then walked over and took the cigarette away from him. Puffing on it again I could smell the fish odor. When I finished the cigarette, I headed down into the cellar and got a handful of potatoes and an onion for supper. I cut them up and threw them in the frying pan with a little lard. Then I lit the propane stove.

"Dad said he got a letter," Leon offered.

"A letter? From who?" I asked, but I knew who he meant. I knew all about it already.

"From Ma."

"So? Big deal."

"Maybe we'll get one."

"I wouldn't hold my breath."

"You just hate her. You always hated her."

"I do hate her. But she still ain't coming back."

"How do you know?"

"Because she's not, that's why."

In the year she'd been gone, our mother had sent us maybe two letters, and not a thing for months. She had recently sent my father a letter, though. I'd come across it in his wallet when I was looking for some money. I considered telling Leon about it but decided not to. He wouldn't believe anything I said against her anyway unless I showed him the letter, and if I did I knew he wouldn't keep his mouth shut and Ambroise would know I'd been through his wallet and there'd be hell to pay.

Leon fell silent. I could tell he was thinking about her, still hoping I was wrong. I went over to him and said, "Want me to make a cake?" He didn't answer. I put my arm around him, cradling his head against my stomach. "How does chocolate cake with vanilla frosting sound? I'll go down to Shaw's and buy some eggs."

He pulled away from me. He was growing up and didn't want me to do things like hold his head anymore. Except at night when he'd have a bad dream. That was different.

"I hope the war lasts," he said.

"What on earth for?"

"So I can join up."

"Why?" I asked.

He walked over to the kitchen window, the one above the sink. It looked out on the driveway, and beyond, to the cove, and across that to the camp on the other side, which you could still make out though the trees had leafed out. "Because I'd like to kill some of those Germans."

"That's stupid," I said.

"It ain't stupid. Harry said his brother killed a bunch of krauts in Italy. Said he got this real nice medal."

"It's stupid," I repeated. "You hear me, Leon Edward Pelletier? I'm not raising you so you can go and get yourself killed for some dumb medal."

"*You're* not raising me. I don't have to listen to *you*."

When Ambroise got home that night he was pretty drunk already and mad, too. He slammed his fist into a wall, hard enough to loosen some plaster. The next day when he was sober he'd feel it but he didn't this night. He sat at the kitchen table, unlaced his heavy work boots. With his socks off, he picked at his toes, peeling long strips of rubbery white skin away from the bottom. The kitchen smelled suddenly like cheese.

"Careful you don't get an infection," I warned.

"Get me the Epsom salts, would you, Lib?" he said. I got the box from the medicine cabinet and some hydrogen peroxide, and I heated some water on the stove. When the water was hot, I emptied it into a pan, poured in some Epson salts, and set it on the floor in front of Ambroise's stinking feet.

"Thanks, Queenie." When he was drunk that's what he would call me: "Queenie, could you get me some clean underwear," or "Queenie, could you go down to Abbey's for some tobacco."

"I packed you a change of socks," I said.

"We were swamping out chain roads all day," he said. "Never had a chance to change socks. We got any beer left?"

I opened the icebox and got him a Ballantine, the last one. I knew what that meant. He had an excuse for heading into town later. By the way he was rubbing the middle of his nose, where it'd been broken, I knew he was pretty tanked up already. That's what he would do, rub his nose, when he'd been drinking. He sat at the small kitchen table and cracked the top off the beer with the jackknife he kept in his pocket.

"You cut that wood, shitheel?" he called to my brother, who

was lying on the couch again reading his comic book. Though it was summer my father brought home pickup loads of hardwood he would cut after work. Getting ready for the coming winter. Split wood cures faster, burns better.

"Yeah, I split it."

Ambroise seemed distracted. He sat there drinking his beer and rubbing his nose, while I started supper. I reheated the potatoes, and put the fish over on one side of the pan. I threw in some onions and a leftover piece of salt pork. During the war, we ate a lot of salt pork, which didn't cost any ration points, as well as pork and beans, chipped beef, potato pancakes, eggs, an occasional chicken from Asa Shaw. In hunting season maybe we had some venison. And fish. A whole lot of fish.

"What're we having?" Ambroise asked.

"Fish."

"What kind?"

"Dace," I said.

"Goddamn dace," my father said.

"Better than eggs and potato pancakes."

"Eggs and potato pancakes. And goddamn dace. Holy shit."

He lit up a Chesterfield and watched the smoke snake upwards. Something was up. I could tell. My father was around forty then, a large man whose size made him always appear uncomfortable confined in a small room like our kitchen. He always seemed more at home in the woods—that was his natural element. When he'd come home after being away for three or four months at some logging camp, I remember he'd have this wild woods smell and he'd pace the house like a cat in a cage. He couldn't sit still, felt more at ease in the cellar sharpening his saws or out in the barn working on the truck. Tonight he sat hunched over at the table drinking the last beer. He had dark skin and olive-colored eyes that turned dull yellow when he was drunk. He wasn't handsome, but he was tall and thick chested, a muscular man with a full head of shiny black hair that made him look as if he had some Indian blood way back (he used to say he was part

Passamaquoddy, and he might have been, for all we knew). Though he never got dressed up anymore, just wore the same green Sweet Orr work clothes every day, there was a picture of him in the album wearing spats and a white straw hat, white trousers with suspenders, one foot on the running board of an old touring car, an arm wrapped around my mother's thin waist. For a lumberjack he cut quite a dapper figure. When I was very young, I can remember my mother talking about how he used to take her dancing to the Hotel Commodore down in Bangor, and how he used to get jealous and start fights with men who so much as looked at her. He had a thin white scar over his left eye that he'd gotten in a fight with some man who'd tried to buy her a drink. He had another scar, this jagged crease, halfway down his nose where my mother had hit him with a gin bottle. After she left I could remember him sitting in the cellar rubbing his nose when he was drunk, as if it still hurt him years and years later, and as if he were still thinking about getting even with her someday.

He'd never had much to say to us, though before Ma left he was all right, would take us fishing with him, and into the woods with him now and then to cut timber. He was nicer then. I even think he loved us, in his own hard, silent way, the way a man given to few words, who was raised in a hard, unforgiving place, can be said to love his children. And he taught us—Leon and me—one thing: the meaning of loyalty, the importance of sticking by each other because we were family. "You're a Pelletier," he had said to us many times. "And don't forget it." So at school Leon's fights became mine, and mine, Leon's. I remember one time when I didn't stick up for him. Some kids down at Abbey's, the Tohay brothers and Timmy Gagnon, were making fun of Leon, and he came home in tears. Ambroise yelled at me, saying, "He's your blood, for Christ's sakes, Lib. Don't let the bastards do that to your own blood."

But Ambroise changed after she left. He grew sullen, bitter, his mouth held tight beneath his mustache. He'd spend most evenings down in the cellar sharpening his saws at his workbench or hanging an ax for the next day's work. Or he'd come home, eat the supper I'd made, then head into town for a few, leaving Leon and me alone. When he was drunk—more and more often now with her gone—he had a pretty good temper. The house in Sheshuncook had holes in the walls from his fist, though except for a cuff now and then he seldom hit us.

Tonight he'd been drinking hard. He sat there, his mouth hung open, swallowing big gulps of air, his shoulders rising up and down with the effort.

"Hey, shitheel," he called to Leon again. "You cut that wood?" It was as if he'd forgotten he'd already asked.

"I told you, yeah," Leon snapped back. "Jesus."

"Don't give me any lip, mister. And how come you're always reading that crap, anyway? War's going on and you're reading goddamn comic books."

"What's wrong with that?" my brother asked.

"You're eleven years old. Christ, when I was eleven I was already driving logs down the Androscoggin. Not sitting on my duff reading that crap."

Leon mumbled a "humph" and rolled his eyes, which was just asking for trouble. To distract Ambroise, I said, "We saw them today."

"You saw who?"

"The Germans."

"Those sons of bitches! Where?"

"Down at the lake. They went for a swim."

My father wagged his head. "Sure. They got it easy, that bunch. I heard they eat meat every lousy day. Like it's old home week. While I got to eat eggs. And goddamn dace."

"Where you working?" I asked.

"Over near Pittston Farm," he replied, staring into the parlor at Leon. "I'll be taking a crew of them goddamn krauts out next week with me. Learning 'em how to cut. Bet they won't know their asses from their elbows about cutting wood. What they know about is killing Polacks and Ruskies."

In a few minutes supper was ready and we sat down to eat.

My father's yellow cat-eyes glared across the table at Leon. For some reason my brother always got under his skin. Maybe it was because he looked just like her. Pretty like her, with long lashes, and these fine features. Leon's softness drew my father's anger like a magnet. As he shoveled the food into his mouth, he said, "You're coming with me next week, shitheel."

"What for?" my brother asked.

"To work—what do you think what for? You're getting too big to be sitting around reading comics. You need to learn a trade."

"I don't want to be a logger."

"What's wrong with being a logger? It was good enough for my old man. And for me."

"I just don't want to be a logger."

"And just what *do* you want to be?"

"I don't know. Something else."

"Well, until you figure out what that is, you can come with me," he said. "And you, too, Lib. Company needs a cookee. I figure you can work all summer. Make some money for school clothes. Pays four bucks a day. You're both old enough to start earning your keep. Christ, for my eighth birthday, Pepé gave me a double-bit ax to keep my ass warm. '*Si tu veux te chauffer le cu, il faut que tu apprenne comment l'user.*' A hard old sonofabitch your grandfather but damned if he didn't have that right."

We sat there for a while, silently eating. Then my father got up, went over to the garbage can, and scraped the rest of his food off his plate. He spit into the sink and hitched up his green work pants. He looked out the window over the sink for a moment.

"Guard over there said the sons a bitches get meat every day. Who the hell's winning this thing, anyway? Them or us?"

Was that what the matter was? I wondered. He was mad at the Germans? Or was it on account of the letter I knew he'd gotten a few days before from my mother? It was hard to say.

"I'll be back," he said, grabbing his sweat-stained cap from the hook near the door. "Don't wait up."

"We need some things," I said, handing him a list of groceries I'd made up. "Stop in town at the A and P."

"You birds eat me out of house and home," he grumbled.

"You eat here, too," I said. "You want to eat you'd better get some food."

Then he left the house. From the sink where I stood doing the dishes, I saw him get in the truck and gun it going down the dirt road. The truck circled the cove, trailing dust behind it. He was probably headed for the Spruce Goose or the Banquet Room down in Piscataquis, an hour's ride over rough logging roads. He'd come back, as he usually did, late, weaving down the road with his truck, and probably without any groceries. Once he came back so drunk he had a tree limb sticking through the windshield. It'd missed his head by no more than a foot. He didn't even know it was there until the next day.

That night Leon and I listened to *Fibber McGee and Molly* on the radio and then news of the war. A bomber had crashed into a trailer court in Portland, killing a dozen people. Field Marshal Rommel had been wounded by Allied aircraft. D day had taken place a few weeks before and we heard about the battles for places like Cherbourg and Le Havre, about the terrible losses the Allies were suffering. But that part of the war didn't mean much to us. What the war meant to us now were those men over in the camp.

I woke up around midnight. It was hot and I couldn't sleep. I got up and went out into the hall. I could hear my father's snores coming from his bedroom, ripping the darkness like a band saw. I went down the hall and stopped just outside his door. I listened for a moment to make sure he was asleep. Then I opened the hall closet and rifled through the pockets of his pants. I took a couple of cigarettes and some loose change I knew he'd never miss. To buy bread and milk at Abbey's the next day. In his wallet I came across the letter I'd already read once before. I took that, too.

I slipped out of the house and headed down the road, walking in my bare feet with just my nightgown on. It was cooler out though still warm. The oiled dirt of the road was even warmer, tacky on the bottoms of my feet. The crickets were making a metallic grinding sound, like a bad starter in a car: *zow-zow-zow*. As I walked along I could hear the grunting and snorting of the bears out behind Asa Shaw's place. I continued around the cove and knew where I was headed only when I'd arrived.

I kept to the side of the road in case anyone from the camp—a guard maybe—came along in one of their boxy little jeeps from a visit to town and wanted to know what I was doing. The camp was brightly lit by floodlights, and I stood in the shadows and watched from across the road.

I saw guards lounging in the four towers, holding machine guns, the sort George Raft and Edward G. Robinson used in the gangster movies. Inside the compound I saw a few soldiers patrolling the grounds with dogs. Earlier in the evening, as I washed the supper dishes and stared out the kitchen window, I'd seen the lights in the big barracks across the cove flickering on and off several times. But now the building was dark and still.

I lit one of the cigarettes I'd stolen, and I sat down on the grass in the dark. I got out the letter. With the light of the match, I read it again. "Dear Ambroise," it began.

> There's no use fooling ourselves any longer and dragging this thing out. I know you are probably still mad at me for what I did, and I don't blame you. I am not asking your forgiveness, for I would do what I did all over again. Why I'm writing now is to ask you for a divorce so I can get on with my life, and you with yours. I know of no other way to put it. I have a lawyer here in Buffalo who will draw up the papers. I'm not looking to get anything, no money and none of the furniture except for my mother's china cabinet and the silverware, which I'd like back at some point because of the sentimental value they

hold for me. The only thing I'm wanting is my freedom. I know the children will be better off with you.
I only hope that when they're bigger they can forgive
me and try to understand that this is the best for all
concerned.

It was signed, "With affection, Denise." At the bottom she
had added, "P.S. Don't try to come after me."

I remember some time after that night waking up to this
racket coming from the parlor. I got up and walked down the
hall. I stood in the doorway watching Ambroise. He was standing
with his favorite double-bit ax in his hands, and my mother's
cherry-wood china cabinet lay in a million pieces at his feet. His
eyes were wild and red-rimmed, like those of a cornered animal.

That night outside the camp, I finished my cigarette and just
sat there for a minute, maybe thinking about her, maybe not.
Across the road, over in the prison camp, I saw what looked like
a light in one of the windows of the big barracks. It was there for
just a few moments, flickering, a candle maybe, then it was dark
again. The windows looked like eyes, shiny and black, like
Abbey's big dark eye. The flies, which were terrible all that summer, started to land, so I turned and headed home, the seat of my
nightgown wet from the ground.

That was the first day. The day the Germans arrived.

7

SUNDAY MORNING, EARLY. I peek in on Leon. He's curled up in a ball sleeping like a baby. I shut his door carefully, go out into the store and put a pot of coffee on. Then I get the woodstove cranking. After that I set up the cash register. From the money bag I keep upstairs in the strongbox at night, I take out the bills, separating them into ones, fives, and tens. I break open the rolls of coins and pour them into the tray. Then I pull on my boots, hat, and down-filled parka, and head outside.

The storm has broken and the sun is trying to cut through the clouds, but the wind is still blowing hard, kicking up gusts of snow. Icicles like jagged fangs hang from the eaves of the store. I get the shovel from the woodshed off the barn and begin shoveling off the front steps. It's a light snow, but deep. Must be a foot on the ground. You're getting too old for this, Lib. Ought to start thinking about selling the place and moving into town. Get some apartment just big enough for Leon and me. We could even do some traveling. I've always wanted to see what other places were like. The Everglades. The Grand Canyon. Maybe even buy one of those RVs the tourist people come in with and just take off. Nothing holding us here. The pair of us, free as birds. I wonder if Leon would like that. Something to think about, I guess.

When I happen to look up I see Roland's tan Blazer out at the road. Without a word he lowers his plow blade, revs the engine, then drives forward. The snow unfurls like a wave crashing on the beach. Roland backs up, drives forward. Again and again until the driveway and parking lot are clear.

After he finishes, I go over to his truck.

"I got some coffee on. I could make you something to eat."

"No, I gotta take my mother to mass. You know her. Hasn't missed a mass in like fifty years."

"Thanks for plowing me out," I say. "And I'm sorry about the other day. I didn't mean to sound like such a bitch."

"No problem. Can I bum a cigarette?"

Roland's been trying to quit ever since Doc Proulx found a spot on his lung. Now he just bums cigarettes. I take out the pack of Merits from my shirt pocket, hand him one.

"I could stop back tonight," he says. "I still got those venison steaks. I could drive my rig up and go to work from here."

"Leon's here, you know." I don't know if having Roland stay over while Leon's around is such a good idea. It complicates things. I want things simple right now. One thing at a time.

"How long's he staying?" he asks.

"I'm not sure. Awhile."

"Does that mean you don't want me coming around?"

"Leon's been sick. He needs me now. Let's see how it goes, all right, Roland?"

"Whatever you say, Lib."

I place my hand on his arm, lean into the truck, and kiss him on the cheek. I taste Old Spice. Roland's not so bad. Just a little pushy, and like all men wanting you to sign your life away on the dotted line. "I just need a little breathing room right now. Till my brother gets back on his feet."

"I'll give you all the room you need," he says. "Gimme a call when you're not baby-sitting." Then he puts the truck in gear and takes off down the road toward Piscataquis.

As I walk back up to the store, I see Leon in the window looking out. He's standing there in his white long johns.

"Brrr," I say once inside.

"Roland been around much?"

"Now and then."

"What's the deal with you two?"

"There's no deal. We're just friends."

"You sleeping with him?"

"That's none of your damn business," I say, annoyed. "You said you were a big boy, could take care of yourself. Well, I'm a big girl, too. Roland's none of your concern."

"Take it easy. I was just asking."

"At least I see you're feeling better. You want something to eat?"

"Sure," Leon says.

I make him some eggs and bacon. He sits at a table and picks at the food with his fork. He doesn't eat much, but I don't say anything. I watch as he glances around the store, eyeing all of Ambroise's old tools, some of which he himself had probably used. Up over the door is Ambroise's favorite double-bit ax, the one he'd used to smash apart our mother's china cabinet so many years ago. But I doubt if Leon remembers that.

Business is pretty slow this morning. I have only a handful of customers. Connie West, who'd been out snowmobiling with his twelve-year-old son, Harry, stops in for breakfast. And a couple of ice fishermen come in. Other than that it's quiet. Leon and I pace cautiously around each other, like a couple of cats in a cage. Trying to give the other some space, trying to get adjusted to having someone else around. Leon mostly stays in his room, comes out once in a while for coffee or butts. Neither of us brings up what happened yesterday on the ride home. Maybe he doesn't even remember it. Maybe that needle in his mind is stuck in some other time. I decide it might be a good idea to head into town for some supplies.

"I got some errands to run in town," I say to Leon, who's lying on his bed. Though it's close to noon, he's still dressed only in thermal underwear. He has on my reading glasses and he's working on a book that has all these crossword puzzles in it. "You want to come?"

"No," he says without looking up.

"Will you be all right alone?"

"Of course I'll be all right."

"I'll only be gone a little while." I turn to leave, then stop. "Oh, I almost forgot. Somebody called for you last night after you went to bed."

"Who?"

"He didn't say."

Leon looks over at me. His eyes are distorted beneath my glasses, large and mushy as jellyfish. "He say what he wanted?" he asks.

"No. Just that he wanted to talk to you. I won't be long. You need me—"

"Just go. I'm fine."

As I ride south into town, the sun glints off the snow. It shatters the light into painful splinters. Lily Bay stretches out below me. It'd gotten cold early this year, and the lake had frozen over solid by November. They're talking a late ice-out, too, maybe not till the end of May. People who make their living from the fishermen are beginning to worry. Spotty Haines said they've already had some cancellations because the late ice-out would make for lousy fishing in May.

I see snowmobilers cutting across the lake's smooth surface, and here and there some ice-fishing shacks with smoke curling out of metal stovepipes. Off toward Piscataquis I can faintly make out Moose Island. Whenever I see it I recall the story my grandfather, Pepé Pelletier, used to tell us kids. A hermit had lived on the island around the turn of the century. He used to dogsled across the ice into town for supplies. One winter he was found in the narrows between the island and the mainland, frozen standing straight up. All his dogs were frozen too, right in line, still in their traces.

In town I stop at the post office first. I drop a letter to Stephanie in the mailbox out front. Bert Osgood, the postmaster, who lives only two doors down, is out front shoveling his walk.

When he sees me he waves, then goes back to shoveling. At the A&P I pick up some groceries. I run into Trudy McCray, Roland's sister, who works part-time as a cashier. She talks my ear off about some bug she'd had, how she couldn't keep anything down.

"Seen Rollie lately?" she asks as she rings up my things. I know her from Tuesday-night bingo. She's the one who sort of fixed Roland and me up, and she likes to keep up on her match-making, see how things are going.

"He plowed me out this morning," I reply.

"How do you like this snow? They're talking another one later in the week. Can you believe that?"

"I guess you got to expect snow in March."

"Hop said some German was in your place the other day?" she says.

"Yeah."

"What'd he want?"

"Oh, I don't know. I got to get going, Trudy. See you."

Afterwards I drive over to Hanson's Mobil, in the center of town across from the library. Billy Hanson comes out to wait on me. He's about my age, a short man with heavy, dark-framed glasses that make his face look confused, like someone who's spent a couple of years in a closet.

"I need a case of oil," I tell him.

"You need a new engine, Lib, is what you need. Or another truck altogether. I got a '85 Dodge half-ton, four-wheel drive. Less than five thousand miles on the rebuilt motor. Let you have it real cheap."

"How about just the oil for now?"

"You're only putting off the 'nevitable."

"I'm pretty good at that," I joke.

He goes inside and comes back out carrying a case of oil. He puts it in the back of the truck and says, "Let me know if you're interested in that truck, Lib. I'll even throw in a pair of retread snows."

When I get home I go through the back door, into the kitchen. My arms are filled with groceries. "Leon," I call. "I could use a hand."

No response. I bring the bags in and set them down on the counter.

"Leon?" I poke my head into his room. He's not there but Mitzi's up on his bed. "Where's Leon, girl?" I notice his hat and coat lying across a chair, so I know he hasn't gone outside. I listen for a moment, and then I hear something. I decide it's coming from upstairs. I start walking up the stairs, but halfway up I pause. I can hear Leon. He's talking to someone on the phone, not quite a whisper but low enough so I can only make out isolated words and phrases.

"No," he says. ". . . you . . . sick . . . I only . . . nothing's changed . . . don't worry."

I wonder if I should call out, make some noise to let him know I'm home, or maybe turn around and go back downstairs and mind my own business. Instead, I hold my breath and try to piece together what it is he's saying. Yet the words remain fragmented, they don't come together into a recognizable whole. I do make out something, though, not so much Leon's words as the tone of his voice: Whoever he's talking to, whoever's on the other end, that person has Leon scared. I don't know how I know this but I do. Something in Leon's voice.

I continue walking up the stairs, making as much noise now as I can so Leon can hear me. When he becomes aware of me, I hear him say only, "I gotta go. No, I gotta go."

"Who was that?" I ask.

"Some guy I met at the VA."

"Was he the one called last night?"

"I don't know. He didn't say."

"I could use a hand getting the groceries in," I say to him.

We go downstairs, and he helps me bring the bags of groceries in from the truck. As I'm putting things away, he stands behind me. He leans against the sink, smoking a cigarette. He's dressed now, flannel shirt, jeans, his new shoes. He doesn't say anything, just stands there with his arms folded across his chest.

"What's the matter?" I ask.

"Nothing."

But I can see that something's on his mind. He takes a long drag on his cigarette, lets it out slowly.

Finally he says, "That German fellow. The one you talked to the other day."

"What about him?"

"He been to see you again?"

"No."

"You haven't talked to him anymore?"

"I told you, *no*." I put some cans away, up in the cabinet. With my back to him I say, "He did leave me a note."

"A note?"

"Last night. He wanted to see me again."

"Why?"

"How should I know? He was looking for Ambroise." I turn to face him. "What's going on, Leon?"

"Nothing," he replies.

"Nothing? Why are you so interested if I talked with him, then?"

"No reason."

Leon picks up a steak knife from the sink and begins casually to run the blade across the stainless steel. It makes an awful noise, one that sets my teeth on edge.

"Don't do that," I say. "Who were *you* talking to just now?"

"I told you, a guy I met at the hospital."

"Did that have anything to do with the German, Leon? That phone call?"

"Now why the hell would that have anything to do with him?" he says, pulling the blade over the bottom of the sink.

"Stop that!" I yell at him. He puts the knife down. "It *wasn't* about the German, Leon?"

"Of course not."

"And what that Kallick fellow is looking for—you don't know anything about that either? You don't know what he's after?"

Instead of answering right away, he turns the faucet on in the sink, fills up a cup with water, and takes a drink. Then he snuffs his cigarette out in the cup: *spssss*. He turns slowly to look at me. "I don't know anything about that, Lib. All's I'm saying is you wanna keep your nose out of it, too. Stay away from him."

8

IT'S MONDAY EVENING. I'm in my bedroom counting the day's receipts and trying to balance the store's books. Just a few weeks away from tax time. Last year I got audited by the IRS. I had to go down to the capital where I was grilled by this anorexic girl in a gray two-piece suit. She kept telling me my records were a mess. So this year I've been a little better. I try to balance the books at least once a month. But I've never had a head for figures. Leon was the one who was always good in math. Maybe I should have him do the books now that he's around. Yet any way you slice it, the place is not doing much business. Must be the economy. Fewer tourists, and the hunters and fishermen are not coming like they used to. If it keeps up like this I may not have much choice about selling the place.

The phone rings. I get up from my desk and go into the kitchen and answer it.

"Hello?" I say.

"Is Leon there?" a man asks. The voice is hoarse, gritty, familiar. It's the man who called the other night.

"Can I ask who's calling?"

"A friend of his."

I go to the top of the stairs and call Leon.

"Who is it?" he asks, climbing up.

"I don't know. Says he's a friend."

He picks up the receiver but looks over at me, waiting for me to leave. I head back into the bedroom. I open the strongbox and take out the canvas money bag, which holds the day's receipts. I empty the money on the old rolltop desk and begin to count the bills—mostly ones and fives, a few tens. As I do, I find myself trying to hear what Leon is saying. He speaks in a hushed tone, though, and I can't make out a thing. Outside in the night I can hear the fierce baying of dogs moving in a pack. The sort of sound they make when they're in pursuit of something: running a deer until its lungs burst and it drops onto the snow, and they fall on it and tear it to pieces.

I'm just finishing up when I feel Leon standing behind me.

"Oh!" I say, looking up at him. "You startled me."

He stares down at the strongbox without saying anything. I gather up the money, stuff it back into the pouch, then place it in the box. Both of us are thinking the same thing, I imagine—the two hundred dollars he stole from me that time. It must be fifteen years ago now.

"Who was that?" I ask.

Instead of answering Leon says, "Can I borrow your truck?"

"Why?"

"I need to go into town."

"Tonight? What for?"

"I gotta take care of some business."

I'm more than a little suspicious. I can just picture him meeting up with one of his old drinking buddies and getting into trouble. Slipping off the wagon. That's the last thing we need.

"What kind of business?" I ask.

"Just some business, that's all."

"I'm supposed to believe that? You sure you're not planning on going out and getting yourself tanked up, Leon Edward Pelletier?"

"Jesus Christ. I told you, I got some business to see to. Besides, if I wanted to get drunk, that's my concern."

"Not as long as you're staying here, it's not."

"All right, I'm seeing somebody about a job then."

"What kind of job?"

"I'm putting in some circuit breakers."

"For who?" I grill him. "That guy at the hospital again?"

"Yeah, as a matter of fact. Don't be so goddamn nosy."

"And what do you need a job for? I can take care of us."

"Hell, on what you bring in from this place?"

Leon grabs the canvas money bag, holds it upside down, and shakes it so the bills flutter down and the coins clink against the Luger in the bottom of the box.

"That Ambroise's?" he says.

"Yeah."

He reaches into the box and picks it up, testing the heft of it in his hand, the way you'd test a rock before heaving it through a window.

"You wanna be careful," I say. "It's loaded."

"What the hell you doing with this, Lib?"

"I just like having it around." I take the gun from his hand and put it back into the box. Then I shut the box, bring it over, and put it away in my closet. "And anyways you're in no shape for a job. Dr. Bedrosian says you should take it easy for a while."

"Fuck him. I feel fine. I don't wanna be a burden on you, Lib. I wanna pull my own weight."

"You're no burden, Leon. You know that."

"You gonna let me borrow the truck or do I have to walk?"

"Twenty miles into town? Tell you what. I need to go to the bank tomorrow. I can give you a ride then."

"He's not going to be there tomorrow. If you're not gonna trust me I might as well pack my bags and leave tonight."

It's a threat, I know, but one that works. I don't want him to leave and he knows it, too. Plus he's stubborn enough to actually try walking into town.

So I relent. "All right. But you got to promise me, Leon. No booze, okay?"

"No booze."

"Bedrosian said any more and you'd be back in the hospital."

"Yeah yeah yeah. Stop worrying, for crissakes."

"I just want things to work out this time. All right." I reach for his hand. He doesn't pull away, lets me take it. His hand is cold. "I can't help worrying, Leon."

"What the hell you worrying about?"

"I don't know. *Do* I have anything to be worried about?"

Leon surprises me by wrapping his arms around me and resting his head on my shoulder. I can feel his breath against my neck.

"Always gotta act like my mother, don't ya."

"Somebody has to."

"Well, stop worrying. Jesus, you'll get an ulcer. Everything's going to be fine. And once I get back on my feet I'm gonna square up on that money, Lib."

"Forget it."

"No, I won't forget it. Plus interest. You watch."

He gives me a kiss on the ear.

"When are you heading in?" I ask.

"In a little while. Could you fix me something to eat first? I think I'm starting to get my appetite back finally."

"That's good, Leon," I say, my eyes beginning to water, which is not like me at all.

"Don't get all blubbery-eyed on me," Leon kids.

"I'm sorry. It's just that . . . I'm so happy to have you back. What would you like to eat, Leon?"

"How about some potato pancakes and eggs?"

"I could make you a steak. Or pork chops."

"Potato pancakes. You always made the best potato pancakes."

"Sure, I can make some. I got some leftover mashed potatoes."

"I'm gonna use your bathroom to shave and get cleaned up."

"There's towels behind the door."

I go downstairs and make Leon some potato pancakes and eggs and bacon. In a few minutes he comes down, clean shaven, his hair slicked back. He's even wearing one of my bulky woolen sweaters, which just about fits him. We're about the same size.

"Well, ain't we the picture. Where'd you find that?"

"In the back of your closet. Do you mind?"

"Go right ahead. But you sure it's not some floozy you're meeting?"

He laughs, the first time I can remember in a long time. He eats with gusto, swirling a piece of bacon in the egg yoke and washing it all down with tomato juice. When he finishes eating, he says, "I'll be back."

"Don't be late," I tell him. "And don't go over forty-five. The road's still slippery in spots. And check the oil before you go."

He shakes his head. From his bedroom window I watch him back out of the barn, turn around, and pull out of the driveway, heading for town. I keep watching him till the taillights sink into the darkness like a stone dropped into still water.

I spend most of the evening sitting in bed working on the baby quilt for Stephanie's little girl, Missy. She was born over a year ago, and if I don't finish the thing soon she'll be too big for it. I'm thinking maybe I can have it done by Easter, which is only a couple of weeks away now. I could ask Stephanie and her family up for dinner. Leon would like that, I bet. Like to have his daughter and granddaughter both here. I could make a big ham, some pies. A regular family gathering. That would be nice.

Every so often I get up and go over to the window and look out—waiting for Leon. Once, around nine o'clock, I see these headlights way off down the road, near Connie West's place. As they approach they seem to slow down, but just as they get even with the dock they speed up again and fly past the store, heading for Millinocket. It's okay, Lib, I tell myself. There's nothing to worry about. He is a big boy. Yet as I look out the window, I think about that other night, so many years ago. Looking out the window and waiting, waiting for Ambroise and Leon to get home. Worrying that something was the matter. It seems like I've spent half my life looking out windows waiting for men to come home.

I work on Missy's quilt some more, but my mind's not on sewing. I make a bunch of bad stitches and have to pull them out and start over. Who's he meeting? I wonder. And why'd he have to go tonight? Around ten-thirty I get up and decide to make a call. I look up the number for the Spruce Goose, though I hope to God he's not there.

"Hello," I say. "Is this Earl?"

"No, this is Benny. Earl's busy right now."

"I want to know if my brother Leon's there."

"Who?"

"Leon Pelletier."

"Just a minute." I hear him yell my brother's name. "Nobody here by that name, lady."

"Was he in earlier?"

"Geez, I wouldn't know. I'm the cook. Sorry."

"Listen, if he comes in you tell him to get his rear end on home."

"I sure will," he says.

I get back in bed, sew some more until my arthritis begins to flare up. Then I put the quilt aside, lay my head back on the pillow, and close my eyes. Up in the attic I can hear the mice scratching around in the insulation, talking their mice talk. *How long has it been?* one of them seems to ask. Another replies, *Forever.* I feel myself begin to slip. I try to fight it at first, but then I give in to it and let myself plunge into something soft and white as cornstarch. I'm somewhere in the woods, surrounded by deep snows. And yet, the funny thing is, there are all these snakes. But not any snakes I've ever laid eyes on. These are perfectly white. Snow snakes, with red eyes and long fangs that drip blood. And they're everywhere: slithering in the snow, piled waist high in drifts. Even hanging from the branches like icicles, stiff, frozen into long rods. They look so wonderful I break them off with my hands and hold them straight out, like wands. As soon as I do, though, they come alive again in my hand, begin to wrap themselves around my arm. They bite me on the wrist until blood wells up and my flesh screams out with what must be poison.

Then somehow I'm way up in the air, floating, detached. It's like I've left my body. I'm weightless. Everything down below looks so small, so remote. A miniature world but one I'm not so sure is mine. I try to make out something familiar—a house, a cove in the lake, some landmark. Something to keep me from getting lost. But nothing down there seems familiar. I keep looking though and finally I spot something I think I know: a square patch of green field, dotted with what look like stones, beside a broad sweep of water that narrows to a thin undulating band: Daggett Cove, I think. Yes, that's it. And my house must be just on the other side. Then I'm falling again, dropping out of the sky.

Then I'm down on the ground again. I'm looking out a window. I see three or four trucks heading around Daggett Cove, their headlights spraying the night. They park in the snow-covered driveway and the men get out and stand there. Their cigarettes glow in the darkness like fireflies. Their smoky breaths mingle with the exhaust of the idling trucks. Dark shapes, in heavy coats and hats. Some carry things in their hands, axes and peaveys. A pair of hunting dogs stand in the bed of one truck, yapping occasionally, their snouts hitting the air for a scent, though no noise reaches me. Not a sound. The men don't move. They might be talking, but from where I am it's hard to tell. They just stand there in the cold, dark night. Finally, two figures, a large one and behind that a smaller one, break apart from the group and walk slowly up to the house. They walk heavily, their shoulders slumped forward. The other men get in their trucks then, pull out of the driveway, and take off down the road toward the cove, their taillights gradually fading into the night. Then I run to the door and open it. The cold night air comes *whooshing* in with a sucking sound, filling the room. And just before I see the ashen-faced boy with the bandaged hand I wake up.

A noise shatters the dream in an instant. On the opposite

wall, I see a weak splash of sunlight, the color of butternut squash, and through the window a rectangle of blue sky. It's the phone ringing. I throw the covers off, get out of bed, my bare feet recoiling from the icy floor, and hurry into the kitchen.

"Yes," I say.

"Are you Libby Pelletier?"

"Yes, I am. Who is this?"

"Ms. Pelletier, this is Chief of Police Chambers." As soon as he says this I feel my pelvis drop away, have this sensation like I'm falling again, like in the dream. I'm plunging toward the earth.

"What's the matter?" I ask, feeling my throat get tight. "Is it Leon?"

"I'm afraid I have some bad news."

"What's happened to Leon? Tell me."

"I'm sorry, Ms. Pelletier. I'm very sorry."

"Is he dead?" I ask, the word twisting into my brain like a screw. "Please, no. Please, God, no."

"An ice fisherman found him out on the lake early this morning."

"No no no," I plead. "How?"

"We found an empty bottle nearby. Looks like he was drunk and slipped and hit his head. Froze to death."

"He was on the wagon. He promised me he wouldn't drink."

"I'm sorry, Ms. Pelletier."

"But why was he out there?"

"That, I couldn't say, Ms. Pelletier. I'm real sorry, though. As next of kin, you'll need to come down and identify the body."

"Yes, of course."

"We got your truck at the station. I could pick you up. Be out there in about an hour."

"If it's no trouble."

"No trouble at all."

Before I hang up I ask, "Where is he? I mean, right now?"

"He's at the walk-in clinic. Doc Proulx is the one pronounced him. If it's any consolation, Ms. Pelletier, Doc said he didn't feel any pain."

"It is. Thank you."

I get off the phone. I stare out the window at the lake. I don't cry. I'm too numb to cry. Then I go and get dressed, and wait for the chief.

Part 2

Part 2

9

THE WALK-IN CLINIC is on Grove Street, across from the high school. The chief takes me into a tiny back room, which smells of ammonia and hand soap, and some other odor I can't fix a name to. Locked in a glass cabinet are all these plastic bottles of drugs. A metal overhead lamp hangs from the center of the ceiling, pouring blue-gray light down onto a stretcher. A white sheet covers Leon, just like in the movies. The chief turns to me and says, "Ready?" As he pulls the sheet back, I brace myself for being shocked. I'm not though. And except for a sound that gets trapped in my throat, I don't even cry. Leon looks as if he's just sleeping, as if, were I to say, "Wake up, Leon. Wanna go fishing?" he'd open his eyes, jump off the stretcher, and come along with me. Except that when I touch his hand his skin feels smooth and cold and not at all human, like the marble in the halls of some large, drafty office building. And over his right eye he has a reddish-blue two-inch gash, the skin around it puffed up like a flower. I touch it gently, as if it could still hurt him somehow.

"Would you like a few minutes alone, Ms. . . . may I call you Libby?" asks Chief Chambers. He's about fifty, a very tall, thin man with sloping shoulders and no chin. He's not a local. They hired him from downstate about a year ago. He has a college degree, I heard, and he doesn't talk at all like a cop. He has kind eyes, the sort of eyes that haven't gotten used to handing out bad news.

"Libby's fine. But no, that's all right," I say. "What's going to happen now?"

"What do you mean?"

"Will there be an autopsy?"

He shakes his head. "Not for a something like this."

"Why not?"

The chief takes a deep breath, looks around the room.

"It's pretty cut-and-dry. This wasn't the first time your brother was found sleeping it off, Libby. According to our records we picked him up about a year ago out behind the old railroad depot. And two years ago he was arrested for DWI and a year before that for disorderly."

"But why would he be out on the lake?"

"After talking with you I called down to the VA. I spoke to a Dr. Bedrosian there. He said your brother could be pretty confused at times."

"Yes, he could. But he was getting better."

"Until he started hitting the booze again."

"What about the cut? You think he got that from falling?"

"That's what it looks like. The lake was sheer ice where we found him. Right off Corbins Point there. We found blood on the ice, too. Doc Proulx said it probably happened when he fell. Plus, he smelled of booze. Given all that, and your brother's record, it's not the sort of thing that calls for an autopsy, I'm afraid. It'd be a waste of time and taxpayer's money. Not to mention the trouble it'd put you through, Libby. Now of course if you insist. Then we'd have to get the medical examiner's office down in Augusta in on it. Could delay a funeral for a long while. Is that what you want, Libby? If it is I'll call right now."

I look down at Leon. "I guess not."

"I think you're making the right decision. You want a few more minutes?" he asks.

"No, I think I'm all set." I lean down and kiss Leon on his cheek. I can still smell the aftershave. I try to think of something to say but nothing comes to mind. "Good-bye, Leon," is all I whisper. Then I cover him up so he's not cold. He always hated being cold.

As we drive over to the police station to get my truck, I say, "One other thing, Chief Chambers."

"What's that?"

"I don't know if it matters or not. But my brother got a call last night. He was supposed to meet some man about a job?"

"Do you know who?"

"No," I say.

"I spoke to Earl Teed this morning. He said your brother was in the Spruce Goose last night for a little while. But he didn't say he was with anybody."

"Maybe he met him someplace else," I say as we pull into the station. The chief hands me my keys.

"Maybe. Or maybe he never met him at all. Maybe your brother just got drunk and forgot all about it. That's the way it is with alcoholics, I'm afraid."

"Did you find anything else out there?"

"Like what?"

"I don't know."

"No, nothing. There were no prints out there. Like I said, it was bare ice. The winds blow pretty hard right off the point. We found your truck not a quarter mile away. Keys still in it. Looks like he parked it there and walked out."

"Why would he do that?"

"I don't know, Libby. I'm awful sorry, though. If I can do anything else you let me know."

All the way home I keep seeing Leon on the stretcher, that gash over his eye. I'm thinking somehow that it was my fault. If only I hadn't let him take the truck. Or if I'd gone with him. Maybe he'd still be alive.

When I get home, before I call Thibodeau's Funeral Parlor to make arrangements, I go into Leon's room. I sit on his bed. It's not made and it smells like Leon. The pillow still holds the indentation from his head. It's hard to believe he's really gone. That his absence isn't temporary, that he won't show up at my door in a couple of months. Under his nightstand I notice the brown grocery bag containing his things. I pick it up and empty it on the bed: all this junk. Some lottery tickets, a set of old car keys, a few mashed chocolate bars, some change, a Swiss army knife, a box containing his electrician's tools—wire cutters, splicers, needle-nose pliers. There's also a coffee can. I take the top off and empty the contents. There are old photographs, some family pictures, clippings from newspapers, receipts, tobacco paper, hand-scribbled notes, estimates for jobs, a warranty for some old muffler he had put on back in the seventies, a few other papers. One of the photos is that one of our mother standing in front of the waterfall. Another, one I'd never seen before, has her sitting on the front porch of our house in Sheshuncook, with baby Leon in a carriage and me behind her. She's very young and she looks dreamily toward the camera, the way young girls do whose minds are way off someplace. All you can see of Leon is his head sticking above the sides of the old perambulator. He's wearing one of my bonnets while I stand by with my hand up to my mouth like I'm about to sneeze. Another picture is of Stephanie and his granddaughter. On the back it says, "Missy, eight weeks old. Who does she look like, Dad? Love, Steph."

I gather up the pile and am about to put them back into the can when I happen to see a yellowed newspaper photo. It's in pretty bad condition, fragile, the picture faded, with cracks in it from where it been folded so many times. However, I catch the headline above it: "Germans Help War Effort." Curious, I spread the photo out on the bed, try to flatten out the creases. It looks like winter. In the background you can make out naked trees and snow the color of oatmeal, and you can tell it's cold because the men in it are dressed in heavy hats and coats, their necks scrunched down into their collars. I look more closely at it. In the front row are the POWs, kneeling or squatting, the white *PW* clearly visible on the sleeve of several of them. They hold axes and crosscut saws. One man has a pulp hook dangling from his hand like an upside-down question mark. They seem so young, most like boys. Could one of these, I wonder, be that German's brother? The interpreter? I look carefully at their faces, one at a time, looking for those hooded eyes, the wide mouth. Yet from this picture I can't tell.

What interests me, though, is the back row. The men, I notice, are company workers, loggers. I count ten of them. They look older than the Germans. While the photo is in bad shape, the faces grainy with age, one face way in the back suddenly leaps out at me, out of the lengthening shadows of that winter day, over the distance of nearly half a century. There's no mistaking the wide nose and dark features, the deep-set, flint-hard eyes: Ambroise. Yes, it's him! And next to him is someone else I'm pretty sure I recognize. Tom Weston. He's wearing a plaid hunting hat, something he always wore, and a mackinaw. He'd worked with and been a close friend of Ambroise for years. The two sometimes would sit in our kitchen eating steamers and drinking, and playing cards until two in the morning. Another, a small bowlegged man who's leaning on a peavey, looks a little familiar but I can't recall his name. I stare at the picture some more, at the other men, but either I've forgotten them or their faces are obscured by the photo. Then, I happen to notice, way over on the right-hand side, halfway between the Germans and the company men, a young cookee. He has a yoke balanced across his shoulders, with two heavy stewpots suspended from each end. He's wearing a hat with earflaps pulled way down on his head, and he's squinting against the late-afternoon sunlight. Even in this picture I can see that he has soft, girlish features and large, rabbitlike eyes. Leon, I think. Yes, it's my brother.

When I turn the photo over I see an advertisement for the A&P in town. It says, "Pork Butts—29¢/lb—No Points!" It must be from the *Herald*. I keep this photo, put the rest back into the coffee can for Stephanie. Then I call the funeral parlor to make arrangements.

*   *   *

Two days later the wake is held at Thibodeau's, in town near McCorkle's lumberyard. I wear the black cotton dress I used to visit Leon in and a black hat I picked up at Flo's Fashion Boutique. The hat has black lace that comes down over my eyes, though I don't need to hide my eyes. I haven't cried yet. I don't know why. I haven't found the secret place where my tears are stored. It's like when Ambroise died. I couldn't cry then, either.

I wasn't sure who, if anybody, would come. Most of the relatives on my father's side are dead, or living far enough away in Canada that I didn't expect them to drive down. And, except for a few drinking cronies, Leon didn't exactly stay in touch with many people from town. I thought maybe some of his old school pals—Luke Gagnon, Harry Klatka, Bub Reynolds—would show up to pay their respects. Or those like Tom Weston or Spotty who'd come out of loyalty to Ambroise.

I doubted if Claire, his ex-wife, would show up. She was living over in East Millinocket now, had her own place doing hair and nails, yet she'd written Leon off a long time ago. I called Stephanie, though, knowing she'd want to come. In fact, I'd called her several times over the past two days, but I kept getting her answering machine. I didn't want to leave a message on it. What could I say? "Your father's dead—you coming to the services?" I ended up just telling her it was urgent and to please call me. She never called, though. So when I enter through the back door, into the small vestibule of Thibodeau's, I'm a little surprised to see her standing there, nervously smoking a cigarette.

"Oh, Auntie Lib," she says when she sees me. She comes over and hugs me.

"Hello, honey," I say. "I'm sorry about your dad."

"Yes . . ." She looks as if she's going to say more but doesn't.

My niece is twenty-nine, small boned like Leon, but other than that she mostly takes after her mother's side. Short auburn hair, a broad, plain face, a small pouty mouth that always made her look as if she'd just gotten some bad news. Not a pretty girl, but sensible and mature for her age. I remember when she was little and would come visit at the store, she'd help me stock the shelves, wash dishes, feed the chickens I had then. She brushed her teeth and said her prayers without being told, was always neat, kept her things just so. A regular little lady.

"What's it been?" I ask.

"My wedding, Auntie Lib." Which was three years ago.

"That long? How's little Missy?"

"Just starting to crawl. Getting into everything."

"I'm still working on that quilt I promised you. In fact, I brought it with me. For something to do." I take my sewing out of the plastic shopping bag and hold it up for her to see.

"That's real pretty, Auntie Lib."

"I got a little behind on it."

"That's all right. I feel bad I haven't been up to see you. Joe's working evenings and it's kind of hard to get away. Plus we're fixing up the house."

"Don't apologize. I know."

We chat about her life for a while. Her husband Joe works for the power company down in New Hampshire. They just bought a two-family house in Portsmouth. She says she's working part-time at a bank and taking night classes to become a paralegal. I remember Stephanie getting baptized right here in town. Old Father Julian sprinkling holy water on her forehead, with me there as the godmother and one of Claire's brothers as godfather. Leon and Claire were living down in Monson. Leon had just gotten out of the service and was working as an electrician's apprentice. Ambroise offered to get him a job logging, but the two had never gotten along, so Leon went his own way. He was making decent money as an apprentice, was able to buy their own trailer, support his family. I'd hoped he would finally be happy, with a wife and new baby. Hoped he would at last have the sort of life he'd never had growing up. But somehow it didn't turn out that way.

"You can stay with me tonight," I say to Stephanie.

"No, I really have to get back," she replies. "Joe took the day off to be with Missy."

"At least come back for something to eat. And I got some things of your father's you might want."

"We'll see, Auntie Lib."

"Come sit up front with me," I say. "Family should be together at a time like this."

We go inside and up to the front, where we both kneel before Leon's casket. Then we take a seat. The room is narrow, no bigger than someone's parlor. I guess they don't expect a crowd. No one else is here. Leon lies stiffly amid the few flowers and pink satin of the casket. He doesn't look like he's sleeping anymore. He looks uncomfortable, as if he's got an itch and can't scratch it. He's swimming in the blue sharkskin suit of his I found up in the attic. The only suit he owned, the one he got married to Claire in. Young Louis Thibodeau, the original owner's son, has done a pretty good job covering up the cut over Leon's eye. You can hardly see it.

"You get my message?" I ask Stephanie.

"No."

"How did you hear about it then?" I ask.

"A friend from town, Molly Driscoll, she heard about it and called me. What happened?"

"They didn't tell you?"

"She heard they found him out on the lake. What was he doing out there?"

"I don't know, hon."

"Do you think he meant to do it, Auntie Lib? Think he was just tired of living?"

"Of course not." I'm not much of a Catholic anymore, but I'm still enough of one to believe in hell. "I don't know why he was out there but one thing I'm sure of, he didn't mean to do this, Steph. If anybody's to blame, it's me. I never should've let him borrow the truck."

"Don't blame yourself, Auntie Lib. You were always helping Dad. He's the one to blame."

"But if I didn't give him those keys."

"He'd have found some other way to hurt himself. And those who loved him, too."

I glance at her and nod.

After a while Mrs. Steele and Patsy Conlon, two ancient ladies from town who wouldn't miss a wake for their lives, show up. It's just the four of us. I can't expect a crowd at two in the afternoon for a midweek service. People have to work. Maybe tonight, I think, though it makes me sad that Leon's life has been whittled down to so little. A sister, a daughter, and two old busybodies looking for something to get them out on a weekday afternoon.

"Remember when you used to come and stay with me and your father?" I ask my niece.

"Yes. I got a kick out of eating at the lunch counter for free. And getting the eggs in the chicken coop."

"You know who built that coop for me?"

"Who?"

"Your dad."

"He did?" Stephanie asks.

"Yeah. Leon was pretty handy, when he wanted to be."

"I never remember him doing much of anything around the house."

"That was later. When he started to hit the bottle. Try to remember the good times, Steph."

"There weren't many of those."

"I know he wasn't always the best of fathers, Steph."

Stephanie looks straight ahead, at Leon, as if waiting for Leon to say something in his own defense.

"I'm sure he loved you, honey."

"Please, Auntie Lib. I'd rather not talk about that."

"Leon was hard to get to know. I don't think even I ever knew him. Not totally anyway. There was a part of him he never let anybody see. It was . . . I don't know. Maybe on account of our mother running off the way she did."

"But you weren't like that."

"I was harder than Leon. He was always soft."

"He never seemed soft to me."

"Not on the outside. On the outside he put up this hard front. To keep people away. Inside he was always afraid."

"Afraid of what?"

"I'm not sure. Of being alone, I guess. Of not being loved. I think that's why the booze."

"He never let us love him. Me or Ma."

"I got this picture back at the house I'll give you, Steph. Leon and me are with our mother on the front steps. Your father's about two years old. You look at that picture and you see this beautiful little baby, all wide eyes and innocence. It'll want to break your heart."

"Please, Auntie Lib," she says, her eyes crinkling like tissue paper at the corners. "It's enough I'm here. That's all I owe him."

"Well, I'm glad you are."

I take her hand and we sit quietly. Only a few other people show up, all women, too. Then again, Leon always had more women friends than men. Trudy McCray and Harry Klatka's sister Bev, who used to have a crush on my brother and now runs the Silver Spoon Restaurant in town. Helen West, Connie's wife, who lives down the road from me. Two women, in their late forties, who look like sisters but who I don't recognize. They both have dull blond hair and huge feet. They hover over Leon for a moment, one of them sobbing softly. Lovers? I wonder. Which one? Both maybe? I think about what I said to Stephanie, how Leon had this part of him he never showed even me.

A very old woman, badly stooped, comes up to me, offers a thin, brittle hand that feels like a bouquet of dried flowers. "You're Libby, right?" she asks.

I nod.

"You don't remember me, do you?"

"I don't think so."

"Mrs. Levesque. Your fifth-grade teacher. Leon's, too."

"My goodness," I say, recognizing suddenly the same stern, brown eyes hidden in the time-scarred face. I can recall the ruler she'd wielded on the back of your knuckles and the way she'd grab the vulnerable flesh beneath your chin to pull you out into the hall if you'd been fooling around.

"How are you, Mrs. Levesque?"

"I get around," she says. "I still remember the time I sent you down to the principal's. Remember that? It was for biting that kid on the ear. What was his name?"

"Gundersen," I say, smiling at the memory.

"Your brother was good in mathematics."

"He was."

"No flies on Leon," she says.

After she leaves, Stephanie asks, "You bit some kid, Auntie Lib?"

"In grade school. He was beating up your father. I didn't know what else to do so I bit him on the ear."

"My goodness," Stephanie says.

"I was a tomboy. I looked after your father. Your grandfather taught us to stick up for each other."

When visiting hours are over for the afternoon, my niece and I get up and head outside. We walk across the dirt parking lot to her car. The early spring day is unusually warm. The snow is melting, creating puddles, and the topmost layer of earth is thawing, turning to mud. Mud season, they call it up here. Everybody's tires and fenders are covered with mud and this whitish film of road salt.

"Come back for a bite?" I ask.

"I can't," replies my niece.

"How about a cup of tea?"

"No, Auntie Lib. I really have to go. Joe's waiting for me."

"But I have some things. That picture I told you about. And some of his personal effects."

"Send me the picture. The rest you can keep."

"Will you come up to visit me sometime?" I say.

"I will."

"Promise?"

"I promise."

"He did love you," I offer.

"He had a funny way of showing it."

"But he did. You have to believe that."

She half nods, then sucks in her mouth in a way that reminds me of her father, the way he would when he was near tears. We hug one last time, and then she gets in her car and takes off. As I watch her head down the road, I wonder if I'll ever see her again. Or will it just be birthday cards, Missy's First Communion picture, letters filled with regrets, and in ten or twenty years her showing up like this for my funeral?

10

I DON'T FEEL like driving all the way home and then having to head back in for the evening service. So I have a few hours to kill. I decide to drive over to the Spruce Goose for a bite to eat. With everything on my mind I'd forgotten to eat, and now my stomach's grumbling. It's early, just a little past three, and most people are still at work. The place has only a few people in it. I sit at a booth near the front window and watch rigs go barreling past hauling their last load of logs for the mills.

"God, I can't tell you how sorry I am about your brother, Lib," says Earl Teed, who has come over to wait on me. He's a tall man in a plaid flannel shirt. His thinning black hair is slicked close to his skull, so it looks like it's been painted on, like a mannequin's hair.

"Thanks, Earl," I say.

"I feel a little responsible. Him being in here that night. But like I told the police chief, he only had one beer. And he nursed that."

"They said he smelled of booze."

"If he did, it sure the Christ wasn't from here. I was on that night and Leon sat over at the bar and had just the one beer. I don't even think he finished it. I hadn't seen him around for a while so we were shooting the breeze."

"Was he with anybody?"

"Not that I remember. He sat there by himself."

"What time did he leave?"

"I'd say around ten. I remember because he kept asking what time it was. Like he had to be someplace."

"But you don't think he was drunk?"

"I can't say what happened after he left here. But, Lib, I swear on my mother's grave, he didn't get drunk here. When he left he was sober as a judge."

"I believe you, Earl."

"What can I get you?"

"Got a menu?" I ask.

"Kitchen's closed till five. Benny ain't come in yet. But I could throw you on a burger or something."

"Sure," I say. "A burger sounds good. And a beer, too."

Outside, I see Ronny Hanson, Billy's son, walk into Pavel's Pharmacy across the street. After a while I see him come out holding a white bag and head up the street toward his father's garage. At the corner I see a man who works for the town shoveling sand from a dump truck into one of those fifty-gallon sand drums. The drum is angled into the air like a cannon. The man wears a green town highway uniform with a white patch on the sleeve. He's standing on the bed of the truck, and with a long-handled shovel he scoops a pile of sand and then tosses it down into the waiting mouth of the drum. He does it over and over, the sand making a deadened *pluff* sound inside the drum. *Pluff . . . pluff . . . pluff.*

I try to tell myself that Leon's at peace finally. That nothing can hurt him anymore. That he'll never be cold or afraid or alone again. I try to find consolation, solace in that. But instead of consolation or solace, there are all these questions. What was the business he had to take care of in town? Did he really go to see somebody about a job? Or was it just a line he gave me so he could go in and get drunk? Yet someone *had* called. Not once but twice, asking for Leon. Was Leon going to see that man, the one with the hoarse voice? Was that just one of his old bum friends? And what on earth was he doing out there on the lake, in the middle of the night? Was he just confused, in a drunken stupor, like the chief said? It doesn't make sense. And I think, too, about how Leon got so upset when he heard I'd spoken to Wolfgang Kallick, the wild look in his eyes when I told him it was the dead German's brother. How he told me, *Keep your nose out of it. Stay away from him.* Like he was afraid almost. I can't help but think that the phone calls had something to do with all this. But what? I glance at my wrist and see the just-healing scabs where Leon's nails had broken the skin the other day.

From my pocketbook I take out that picture of the loggers. I spread it out on the table. Why did Leon keep this? He hated logging, hated anything to do with Ambroise. My face is only inches from the picture when Earl says, "You want anything on that, Lib?"

"What?" I ask.

Earl is standing over the table, looking down at me.

"Any onions or lettuce on that?"

"Oh. No. Plain is fine."

"Here you go," he says, setting a plate, a bottle of ketchup, and a beer in front of me. "What's that, Lib?"

"Some old picture of my father's logging crew," I say. "It was in the *Herald,* from back during the war. You wouldn't happen to recognize anybody in it, would you, Earl?"

Earl picks up the picture, angles it toward the light. "Not a very good picture." After a while he says, "There's your old man, ain't it?"

"Yes, that's him. Anybody else?"

"Naw. It's too faded. Why you interested?"

"It was Leon's," I say. "Just curious."

"You should go over to the library. Ask Roberta. They have some of the old *Herald*s over there. Maybe if you was to find the original it might have the names listed. Or at least a picture in better shape you could make out who the hell's in it. By the way, what time are visiting hours tonight?"

"Seven to nine."

"I'll try to get over later," says Earl. "If it ain't too busy."

When I take out my wallet to pay he says, "Your money ain't no good here, Lib. Least I can do."

"Let me ask you something, Earl."

"Sure."

"Did Leon seem all right to you?"

"How's that?"

"You know, confused. Like he wasn't all with it."

"No. He seemed like the same old Leon. Hell, we were talking about the Red Sox's chances of blowing it again this year."

"You said he kept asking what time it was. Did he say anything about where he had to go?"

"Nope. Nothing."

When I finish eating I go outside and get in the truck. It's just after four. I still have a couple of hours on my hands. I drive through the center of town. I can see Billy Hanson in the office, his feet up on the desk. He's eating a sandwich. A sign in the window of Mercier's clothing store says, "We Support Our Desert Storm Troops." As I'm about to pass the library, I decide to pull over and go in.

"I thought you closed at four," I say to Roberta Pike, who's standing behind the main desk. The woman's been the librarian since about Eisenhower's second term, and the town gossip since way before that. She's my age, a big, gawky woman with a thyroid problem: bug eyes, thinning hair. And like me she's an old maid, except I don't think she's ever been with a man. She makes up for it by knowing all the dirt in town.

"Thursdays we stay open till seven," she says. "I'm so sorry about Leon."

"Thanks."

"I hadn't seen him in years. Didn't even know he was back in town."

"He just came up to stay with me."

"I was wondering," she says. She leans over the desk toward

me, slides her reading glasses down her nose, and glances over my shoulder, as though she's worried someone will overhear what she's about to ask me—we're the only ones in the place, though. Her breath smells sour like old books. "Was he really depressed?"

"Where'd you hear that?"

"That's what some people are saying."

"What else are they saying?" I ask, angry that they're spreading rumors about Leon.

"Just that he was having some problems up here," she says, tapping her temple with one of those rubber page turners.

"He didn't kill himself, you understand, Roberta. Leon wouldn't have done that."

"Of course he wouldn't. But alcoholism sure is a curse. And you, poor thing, you'd certainly know about that. What with Ambroise—"

"Roberta," I say, cutting her short, "where would I find old copies of the *Herald*?"

"We have the past three months over on the shelf."

"I mean, really old. From during the war."

"Vietnam?"

"No," I say. "Second World War. I'm looking for articles about the POW camp."

Roberta stares at me over the top of her reading glasses, grinning her big horsey grin. She has a smudge of pink lipstick on her front tooth.

"What's the matter?" I ask.

"You're the second person's been in looking up the camp."

Though I have a pretty good idea who the other was, I ask anyway.

"This older gentleman came in a couple of days ago," Roberta says. "He was interested in the prison camp, too."

"Did he say what for?"

"No."

"Do you have copies of the *Herald* from back then?"

"Some on microfilm. Just a sec," she says, holding up an index finger.

Roberta goes over to a small metal file cabinet. She looks something up, then heads into the room behind her desk. She returns with a small gray box.

"Here we go," she says. "This roll begins with 1943. They started the camp the next year, I believe."

Roberta opens the box, and then sets me up on the microfilm machine, which is over near the encyclopedias.

"If you tell me what you're looking for, I might be able to help," she says. "I'm not too busy right now."

"To tell you the truth, I'm just poking around." I don't want her looking over my shoulder, asking questions.

"Well, here's your focus adjustment. And this knob is your fast-forward. If you need any help, just give a yell."

"Thanks."

I turn the knob that sends me skimming through the past. I begin with the June 1944 issues, when they opened the camp. I don't exactly know what I'm looking for, what I expect to find. Except that I want to find out who else is in that logging photo with Ambroise and Leon—though why that seems important now I can't say either.

I haven't gone very far, however, when I come across the first mention of the camp. A headline on the front page of the June 22, 1944, edition reads: "The Germans Have Landed." Beneath it is a picture of a group of Germans getting off at the train depot in town. The article is about the camp and the journey the prisoners, part of Rommel's Afrika Korps, had made from Africa.

I skim several more issues before I come across another mention of the camp. This one is about a dance the Women's League was putting on for the prisoners and servicemen. It was to be held in the camp mess hall. Jane Potts, the mother of a girl I'd gone to school with, was quoted as saying, "They're just regular boys, like yours or mine. They need something to take their minds off the war, too." A few issues after that there's something about Senator Brewster, a Maine senator back then. He was lobbying in Washington to have the POWs' stay lengthened after the end of the war to have enough labor for the paper industry. There are a few other articles about Sheshuncook: one about a local soldier, badly wounded in Italy, being stationed at the camp as a guard; another about a potluck supper for the military personnel. There was one about a hunger strike the POWs were going on to protest increased pulp production quotas. For each prisoner they were raising the quota to "one cord per man": "*Eine Klafter pro Kopf!*" said the indignant camp spokesman, somebody named Lagerführer Heydt. I can remember they were always raising the quota every few months and the prisoners grumbling and sometimes going on strike. And Ambroise coming home mad as hell, both at the Germans for the strike but even more at the mill bosses for expecting more than he could deliver with the inexperienced help.

Though I don't find the logging picture, I do come across something interesting in the February 8, 1945, edition:

NAZI ELEMENT BLAMED FOR DISTURBANCES

Recent disturbances at the Sheshuncook POW compound are being blamed on hardened Nazi elements within the camp, so say authorities. Two prisoners were taken to the camp infirmary where they were treated and released after receiving minor wounds suffered in an altercation between inmates at the government facility situated on the north shore of Moosehead Lake. A third prisoner had to be admitted to St. Joseph's Hospital in Bangor. His condition was not immediately known.

The fight broke out between rival groups of prisoners in the camp mess hall. A spokesman for the camp said several Nazis were championing Adolf Hitler's recent rallying cry for their countrymen to "die in their tracks in defense of the Fatherland," when the outbreak occurred. Some furniture and several windows were broken. It was also rumored that a fire was started in the basement of the barracks, which houses the prisoners' laundry. However, that rumor could not be confirmed. Damage, estimated at several hundred dollars, will be paid for out of the prisoners' canteen credits.

Guards wielding baseball bats and carrying tommy guns were called in to quell the melee. It took them nearly an hour to clear the mess hall and get prisoners back to their barracks. Several Germans were placed in solitary confinement. Meanwhile camp commander Major Denton Ryker is conducting an ongoing investigation of the incident, one of several in the past few weeks. "You can be sure, the ringleaders of this will be found and punished," he said. "We're not running a boys camp here." When asked if he thought the way the war was going for Germany had added to the tensions in camp, he noted, "It's certainly possible."

After a while my eyes begin to hurt. I get up and go over to the water fountain at the back of the library to get a drink. I feel a little dizzy. The sudden jump from past to present makes my head spin. I cup my hand and throw some water on my face. Outside, I see a large black dog chained to a tiny doghouse. The dog has a narrow, flat head, like a snake, and his ribs poke out through his coat.

I can't say I remember that fight in the mess hall. What I do remember, though, was another fight, between two prisoners in the woods while the guards stood by watching. And, of course, that bitter cold Christmas evening when Major Ryker marched the Germans out into the woods after they'd worked all day. Some prisoners had tied a homemade Nazi flag to a big spruce tree, as a joke or something, and no one noticed it till somebody called the camp to complain. I remember Major Ryker punishing the prisoners by marching them out to the cutting site to chop down the tree. I hadn't thought about it in a long time, but I can recall suddenly how cold that afternoon was, sitting in the truck while the major addressed his prisoners, the small wire spectacles he wore. I wonder why I hadn't told Kallick about that. He'd asked if there had been problems at the camp. I could've told him about that.

The dog begins to bark, his muzzle angled toward the sky. He seems to snap at the air, biting it, trying to rip a hole in it.

I go back over and continue skimming through the winter issues of the paper. I'm almost ready to quit when I come across an article at the bottom of an inside page. It's wedged between an ad for Kil-Ve lice powder on sale at Pavel's Pharmacy and an article on how the extremely frigid weather had cracked water pipes at the town hall. The headline reads: "Nazi Prisoner Escapes."

This past Tuesday a German POW from the Sheshuncook camp managed to elude guards and flee into the woods north of Moosehead Lake. Sources at the camp said the escape took place around five o'clock in the evening in a very remote area near Pittston Farm. The prisoner was being transported back to the POW camp when he slipped away from a work detail and fled into the woods. He is believed to be headed west, toward Jackman and the Canadian border. Search parties using dogs scoured the woods northwest of the lake but, as of this writing, were unsuccessful. Camp commander Major Ryker said the search will continue until the prisoner was apprehended. Major Ryker said that the prisoner poses no threat to the community. However, First Selectman Ed Desauliers was quoted as saying, "This is exactly the sort of thing we worried about when they said they were going to stick a bunch of Nazis in our town. Now who's going to protect us?"

The prisoner was identified as Corporal Dieter Kallick, 23, a former member of Rommel's vaunted Afrika Korps. He is described as being 6'1" and 150 pounds, with dark hair and an Italian complexion. He was wearing work clothes with the letters P and W on his sleeves, though he may have escaped with additional articles of clothing. He speaks fluent English and is not believed to be armed or dangerous, but Elton Bishop, chief of the Piscataquis Police Department, cautions civilians from trying to apprehend him single-handedly. "He's still the enemy. And that makes him dangerous." A $100 reward is being offered for information leading to his capture. If anyone sees a man fitting the description of Kallick, he should call the police department immediately.

When I finish reading the article, I turn to the top of the page to see the date: Wednesday, March 14, 1945. The article said the escape took place on Monday, two days earlier—March 12, 1945. *Leon's birthday*, I think. I remember baking a cake that night and going down to Abbey's to buy a canned ham to fix for supper. I had his present all wrapped. I'd knitted him a sweater I started that fall. I still remember it: green with white reindeer across the bottom. I'd bought the pattern at Montgomery Ward over in Bangor. But Ambroise and Leon had stayed out to help the soldiers search for the German and didn't get home till late. By then the ham was hard as a rock, and we didn't celebrate his birthday till the next night, and then it was just Leon and me. Ambroise had gone into town. I remember that night, though I haven't thought about it in ages.

I look through some more issues of the *Herald* to see if I can find anything else about the escape. I remember they'd found the body sometime after ice-out, which would have made it late April or May. We heard he'd probably fallen through the ice and drowned. We'd heard a lot of things, but that's what most people around here thought happened. It was what made the most sense. I look for that logging picture, too, but the film runs out suddenly, and the end begins flapping wildly in the machine, like a chicken held by the leg. I try turning the reverse knob, but I soon find myself with a pile of film on the floor.

Luckily Roberta is there to help me.

"I didn't know what to do," I say, embarrassed, the blood rushing hotly to my face.

"That's all right." Expertly, she rethreads the film, then turns the knob the other way to rewind it. "Find what you're looking for?"

"I'd like to see the film for the papers after March 1945."

"That's it."

"What do you mean?"

"Town ran out of money to have them put on film," Roberta explains. "We do have some old copies in the basement."

"Would you have the ones after March down there?"

"We might. I don't know. It's a mess, but you're welcome to go through them if you want."

"Maybe some other time," I say. "Roberta, did you show this photo to that German fellow?"

"What German fellow?"

"The one you said was in here looking up the camp."

"I don't believe he was German," Roberta replies.

"A short, heavyset man? With an accent?"

"No, this one was tall, and I wouldn't say he was heavyset. And he didn't have any accent that I could tell."

"What did he look like?"

"He was tall. Mid-sixties, I'd guess. A distinguished-looking man. Oh, one thing I do remember about him."

"What's that?"

"He was missing the tip of his index finger. I remember noticing when he was working the microfilm machine."

"You ever see him before, Roberta?"

"I can't say I have. Why?"

"No reason."

"Isn't that the oddest thing, though?" she says. "I mean, there haven't been more than a handful of people in forty years interested in this old stuff. And now I get two in the past week."

She looks at me, waiting for me to tell her why I'm so interested. But all I say is "Thanks," and leave.

The sun is just setting when I go outside and get into the truck. I sit there for a moment, thinking, wondering what I'm thinking. Who else was interested in the camp besides Kallick? The dog behind the library has fallen silent. The only noise I can hear now is an impact wrench zipping away over at Hanson's garage. The sound of metal coming undone, flying apart: *brrppp, brrppp.*

I take the newspaper photo out of my pocketbook, carefully unfold it, the paper as brittle as a dried leaf in my hands. I study it closely, staring at the Germans now. Except for the P and W on some of their sleeves and for one or two who wear the floppy Afrika Korps cap, they don't look like prisoners. You could easily take them for the sons or younger brothers of those in back.

I find myself staring at one German in particular. He's in the middle, kneeling. He's holding a crosscut saw—*die Schrotsäge*—in front of him, the way you'd hold a guitar, and he's gazing not *into* the camera but off to the side, as if something had caught his attention and pulled his gaze away from the photographer at the last second. His Afrika Korps cap is pulled down at a sharp angle over one eye so part of his face is hidden. He appears darker than the other prisoners, in fact, doesn't even look German. His eyes are fleshy, and he has the Slavic looks of some of the Czechs that were in the camp. I think, *Maybe. Maybe it is him.* I hunt around in my purse until I find the picture Kallick had sent. I take it out and lay it side by side with the newspaper photo. While neither picture is that clear and while the person in the newspaper photo is older, no longer a boy, I can still make out the faint resemblance between the two. In fact, the more I look at the two photos, the more convinced I am that I could be looking at the same person. The interpreter. The one who escaped on March 12, 1945.

11

As I PULL into Thibodeau's Funeral Parlor, my headlights freeze a group of men standing in the parking lot. Leaning up against their trucks, they smoke cigarettes and pass a bottle around in a paper bag. That's what men at funerals around here do. While the women sit inside and sew and gossip and keep the dead company, the men stand out here and talk about fishing or the Celtics. Roland, I can see, is one of them. When he sees me he separates himself and comes limping over. He's got on a too-small yellow sports coat that makes me think of an overripe banana about ready to split open at the seams. As he sticks his head in the window, I'm almost knocked over by the sweet rush of his aftershave.

"I stopped at your place on the way home from work," he says.

"I didn't go home. I stayed in town. Who's over there?"

"Some of the boys. Al Royce and Hop and a few others. Jack Duchene wasn't sure you wanted him here."

"Doesn't make any difference to me."

"He thought you were still mad at him, Lib. What are you going to do afterwards?"

"I don't know. Why?"

"Trudy and a few of the girls brought some food over to my place. They want you to stop over."

"I'll have to see. I'm kind of tired."

"You oughta at least stop by. They made enough to feed an army."

Inside, Roland sits with me up front.

"Your brother looks good," he offers. "I mean, considering."

"Considering what?" I ask.

"Well, just considering."

I look at Leon. "I guess so."

"They have any idea what he was doing out there?"

"No."

"That's the goddamnedest thing."

There are more people tonight than at the afternoon service. Some I haven't seen in ages, old friends of Ambroise's, distant relatives—like our crazy cousin, Joe Provost, who used to live out in a hut in the woods and eat roadkills. While others I've never laid eyes on at all. They pass in front of me and shake my hand, mumble something about Leon. How he'd done the wiring for this person's house. Harry Klatka says they used to call Leon "Pushy" back in grade school, something I'd never heard before. Someone else says Leon used to date his sister before he started going out with Claire.

Jack Duchene shuffles in to pay his last respects. He comes up to me, his little rat eyes not getting above my chest, says, "Sorry," before moving along. After a while, Tom Weston comes by. He hobbles up to the casket with a cane, stands there for a moment. Then he comes over and gives me a hug.

"God, it's been a long time, Lib."

"Yes," I reply. "Last time was at your Peg's funeral. Ten years ago?"

"Twelve."

"Is it that long?"

"Yeah. Twelve years this June."

Tom hasn't changed much. A little grayer and thinner, but still tall and straight as a board. In fact, it's not so much the wrinkled face in front of me I see as that other, youthful one in the logging picture. I wonder if he'd know who was in it.

"That was a terrible thing happened to Leon," he says. "Your brother was a good kid."

"Yeah," I reply. "Tom, do you know Roland St. James?"

"St. James. There was a St. James used to log with the Brown Company," Tom says.

"That was my father."

"Yeah, I knew your old man. Harold, wasn't it?"

"Howard," Roland corrects.

"Sure, I remember. Your old man still alive?"

"No, he passed away a few years back."

"Well, glad to meet you. Lib, if there's anything I can do, anything at all, don't be afraid to give a yell."

"Thanks. I will, Tom."

After Tom leaves, Roland asks, "You gonna stay for the whole wake?"

"I ought to."

"Christ, I hate these goddamn things," he says tugging at his tie. I don't know whether he means the tie or the wake.

"You don't have to stay if you don't want to, Roland."

He picks my pocketbook up off the floor and starts hunting through it.

"What are you doing?" I ask.

"Looking for some smokes."

I picture him coming across that photo Kallick sent me and wondering what I was doing with it.

I slap his hand. "Get out of my pocketbook. I'll get 'em for you."

I hand him a cigarette and some matches, and he says he's going outside for a little while.

After he leaves, I get my sewing from the bag on the floor and begin working on Missy's quilt. It occupies me, keeps my mind busy. It was Tom Weston's wife, Peg, who got me interested in sewing. Those times we used to stay with her after my mother ran off. It was she who taught me how to baste and backstitch, how to quilt and cut out a pattern, how to hem pants and darn socks, things to run a household. When Leon would be sick with a fever, I'd sit in his room at night and sew. Sitting here now I think of that sweater I'd made him for his twelfth birthday. March 12, 1945. The night the German escaped. I'd worked on the sweater for weeks. I remember how he didn't even get to open the box on his birthday. It wasn't till the next morning, and when he tried it on the sweater turned out to be too small for him after all. It was as if he'd gotten too big for it overnight. There was something else different about him, too. I couldn't say exactly what, yet when we walked around the cove to Abbey's to catch our bus for school, I sensed it, felt it the way I'd felt my own period coming on a few years before that. There was something different about Leon, a hard, closed place inside him, one that had never been there before, but would be there from then on, that would get harder and more closed as the years went by.

I remember another birthday too, years later. Claire had already kicked Leon out and he'd come to stay with me. He'd just turned forty, maybe forty-one. I forget exactly. But I remember I was in the kitchen making a birthday cake for him. He was in his room reading. "Leon," I called from the kitchen. "Remember what I made you for your twelfth birthday?"

"You gotta be kidding," he said.

"I knitted you that sweater."

"What sweater?"

"It was green with white reindeer across the front. I worked on it all that winter."

"I thought Ma made me that."

"She never made you a damn thing. It was me."

I walked over to his room. I stood in the doorway, beating the batter with a spoon. Leon was lying on top of the comforter, a book on his chest. He had his thick reading glasses on, and they made his eyes as big as clamshells. He was wearing the long johns and the pair of slippers I'd already given to him as birthday presents. He didn't look up from his reading, a travel book about Alaska.

"What's that for?" I asked.

He shrugged, then said, "I might be looking to make a change."

"Why?"

"I just might, that's all."

"Don't you like it here?"

"It's all right."

"What's up in Alaska anyway? You never liked the cold."

"They got plenty of work up there."

"There's work here if you want it."

"Shit. Pumping gas and pouring coffee for every asshole that comes down the pike. Forget it."

"You could get something else if you wanted. In town."

He glanced over the top of his glasses at me. "There's nothing for me here."

"Why?"

"There just ain't. Never was."

Leon could get in these black moods all of a sudden. One minute he'd be happy-go-lucky, then the next fly off the handle for no reason. When he was in one of those moods I'd have to step around him like I was walking on eggshells. It was then that he usually fell off the wagon. I figured I'd change the subject. "What kind of frosting you want on your cake, Leon?"

"Don't make a rat's turd to me."

"How about coconut? You always liked that."

"Whatever you want."

"I'm surprised you don't remember that sweater." I stopped stirring the batter. I dipped my finger in and tasted it.

Leon finally looked up again. "Now why would I remember that?"

"I gave it to you on your twelfth birthday."

"So?"

"It was March twelfth, 1945. You were twelve on the twelfth."

"Big deal. Everybody's something on some damn date."

"You didn't get home till late that night. Remember?"

"Of course I don't remember."

"You were out with Ambroise, in the woods. I started to get worried. I remember sitting in the kitchen looking out the window for his truck. When you finally got home your feet were nearly frostbitten. We had to soak them in a basin."

"I don't remember any of that. You're just making it up."

"No, I'm not. You were out late with Ambroise. And the others." I stirred the batter some more, looking down at Leon's bony ankles. "They were searching."

Leon put his book down. "Searching for what?"

"For the German who escaped. Ambroise's crew went out with the soldiers."

"How do you remember that?"

"I don't know. Probably because it was your birthday. And you were late and I was afraid something had happened."

Leon shoved his glasses up on top of his head. His eyes were suddenly small and wet looking. "You're fuckin' crazy, you know that."

"Why?"

"You just are. That's why nobody ever wanted to marry you. Nobody could put up with you. You'd drive 'em crazy. Just like you're driving me crazy."

After that I never brought up the "German business" to Leon again. He seemed to have his reasons for not wanting to talk about it and I didn't want to push him.

The room seems suddenly smaller, as if the walls are closing in on me. I need to get out, get some fresh air. I put my sewing down and go outside and join Roland, who's standing on the back porch.

"I was just coming back in," he says.

I light up a cigarette. There's a sweet odor in the air. "What's that smell?"

"Cedar. Lumberyard must've got a new shipment of fence posts."

"This weather going to hold?"

"Fake spring. I heard another front's coming down from Canada by the weekend. They're talking a coupla feet maybe."

We wait on the back porch of Thibodeau's, looking out across the parking lot toward McCorkle's lumberyard. At the edge of the parking lot, the group of men stand beside their pickup trucks, talking, laughing. It's dark and I can only make out their cigarettes flaring now and then. Occasionally someone's laughter drifts up toward us.

"What're they saying, Roland?"

"What do you mean?" he asks.

"You know. About Leon."

"Oh, let 'em talk. Don't worry about it."

"But what *are* they saying?"

"It's just bullshit, Lib."

"Roland, tell me what they're saying."

"Well, somebody said he was out there buying booze."

"Booze?" I ask. "Why wouldn't he just buy it at a liquor store?"

"Not if it was still whiskey. Coupla people got stills out in the woods. Lucien Turgeon up on Burnt Jacket sells it. The Feds raided him just a while back."

"You hear anything else?"

"Naw. You coming over the house?"

"I don't think so."

"You ought to pick up some food. So you won't have to cook."

"I'll stop over tomorrow. After the funeral."

"I'm gonna be one of the pallbearers."

"Thanks, Roland."

"No problem. I'm gonna take off then." Before he leaves Roland gives me a hug and says, "There's nothing you could've done."

"About what?" I ask.

"Leon. I know that's what you're thinking."

"How do you know what I'm thinking?"

"I know you. Know how your mind works. Nobody put the bottle to his lips and made him drink. You did all you could."

"If I did everything I could he might still be alive."

"That's just what I mean. Don't go beating up on yourself."

"See you," I say.

After Roland leaves I finish my cigarette and toss it into the parking lot. I stare out toward the group of men. The scene suddenly makes me think of the dream I've been having. About the men standing out in the driveway. As I'm thinking about the dream, a late-model Buick pulls into the lot. A man gets out and comes walking up. It takes me a moment to realize who it is.

"Good evening, Frau Pelletier," says Wolfgang Kallick, offering his chubby hand. I don't take it, and his hand slowly settles on the porch railing.

"What are you doing here?" I ask, recalling how Leon had warned me to stay away from him.

"I was trying to get in touch with you. Your neighbor, Herr West, told me the bad news. My deepest sympathies, Frau Pelletier."

"But why are you here?"

"Did you get my note the other night?"

"Yes. But I've had other things on my mind."

"Of course."

"Like I already told you, Mr. Kallick, I don't know anything about your brother. I can't help you. I wish you'd just leave me alone."

"Could we talk? Just for a few minutes? I must leave for Germany soon and I do not have much time."

"No, I don't think so. I'm not in the mood for talking right now."

"Perhaps tomorrow? Just for a little while."

"I'm burying my brother tomorrow, Mr. Kallick. You have to understand."

"Certainly. I understand, Frau Pelletier. I hate to trouble you at such a time. But . . . but I never had the chance to bury my brother. I am only asking for a few moments of your time."

"Mr. Kallick—"

"Please, Frau Pelletier. Did you love your brother?"

"Of course I did. What kind of question is that?"

"I loved mine, too. Help me. Please. I have no one else to turn to."

I suddenly feel his sadness as a tightening in my chest, as if someone had reached into me and was kneading my heart with strong remorseless fingers. His pain is somehow linked to my own: his brother's death and Leon's connected in some strange way. He must sense I'm wavering.

"I need to show you something, Frau Pelletier," he adds.

"What?" I ask, wondering if it's just a trick to get me to say yes to him.

"It would be better if I showed you when we talked."

I stare at him, trying to see if he's telling the truth.

"All right," I say finally. "But not now."

"When?"

"Give me a few days. I need some time alone. I'll call you."

"Thank you, Frau Pelletier. *Vielen Dank*. And please accept my deepest sympathies." He holds his hand out again. This time I accept it.

On the ride home I stop at Corbins Point, on the east side of the lake. It's a popular necking spot for teenagers. I shut the truck off and grab the flashlight from the glove compartment. I get out of the truck and shine the light around on the snow. It's covered with beer bottles and paper six-pack cartons and the ashes from bonfires. Down toward the lake, half buried in snow, are the hulking remains of an old car. It looks like an old Rambler. Its windows have all been smashed out, and rusted bullet holes pepper the sides. I walk past it heading for the lake. There are footprints and snowmobile tracks everywhere.

When I get down to the lake, I head straight out, toward some lights on the other side. I find the ice smooth, a little slick in spots from the day's unusual heat wave. But it's already starting to refreeze. I can feel the ice crystals crunching under my shoes.

The night is clear, the stars tiny fragments of mica glittering in the sky. A brisk wind comes slipping in from the northwest, down past Mount Kineo, over Lily Bay. I can smell pine and for some reason the faint odor of fuel—maybe where a snowmobiler spilled some gas. It crosses my mind that this time of year, especially after a warm spell, there can be weak spots in the ice. That every year somebody goes through. But I keep walking anyway, heading, though I don't know why, toward those lights on the other side, which must be over on Black Point. They're like a beacon.

After I'm out pretty far, I stop, shine the light around on the ice. I'm looking for something, though I'm not sure what. Blood? Something of Leon's? Something to tell me why he was here. Maybe something the police had missed, something to tell me what that *business* was he had to take care of. I search the ice for a while, but of course I don't find anything. It's a huge lake. Like searching for a needle in a haystack. I don't even know why I came out here.

As I head back to the truck I have this odd thought. It's about Leon. He's lying in his casket down at Thibodeau's, alone, in the dark, and he's scared. Scared of the dark. The way he used to be afraid to sleep alone sometimes. It's crazy, I know. Leon's in a place beyond fear. But I can't shake the image. I can picture his eyes darting around the dark funeral parlor. He's afraid and he's calling out for me. And there's nothing I can do. Not a thing.

12

THE NEXT DAY I say good-bye to Leon for the last time as we lay him to rest in the cemetery out on Ridge Road. It's colder out today and raw, with a light drizzle that freezes as soon as it hits the ground. A front's coming in from Canada, bringing with it more snow by the weekend. Leon's grave lies beneath a scarred old cedar tree, and right next to Ambroise's, which lies next to my grandfather's. Pudgy and boyish-looking Father Rodino, who has never met Leon, says a few things about him, about his soul, how it had been weary and seeking rest. A weary traveler, he calls him. And I think how that fits Leon. Father Rodino ends by saying, "Lord, we commend the soul of Leon Edward Pelletier to your loving care. May he rest in peace. Amen."

Afterwards we go over to Roland's place, over on Indian Pond. Al Royce and his wife Helen, Trudy and Hoppy McCray, and Roland and I stand around drinking coffee and eating potato salad and these small olive-loaf sandwiches Trudy made. In the kitchen Hop's talking to Al about layoffs over at the mills. The economy and everything. How there's talk about them letting several hundred people go.

"Logging ain't like it was in the old days," Hoppy says. "They don't give a shit about me and you."

I'm standing near the sink looking out. I feel a chill coming on, an ache deep in my bones like I'm going to be sick. Outside, I watch a blue jay in a tree, squawking, giving a squirrel hell about his eating out of the bird feeder. The driveway has these deep ruts cut into the frozen mud. I think of that muddy spring day twenty-six years ago. When the men Ambroise was working with then pulled into the driveway to tell me he had been killed. I was standing at the sink cutting carrots. Even before they came in and told me, I just knew something bad had happened. I thought then, as I do now: Isn't it always the way, the men go out and get themselves run over by a tractor or drink themselves into the ground or get themselves killed in the mud of some field in France or the sands of Iraq, and it's the women who get stuck holding the bag, who have to stand over the grave, silently cursing them for leaving them so alone; it's the women who have to get up the next morning and make the coffee and patch things up and keep on with the tedious business of living. And I think maybe I can understand why my mother grabbed the chance when it came and left, so she wouldn't have to be the one grieving over the dead, the one holding the bag for the men.

"It was never any goddamn good for the guy in the woods," Al says. "You go out and bust your ass to get them the wood."

"Or your knee," Roland tosses in.

"Fuckin' got that right," Al says.

"Let's clean it up," Helen says. "It is a funeral, you know."

"Sorry, Lib. But what I'm saying is these stinking SOBs don't give a damn what happens to you."

"It's always been that way," Roland says.

"Yeah, but at least you'd see the owner on the street," Hoppy counters. "He was part of the town. Now they live down in Boston or Atlanta and could give two shits you don't have a job. They don't even know who you are."

"You're just a number to those bastards," Al replies.

"They're not going to lay you fellows off," says Trudy. "No way." But you can hear the worry in her voice.

"Who's to say what they'll do?" Hoppy says. "I'm fifty-eight. Who's gonna hire me?"

"Won't happen, so don't worry," his wife says.

"Who's worrying? I'll just go fishing," Hoppy jokes. Trudy, though, doesn't think it's funny. She chews on a fingernail.

I slip out of the kitchen, heading for the front hall closet where my coat is hung. Roland comes after me. "How're you doing?" he asks.

I shrug.

"You want a beer or something?"

"No," I reply. "I have to get going."

"What's the big rush? You ain't gonna open up the store? Not today?"

"I don't feel too hot. I think I'm coming down with something."

"Trudy had the flu."

"Maybe that's what I got. I should go home and get in bed."

I grab my coat.

"Aren't you gonna say good-bye to everybody?" Roland says.

"Tell them I wasn't feeling well, would you? And tell them thanks, too."

"Hop and Trudy are going to the Legion potluck on Sunday. You want to come?"

"I'll have to see how I feel. I'm not really up for doing much yet."

"You need to get out."

"I just buried Leon today. Give me some time. *Please.*"

When I leave Roland's place, instead of heading home I take a left and drive north on Route 15, along the west side of the lake. About eight miles north, just past the railroad bridge, I turn down Cove Road and head toward Misery Point, which somehow strikes me as appropriate now. I'm not sure which house is his, so I start looking at the mailboxes. It's been a long time since I've been to Tom Weston's house. Finally I spot his mailbox. He lives in a small frame house covered with green tar paper and a front porch that's propped up on cinder blocks. There's plastic over all the windows and straw over the bulkhead. In the front yard a rusted outboard motor lies half buried in the snow next to an overturned wooden fishing boat going to hell. It's probably a boat he and Ambroise used to fish in.

I pause for a moment before knocking. What do you think you're doing? I ask myself. Go off half-cocked like this, who knows what'll happen? Oughta just leave it alone. I knock anyway. Inside, I hear the high-pitched yipping of a dog, then somebody is at the door peering out. It's Tom. He opens the door, squints down at me. "Libby, what the hell you doing here?"

"Just came for a visit," I say.

"Well, come on in."

Walking with the help of a cane, he leads me down a hall and into the kitchen. A small frizzy-haired dog jumps at my feet. Tom takes a swipe at it with the cane, misses. "Scoot, you little son of a bitch. Or I'll brain you," he curses. The place smells like a widower's place: garbage that's been sitting too long, dust, feet. I'd always liked Tom. He was good to me and Leon. He'd never had kids himself, and whenever he'd stop over the house he'd always give us a nickel or a pack of gum, or something his wife Peg baked or sewed for us.

"Have a seat," he says. We sit at a small table that has a bowl containing a single brown banana. "Can I get you something?" Tom asks. "Tea? Or would you like something stronger? I might have some whiskey someplace. I'm not supposed to touch the stuff myself anymore."

"No, thanks," I reply. "I can't stay long."

"I'm so sorry about your brother. I remember when he was no bigger than my knee. The two of you staying with me and Peg."

"I remember."

"I hadn't seen Leon in ages. Course I don't get around much anymore. Not with this thing," Tom says, slapping his hip.

The little dog begins to frantically scratch a spot of linoleum. He pauses for a moment, sniffs the spot like there's something beneath the floor, then goes back to scratching.

"Cut it out, you stupid bastard," Tom yells at the dog, but it ignores him. Tom picks up the banana and heaves it at him. It misses, but it gets his attention and he lies down on the floor. "Does that all the damn time. Someday I'm gonna put him in a bag with some rocks and throw him in the lake," he says. "So what're you doing these days?"

"I keep out of trouble."

"You still running the store up there?"

"Yeah. Not getting rich but getting by."

We talk for a little while, about the store, his hip problems. He says they want to do a hip replacement, but he's not about to have them sticking plastic in him. "I prefer bone to plastic. Even old bones," he says, smiling. "Now I know you didn't come all the way down here to talk about my goddamn joints."

"No. I wanted to ask you something, Tom. You worked with Ambroise up at Sheshuncook."

"Sure did. We cut for two, three years up there. During the war and after."

From my pocketbook, I bring out the logging photo. I slide it across the table at him. "It's not very clear, I know. But I was wondering. Do you recognize anybody in there?"

"Well, let me get my specs," he says. He gets up and hobbles out of the room. When he returns he has a pair of glasses balanced on the end of his nose.

"These were Peg's," he says. He glances down at the photo, rubs the gray stubble on his chin. "Picture's lousy. Where'd you get this, anyway?"

"From Leon," I reply. "It was among his things."

He continues looking until his eyes seem to catch something and light up. "There's yours truly in the back row. Christ, I was just a kid there. And who the hell's that over here? Looks like Ross." He points to a man with a mustache and a square, good-looking face. "What was his first name? . . . Freddie. Yeah, Freddie Ross. And right here, that's gotta be Goose Mitchell." Tom points at a tall, thin man who has a small head covered by a woodcutter's toque and a long neck. "You can tell by the neck. That's why we called him Goose. Over here . . . let's see . . . that could be Willard Walker." He pauses for a moment then, tilting his head back. "That your old man's puss there?" he says, pointing to Ambroise.

"Yes," I say. "That's my father."

"Thought so. Goddamn Ambroise. Christ, this brings back memories. He ever tell you about the time me and him went down to Bangor one night, got good and tanked up, and wound up in jail?"

"No," I say.

"We didn't even know for what. I woke up with two shiners and didn't remember a thing." Tom looks across the table at me and shakes his head. "You do crazy shit when you're young. And you pay for it later." He slaps his hip, as if that's his payment.

"Can you name anybody else?" I ask, trying to get him back from memory lane. "Who's this young kid here next to Mitchell?"

Tom glances at the picture, then says, "Don't think I know him. We took on a lot of drifters during the war. They'd work for a few weeks, pick up a couple of paychecks, then take off. There were better-paying jobs to be had down in the shipyards at Bath. Bad business, some of those fellows."

"Why?"

"You never knew what you were getting. People on the run from the law. Couldn't count on them the way you could somebody local. Somebody with roots."

"How about this man next to Walker?"

"You got me. Now this fellow here," he says, pointing at the man holding the peavey. "I'm pretty sure I know him. A stumpy little fellow, bowlegged as a whore. Nap, I think."

As soon as he says it I recall my father mentioning the name, remember him around the camp. "Nap LeRoux?" I say.

"Yep. That's it. His full name was Napoleon Bonaparte LeRoux. This great big handle on this little sawed-off runt. He died just a few years back. I remember seeing it in the paper."

"How many others are still alive?" I ask.

Tom leans back in his chair, scratches his neck. "Let's see. Goose Mitchell was killed in a car accident over in Jackman some years back. Willard was living down in Skowhegan last I heard. And Freddie Ross was downstate, too. In Augusta, I believe. He'd gotten out of logging and bought a hardware store, as I recall. But that was years ago. Who knows where the hell they are now? Listen, I'm gonna make me some tea. Sure you wouldn't want some?"

"Okay, if it's no trouble."

Tom gets up and goes over to the sink. He picks the kettle up off the stove and begins to fill it with water.

With his back to me he says, "Those other boys in that picture. They were the Germans."

I can't tell if it's a question or a statement of fact.

"Yes," I offer.

"Some fellow stopped by the other day. A German. He was asking about the camp, too. This have anything to do with that?"

"What did he want?"

"If I could remember anything about it. The camp and all."

"What did you tell him?"

The dog is beginning to scratch the floor again, but Tom doesn't seem to notice now. He keeps his back to me so I can't see his face. The water has already filled up the kettle and I can hear it overflowing, running down the drain.

"I didn't have much to do with the Germans," Tom says. "Mostly I was driving the Cletrac, laying out tote roads for your old man's crew. Once in a while they'd give me one to help swamp a road. Or do some work on the tractor. Those boys were real handy with engines. But other than that I didn't have much to do with them."

"Do you remember any of them? At all?"

Tom finally shuts the water off. He puts the kettle on the stove and turns on one of the burners. It takes several seconds before the pilot light catches, and when it does there's a loud *wrrrf* sound. "There was one kid. This young farmboy. Wasn't even a kraut. He was Czech."

"A young blond kid?" I ask. "A teamster?"

"Yep, that's the one. Name was Ernst. Don't remember his last name. He knew his way around horses, that boy did. Lunchtime he'd unharness the teams and brush 'em off. Wouldn't eat until they were fed. He wrote me a couple of letters after the war. Said how bad things were over there and how good he'd had it at the camp. Asked if I remembered the time I'd had to shoot a horse. You see, one of his team had broken a leg and I had to kill the poor bastard. That kid took it bad, like it was his pet or something."

"Any others?"

"No," he replies. "It was a long time ago. All in all, they were pretty decent fellows mostly. You had your bad apples, of course, but most were all right. Good workers. I got along all right with them. Some folks around here didn't. Thought we should hate 'em just because they were German. I couldn't understand that way of thinking. They were just kids most of them. It wasn't their fault." Tom sets out two cups, places tea bags in them. "How come you're so interested in the camp?"

"Just curious, I guess."

"Didn't you and Leon work up there for a little while?"

"Yeah. Not long. I worked as a cookee."

"What do *you* remember?"

"Not much."

"That's what I told that German fellow. Not much *to* remember. I did my job and kept my nose out of the rest of it."

"The rest of it, Tom?"

"You know, the politics. Us and them. Christ, the way I saw it we were all just trying to earn our bread. Get through as best we could."

"And some didn't see it like that?"

"No, they didn't. But I'm just speaking for myself, mind you."

When the water is boiling Tom fills the cups and brings them over to the table. He sits down and starts talking about Ambroise, when the two of them were young, working in logging camps together, going hunting. He talks about my mother, too. Tom's one of the few people around who still remembers her.

"What was she like?" I ask. I guess my hatred of her has slowly changed more to curiosity. Another sign I'm getting old—hatred is for the young who have the energy for it. A couple of weeks ago I'd even dreamt of her. In the dream I was a little girl again and she was braiding my hair. I'd never had long hair—not long enough to braid, anyway—but in the dream I did. It felt good. I remember her smelling of Lux soap and baby powder, and the feel of her hands against my scalp.

"Denise was a looker, all right," Tom says, sipping his tea. "She liked to have her fun, too. Everybody wondered how Ambroise hooked up with her."

"Why'd she run off?"

"I don't know. She was the sort of woman I guess felt trapped here. Needed more than a place like this could offer."

"She left two kids behind."

Tom shrugs. "I'm not saying it was right. I'm just telling you why, Libby. Ambroise was never the same man after she left."

"I guess not."

"That's when he started hitting the bottle."

"He did pretty good before that," I say.

"Worse after. She broke his heart."

"You mean somebody wasn't there to do his wash and make his meals."

"No, I mean it. I think he kept waiting for her to come back. Tell me, how come you never got married?"

"I don't know. Nobody ever asked," I say, laughing. "Besides, I guess I was more like her than I thought. Liked having my good times too much to ever settle down with just one man."

"Pretty girl like you should've got married."

"You're still a bullshit artist, Tom," I say. Out of habit I lift my hand protectively to my mouth.

"You were. I mean it. That little scar didn't mean nothing."

"Seemed to then."

"I remember the young fellows at work talking about you. I used to tell 'em, 'You watch yourself, Ambroise'll break your god-damn neck.' You know Ambroise. He had a temper."

"He had that, all right."

"You should've had a family of your own. Shouldn't've had to baby-sit those two all them years."

"I'm not complaining," I tell him. I finish my tea. "I have to get going, Tom."

At the door he says, "Don't be a stranger now."

"I won't," I reply. I pause for a moment. "One other thing, Tom. That German that drowned . . ."

"Yeah," he says.

"The night he escaped. I remember some company men going out with the soldiers, looking for him. Was my father one of them?"

Tom's gray eyes don't meet mine. He looks past me, out to the road, squinting against the snow.

"I don't remember," he says.

"You don't remember that night? Or if my father was with them?"

"I don't remember—*period*."

I get the sense he doesn't want to talk about it. So I thank him and head down the steps. I'm halfway to the truck when Tom calls to me.

"Libby," he says.

I stop and turn around. He looks down at me for a moment, then says, "Best to let all that alone, Lib."

"All what, Tom?"

But he shakes his head and adds only, "Take care of yourself."

It's not true what I'd told Tom. I'd had my chances not to be an old maid, to prove my mother wrong. A few years after the war I was working first shift in a shoe factory down in Dexter. I was seventeen. Jughead Buzzell, a shift supervisor, spent a lot of time around my machine, talking, flirting. He would overlook a bad stitch, even though he was pretty hard on the other girls. He was twenty-four, just out of the service. He had reddish brown, Indian hands, stained from working with the leather dyes, and a head too large for a man only five six. That's why some of the girls called him Jughead, but behind his back. His real name was Clayton. He used to drive a Packard. After work sometimes he'd take me to the Commodore over in Bangor. For a small man he sure knew how to dance; he was light on his feet. In the dark corner of the dance hall he'd spike my Coca-Cola from a flask of rum, even though I was still too young to drink, and slide his hand along the inside of my leg.

He was the first boy I let go all the way. We made love on the scratchy backseat of his Packard. He would stick his tongue in my ear and say I was beautiful, tell me other things that smelled of rum. Afterwards he'd bury his face in my neck like he was going to cry. He wanted to marry me in the worst way so we could have our own bed instead of a backseat. He used to pick me up just past Abbey's store. He never came around the house, I guess because he was afraid of Ambroise, and probably not without cause. When he asked me to marry him, I told him I couldn't, not yet anyway. Leon was still home. He needed me. I couldn't imagine how he'd get along with just Ambroise to look after him. I told him to wait. Two, three years maybe. Then Leon would be big enough to take care of himself. But Jughead couldn't wait. He married another girl from the factory and had about a dozen homely kids with big heads. Last I heard he was running a video store in Bangor.

Then there was Frank Cobb. By then I was waitressing in town, at the Banquet Room. The place that used to be out near the airfield. I wasn't a spring chicken anymore, in my thirties already with hard lines setting in around my mouth and a feeling every time I looked in the mirror that my mother was right—I would end up an old maid. I'd had my share of men since

Jughead, but there'd been nothing serious. Nothing you could make a life out of. I was still living at home even though Leon had long since left for the service. Ambroise had been hitting the bottle steady and hard for years and had lost his job at the paper company. He was doing mostly jobber work now, when he could get it. He'd put together a crew and contract out to whoever would hire him. Sometimes he'd even sign on as a swamper, bulldozing roads for somebody else's crew—quite a comedown after being foreman all those years. He'd make just enough to get by. Log for a few months, get paid, then go on a binge till the money ran out. I was the only one bringing in steady money.

Frank Cobb had red hair and freckles, and lashes so light it almost looked like he didn't have any. Not handsome but dependable. Had a nice smile that made you want to trust him. He ran a charter plane service, flying sportsmen into these remote lakes up north. He used to take me up in his small pontoon plane. I'd never been in a plane before. He used to do all these crazy things, like dives and rollovers, once even a loop. I was afraid at first, thought we'd crash into the lake. But he was pretty good and after a while I got used to it, even liked being up in his plane. Below, everything looked so different. I'd try to pick out things I had spent my whole life next to—Daggett Cove, Abbey's store, the little cemetery down there—but up in his plane everything looked so different, so unfamiliar. Frank would look out of the cockpit window and say, "Lib, down there everything seems so goddamn important because it's all you can see." He'd grown up in Maine but he'd traveled around a lot, wasn't like so many of the men I'd known. He talked about heading off someplace different, someplace where it wasn't so cold and everybody didn't think the world stopped at the end of his nose. He talked of going out to Arizona. He'd been stationed there back during the war. He said it was warm and dry there, and you could see for miles. The sun, he explained to me, just didn't set—it melted into the mountains each night, as if it were part of the earth, not something millions of miles away.

Frank finally said he was going out west, and did I want to come along. He'd talked about it a lot before, though, and I thought it was just that, talk. But this time he meant it. He was really leaving, he said. Going to fly his plane out there. I told him I'd have to think about it. It was a big step. I didn't know if I could leave. What was out west anyway? How was it any different from here? And besides, there was Ambroise. Who would do his cooking and cleaning? Who would see to it that he didn't drown in his own booze-vomit? I tried to convince myself I didn't owe Ambroise a thing, that I'd wasted enough of my life on him already. But every argument I came up with didn't sound convincing. Then again, maybe it had nothing to do with Ambroise. Maybe I was just too afraid of leaving what I knew and Ambroise was just an excuse. I don't know.

I kept hoping Frank was just talking and I wouldn't have to choose. But I ended up waiting too long—*again*. One day Frank Cobb just flew off in his plane and I never saw him anymore. He wrote me once or twice, asking me to come out, but I never wrote back. I didn't see the point. I knew I'd never go. I pictured him making love with another woman as they watched the sun melting into the mountains. But I kept his picture in my wallet, just in case he returned. The funny thing was it was only a few months after that that Ambroise fell under the tracks of that Caterpillar tractor. But then it was too late to go. I took it as a sign that I wasn't meant to leave this place.

After Ambroise died I went through his things. I found the divorce papers, from a lawyer in Buffalo, New York. Some old pictures. One of my mother, on the back of which it said, "All my love, Dee." The Luger was there too, as well as a clip full of squat 9mm shells. I found the deed to some land way up near Madawaska, left to him when his sister Eunice died, and an IOU for two hundred dollars from a man named Maxim LeBoeuf. There was also a small insurance policy, which I thought funny because Ambroise was not the sort of man to worry about such things. I ended up selling the house to a young couple from downstate who were looking for a vacation home. I didn't have any attachment to that place. I gave Leon half of everything, which he squandered on booze and high times, and a new Lincoln he ended up wrapping around a telephone pole. With my half I bought the McDonough store over on the east side of the lake. I was tired of waitressing and liked the idea of being my own boss. But as soon as I bought it I knew I would never go anyplace else. I knew that whatever would happen to me would happen here, would seek me out, or it wouldn't happen at all.

13

AFTER I LEAVE Tom's house, I stop at Saint Adelbert's, the new Catholic church near the rest home. I haven't been there in a long while. The last time was two Christmases ago, the Feast of the Immaculate Conception. The inside is bright and airy, paneled in flesh-tone knotty pine. The old church, St. Cecelia's, burned down a few years back. The new church has no dark corners, no shadows, no mystery. You leave your sins at the door when you come here. I've never liked St. Adelbert's, nor for that matter the new priest, Father Rodino, who replaced Father Julian. Father Rodino is young and overweight and smiles like a politician, and worries more about the rec basketball league than he does about your soul. I preferred old Father Julian, a gaunt man with sharp eyes that drilled deep into your soul looking for foulness, for secret sins. In the confessional when you thought you'd finished, when you'd dug as deep as you could go, he would always say, "And what else, my child?" And of course there *was* always something else, something deeper, something you'd hidden even from yourself.

I sit in a pew in back. The church is empty except for a boy up at the altar. Red-haired, with slow, precise movements, he's setting up for tomorrow's mass. He knows I'm watching him, and his careful attention to detail is for my benefit. The late-afternoon light cuts at an angle through the stained-glass stations of the cross, enters the church softly in broken, dust-filled bars. I take out my rosary beads. I pray for Leon, for his soul. "*Glory be to the Father and to the Son and to the Holy Ghost; As it was in the beginning, is now, and ever shall be: world without end. Amen.*" I haven't prayed in so long the words sound strange in my mouth.

From my pocketbook I take the photo out. I unfold it and angle it toward the fading light. I get out a pencil and put light Xs—so light, in fact, only I can make them out—above the faces of Goose Mitchell, Nap LeRoux, Ambroise, Leon. Dead men. Above Tom's face I start to put an X, though he isn't dead, but then decide to change it to a question mark. That leaves five in the back row, five who might still be alive, three of whose names I don't know. I stare at the three faces for a long time. I think if I stare long enough, I'll suddenly recall one of them. A man who'd come over to the house with Ambroise. An old drinking crony. Maybe someone I can remember from that summer I'd worked up there. But no matter how hard I stare they remain strangers to me, just faces looking out from the past.

Then I look at the Germans. After starting to work with my father that summer, I'd taken a book out of the library. It was on speaking German. I was careful about anyone seeing me with it, afraid that someone might wonder why I was trying to learn *their* language. I never got very far but I did pick up a few words, some phrases. Things I would overhear the guards say to them, or the Germans whisper to each other: *Ich verstehe, Es ist jetzt sehr kalt, Wie sagt man auf deutsch?, Und was haben Sie dann vor nach dem Krieg?* Their words always sounded like secrets to me. I can remember once a prisoner in the woods say to another, "*Sie hat einen schönen Arsch,*" and smile at me. They'd said it right in front of me, assured I wouldn't understand. Overhearing them talk in German and knowing what it meant sometimes, I felt it was a little like having your ear pressed to someone's door.

I look at the German with the Afrika Korps hat. *Maybe*, I think. *Maybe it's him*. The eyes are similar, and the mouth could be his. But the picture's so faded, it's hard to say. Memories swirl around me, stirred up as if by a sudden gust of wind. I tell myself, the way Father Julian would, "What else, Libby? What else do you remember?"

I remember it was cool out, the ground dew-covered that first day I went to work with my father. The sky was clear and later in the morning when the sun got above the trees it would be hot. It was summer and I'd forgotten to bring a jacket. Goose bumps rose on my arms and I shivered as we waited in Ambroise's truck just outside the camp gates. Nearby in a small sentry box, a guard sat reading a paper. Every once in a while he'd look up, stare at us, then go back to reading. Just on the other side of the barbed wire, prisoners, sleepy eyed, wearing light khaki uniforms, some in shorts, were loaded into the back of a large canvas-covered Great American Paper truck. They sat on two wooden-plank benches. An army guard with a clipboard in his hand took a head count as they boarded. That would be the routine. They took a head count twice a day, on leaving and on returning to the camp. We were close enough to see that some of the men had scars on their faces. One wore a black eye patch. The only eye patches I'd ever seen before were in the movies, on Errol Flynn.

When the truck was full, the guard with the clipboard climbed up in front with the driver and we pulled out through the gate and they followed us. Bringing up the rear was a jeep with two more guards who had guns slung over their shoulders. We drove up the road from the camp, past Abbey's store. Old man Abbey and some of the locals stood out in front watching us as we went by. When we reached the main logging road we turned west toward Pittston Farm, about ten miles away.

Ambroise was smoking a cigarette and rubbing his nose. Leon sat in the middle and kept looking nervously back at the truck.

"You keep clear of those krauts," Ambroise warned us. "Don't talk to 'em."

"What if they talk to us?" Leon asked.

"Just mind your own business."

After a while we pulled onto a smaller tote road and headed into the woods another couple of miles. This is where Ambroise's crew was cutting. A thick stand of spruce and fir, broken only occasionally by second-growth hardwoods and stretches of forest-fire burn, went on as far as you could see. Ambroise said they'd be cutting here for a long time. Maybe until the war ended.

We stopped at a cleared yarding area, where two company men were sitting on the tailgate of a pickup, drinking coffee from tin cups. The transport truck had fallen far behind us. Twitch roads had been swamped out up into the woods in several directions from the yarding area, and a man on a Cletrac dozer was at work clearing another. One team of horses with their driver was already twitching logs from the woods into the yard. Ambroise pulled up alongside the other truck and got out. He walked over and started talking with the two men, while Leon and I waited in the truck. I watched a hawk circling lazily overhead, and somewhere in the woods a blue jay was screeching noisily.

After a while the company truck came whining up the tote road. When we saw it, Leon and I got out of the truck and joined Ambroise and the two other men.

"Here they are," Ambroise said. "Hitler's whores."

The truck stopped and two guards got out, one with the clipboard and the driver. The other guards following in the jeep came up and flanked them, their tommy guns slung over their shoulders. They had the prisoners get off the truck and form two lines, one behind the other. There were about twenty-five Germans. They were quiet, squinting at the woods and the sky. All of them had a P and a W written in large white letters on each shirtsleeve.

I nudged Leon and pointed at the fat, red-faced German who stood in the back row. Up close his face was the color of potted ham.

"Okay, listen up, gentlemen," said the guard with the clipboard. "C'mere, Fritz." One of the prisoners stepped out of line and stood beside the guard. As soon as the guard began to speak, this prisoner quickly translated what he said into German.

"I'm Sergeant Moore," the guard said. Then in clumsy German, he added, "*Ich bin Amerikaner.* I'll be in charge of security here. I want to make things very clear to you, so there's no mistake." He paused to let the interpreter translate into German before continuing. "If you work hard you'll be treated fairly. I don't permit any slackers. We have a job to do and we're gonna do it. If you want to eat you'll work. Another thing—if you try to escape you'll be shot." As he said this he took out the big automatic pistol from the holster on his hip, aimed it at the sky, and fired. The noise shattered the early-morning quiet. Several of the Germans cried out, startled. I felt myself jerk.

"*Verstehen?*" the guard said, pleased with the reaction he'd gotten. "Once you're at the job site, however, you'll take your orders from this gentleman here," he said, pointing at my father. "Mr. Pelletier." The POWs looked over at Ambroise, and then at Leon and me. Leon moved closer to me.

After that the guards had the men pick up saws and axes from the back of our truck. Then they marched the prisoners a short ways into the woods.

My father had the guards gather the men around a big spruce tree where he gave them a stump speech about cutting. It was the kind of speech he would give to inexperienced men coming to work for the first time. "I'm gonna show you how to fell a tree, boys," Ambroise said, the interpreter turning my father's words quickly into German. "Pay attention." With a double-bit ax he made an undercut on one side of the tree. "Undercut," he said, and the interpreter translated. He then took a crosscut saw from one of the prisoners and said, "Now does anybody know how to use this?"

"*Ja. Die Schrotsäge,*" a young boy called from among the group of Germans. He pointed at the saw my father held. "*Die Schrotsäge.*"

"C'mere," my father said to the young German, a stocky boy who walked heavily on the heels of his feet. "You got some experience cutting logs?"

The interpreter translated the question and then the man's response. "His name is Oswald. He says he worked on his father's farm cutting timber."

"That's good. I'll count on you to help the rest of these stupid bastards. You'll be my right-hand man, *ja*, Oswald?"

"*Ja, ja*," the man said, smiling broadly.

Ambroise and Oswald began sawing through the big spruce, which must have been sixty feet tall. All the while the interpreter went on explaining in German. When the backcut almost met the undercut, Ambroise said, "Okay. Stand back now. Sometimes a tree'll jump its cut. So you have to be careful if you don't want to get hurt." The tree gave out that almost human groan trees do right as they begin to fall, then the wood buckled and snapped, and the tree started to go down. "*Timmmber!*" Ambroise yelled. When it slammed into the ground, it kicked up a spray of dust and needles. In the sweet-scented quiet that followed, the men glanced at each other, impressed.

"Make sure you always yell *timber* when a tree is about to fall," Ambroise warned. "So people can get the hell out of the way. Now ask 'em if they got any questions."

"*Übrige Fragen?*" asked the interpreter. No one said anything at first. One man finally raised his hand meekly, said something in German.

The interpreter, smiling awkwardly, said. "He says he has to relieve himself."

"Tell him to pick out a tree," Ambroise said. "Any tree he wants."

The German said something, and the other Germans started snickering.

"He is frightened of . . . of bears," said the interpreter.

The company men and the guards joined in the laughter. "Jesus H. Christ," Ambroise cursed, shaking his head. But then he, too, broke into a smile. "Bears! Well, you tell him, if he sees a bear to do what we do around here."

"What is that?" the interpreter asked.

"You piss right on 'em. That scares the hell out of a bear."

The interpreter put his hand to his mouth, smiled, then translated into German. The prisoners laughed again. Then the interpreter tilted his head a little and glanced in our direction. He might have been looking at me. At least I think he was. I didn't know his name. I would never know his name. He was just the interpreter. A tall, slender boy, a little older than some of the others, nearly a man already, with dark, tightly curled hair and fleshy eyes. Not quite handsome but sophisticated looking, like those men you might see in the *Saturday Evening Post* for an ad for hair tonic. He had a knowing expression, especially something about the lips, a faint half-smile that made you think he was amused at something that only he thought was funny. That was Kallick's brother, though I would never know him as anything other than the interpreter.

I would see the inside of the camp for the first time later that morning. Ambroise kept Leon out in the woods with him as a bull cook, a general camp helper, but he had me working with Pop Flynn. I knew Pop a little. He used to drop my father off from work sometimes. He was only a little older than Ambroise, yet he'd always seemed much older, wrinkled and slump shouldered. That's why they called him Pop. He had only one arm, had lost the other in a logging accident. He couldn't log anymore so the company let him drive the truck—what used to be called a wangan in the old logging camps. A thing that carried tools and supplies and food out to the men in the woods. I was to help him bring the prisoners their meals, do odd jobs, bring back fresh tools.

"Old man's got you kids working, huh?" Pop said as we drove back to the camp to get the noon meal.

I nodded, watching Pop steer the truck with the stump of his left arm while he shifted with the other. He would nearly slide off the dirt tote road before grabbing the wheel just in time. Once we were nearly flattened by a rig coming down another tote road with a full load of logs. Pop swerved at the last moment and then cried, "Watch where you're going, y' horse's ass."

When we arrived back at camp again, the sentry opened the gate for us and we drove on through. The grounds were flat, muddy in spots, almost barren of trees except for over toward what had once been the blacksmith shop for the old supply farm. A bulldozer had leveled everything except for the original farm buildings. It smelled of sewage. Several prisoners were digging over near one of the outbuildings, a trench of some kind. Others were whitewashing the mess hall and another building. One group was just lounging in the shade of some swamp maples near a newer structure that I would later learn was the infirmary.

"See them," Pop said, pointing at the ones in the shade. "We can't make 'em work."

"Why not?" I asked.

"Them's officers. Genever Convention says we can't make the bastards work. Me and you have to but they get to sit on their kraut asses all day."

We drove over to the building that housed the mess hall. As we started to get out, Pop said, "Now you let me do the talking. These krauts ain't so bad once you show 'em who's boss."

I followed Pop into the kitchen, which was at the back of the mess hall. A thick-bellied man in a sleeveless T-shirt was stirring something in a big kettle. The kettle sat on a black wood cookstove. When the heavy man turned around, I saw that he was wearing a dirty apron. His face was sweaty and he had big pouches under his eyes. But he looked friendly.

"*Guten Tag, Herr Flynn*," the cook said, coming over to greet us. He acted as if he and Pop were old friends, though they could only have known each other for a few days at most.

"How's it going, Jurgen?" He pronounced the J.

"*Mir ist sehr warm*," the cook said, wiping his brow with his hand and throwing imaginary sweat on the floor.

"*Ja, ja*. Hot as a bitch in here," Pop replied. "Cool outside, though." Both men laughed at that, though I don't think the

German understood much English. "Libby, this fat-ass bastard's Jurgen. The cook," Pop said without lowering his voice. The cook continued to smile at Pop, nodding his head. "Me and him's pals. Right, Jurgen?"

"*Ja*, pals," said the fat cook. Then he pointed at me and said, "*Die Fräulein?*"

"Oh, I got me an assistant." Then to me he said, "Jurgen here knows how to take care of his pals. Ain't that right, Jurgen?" The cook kept smiling, saying "*Ja, ja.*" Then he held up one finger and hurried over to the stove. He opened the oven door and took something out. When he came back, he was holding something wrapped in newspaper comics.

"*Pfannkuchen*," said the cook, putting it to his nose. He had Pop smell it, too. "*Es riecht gut.*" It smelled sweet and warm, like pancakes. The paper was grease stained.

"*Danke*," Pop said, stuffing the bundle into his shirt. He winked at me.

"*Das Vergnügen ist ganz meinerseits*," said the cook, patting himself on the chest. "Mein pleasure."

"We'd better get a move on, Libby. Those boys'll be hungry."

Pop went out to the truck and brought back an ax handle. We put it through the kettle's handle and we each took an end. It was heavy. We brought it out and set in on the floor in the truck. Then we carried out a box of dark-bread corned beef sandwiches, a basket of apples, and another kettle filled with strong, dark tea. On another trip to the kitchen we brought out the utensils, metal plates and cups, and wooden spoons. The prisoners, I was to learn, received no knives and forks when they ate in the woods. The army feared it would be too easy for them to be stolen and made into weapons. Then Pop told me to go out and wait in the truck while he went over to talk privately to Jurgen.

When Pop returned he took the bundle Jurgen had given him out of his shirt and put it on the seat. "I give him some things to read. Old newspapers and magazines. Some of these boys ain't heard any news about home in months. Now he takes care of me. Course, you don't have to go saying anything to your old man now, you know. Wanna bite?" he said.

I shook my head.

"Suit yourself," he said, tearing into the meat pancake.

After that we headed over to the maintenance shop, on the south end of the compound. One paper-company man worked here along with a couple of German assistants. They tuned up the power saws and resharpened crosscuts and buck saws, and rehung axes whose handles had been broken. The first few months the prisoners broke a lot of ax handles and drove saw blades over rocks to dull them. Ambroise said it was to get out of work. But they learned that they wouldn't meet their half-cord-per-day quota and would have to stay longer in the woods or work on Sundays. Slowly they began to take care of their tools.

We loaded the truck with equipment and headed back out to the work site. Pop showed me how to set up for lunch. We made a small fire and hung the kettles of soup and tea on spruce-bough supports over it. We laid a plank across two sawhorses for a table and set the rest of the food and utensils on it. It wasn't fancy, but to hungry men it was enough. At noon Ambroise whistled for the men to stop for lunch. They came over, and the guard had them form a single line. The men came through it, picking up their metal plates and cups and grabbing a sandwich and an apple. I was in charge of dishing out the soup. Pop told me to skim it off the top, to go easy on the vegetables and chunks of meat on the bottom.

As the men came through I kept my eyes down, mostly on their bowls, afraid to spill anything. I didn't look up much. I noticed things like if they had big feet or if they were bowlegged. Or their hands. I noticed their hands a lot. Some of them had large hands with tattoos of palm trees or swastikas on the back. Some were missing fingers. Most were tanned from being in the desert in Africa. Some of the men wore wedding rings or fancy ones I'd assumed had something to do with the German army. Most of them were very polite. They would say, "*Danke, Fräulein*," or "*Guten Tag, Fräulein*," before passing on. But even then I didn't look up. Their voices were soft and nervous, as if ready to break into laughter almost, like those of high school boys out on a first date. And I noticed that machine-shop smell they carried with them, a heavy smell like machine grease.

Leon and I ate off by ourselves a little ways, just on the edge of where the company men sat. We could hear them—Ambroise, Pop, Tom Weston, and the others—talking about the day's work. Where they'd be cutting next week, would they make their cord quotas. It was funny, but they hardly spoke of the war, of all the things that had been happening for the past several weeks following D day. It was as if the war didn't exist for them any more than it did for us kids or for the Germans. We had our own, quiet, solitary life here. The Germans sat in a larger group in the middle of the chain area—the section of woods to be cut in a week. One guard stood at each of the four corners around them, their guns at the ready. Later, as they realized no one was going to try to escape, the guards got to be pretty relaxed. They would set their rifles down and sometimes doze off in the woods. But for now at least they were alert and kept the Germans huddled tightly together.

I watched the prisoners. Except for one or two who were older, maybe in their late twenties, the rest looked even younger than I'd thought that first day down at the lake. In German they talked nervously, in whispers, their eyes lighting up as they laughed secretively, the way boys in the halls at school laughed. Some, their shirts off, had bare backs that were sweaty and white in the noon sun, or splotchy from the blackfly bites or where branches had scraped them. Others unlaced their boots and picked at their feet. One man had a harmonica and began to play something, while another, not knowing all the words, partly sang, partly hummed along. The music seemed to make the woods very small suddenly, like we were all sitting in someone's parlor, not out in the woods.

Soon Ambroise stood up and whistled shrilly. "*Achtung*, boys.

We got wood to cut. Leon, you go back with Libby. Have Pop drop you home. I might be late."

After we cleaned up and put out the fire, we headed back to the camp. On the way Pop pulled over to the side of the road and poured a good helping of what was left of the soup into a thermos he kept under the seat.

"Why the hell should those boys eat like kings?" he said. "You're welcome to some, too."

I did take some, and Leon and I ate it for supper that night. Ambroise didn't come home until late, and when he did he was in no shape for eating. The German soup was very good. It had carrots and onions and little pieces of white sausage in it. We hadn't had anything like that to eat in ages.

For the next several weeks the POWs slowly got the hang of logging. When they were yarding wood, dragging the logs by horse to a central area, Ambroise broke them into cutters, teamsters, sawyers, and cant-dog men. Each learned one skill so they could get good at it. The cutters felled the trees, while the teamsters, men with a farm background, often the Czechs, used horses to twitch the logs back to the yarding area. There the sawyers cut the logs into four-foot lengths, and the cant-dog men then loaded the wood into piles for the winter hauling-off season. And a couple of prisoners who'd worked as mechanics in the army kept the tractors and power saws in running order. I learned what a prisoner meant when he called out *der Wendehaken* or *der Benzinkanister* or *die Motorsäge*, and I had to go back to the truck to get it.

Yet even though they were picking up logging, by the end of July each man was barely making his half-cord-per-day quota and there was talk over at the mills of raising it to three-quarters. The mills needed more pulp for paper, gobbling up the forests to print more stories about the war, I guess. Part of the problem was that the POWs had to work under the tight security the army had insisted on at first. Like the townspeople, they were afraid of escapes. The prisoners weren't allowed to move freely to cut trees, but had to stay inside the chained cutting area with guards stationed at the four corners. They couldn't go back and forth to the yard, but had to have one of the guards escorting them, and they couldn't stump-cut the wood in pairs, the way our own cord cutters worked. This slowed things down. But it was also that many of the Germans just didn't take to logging naturally. A lot of them were city boys, and handling an ax wasn't something they picked up easily. With others, though, you got the feeling they just didn't want to learn. It was as if they thought they shouldn't be helping us, that we were still the enemy.

Ambroise tried everything he could to get them to work faster. He gave them stump speeches about how to cut and haul, how to swamp out areas for the horses. He made sure the Germans had plenty of fresh saws. He sent Pop and me back to the maintenance shop two or three times some days, and had one of the German mechanics at the site to repair the power saws. He even let them take morning and afternoon breaks, something he didn't do with his own men. Sometimes on really sweltering days he would have us bring back some lemonade or tea to drink. If a prisoner got hurt we would take him back to the infirmary with us, and when we returned we'd have his replacement. And if the prisoners made their quota before five in the evening, Ambroise had the company truck take them back to camp, and they had the rest of the day off.

At first he had to give instructions to the interpreter who translated for the senior prisoners who in turn passed the orders along to their subordinates—that was the way the army said he was to do it. But many of the senior prisoners knew nothing about forestry, and so it was very slow and cumbersome. Soon Ambroise took to using those prisoners who had experience logging, no matter what their rank, which the Germans didn't seem to appreciate. And when all else failed he resorted to yelling and cursing at the prisoners, hoping that would get them to work harder and faster.

"No, not like that, you stupid son of a bitch," he'd yell when one of the Germans did something wrong, say, made the undercut too high or ruined a new saw blade by cutting the backcut too deeply. The interpreter would start to translate my father's curses but give up quickly, realizing that it was probably best left in English. "Like this, Fritz. See?" he'd explain, pulling the saw out of the hands of some German and demonstrating how to do it right. *"Verstehen?"*

On the ride home at night Ambroise would say to us, "I swear to Christ they're doing it on purpose. Nobody can be *that* stupid."

Yet he respected, even liked, some of the prisoners. The teamsters, for instance, mostly boys who'd grown up on farms and knew their way around horses. One was the Czech boy Tom Weston mentioned, who would care for the horses before he himself ate. Another was the fellow named Oswald. I don't know if that was his first or last name. They just called him Oswald. A short, powerfully built boy—nineteen or twenty—who walked like a bear on its hind feet. Ambroise made him a sort of assistant foreman, putting him even over some of the senior prisoners. In the morning my father would tell him, through the interpreter, what sections he wanted cut and Oswald would direct the other prisoners. Like Ambroise, he would yell and curse, only in German, at his own countrymen. He'd wave his long-billed Afrika Korps cap and clap his hands. *"Nein, nein,"* he'd cry. The other Germans, you could see, resented him, didn't like him working so hard for the Americans. They didn't sit with him at lunch and grumbled when he ordered them around.

I worked with Pop Flynn all that summer. Each day we'd have to bring the men ten or twelve rehung axes as well as half a dozen new saws, and the occasional replacement for an injured man. Over at the kitchen we picked up the day's noon meal. Jurgen the cook or sometimes his young helper would have something for Pop wrapped in old newspaper, and Pop would give him something in exchange. A newspaper maybe or sometimes something the prisoners couldn't get in the camp canteen, a girlie magazine or maybe a bottle of still-whiskey. Or American cologne. For some reason the prisoners liked that.

Later, as Jurgen got to know me, sometimes he'd slip me something, too. He'd wink and say, "*Für die Fräulein. Ja. Regensburger. Gut, gut.*" Then he'd place a finger dusted with flour to his lips and smile, showing long yellow teeth. Our little secret. He might give me a pastry or some meat pie, maybe some sausages stuffed in the center of a heavy loaf of pumpernickel bread. Sometimes he'd ask me to sample a piece of beef he'd been boiling, something, given the war rationing, we never had at home. The food he gave me was always delicious, better than anything we ever had, better even I'd say than what was on the tables of most people in town, even the well-to-do. At first I would devour the food in the truck on the way back to the woods, the way Pop did. But then, feeling guilty that Leon and Ambroise would be eating eggs for supper, I started to bring some of the things home.

"Where'd you get this?" Leon asked one night when I set a plate of pale, thick sausages on the table.

"From the German cook," I replied.

Leon jabbed the sausage on his plate with a fork. "How do you know it's not poisoned?"

"It's not."

"How come he gave you this stuff?" Ambroise asked.

"He's just being friendly."

"Didn't I tell you not to get friendly with those krauts?"

I said, "He had a little extra so he asked if I wanted some. If you want I'll tell him no."

"I'm just saying to watch your step is all," Ambroise warned. "They're still Nazis. And besides, most of them boys ain't laid eyes on a girl in a long time. No telling what those Jerries might have on their minds."

"I'm gonna be fifteen," I said. "I can take care of myself."

Ambroise thought for a moment. "She ever get around to telling you about . . . you know . . . men and women?" She, of course, was my mother. And no, she hadn't explained how it was, except to say that a little perfume behind your knees never hurt. And lipstick would do wonders for someone with my handicap. But I knew already about men and women, though at fourteen I was still a virgin. The only advice my father had ever given me about boys was once when he was drunk and I was helping him into bed. He told me that when they come sniffing around to keep a penny held tightly between my knees.

And I remember at the end of that summer, right before I went back to school, one of those German boys was killed. You could blame it on the weather, I guess. It had gotten cooler suddenly, bringing heavy, fall-like rains that turned the tote roads into muddy cow paths. Trucks sank into mud up to their axles, and horses lost their footing twitching their loads back to the yards. Ax blades careened dangerously off wet branches, and saw blades got stuck in swollen wood. It was an awful time to be logging.

This day Pop and I had just arrived at the cutting site with lunch. We were pretty far in the woods now, out past Sheshuncook Lake, and the driving was tough. It took an hour and a half to get there, in good weather. The roads now were rutted and slick from the rains. Even with four-wheel drive it was difficult getting in. We were setting up for lunch in a yarding area not far from where they were cutting that day. Suddenly, the fellow called Nap came running through the woods at us. He grabbed one of the planks we were using for a table, spilling the kettle of soup on the ground.

"What the fuck?" Pop cried.

"Need this," Nap said, turning and running back into the woods with the plank under his arm.

Pop and I followed him. We ran up a small hill and then across an open, swampy area that had been clear-cut. I remember slipping, banging my knee against a stump, ripping my pants, but not feeling the pain until later. At the far side of the clearing a group of prisoners, company men, and guards were standing around. When I got close enough I could see that a man was in the middle of the group, on the muddy ground. A big spruce log was lying across him, pinning him. He was twisted like a corkscrew, with his legs face down but his torso half turned around so he was almost looking up at the people above him. It looked as if he had started to turn when the tree struck him and drove him into the soft earth. One arm was pinned beneath the tree, but the other was free and clawing frantically at the bark. His fingernails were raking it. His mouth was open, trying to form words, but the only thing that came out was a gurgling sound and this a bloody froth. Blood eased out his ears, too. He looked up at us, his eyes flitting from one face to another, pleading. It took me a moment to realize that it was the prisoner called Oswald.

Ambroise and another company man used the big two-man power saw to cut him out. When they'd cut through the section that was on top of him, they threaded ropes beneath it and about a dozen men grabbed the ropes and lifted the log straight up, enough so they could pull the man out.

His free arm, the one that had been grabbing at the tree so frantically, now lay limp at his side. His eyes, too, had slowed. In fact, they didn't even search any of the faces over him. They seemed to look past us, at the sky overhead, with this grim concentration. I looked up too, to see what was of such interest to him. It was drizzling, and the sky had thin ribbons of lower-hanging clouds. They were suspended at treetop level. Maybe he was looking at them. I had never seen anyone die before, but I knew that this man lying in front of me was slowly trying to die. And dying suddenly seemed as if it was something very hard to do, as if you had to concentrate to get it done.

One of the Germans, a former medic, had him lifted onto the plank Nap had taken from us. The froth around his mouth now had turned to thin trickles of blood that slid down each cheek and dropped onto the muddy ground. The medic asked for some belts, and several prisoners took theirs off and handed them to him. With the belts the German strapped the man to the plank and then several of the prisoners lifted him up and carried him back to the yarding area. They placed him in the bed of our pickup truck. Then my father told Pop to bring him back to the infirmary.

The German medic and two other prisoners sat in the back of the truck along with one of the guards. They hovered over the man, trying to comfort him. Yet it was obvious, even to me, that the man was in a place beyond his needing any comfort. His eyes had by now lost their concentration. They were flat and wide, the pupils wide as pennies. The only thing that seemed pained was his breathing. His chest rose and fell unevenly, and there was an awful sucking sound each time he tried to take a breath. It was a noise your boot would make when you tried to pull it out of the mud.

Before we left the yarding area, the interpreter got in the truck. I remember he got up in front with us. He was to go back and take down the statements in English of the other Germans who'd witnessed the accident. I expected Pop to floor it going back to camp, but he didn't drive any faster than normal.

"I guess there's no sense busting a gut getting back," Pop said across me to the interpreter.

"No," the German replied. "I think not."

"What the hell happened?"

"I am not sure. Perhaps he slipped in the mud."

"Anybody yell *timber*?"

"No, I don't think so."

"Jesus. When you're logging, you can't fall asleep. No siree Bob," Pop said, holding up his empty sleeve as proof. "I was running an old Lombard steam engine back in the twenties. Put my hand where I oughtn't ta of and took it clean off at the elbow. Did you know him?"

"Yes," replied the German. "We had been in Africa together."

"You see much action?"

The German glanced down at his hands. They were long and

slender and tanned. The palm of one hand had a pink, still raw scar from where he'd been cut earlier that summer. I remembered that incident, too. I had helped him bandage the wound. He'd lost a lot of blood and his face had turned ashen, as if he were going to pass out. I had gotten the first-aid kit from the truck and some rags and had helped stop the bleeding. Then Pop and I took him to the infirmary. Now we were taking another German there, though this one was beyond any help the infirmary could offer.

I looked down at my knee, which had begun to throb. My overalls were ripped and my knee bloody.

"Cigarette?" the interpreter said, taking out a pack of Old Golds from his shirt pocket and offering it to Pop.

"*Danke*," Pop said, taking a couple.

As the pack of cigarettes passed back in front of me, the German's hand paused for a moment, unsure whether he should offer me any.

"Sure," said Pop. "Lib's a big girl. Ain't you, Lib? I seen you sneaking a smoke or two out in the woods, when your old man's back is turned." I took one cigarette and put it in my shirt pocket. I said, "*Danke*," and the German smiled and said, "*Das Vergnügen ist ganz meinerseits, Fräulein.* You know what that means?"

"Yes," I replied. "The pleasure is all mine."

"Ah. *Sprechen Sie Deutsch?*"

I shook my head. "A few words is all."

I didn't say anything about getting that book from the library on speaking German. I looked over at him. His eyes were a bluish gray, the color of the sea on a blustery day. He stared back at me, and I found myself putting my hand to my mouth. I blushed, felt my face redden the way it did when someone would stare at me.

"Isn't that something," Pop said after a while.

"What is?" the interpreter asked.

"Well, here this fellow goes through all that fighting and then a goddamn tree drops on him. Kind of makes you wonder, don't it?"

The German shrugged, smoked his cigarette, holding it

between thumb and forefinger, the way I'd seen the other POWs smoke.

"You've hurt yourself, *Fräulein*," he said.

I looked down at my knee again. "It doesn't hurt," I said.

"You should have someone look at it," he said.

Before we got back to camp the German medic pounded on the back window and made a sign—a shake of his head followed by two upraised hands—to indicate the man had finally died. I turned around and looked. The dead man, Oswald, lay on his back. Every time we hit a bump his head would flop one way and then the other, as if he were trying to say no to something. His eyes were still open and completely blank, like stones.

When we reached the infirmary the camp doctor, an American soldier, came out and helped the prisoners carry the limp body inside. Pop and the others followed them in to give the official story. I stayed in the truck. One German POW came up to me and asked, "*Ist er todt*?" I nodded.

The next day they had the funeral and the prisoners had the morning off from work. We drove around the cove and headed over to Abbey's for coffee. Pop Flynn was there, and so were some of the locals. Everybody went out onto the front steps when the prisoners came marching by. It was something to see, all right. Though it was raining out, they were all dressed up, military uniforms and medals and everything. They marched with those goose steps we'd seen in the newsreels, their polished boots clicking—or at least in my memory they did. It was as if they were marching past Hitler, in Berlin or Nuremberg or someplace like that. Only it was here, in Sheshuncook, Maine, in front of Abbey's store.

Eight men carried the plain pine, swastika-draped casket on their shoulders, arms interlocked. As they passed by, one of the locals, Vance Tohay, called, "How do you like that, you bastards?" Tohay had recently lost a son in Europe and he never had anything good to say about the POWs. He was one of those who thought they had it too easy, should be fed bread and water, and worked until they dropped.

But Ambroise said, "He was a good logger. He did what I asked him to and didn't bellyache."

"What the hell, Ambroise?" Tohay said. "You getting soft on these Nazi bastards?"

"I ain't getting soft. I'm just telling you this one did his work and didn't give me any problems. In my book he was all right."

We watched the POWs march down the road toward the small village cemetery. I remember thinking, *He's not going to go home—ever. The rest will but he'll stay here as a reminder to us that this happened, that there'd been a war and a camp, that some men had paid for this with their lives.*

14

I CAREFULLY FOLD the newspaper photo and stick it back into my pocketbook. My head is pounding now and I feel hot, like I have a fever. I must be coming down with something. I should go home and go to bed. That's what I should do. Before I leave the church, I walk up the aisle to the altar to light a candle. For a long while after Ambroise died, though he wasn't a practicing Catholic, I used to light candles for him. For his soul. I don't believe in everything they taught you when you were young, but I still believe in hell, still believe that you pay for your sins, if not when you're alive then after you're dead. Yet when I get up to the altar I find there are no candles set out. The altar boy sees me, leaves what he's doing, and comes over to help me.

"You looking for candles, ma'am?"

"Yes."

"I'll go look in the supply closet," he says. He's about twelve years old, pudgy, with a broad face covered with freckles the size of pennies. If he had no clothes on you could see him as one of those floating angels in the old pictures, the ones playing trumpets at the birth of Jesus. He comes back in a minute with a box of new candles. "Here you go."

"Thanks."

"Not too many people light candles anymore."

"Not as many souls need saving, I guess." The boy nods thoughtfully.

"Is Father Rodino hearing confession today?" I ask. I figure as long as I'm here I might as well make confession. I haven't made it for a long time.

"Father heard confession from one to three today. But I could go see if he's got time now."

"Never mind. That's all right. Some other time."

I light a candle for Leon, then one for Ambroise, too. I get down on my knees and say a prayer:

O God, the Creator and Redeemer of all the faithful, grant
to the souls of Your servants departed full remission of all
their sins, that, through our devout prayers, they may
obtain the pardon, which they have always desired. Who
live and reign, world without end. Amen.

At home Mitzi comes over and lays her head on my lap, wanting me to pet her.

"Not now, girl."

She keeps nudging my hand with her muzzle.

"Go sit," I snap at her. She goes over to the sink and lies down.

I change into my flannel bathrobe. I pull on two pairs of wool socks, but I'm still cold way down in my bones like a dull ache, the sort that's never going to go away. I check my temperature and find I'm running a fever of 103. So I take some Tylenol and then go and put the kettle on for tea. I sit at the kitchen table and glance out at the blue-black patch of evening sky I can see through the window. The house seems so quiet and still, the sort of deep stillness that follows a sudden noise. Only then does it hit me that he's gone, really gone this time. I think about how they've all left. What started with my mother's leaving is now complete: I'm all alone. Just like she predicted I would be.

When the kettle starts to whistle, I fix myself some tea. I add a little honey and lemon, then a splash of whiskey to help me sleep. As I sit there sipping my tea, I find myself trying to believe it was just an accident. Just like Chief Chambers said. Leon *could* have been drunk and confused; he *could* have fallen and hit his head on the ice; it *could* have happened just that way. I tell myself this over and over, as if by saying it enough I'll believe it and that infernal racket in the back of my head will stop. It's finished, Libby. Whatever it was you were looking for, you should just forget it now and get on with your life. Leon's dead. Nothing you do, nothing you find out, will change that.

But something doesn't sit right with me, doesn't make sense. "Best to let that business alone, Lib." What did Tom Weston mean by that? He said he'd done his job and kept his nose out of it. Out of what? When I asked him what he remembered of that night he seemed annoyed, like he didn't want to talk about it. Did he know something about the German's death? And did that have anything to do with how weird Leon was acting right before he died, with that business he had to take care of in town?

Stop it, I tell myself. This is crazy—*really* crazy. It's the fever got you thinking this way. I feel myself being pulled. It's like I'm in the middle of a fast-moving stream, with the water rushing around my legs, trying to sweep me along. I have just a toehold keeping me from being pulled under. If I slip or give in to it, who knows where I'll end up? Go to bed, I tell myself. Just get in bed and go to sleep, and when you wake up in the morning with a clear head, you'll see things differently. You won't be thinking like this.

Despite the warning, I go over and pick up the phone, dial information. When the woman comes on I ask for the numbers of Willard Walker in Skowhegan and Freddie Ross in Augusta. It's a long shot that they're still there, but what do I have to lose? The information lady is able to give me Walker's number right off but says there are several Rosses listed in Augusta: a Fred P. Ross, an F. T. Ross, a Dr. Frederick Ross, and an Alfred Ross.

"Which one you want?" she asks.

"I'm not sure. Can you give me all of them?"

"I'm only supposed to give two numbers at a time."

But she ends up giving me the numbers anyway. I decide to try Walker's number first. I let it ring about ten times and am about to hang up when a woman picks up.

"Hello," she says. She has a high, quivering voice, as if a feather is tickling it down inside.

"Mrs. Walker?" I ask.

"Yes?"

"Mrs. Willard Walker?"

"That's me. What can I do for you?" She doesn't sound from Maine. She sounds more like somebody from Boston.

"I'm looking for the Willard Walker that used to work for Great American Paper."

"That would be my husband," the woman explains. "He passed away, though."

"Oh," I reply. "I'm sorry to hear that."

"Yes, four years now. Is there something I can do for you?"

"No." Then I add, "Wait, maybe there is. Did your husband work at the POW camp up in Sheshuncook?"

"The what?"

"There was a German prisoner-of-war camp up on Moosehead Lake. The paper company used the prisoners for labor during the war. Did your husband work up there then?"

"He might have. I really wouldn't know."

"He ever mention any of the company men he worked with?"

"I don't know too many of his old acquaintances. You see, I'm his second wife. We married about fifteen years ago. He used to get together occasionally with a couple of men he logged with from the old days. Let's see. One was named Rabin."

"Wally Rabin?" I ask. I can remember Ambroise mentioning that name a few times. I wonder if he might be one of the other men in the picture.

"Yes, I believe that was his name. You could talk to him."

"You wouldn't know where he's living?"

"I think in Orono. But that was a few years ago."

"You said there was somebody else."

"Oh, yes. I seem to recall it began with a D. Daigle, Ducharme. Something like that. The three of them used to get together and play poker. But like I said, it's been a while."

"Thank you, Mrs. Walker."

I try the list of Rosses next. There's no answer at one. The second one, F. T. Ross, turns out to be Felicia Ross. The third on my list is a Dr. Frederick Ross.

"Hello," I say. "I'm looking for a Freddie Ross."

"I'm Dr. Ross," the man replies. "Is this an emergency?"

I listen carefully to the voice, but it's not one I've ever heard before. "No, nothing like that," I say. "I'm calling to see if you ever worked for Great American Paper, Dr. Ross."

He pauses on the other end, then says, "What is this about?"

"My father was a foreman with Great American," I explain. "I'm looking for a man named Freddie Ross who might have worked with him during the war."

"Oh, yes. Of course," says Dr. Ross. "You must mean my father. Freddie Ross Senior. He used to work at the paper company."

"Any chance I could speak to him?"

"I'm afraid not. He's dead. What did you say your name was?"

"Libby Pelletier, from up in Piscataquis. My father was Ambroise Pelletier. He was a crew foreman."

"What did you want with my father, Miss Pelletier?"

"I wanted to know if he worked up in Sheshuncook during the war?"

"Isn't that where they had the prisoner-of-war camp?"

"Yes."

"I don't know," replies Dr. Ross. "Pop may have. Why did you want to know?"

"It's a long story. Would you know of anybody else who worked up there with your father?"

"No, I wouldn't. Sorry."

Before I hang up, I decide to ask if he happened to know my brother.

"I don't think so," said Dr. Ross. "No, the name doesn't ring a bell. Then again, we weren't from Piscataquis."

"Well, thank you. Hope I didn't disturb you, Dr. Ross."

"That's quite all right. Sorry I couldn't help you."

Next I call and get the number for Wally Rabin, who's listed as still living over in Orono. A little girl answers and says her grandfather isn't home. I ask when she expects him back and she replies, "May. That's when Gramps comes back from Florida."

"Would you know where I could reach him down there, sweetie?"

"Just a minute," she says. "I'll get my mom."

A woman comes on the line. "You want to get ahold of my father?" she asks.

"Yes. I'm an old friend of his." A lie, I know. "Would you have his number?"

"Just a minute," she says. "Here we are." She gives me the number in Florida.

"Thank you," I say. After she hangs up I dial the number. I picture warm beaches and palm trees, people soaking up the sun like oranges.

"Is this Wally Rabin?" I ask when a man answers.

"Yeah. Who're you?" Though I can vaguely recall what this man looked like—he had light curly hair and a face that was always broken out with hives—his voice isn't familiar.

"My name is Libby Pelletier, Mr. Rabin. My father was—"

"Ambroise Pelletier," he says. "I remember him. What can I do for you?"

"You worked for my father, didn't you?"

"I sure did. We go back a long time."

"You work for him during the war?"

"Hell, no. I wish I had, though."

"Why is that?"

"I was getting my ass chewed up in the Pacific. No, I started for the company after the war. Forty-six. Worked as a cant-dog man loading sleds, then moved up to head sawyer. Finally assistant to your old man."

"You remember my brother Leon?"

"Sure I remember him. He was quite a bit younger than me. Your father had him working as a bull cook, didn't he?"

"Yes. You remember anybody else from those days?"

"Oh, Christ. There was Willard Walker and Tom Weston. Pop Flynn, the old one-armed guy. Nap LeRoux. The Mitchell boys."

"Anybody else?"

"I can't remember. It's been a while. They'd probably have records over in Millinocket. You could check there."

We spoke for a while about the old days, about Leon and my father. Then I said, "Thanks, Mr. Rabin. Good-bye."

Before getting into bed, I look in the fridge and get some leftover stew, and empty it into Mitzi's bowl. She gobbles it up, her ribs heaving. "Good girl," I say. Then I lie down. The sheets are freezing, and I rub my legs back and forth trying to get warm. I don't fall asleep right away. I toss and turn for a long time, thinking about Leon, about the faces in that picture with him, wondering what, if anything, I should do next.

In the middle of the night a noise awakens me, pulls me headfirst from a dream. In the dream it was night and I was walking barefoot over ice. Yet the ice wasn't cold, it was hot. Burning hot. Each step I took hurt, singed the bottoms of my feet. It was like walking over the hot sands at the beach. I sit up on the side of the bed, trying to clear my mind. The bedside clock says 1:32. It takes me a moment to realize the noise is the ringing of the phone. I get up, go into the kitchen, and answer it.

"Hello?" I say.

Silence for several long seconds.

"Hello? Who's there?"

Whoever's on the other end still doesn't say anything, but for some reason I can tell it's a man. Maybe because I can hear his beard scratching against the receiver, or maybe it's his breathing. I don't know. But I know it's a man.

"Kallick?" I say, thinking, for some odd reason, it might be him. "Is that you?"

There's silence for several more seconds. Then the voice on the other end asks, "Now why would you be expecting him?" It *is* a man's voice, and as soon as I hear it I know I've heard it before: a gritty, raspy voice. A voice filled with glass slivers. It's the man who called looking for Leon. I'd recognize that voice anywhere.

"Who is this?" I ask.

"Never mind. What did he want?"

"What did *who* want? What are you talking about? Do you know what time it is, for heaven's sakes?"

"Don't play stupid with me. You know who I mean. That god-damn kraut."

"I *don't* know what you're talking about. I'm going to hang up, you hear me."

"I know you talked to him. What'd he want? Was he asking about his brother?"

"Who are you? What do *you* want?"

"Stay away from him. You understand?"

"Are you threatening me?"

"I'm just telling you to keep your nose outta where it don't belong."

"You're the one who called Leon, aren't you? You're the one he went to see that night."

"It don't concern you, lady. You stay out of it, you know what's good for you."

"What doesn't concern—" But he hangs up on me. I'm left with the phone pressed against my ear, the other end sounding like the black bottom of a well. My feet are turning numb on the cold floor, and my head is going *woh-woh-woh*.

15

WHEN I WOKE up the next morning it was snowing again. I could see it as I got up to go to the bathroom. The snow was coming out of the northeast, down over Hardwood Mountain, then shooting across the bay. Wave after wave. My head was spinning, reeling. I still felt hot, ached all over. I took some more Tylenol and got back in bed. I stayed there all day, didn't open the store. I was out of it most of the time, dreaming, feverish. I could hardly tell what was a dream and what was real.

One time I woke up and Leon was in the room with me. He was young again, just a skinny boy. He was wearing that sweater I made him, the one with the reindeer. He was lying down, on something like a bed but not a bed either. What it turned out to be was a solid block of ice. It was melting, making dark puddles of water on the floor. Leon was quiet, but his eyes were wide open and staring up at the ceiling. I said, "Leon, what's the matter?" He didn't answer. When I went over to him and looked down into his face, it was like looking into the middle of a fire. "Leon," I said. "Leon, what happened?" But he remained silent. And when I touched him, his skin felt so hard and cold and lifeless, like the plaster walls in a room sealed off for the winter. Then a voice behind me asked, *"Ist er todt?"*

The phone rang several times but I didn't bother answering it. Vaguely, I remembered the night before, the caller, though I wanted to chalk it up to being just a bad dream. Or the fever. I guess I hoped that if I went back to sleep I'd wake up and every-thing, all of it, would just be a bad dream.

My fever finally breaks this morning, though I still don't feel too good. I get up and throw on my bathrobe. I make myself some chicken broth and a little dry toast. The house is freezing, yet there's no wood in the wood box. So I have no choice but to go outside and get some more. I throw my coat on over my robe, pull my boots and hat on, and go outside.

It's still snowing. There must be two feet on the ground already. I haven't seen it snow this hard since the big storm of '78. The gas pumps out front are nearly covered in drifts, as is the boathouse down at the dock. The road out front is nearly impass-able. I haven't heard anything go by, not even a town plow. People are sitting tight, I guess, not wanting to get stuck out in this.

I'm out in the lean-to off the barn, splitting wood. The back of my head throbs every time I take a swing with the maul. It's green wood, mostly red and white oak, some ash and birch mixed in. Roland dumped it here a few weeks ago to see me through the winter. The oak pops at the touch of the blade but the ash is stubborn. It fights me, catches hold of the maul and won't let go. Every so often I have to take a wedge and drive it in with the sledgehammer to free the maul. As I'm trying to yank a piece of wood apart, an inch-long sliver embeds itself in my palm. I wince as I pull it out.

Mitzi is standing just inside the overhang, snapping at snowflakes as they drift down. Her muzzle has a white beard of ice crystals hanging from it. I think about the other night. "It don't con-cern you. Stay out of it." I wonder who this caller is and what he wants. Is it the same man Leon went to see that night? Maybe the one Roberta said was in the library? So why is he threatening me? I wonder if I ought to call the police. My mind is racing, pounding.

I pick up the wood I've split, as much as I can carry, and head for the store. Out on the lake the wind is driving the snow. Small funnels erupt here and there, swirling madly like a swarm of white bees. In the distance Mount Kineo is lost behind a sheet of white. As I look out over the lake I see this dark speck against the white background. Slowly, the speck grows. A dog, I think, but even a dog would have better sense than to be out in this. The speck gets bigger and bigger. Finally I recognize it as someone riding a snowmobile, but the wind drowns out any noise. Mitzi, however, catches something and growls once. My heart begins to race: *Get the gun.* But the snowmobile is too close. It zips past the boathouse, up over the road, and comes to a stop in front of the gas pumps, snow swirling madly around the driver. He cuts the engine and gets off. It's Spotty Haines.

"You lost your marbles? What the hell you doing out in this?" I call, though I've never been happier to see anyone.

"Got antsy sitting home." He pulls up his goggles, smiles. "You got a fresh pot on?"

"Fresh enough," I say.

"Need a hand?" He goes over to the lean-to and grabs an armload of wood. Once inside, he says, "I'm sorry I didn't get down for Leon's funeral."

"That's all right."

"Hell, I didn't even hear about it till yesterday. I'd gone snowmobiling with a few guys up to the Saint John. I tried calling yesterday but I guess you weren't home. What the hell happened?"

"They say he was drunk. They're thinking he must've fallen and hit his head on the ice."

"What the hell was he doing out there?"

"They don't know."

"I'm real sorry, Lib."

I pour two cups of coffee. I sit down at the counter next to him and light up a cigarette.

"Did you know I was with him and Ambroise when he shot his first buck?" he says, sipping his coffee.

"No, I didn't."

"Sure. Leon got himself a nice little spiker. Out near Canada Falls Lake."

Spotty takes out a jackknife and begins to clean his nails. His hands are cracked and scaly, without any flesh. All bone and tendon, like chicken's feet.

"By the way, Lib, that kraut fellow catch up with you?"

"He stopped by," I say.

"What did he want anyway?"

"I don't know. Guess he thought maybe Ambroise had known his brother?"

"Did he?"

I shrug. "Maybe. He could have. Don't see how that matters much now, though."

"I suppose not. He tell you anymore'n he told me?"

"He . . . no, not really." I take a drag on my cigarette, feel the back of my head pounding. "Spotty, you remember some of the old-timers used to work with Ambroise?"

"Yeah, some. Why?"

I go into the kitchen and get my pocketbook. I come back, take out the photo, and lay it on the counter in front of him. "Take a look at that."

"Humph," Spotty says, looking it over. "That kraut give you this?"

"No. I found it with Leon's things. Leon's the one with the yoke over his neck, carrying the pots. It's Ambroise's logging crew."

"Sonofabitch. So it is. This's from back during the war."

"Yeah. I'm looking to find out who these three are," I explain, pointing at them. "You said you had such a good memory. Recognize any?"

"The picture's lousy," Spotty complains, scrutinizing it closely. He turns it this way and that to get a better look. "This fellow looks a little like one of the Mitchells."

"You sure? Tom Weston told me this one was Goose Mitchell," I said, pointing to the tall man with the long neck.

"That is Goose. This one here might be his little brother Alf. I'm not positive, but they both worked for the paper company.

Coupla crazy fuckers, those two. Goose held up a liquor store downstate and served some time."

"Is the other one alive? Alf?"

"Last I heard he was. Living over in Jackman. They got him for shooting a bear over at the town landfill. Ask Harve about him sometime."

"He still over there?"

"That was seven, eight years ago. He could be dead for all I know."

"How about the other two?"

"Hard to say."

I snuff out my cigarette and glance down at my hands. They remind me of my father's—short, square hands, with the same pattern of veins on the back. Ambroise's were smooth with thick calluses, like polished leather. I look at my own palm, at where the wood sliver broke the skin. There's a dark line of blood just under the surface of the skin. I think of the interpreter's hand, the deep gash he'd gotten from the power saw.

"Uh-uh. Picture's too faded," Spotty says after a while.

"How about this young kid here?" I ask. "Next to Goose Mitchell?"

Spotty takes a sip of his coffee. He stares at the picture some more. "Doesn't ring a bell. These other ones in front. They were the krauts."

"Yes," I reply, taking the picture away from him and slipping it into my sweater pocket.

"That reminds me," he says, snapping his fingers. "Remember the other day I told you there was something else."

"Yeah," I say. I watch Spotty work the knife blade under his nails. I feel a narrow band of pressure above my eyes, tightening. Like a winch chain being drawn in. Spotty takes his sweet time before he speaks again.

"When I heard about Leon I remembered it. Something clicked in my mind. You remember Pop Flynn? Fellow with one arm."

"Yeah."

"Me and Pop used to do a lot of fishing together. Best one-armed fisherman I ever saw. Sonofabitch would cast out and then if he got a bite he'd tuck the rod up under that stump of his and—"

"That's what you wanted to tell me? That Pop was a good fisherman?"

"Keep your pants on. Anyways, one time me and him are over in Socatean Bay. You know where that is?"

"Yeah, I know."

"We were way up in the bay, right in the middle of all those little islands there. We weren't catching shit but we were in Pop's boat and he didn't want to leave. He kept pulling us in and out of all these little coves, like he was looking for something. Finally he points to a spot about a hundred yards from shore and says, 'That's where they found him.'"

"Found who?" I ask.

"That's what I said. I don't have a clue what the hell he's talking about, so I say, 'Who the hell you jabbering about?' And he says, 'The kraut from the POW camp.' Just like that."

"What else he say?"

"Nothing."

"Nothing?"

"Not another word about it. He was half in the bag so I didn't pay it much mind."

"So what's your point?"

"They *didn't* find him in Socatean Bay. They found him down off of Kineo."

"How do you know that?" I ask.

"I remember. A coupla fishermen came across the body after ice-out and it wasn't in the bay. It was down off Hardscrabble Point. Toward Mount Kineo."

"Why did Pop say that, then?"

"Who the hell knows? But the currents run south, from the bay down past Hardscrabble."

"So?"

"So if a body went through the ice up in the bay it might just drift down to Hardscrabble."

"I don't see how it makes a whole lot of difference either way," I reply. "He could drown as easily one place as the other." But something clicks in the back of my head: Socatean Bay.

"Not in March," Spotty says.

"Why not in March?"

Spotty gets up and goes over to the window. He looks out at the lake.

"You couldn't a drowned out there even if you wanted to."

"We could've had a warm spell."

"Not that year."

"I suppose you remember that year."

"Matter of fact, I do. That winter was worse than this one. The lake froze early and didn't thaw till late May. One of the coldest goddamn winters we ever had around here. I still had traplines then and there wasn't a stream or beaver pond around these parts not froze over solid. I mean, *solid*." He raps his knuckles on the windowsill.

"Maybe he went through black ice. A current or something. You're always hearing that happen. Even when it's real cold."

"Humph."

"He could've gone through a crack from where the ice heaved. A lot of things could have happened."

Spotty continues looking out the window. Finally he comes back over and sits down again.

"What is it you're saying, Spotty?"

"I'm just saying it don't make sense him going through the ice like that."

"A lot of things don't make sense," I say. "That doesn't mean they don't happen."

"There was a lot of bad feeling against those krauts near the end of the war. Especially after what they did to our boys in Belgium. You were too young to remember that."

"I wasn't too young."

"Dirty sons of bitches took our GIs—prisoners, mind you, just like they was—and shot 'em in cold blood."

"I remember."

And I do. I remember how when people found out what they did to our soldiers in the Battle of the Bulge, they started grumbling about the Germans in camp. How we were too easy on them. How we should make them pay. Mrs. Gagnon, whose husband was killed in France, would stand outside the fence, cursing the Germans and heaving rotten fruit at them. Others, people who had had nothing against the Germans before, now began to hate them, to really hate them.

"You want to know what I think?" Spotty says.

"Not particularly."

"My bet is one of those guards had a buddy or a brother, something like that, get it over there. And one day when nobody was looking he took that kraut and . . . *auf Wiedersehen*—in the drink he goes. Wouldn't surprise me a bit."

"That was just wild talk back then."

"More'n talk, you ask me."

"That's crazy, Spot," I say. But it suddenly doesn't seem so crazy. It doesn't seem crazy at all. Those soldiers would've had a reason for wanting some revenge. Some of them had fought in Italy and in Africa. Maybe they hated the Germans enough to kill. Who knows?

I get up and go behind the counter. I put my cup in the sink and run some cold water on my hands and splash it over my face. I feel dizzy and my knees feel rubbery all of a sudden.

"You okay?" Spotty asks. "You look kinda pale."

"I don't feel too good. I've got a touch of flu."

"You ought to go lay down. Ain't gonna get any business today anyway."

"I think I will lie down."

"I'll split you some more wood."

"You don't have to do that."

"No problem. Go lay down."

My spine feels like a cold metal rod driven lengthwise down through my back. I take some more Tylenol and lie down. I close my eyes but I can hear Spotty splitting wood outside. My mind keeps running out of control, like an engine that needs to be timed. Stop thinking. Stop remembering. The German drowned in the bay. What makes me think I know something about Socatean Bay? What was it now? I lie here trying to remember, at the same time hoping I won't.

I remember this: A few days after the German escaped, I was in Abbey's store. Ambroise had given me a couple of bucks and sent me down to get some things, oleo and tobacco and some bread. It was after supper and dark already. Some men were sitting on the car seat, near the woodstove in back, talking to Charlie. I knew they were talking about the escape. It was all anyone in Sheshuncook or, for that matter, down in the town was talking about. There had been no escapes, at least no real ones anyway, for the first nine months the Germans had been here. One prisoner had made it out to Route 15 and had hitched a ride into town. He'd gone to a movie and then was picked up by the police when he tried to go into a liquor store and buy something with his canteen coupons. Two others had hid out in the woods overnight, but they had walked to camp voluntarily the next morning, half frozen and glad to be back. But those weren't real escapes. They were just the tricks of boys bored with prison life and playing a little hooky. This was the first real escape, and it was big news around here.

As I was paying Charlie, one of the men said to me, "Ain't you scared going out by yourself, little miss?" He was a slender man with dark hair slicked back with Vitalis and long, bad teeth. I often saw him in Abbey's though I didn't know his name.

"Why?" I said.

"'Why?' she says," the man repeated, laughing.

"You know what that goddamned Jerry'd do to you," said

another of the other men there that night, a thick-jowled man named Fats Farrell. He ran the Sheshuncook Inn, a large Victorian with faded yellow paint, a place overlooking the lake. In its heyday it attracted vacationers from as far away as New York and Washington. But now it was run down and Fats mostly rented rooms by the week to loggers or hunters.

"You be careful," Charlie said as I lifted my sack of groceries. His one glass eye was aimed at my belly button, the other at my forehead.

Though I wasn't usually afraid of the dark, I remember as I walked home that night listening to my footsteps crunch on the compacted snow. Thinking I had heard more, other footsteps, noises in the dark woods just off the road. And not the bears, who would have been hibernating this time of year. I pictured the German, at that moment still this faceless prisoner, just one of *them*, with frostbite sores on his lips, hungry, driven to desperation by the brutal Maine winter.

When I got home Ambroise was in the cellar sharpening a saw in a vice. The grinding of the file going between the saw's teeth made the whole house shake—*grrr . . . grrr . . . grrr*, like some giant monster scraping his claws along the foundation.

"They were talking about the escape," I said to him.

Without looking away from his work he asked, "Who was?"

"Charlie and Farrell and the others. They say he's dangerous."

"What do those birds know? They got nothing better to talk about."

My father ran the file through the teeth—*grrr . . . grrr*. He hadn't said two words about the escape. When I would ask him about it, he'd rub the bridge of his nose and ask me what's for supper. As I stood there I wondered why he wasn't worried about me walking home alone in the dark.

"Do you think they'll catch him?" I asked.

"Maybe." *Grrr . . . grrr.*

"Which one was it?"

He stopped filing then and turned around. His eyes shone

that chicken-fat yellow they did when he was drunk.

"How the hell would I know which one?" he replied. "Did you get me some tobacco?"

"Yes."

He went back to his work and I started to head up the cellar stairs. He called to me when I was halfway up.

"Libby," he said.

"Yeah?"

"I wouldn't worry about that kraut."

"No?"

"I bet he's already to Canada by now."

"You think so?"

"I wouldn't be surprised."

I paused on the stairs for a moment, then quickly headed up and closed the door behind me.

That winter I didn't work at the camp much. Leon continued working, after school sometimes and on Saturdays. Ambroise was still trying to get him to learn the trade. But they'd hired a full-time cookee and didn't have any need for me. So I didn't really have much to do with the prisoners or the camp. Yet I recall going to work one Saturday in April. The new cookee had called in sick. It was a couple of weeks after the German had escaped. Pop and I were in the truck heading out to bring the prisoners their lunch.

"Which one was it?" I asked. Not having worked there since Christmas, I wondered if I'd even remember any of their faces.

"Which one was what?" Pop replied.

"The one that escaped?"

Pop jammed the shifter in gear, swore. "That dark-haired one. Looked like a wop," he said. "Rode with us for a little last summer."

I knew the one he meant. The interpreter. He'd worked with us for a while after he'd cut his hand with a power saw. I'd sat next to him in the truck a few times. I wondered why Ambroise hadn't known which German had escaped. After all, it had been his interpreter. But I figured that just showed how Ambroise never really thought of those boys as anything more than cord cutters.

"Why would he run now?" I asked Pop.

"Why?" Pop laughed. "You'll have to ask him that."

"He won't last long in these woods," I said.

"That's his problem."

"But they say it's almost over."

"Maybe he didn't like the accommodations."

I didn't understand it. The camp didn't seem so bad to me. Except for the barbed wire, it wasn't much different from the life that most of the loggers led here. Going into the woods every day, cutting wood, going home at night. Working, eating, sleeping. Of course, they didn't have wives or families and they didn't have their freedom, but the war, everyone was saying, would be over soon, in a matter of months.

I remember for weeks afterwards people in the village and even down in the town talking about the escaped German. It was *the* news. At first it was with a real sense of fear, at least for some. Like Spotty said, people took to keeping guns next to their beds, and women and children were warned about going out alone—"on account of the German." People talked about it in Abbey's store and at the Sheshuncook Inn, and in town at the gin mills that Ambroise sometimes took Leon and me to. The kids talked about it at school: There was always somebody who'd seen a suspicious-looking man crossing the railroad tracks over near Brassua Lake or footprints in the snow behind someone's house. Once in a while you'd see soldiers with dogs searching in the woods for him. They even brought in trackers, men who knew these woods and every hunter's cabin around for miles.

And everybody had a theory about the German. At first people said he'd get cold or hungry and probably come in on his own in a few days. And when that didn't happen they brought up other possibilities. Asa Shaw's wife, Milly, a nervous woman who always had a bad case of shingles, said she'd read an article in *Life* by no less an authority on the subject than J. Edgar Hoover himself. She explained how the article said *escapees*—which she made sound like *SKPs*—would try to catch a freight train to some port city, in our case some place like Quebec or Boston, and then try to get on a ship to South America where they might make it back to Germany. Charlie Abbey said the kraut might try to hole up someplace—in a hunter's cabin or abandoned logging camp—and wait for warmer weather. Vance Tohay, the man who'd lost a son, said if he laid eyes on that son of a bitch, well, he'd be a hundred dollars richer and there'd be one less kraut to ship back to Germany. While still others, when the subject of the escaped German came up, would roll their eyes or nod, and say something to the effect that their money was on the German already being dead.

But as the weeks melted into months, the escaped German became just another topic of conversation, the way you'd talk about ice-out or the approach of fishing season, or how the war was going. Sometimes at night, doing the supper dishes or lying in bed, I would think about him, *out there*, somewhere in the night. *The escaped German*. That's how I thought of him—*tried* to think of him anyway. It was easier not putting a face or a name to him. Occasionally, I might picture the one who'd sat next to me in the truck, recall what his eyes and hands looked like, his voice, that smell. But as time passed his image in my mind grew fuzzy and I did nothing to stop it.

After a while things settled down. The big news by May of course was Germany's surrender. V-E Day. That's all you heard, in the papers, on the radio. That and the news about the dead. Hitler. Roosevelt. All the other deaths, too, the ones in the camps as well as on the battlefield. Death, death, and more death. The smell of it was heavy over the town. It hung over people's lives like a cloud from a forest fire, raining down ash and soot, sometimes red-hot cinders that scorched and burned. People wanted to know when their boys and husbands and brothers would be coming home, if they were safe, if they'd been excluded from all that death. They weren't too concerned anymore about one German who'd been foolish enough to escape.

So it didn't really make much news when they found a body in the lake after ice-out. If they said anything at all, people said it served the son of a bitch right. He shouldn't have tried to escape. A lot of people felt the way Vance Tohay did: just one less German we'd have to ship back after the war. One more death—especially one on *that* side—didn't really seem to matter. If anything it sort of evened up the score just a little. And when the word out of the camp infirmary was that it had been classified a drowning, that pretty much closed the subject right there, even if some rumors continued to circulate. Especially in Abbey's, where when talk of the German came up, the men would trade glances and say it was the strangest drowning they ever saw.

"What are they going to do with them now?" I asked Ambroise one night at the supper table. It was after Germany had surrendered.

"I guess they'll be shipping 'em back right after we beat the Japs," he said. "Our returning boys'll need the work."

But it turned out to be nearly a year before the Germans went home. They stayed here, cutting wood and keeping the mills in pulp. The politicians and the army, I guess, wanted to make them pay for causing all that death. I remember working again as a cookee that summer of '45 and noticing that things had changed. Where the Germans had once looked like young boys with an expression of sadness or confusion or possibly, on a few, of proud defiance, they now all looked like bitter, shrunken old men for whom life had soured. I was amazed at the change. When I filled up their soup bowls they would no longer say, "*Danke, Fräulein*" or "*Guten Tag, Fräulein.*" They would just stare at me with eyes filled with this silent, barely contained rage—like those of a caged animal, one that was used to the cage but one that would rake your hand if you came too close. Germany had been beaten, *they* were beaten, but they still weren't allowed to go home. As the months passed they grew to feel for us something I'm certain they hadn't at first: hatred. We'd taught them that and we'd taught them well.

Then finally in the spring of '46 they were going home. They were packed in trucks one day and shipped down to Piscataquis to the train station. The camp stayed opened for a while afterwards, but then the servicemen left, too, and the prison became a ghost camp. When you'd walk by it at night the empty guard towers looked suddenly out of place, spooky and solemn. The barbed wire rusted and caught unsuspecting birds in its steel talons, and at least one deer was killed trying to bolt through it. Pretty soon the fence and the guard towers were bulldozed by the paper company. The buildings were converted back into storage for hay and grain, but by the fifties dozers and skidders were replacing horses, and soon the buildings, too, were abandoned. Trees grew up and windows were used for target practice. Fearing a fire, the company finally knocked the remaining buildings down and that was that. People tried to forget we'd ever had a POW camp here. The only reminder of the Germans' stay was the small graveyard along the river. Off by themselves, near a willow leaning over the water, were the German graves. I remember going there once or twice to look at them. Out of curiosity, the way you might go to see a rock in the river that was supposed to hold a dinosaur footprint. Plain, flat, stone markers that contained only the men's names, their rank, their date of birth and death, and way at the bottom, the single word *Soldat*, as if their entire existence had been reduced to that: soldier. That's where they'd buried the escaped German. But by then his death was like a drop of water in the flood of death that had come in the wake of the war. It wasn't very important anymore.

Late tonight the phone rings. I hesitate before answering it.

"Hello?" I say.

No answer. Outside I hear the wind howling and the snow pelting the house like someone was tossing gravel at it. Mitzi stares at me from the kitchen doorway.

"Hello?" I repeat, my words tumbling, rattling like stones down a metal pipe. "Who is this?" More silence: deep, cavernous, as if it could swallow me up.

Then I hear it—that breathing. Raw, hoarse, as if I'm down inside his lungs.

"What do you want? Why are you calling me?"

Finally the voice says, "You know why I'm calling."

"I don't. I swear to you I don't."

"Stay clear of it. It don't concern you."

"Did it concern Leon?" I ask. "What did it have to do with him?"

"You watch your step, lady," he says.

"You were with him that night, weren't you?"

"Stay out of it."

"What happened? What happened to my brother?"

"If you know what's good for you."

"What happened to Leon, goddamn you?"

But he hangs up.

I go over to the outside door and check the lock. Then I walk down into the store and double-check the doors there, too. Finally I head back upstairs and into my bedroom. I lock my door and pull the shades. From the closet I take out the strong-box and set it on the table. My hands are shaking. I open the box, but when I lift the money bag I see that the gun isn't there. Leon must've taken it, I think. He was the only one who knew it was there.

16

MONDAY MORNING.

I hear this grinding noise—*grrr*, *grrr*. For a moment I almost think I'm back in the house up in Sheshuncook and Ambroise is in the cellar sharpening a saw. But then I realize the noise is coming from outside. I get up, throw on my robe and slippers, and go over to the window. Outside, I see Roland's pickup truck. He's plowing my driveway. Seeing me in the window, he waves, holds up one finger to tell me he'll just be a while more.

By the time I get dressed and head down into the store, he's already pounding on the front door. When I open it, he's standing there, his thick lips cracked from the cold, his cheeks pink. He has a package under one arm.

"I tried calling," he says after I open the door. "Where you been?"

"Sick. Wipe your feet," I scold him.

"I was getting a little worried. Tried calling Saturday and again yesterday. Don't you answer your phone? Figured I'd drive up this morning and make sure you were all right." He smiles, his eyes glistening.

"I was sick the past two days. But I'm feeling better now."

"Here, I brought you those venison steaks," he says, holding out the package to me. "Karl Olender, the fellow in here the other day, he hit a deer with his truck."

"Thanks. No work today?" I ask.

"No. Roads are closed down. Whole state's just about shut down."

"What did you do last night? You go to the Legion supper?"

"No. I stayed home and watched the Celtics."

"You eat breakfast yet?" I ask. "I could make you some."

"You sure it's no bother?"

"No bother."

I open the package of meat and take out one steak wrapped in light yellow butcher's paper. I defrost it in the micro, then turn on the grill and put the steak on. I place the rest of the package in the freezer and then make a pot of coffee. I fry up half a dozen eggs and some home fries. Roland's a big man, goes over two hundred pounds, and he can eat a lot. I like a man with a good appetite. He sits in a booth, the same one Wolfgang Kallick sat in the other day. Every once in a while I catch him looking at me.

"What's the matter?" I say.

"Nothing? You hear about Al Royce?"

"No."

"He ran his rig off the road Saturday during the storm. Near the dam."

"He all right?"

"He's fine but his rig is all busted to hell. Just had the thing painted, too."

I set Roland's breakfast on the table and then slide in across from him. I have only a cup of coffee in front of me. I light a cigarette.

"Ain't you gonna eat?" he asks.

"I don't feel much like eating."

"Don't they say, 'Starve a cold and feed a fever'?"

"You got it ass-backwards."

"Still, you ought to eat something."

"What are you, my mother?"

Roland pours a ton of ketchup on his potatoes. Then he covers everything under a flurry of salt. He cuts a piece of steak, runs it through the egg yoke, and shoves it in his mouth. A vein in his forehead swells as he chews.

"Good steak. Karl had Walt Monroe butcher the thing for him. A doe."

"The cold's driving them down out of the mountains. I found one out back the other day. Dogs had run it. Tore the thing all to hell. That's why I'm keeping Mitzi tied up."

"Only one way to curb a dog from that," Roland says. "A bullet."

He takes a piece of toast and mops up the yoke. Then he washes it down with coffee. When he finishes he leans back, scratches his belly. He's got a scab of egg yolk on his chin.

"That hit the spot. Wanna hear something, Lib?"

"What?"

"You know your friend?"

"What friend?"

"That guy was in here the other day? The German?"

"He's not my friend," I say. "But what about him?"

"He's nosing around town."

I say, "Well, it's a free country."

"Kevin Nance said he was over the police station asking questions. Evidently his brother was the one died over here. Did he tell you that?" I nod.

"I was just eight or nine then but I remember my folks talking about it. I asked my mother. She remembers when the German escaped. Said everybody was on the lookout. This one's got a lot of nerve, you ask me?"

"Why?"

"Coming over here and snooping around. Like it was our damn fault."

I pause with my cigarette halfway to my mouth.

"Like what was our fault?" I ask.

"All of it. The whole goddamn thing—the war, the camp. His brother running off like that. Nobody put a gun to his head and made him run. Can I bum a cigarette?"

I give him one, and he taps the end on the table. I think about the man who's been calling. I wonder if I ought to tell Roland. If maybe I shouldn't go to the police.

But what exactly can I tell them? What do I know for sure and what's just in my own crazy imagination? And yet I sense something else holding me back, something that has to do with that night, with Ambroise and Leon and those logging men out in the driveway.

Instead I ask, "When did you start for the company, Roland?"

"Sixty-three. The year Kennedy was killed. Two years and I'll have thirty in. Can take early retirement then."

"Was Ambroise still there then?"

"No, he was gone by the time I came. Wally Rabin was a crew foreman then. I worked with him till I hurt my leg."

"But you'd have known some of the old-timers."

"Some."

"I want to show you something." I get my pocketbook and show him the picture. I ask him if he knows the two I don't have names for in the back row. He moves his plate aside, wipes his hands on his shirt.

"Jesus. When was this taken?" he asks.

"During the war."

"That was way before I started," he says.

"I know. I just thought maybe some of those fellows were still with the company when you came on."

"It's hard to say. The picture's so old. This one, he looks a little like Desauliers."

"Who?"

"Beany Desauliers. He was still working for the company when I started."

"Is he still alive?"

"No, he's been dead for years. I went to his funeral. Lung cancer," Roland says, crushing out his cigarette.

"Wasn't there a Desauliers that was first selectman for a while?" I ask, recalling the article I'd read in the newspaper. "Back during the war."

"Yeah. That was this one's brother. He's down in the rest home in town."

"Did he work up at the camp, too?"

"I wouldn't know. Everybody and his brother worked for the company at one time or another. Why are you so interested?"

I shrug, take the photo back. "What are your plans today, Roland?"

"I don't have any. Why?"

"Me neither. I could make us a nice dinner. A couple of those steaks. Watch a little TV."

"Sounds good to me."

I suddenly like the idea of having Roland around now.

Roland's right leg has a pale white dent running vertically down his thigh and over the kneecap. Two parallel scars, crisscrossed by stitch marks. It's where a power saw chewed up his leg, forced him into driving a rig. Though I can't see it beneath the covers, I can feel the bumpy territory with my hand. The skin is knotted but oddly smooth, too, and hairless. It feels like the scar on my upper lip. We both have our handicaps. I run my fingers over it and watch him as he sleeps. His mouth is open and he's snoring. His breath smells warm and sour, like butter melting in a pan. Every once in a while the rhythm of his breathing changes and his eyes flutter beneath his lids. I wonder what he's dreaming, where he is right now. Roland's body feels nice against me—warm and solid and comforting—and made up, I somehow feel, completely of the present. It'd be so nice just to stay here, never get up.

It's near twilight. Through the window I can see the pink, swollen underbellies of clouds. I get out of bed, quietly, so I don't wake him. I throw on my robe and slippers and head down into the store. I don't chance calling from upstairs. I go over to the pay phone near the rest rooms and open the phone book. I look to see if there's an Alf Mitchell over in Jackman. There are several Mitchells but not one named Alf. I get a dime from the jar over the sink and call the operator. She tells me the same thing. No Alf

Mitchell. Maybe Spotty had it wrong, or maybe he doesn't have a phone. Maybe he moved. Maybe he's dead. Who knows?

Next I look up the number of the nursing home in town. A young woman answers, right in the middle of laughing at something.

"Excuse me," she says, trying to suppress her laughter. I don't know why, but hearing her makes me almost want to laugh too. "Piscataquis Rest Haven," she says finally. "Can I help you?"

"Is there an Ed Desauliers there?"

"Just a minute." I hear her talking with someone in the background and then more laughter. "How do you get yourself into these things?" she says. In a moment she comes back on the line and explains, "Yes, we do. You want me to connect you to his room?"

"Please."

After a while someone comes on the line. "Hello," says an old man's voice, thin, high pitched like a woman's.

"Is this Ed Desauliers?" I ask, whispering so Roland won't hear me.

"Yes. Who'm I speaking to?"

"My name is Libby Pelletier. My father was Ambroise Pelletier."

"Who? You'll have to speak up."

"My father was Ambroise Pelletier."

"Ambroise, you say?"

"Yes. Did you know him?"

"Sure I knew Ambroise."

"Did your brother Beany work at the paper company with him?"

"Hell, yes. For years. Beany worked on Ambroise's crew till they made him a foreman, too."

"They both worked up at the POW camp, didn't they?"

"You say the camp?"

"Yes. Didn't your brother work with the POWs?"

"I don't think so. In fact, I'm sure he didn't."

"But I have a picture, Mr. Desauliers. It shows your brother standing with the prisoners."

The old man doesn't say anything for several seconds. For a moment, I almost think we've been disconnected.

"Hello? Mr. Desauliers?"

"You must be mistaken."

"I have a picture of him."

"I don't need to see no picture. Beany was working over to the mills during the war. He had nothing to do with those Germans."

"Would you happen to know who else worked on Ambroise's crew up there?"

"No, I wouldn't." The old man coughs, clears his voice.

"Could I show you the picture? Maybe you'd remember if I showed it to you."

"I would doubt it very much."

"Why's that?"

"Christ, you're talking fifty years ago."

"Forty-six," I correct. "I could stop down."

"I don't think so."

"Why not?"

"I just don't, that's why."

"Mr. Desauliers—"

"You listen here, young lady," he says, his tone turning suddenly harsh. "My brother had nothing to do with that."

"With what, Mr. Desauliers? He had nothing to do with what?"

"I don't want you calling here anymore."

"Mr. Desauliers."

"Do you understand?"

"But—"

He's hung up.

I'm suddenly freezing. The backs of my arms go rough from goose bumps. I head back upstairs and crawl in beside Roland. I cling to his warm, broad back the way you would to a life jacket.

In his sleep he mumbles something. At first I try not to listen. It's like putting your ear to a closed door, like eavesdropping. Yet when he says it again I can't help but hear. "Faye, honey," he says. His dead wife's name. And suddenly it's like she's there in the room with us. A ghost. He says, "There's water in the cellar, Faye. Pump ain't working." I'm listening in on a conversation with the dead.

17

I'M AT THE GRILL fixing breakfast for Roland, Harve Michaud, a couple of power-company guys who'd been working on a downed line just north of here. A rig carrying chickens had taken out a pole. They're talking about the accident. One of them says, "Christ, there was feathers and blood all over the snow. You shoulda seen it." I got my back to them when I become aware of someone standing over near the cash register. When I turn I see Wolfgang Kallick. I feel myself stiffen.

"I was waiting for your call, Frau Pelletier," he says to me.

"I've been busy," I reply.

"You said you would call."

I leave what I'm doing and go over to him. I look over at the others. Roland is staring at me, wondering what's up. "You shouldn't have come here."

"I could not wait any longer. I am leaving for Germany tomorrow. I needed to speak to you once more."

"I have nothing more to say to you. I told you what I knew. Can't you understand. It was a long time ago."

"Please, just a few minutes, Frau Pelletier."

"No. Now please go."

"But Frau Pelletier, you said—"

"Just go. I'm sorry."

Suddenly Roland is standing next to Kallick.

"Is he giving you a hard time, Lib? You heard the lady, pal."

"I can handle this, Roland," I say.

Roland pokes a finger in the middle of Kallick's chest. "If you knew what was good for you you'd get your fat kraut ass in that car and get out of here."

"Roland, please." Then to Kallick I say, "I think you'd better go."

I spend all evening telling myself I don't owe him anything. What's he to you anyway? He'll leave soon, go back to Germany where he belongs. Then this'll all blow over. It's got nothing to do with me. It was something that had happened a long, long time ago. But in my mind I hear the words *Was ist passiert? . . . what happened?* I think, too, how it won't just blow over. That after he goes Leon'll still be dead, and I'll still have all these questions. Kallick's brother and Leon, it's *all* bound up together somehow. I feel that frightening pull on me again, drawing me toward something, something big and dark and terrifying, like an undertow in the ocean drawing you out into deep water, pulling so hard at your legs that you end up wanting to give in to it.

I get dressed and tie Mitzi at the bottom of the stairs. Then I head out to the barn. It takes me a while to put the chains on the truck and then I have a hard time starting it. I have to jump it with a spare battery I keep in the barn. When I finally reach Frannie's Cabins on the northwest side of the lake, it's nearly nine o'clock. The place is off to the right, down a slight incline. Six small cabins facing the lake like ducks drying their feathers. Frannie Peters, the daughter of a woman I went to school with, runs the place. She lives with her family in the big house at the end. It has lights on, looks warm and cozy, and I picture them sitting around watching TV—a regular family.

I pull in and start looking for the red Buick, which I find parked in front of the last cabin. I shut the truck off and go up and knock.

"Frau Pelletier!" Wolfgang Kallick exclaims when he opens the door. He's dressed in a terry-cloth robe and slippers. He has a dab of shaving cream on his earlobe. For a moment he just stares at me, those blue eyes of his showing surprise and relief at the same time.

"I decided we needed to talk after all," I say. He asks me to come in but I tell him not here. I don't want anybody seeing us together.

"I know a place where we can talk in private," I say.

"I'll get dressed," he says.

In five minutes we're on the road heading north. He's brought a briefcase with him. It sits on the seat between us.

"Where are we going?" Kallick asks.

"This place I know."

I drive Route 15 west. Neither of us talk, although the silence is something you can touch. I look straight ahead, but out of the corner of my eye I catch the outline of his thick head in the dash lights, his small birdlike nose. I can smell him—that musty smell I noticed the other day. Not of hot grease and metal but that mothball odor. He breaks the silence only once to say, "It is good at least the snow has stopped." I just nod, keep driving. The chains make a far-off rhythmical sound.

After a few miles I take a right and cross the bridge over the Moose River, heading north now. I stay on this road for a while, then turn onto an old logging road that goes out to Brassua Lake. The road has been plowed but still has drifts of snow. The wheels spin freely at times even with the chains, and the truck fishtails toward the drainage ditch. In the headlights the naked trees shine bone white, like fingers sticking up out of the deep snow. Finally I reach the hunting lodge of a lawyer from Boston. He pays me to keep an eye on it, to clean up after he leaves. I have a key, and when he's coming he has me open it up and stock it with food from the store, make sure there's enough wood. The driveway hasn't been plowed, so I park on the road.

"Is this yours?" Wolfgang Kallick asks.

"No. I just look after it. We can talk here."

I glance back up the road behind us. It's quiet and dark, not a sign of anybody. I grab the flashlight from the glove compartment, and we struggle through the deep snow to the door. Wolfgang Kallick slips once and I catch him under the arm. He's heavier than I thought, but solid, muscular, not fat.

"Thank you," he says.

Inside, this cool, sharp odor greets us—the smell of gun oil and wood smoke. The lights are run by a generator in the shed out back, but I don't feel like fooling with that. Instead I get the kerosene lamp from the mantel and light it. The flickering light throws eerie shadows on the walls, bare except for a single fraying deer head with dusty, gray eyeballs. I think of old Abbey's glass eye. The main room—kitchen and living room—is plain, just a few wooden chairs, a ratty couch with a green army blanket thrown over it, a kitchen table made out of a single pine slab with four spindly legs sticking out of it like those of a crab. In back, I know, is a bedroom with bunk beds. Sometimes the lawyer from Boston comes here with other men to hunt. When I clean up, I find beer cans and cigar butts and girlie magazines after they leave. Sometimes, though, he brings a woman I know is not his wife. I once found lacy panties under the bed and Tampax in the garbage. He knows I'll keep my mouth shut.

"Sit there," I say, pointing at the table. "I'll get the fire going."

I go over to the woodstove and ball up some old issues of the *Boston Globe*. I shove some kindling in, then a few sticks of birch and ash, open the damper and light it. When it's going good I go over and sit across from him. His briefcase is on the table. It's old, the leather cracked. I wonder what's in it. He said he had something to show me. Neither of us say anything for a while, and the quiet makes me uncomfortable. I light up a cigarette and use the lid of a peanut butter jar for an ashtray. Kallick takes out his pipe. He carefully cleans out the bowl with a small knife. I watch his hands, those fat but nimble fingers. They work the knife with the precise movements of a wren building a nest. Remembering his card, I ask him what an *Uhrmacher* is—it's more just to keep the silence from overwhelming us.

He smiles. "One who repairs watches."

"How long have you done that?"

"All my life. I apprenticed right after the war. I don't know why but they needed people to fix watches. No one had jewelry after the war. Everyone pawned it for something to eat."

Finally I say, "You don't believe your brother drowned?"

"I received an official letter from your government shortly after the end of the war. They said the autopsy showed he had drowned."

"Then why are you here? Why isn't that good enough?" I can feel something like anger slipping into my voice, rising in my chest like a hot bubble trapped behind my sternum. In the back of my mind a thought runs something like this: If he hadn't come and started stirring things up, maybe Leon would still be alive.

"Since he knew my brother, Herr Wattenberg was asked to identify his remains in the camp infirmary. He said it looked as if he had been beaten."

"Beaten?" I say.

"*Ja*. He said that Dieter had marks on his face and head. Bruises." Leon on the stretcher, that gash over his eye.

"He was in the lake for a couple of months," I explain. "A lot of things could've happened. He could've been hit by a boat propeller."

"I suppose."

"Why would the Americans say he'd drowned if he didn't?"

"I do not know. Herr Wattenberg said there were rumors around the camp. That he had been . . . silenced."

"By who? Why?"

Kallick places the tips of his fingers together lightly, forming the shape of a cat's skull. "Herr Wattenberg said there were problems at the camp. With the Nazis. Dieter had never really fallen for all that. Even as a boy he hated them. Did your father ever say anything about the Nazis in camp?"

"I don't know. Maybe a few things. You think *they* had something to do with your brother's death?"

"Who can say? Why would he run away? The war was almost

over. He had to have known that. It was suicide to run off like that."

"Maybe he was just tired of being a prisoner," I say. Yet as soon as I say this I recall asking Pop Flynn that same question years and years before: *Why would he run now? It's almost over*.

When I look up he's staring at me with those blue eyes—his little beak of a nose straining, the edges of his nostrils rimmed with white.

"What I still don't understand," I say, "is what all this has to do with me, Mr. Kallick? My father's dead. He's been dead for a long, long time. You should be talking with the military. Or with those prisoners that were at the camp. If you think they had something to do with it."

"I have tried. But many are dead. Others I cannot locate. Those I have either will not talk about it or say they do not know anything."

"How am *I* supposed to help you?"

Kallick takes a long puff on his pipe, lets the smoke out slowly. "Did you work at the camp, Frau Pelletier?"

I wonder how he knows that. Did that Wattenberg tell him about me? I don't recall a prisoner by that name, but he could've remembered me, I guess. Or maybe someone from town told him. Or maybe there are records over at the company showing me on the payroll? I don't know. I imagine it wouldn't be that hard to find out, but it surprises me nonetheless.

"Yes," I say. "For a little while."

"How come you did not tell me that the other day?"

"Because you didn't ask me. You asked about my father."

"Do *you* remember my brother, Frau Pelletier?"

"It was a long time ago," I say. "I was just a girl."

Kallick opens his briefcase. He takes out an envelope, removes a picture, and slides it across the table at me.

"That is my brother," he says. "Dieter."

It's the picture he'd sent a year and a half ago, the one I still have in my wallet. It shows a skinny young boy on a pair of skis.

His face is pale with a broad forehead and black shadows for eyes. He has that faint half-smile on his face.

"He was sixteen there," Kallick tells me. "Do you recognize him, Frau Pelletier?"

I stare at it for several seconds. "I . . . it's possible. He looks like the one that interpreted for my father's crew."

"Dieter was an interpreter. He spoke good English."

"Yes, I remember him now. A little. Is this what you wanted to show me, Mr. Kallick? This picture?"

"And this," he says, taking a small black book from his briefcase. He places it on the table between us. Like the briefcase, its leather cover is worn and cracked. It looks like a Bible.

"Is that a Bible?" I ask.

"A *Tagebuch*. A diary. Many soldiers kept them during the war."

"Is that . . . your brother's?" I ask.

"*Ja*. Of his imprisonment."

"Where'd you get it?"

He doesn't answer right away. He takes out his glasses. Then he picks up the small book and starts flipping through the pages, which are yellowed and covered with tiny, faded handwriting done in black ink. He stops, then turns back a few. "Here we are. Wattenberg had saved it along with some other personal effects of my brother. He had kept it all these years and gave it to me. May I read something to you, Frau Pelletier?"

"Whatever," I reply, but I feel this hard lump in my stomach nonetheless.

He begins to read, slowly, occasionally stumbling over some English words, unable to make out others at all. He uses his stumpy finger to follow the tiny scrawled writing.

14 July 44: Cut my hand the other day with . . . die Motorsäge. Spent some time in the clinic and have been given light duties for the time being. Get to ride in the truck with the Ami driver. Our job is taking tools back to the repair shop at camp, and when we return we bring the men the noon

meal in the woods. Work is certainly easier than cutting timber and the
old American is not so bad. Herr Flynn.

Kallick stops reading, looks up at me. "Do you remember a Herr Flynn?"

"Yes," I reply. "He was a driver. Pop Flynn."

Kallick then picks up where he left off.

Has only one arm but drives through the muddy roads like the devil. A dirty mouthed little man who does not bathe. First day he warned me: "I may only have one arm but I can cut the balls off a fly at twenty feet with this," he said, showing me the hunting knife he keeps on his hip. Said he'd killed many of us "Jerries" in the first war at Belleau Wood. When we bring the men their lunch, sometimes we stop by the side of the road and eat our fill before we reach the cutting site. Seconds too. A starving . . .

Kallick turns the page and seems to momentarily lose his place.

"Mr. Kallick," I interrupt.

"Just a moment, please."

"What has this to do with me?"

"Please," he says, glancing up from the pages of the book. His eyes look hollow, like the empty shells of a robin's eggs sitting in the plump nest of his face. Then he dives back in, searching, hunting for the lost thread of the diary. "Here we are."

22 July 44: A young American girl works with Herr Flynn. The daughter of one of the supervisors. First girl I have actually spoken to since Italy. At first she thought we were all monsters. When we work together she keeps her distance. As if I am a leper. If I accidentally bump her she pulls away as if bitten. But think she is only very shy. Have traded her some canteen cigarettes for a magnet (may come in handy). Sturdy peasant girl, like some milk-maid from the Erzgebirge, but sweet. When I cut my hand a few days ago, it was she who helped me bandage it. Would dare not look me in the eye though. "Thank you very much, Fräulein

Nightingale," I said. Which quite embarrassed her. Poor thing has . . . die Hasenscharte.

"A what?" I ask, though somehow I already know what it means.

"This," Wolfgang Kallick says, touching his lip.

So that's why he'd been staring at my mouth, how he'd known I'd worked with his brother.

Wolfgang Kallick takes his glasses off, shuts the diary, but keeps one finger in as a bookmark. When he glances at me, his eyes look as if he's just come out of a dark room. I look at his face, and beneath the creases around his eyes and the liver spots and the added weight, I can see that resemblance to his brother.

"That was you, was it not?" he says.

"Yes." I light another cigarette, press my hands flat on the table to keep them from moving. "How come you didn't show me that the other day?"

"How come you didn't tell me you knew him?"

"I never really *knew* him," I explain. "He was just somebody I worked with for a little while a very long time ago."

"But you remember him now. A little?"

"A little, yes."

"Can you tell me what you *do* remember?"

"You mean, how he died? Is that what you mean?" Kallick doesn't say anything. "I don't know that. I swear I don't. As far as I know he drowned, just like they said."

"Tell me whatever you can. Anything." Kallick reaches across the table and touches my hand. His hand is warm and smooth, and somehow comforting. "Anything at all, Frau Pelletier."

"I remember his hand," I offer.

"His hand?"

"Yes. The day he cut it. I did give him some bandages. Just like it says there."

I pause and he says, "Please. Go on."

"It was a long time ago and I don't remember that much. I really don't."

"I understand."

"Where do you want me to start?"

"Wherever you would like, Frau Pelletier."

"I remember the blood, when he cut his hand. Pop Flynn took him back to the infirmary. He was bleeding pretty good. When you're a kid you remember blood. Blood sticks in your mind. A power saw had raked him along the palm, just like he'd written there. They'd just started the prisoners using power saws, hoping to increase cord production. Is that the sort of thing you wanted to hear?"

"*Ja*," Kallick says. "Tell me everything you know. Don't leave anything out. No matter how insignificant it might seem. I want to know what his last days were like here."

Kallick sits back in his seat, folds his hands across his large stomach, and listens as I tell him what I remember about his brother.

18

I'D BEEN WORKING at the camp for a few weeks as a cookee. The prisoners still weren't producing as much as the mill bosses wanted, so they started them in using power saws. My father was against it. He thought it was dangerous, that somebody would get hurt. Not that he loved Germans, mind you. Nobody around here did. But my father always took care of the men who worked for him. The mills, though, needed more pulp and decided to risk the prisoners to get it. They thought, so what if a few Germans got hurt? You got to understand, people figured they—you people—had started the war. Whatever happened was your responsibility. I'm not saying that was right. Just that it was how a lot of people saw it.

Your brother wasn't the only one got hurt. Several prisoners got cut up pretty bad in accidents. A few lost fingers. The day your brother was hurt, Pop and I had just arrived at the cutting site. We were getting ready to set up for lunch when your brother came walking across the yarding area up to our truck, his hand covered in a bloody rag.

He said something like, "I am to go back to the clinic with you." I recognized him. I'd seen him before a few times. He was the interpreter for my father's crew; he spoke good English. I didn't know his name. In fact, I never knew his name—not then, not even later after he escaped. He was just the interpreter. A tall, skinny kid, with dark curly hair. He didn't look much like that picture you showed me. Except for maybe his eyes.

Pop told him he'd bring him back after lunch. I said to Pop it looked like he was bleeding pretty good, that maybe we ought to bring him back now.

"He can just hold his horses. I ain't gonna make two trips for any goddamn kraut."

Your brother just stood there, uncomplaining, as we started to set up for lunch. The rag around his hand was completely soaked with blood, and he was holding his hand up in the air to keep it from bleeding more. His face was pale and he didn't look too good. He looked like he was going to pass out. So I went over to the truck and got the first-aid kit from the glove compartment. I took out a role of gauze and some tape, and went over to him. I told him to sit down and I unwrapped his hand. It was cut pretty bad. There was a lot of blood. I could see the muscles and tendons when he moved his fingers. I wrapped his hand in gauze, then put some tape around it. But it was still bleeding. He needed stitches.

Ambroise came by in a few minutes. "How come he's still here," he said to Pop.

"I figure I'd take him back after I finish lunch," Pop replied.

"Just leave everything and take him back now."

"Ambroise, that means I'll have to make two trips."

"Then make two trips. He's cut bad."

"What about lunch?"

"Libby can set up. I'll have one of the prisoners give her a hand."

My father took care of his crew. He was always fair to the men who worked for him. Ask anybody around here, they'll tell you Ambroise Pelletier was always fair.

We didn't see your brother for a couple of days after that. The next time we did, Ambroise told us he'd be helping us for a few days, until his hand had mended enough to go back to work. He rode in back of the pickup truck as we drove from the camp to the woods. Except for a few words, we didn't do much talking to him. We weren't supposed to. Besides, your brother was quiet. Pop told him what to do and he did it. He was a good worker, I'll say that for him. You only had to tell him once to do something and he understood. And he never complained, not about his hand or riding in back or the flies or the heat. If Pop told him to lug a kettle of soup a half mile into the woods for his fellow prisoners, he did it, and with only one good hand, too. Not that it would've done much good to complain, but still he seemed to accept things the way they were.

One day while we were coming back from the woods, it started to rain. Pretty soon it turned into a downpour. I looked out the window and saw him back there, soaked to the bone.

"You think he could come up here?" I asked Pop.

I thought he would say no but he let him.

"Thank you," your brother said. He was very polite. I remember sitting in the middle, shoved way over toward Pop, straddling the shifter with my knees.

"Where'd you learn to sprechen so good," Pop asked him.

"I studied in England," the interpreter replied.

"I was over there in 1918, after the war."

I remember Pop asking him things about the war, about Rommel. What it was like to live under Hitler and what he was going to do when it was over. Things like that. From then on, he rode up front with us.

Your brother didn't work with us very long, though. A few days, maybe a week. I don't recall exactly. I do remember, though, that before he rejoined his own yarding crew, something happened. There was a fight between two prisoners. It was right after lunch. We were cleaning up, putting things back into the truck when it broke out. Two Germans were hitting each other. They were rolling around on the ground, punching and kicking and grunting. One finally pinned the other and was striking him in the face. The rest of the prisoners were standing around cheering. The guards just stood by, letting them fight. My father came up and told the guards to break it up, somebody would get hurt and he'd be short a cutter. I remember they told him they would in a minute. They said, "Let the krauts get it out of their system, Mr. Pelletier." After a while the winner stopped hitting the other prisoner and let him up. The one who'd lost had a bloody face and got up slowly, swearing in German.

In the truck riding back to the camp afterwards, Pop asked your brother what that was about.

"Oh, the same old thing," he said, taking out a pack of cigarettes. He reached across me and offered one to Pop.

"Danke. What do you mean?" Pop asked, taking the cigarette. He held the steering wheel in place with the stump of his left arm.

"Even here they run things."

"Who's they?" Pop asked.

"The Nazis?"

"That's what they were fighting about?"

"Sort of. It's more complicated than that."

"I thought all you boys were fighting for the Fatherland."

"Some more so than others." Your brother took a drag on his cigarette and glanced out the window. "I am a German. I fought for my country. But I am not a Nazi. The Nazis here are only a few. But they are strong. Just like at home."

I listened closely. I had never known there was a difference. I thought, like most people in town, that one German was like the next. They were all Nazis. They were all terrible and all of them were our enemies. But this one was saying there was a difference.

"Why don't you go to the CO?" Pop asked.

"If you go to the authorities you had better watch your back. Besides, Major Ryker may even prefer the Nazis."

"You're kidding?" said Pop.

"It's true. In the camp in Africa the British commander preferred dealing with them. They didn't allow complaints and they kept their troops in line. It made it easier for the British. If you speak out, you're called a troublemaker. Nazis do not cause any trouble. They are very good at following orders."

"That's a hell of a thing," Pop said. Your brother fell silent, looked out the window.

When his hand was better, he went back to working with his own yarding crew. I would see him from time to time. When he would go through the chow line, he might smile at me and say, "Good day, Fräulein," or "How are you today, Fräulein?" I'd return the hello or give him an extra apple or cookie, but that was all. We weren't sup-

posed to talk to the Germans. You could get in trouble for that. I was only being friendly. That was all.

In late August one of the Germans died. I never knew much about it. An accident, we'd heard. A tree had fallen and killed a man named Oswald. He had been my father's right-hand man. I had to go along as we drove him to the infirmary, but he died before we got there. It was some time after that when we began to hear things. Rumors. That maybe it wasn't an accident. Like your brother said, I guess there were some problems at the camp, though what the Germans did to each other wasn't of much concern to most people—just as long as they cut the wood. But the paper company had increased the cord quota and the POWs began to grumble. They went on a work strike. There was some fighting, some problems with the men. I could see it on their faces.

A few months afterwards, I was in Abbey's, that was the general store in Sheshuncook, a little ways down the road from the camp. I was back in school then, so I didn't have much to do with the camp anymore. What I heard was what everybody heard. On this day a camp guard was talking to some of the locals there. They were discussing how the Germans were taking their sweet time, not even trying to reach the new cord quota, even though Major Ryker, the commanding officer, had begun to crack down. He was making them work on Sundays and was punishing slackers by placing them in the guardhouse on restricted diet.

"I don't know though," said the guard. "They're damned if they do and they're damned if they don't."

"What're you talking about?" asked Charlie Abbey, the store's owner.

"Well, you make quota and you're sticking your neck out."

"How's that?"

"After what happened, I'd rather eat bread in the guardhouse than have a tree fall on me."

It took me a moment to realize they were talking about the prisoner named Oswald. He'd died more than two months before, but it was the first time I'd heard anything about it not being an accident. He'd been a good worker for the Americans, and maybe, I began to think, the others had held that against him.

When the snows came that December the company started hauling off the wood they'd cut the previous summer and fall, dragging it by sled and then by truck to the mills. Because they'd fallen behind their production schedule, they had to work on Christmas. I remember going to work that day because my father needed me and my brother Leon to help out. Jurgen, the cook for the prisoners, had prepared this special lunch for the men, and my brother and I helped Pop bring it out to them. It was brutally cold that day, with the wind blowing hard. It was so cold the men didn't even sit down but ate their meals squatting beside fires they had made in the snow.

By midafternoon even though we hadn't reached our cord quota, Ambroise had the men knock off work. He worried about them getting frostbite. So we packed up and the prisoners were loaded into their truck and driven back to camp. When we got to the gates, however, I could see something was wrong. The men were unloaded and counted as they always were, but they weren't allowed to go through the gates and back to their barracks. The guards were talking among themselves. Pop and my brother and I watched them from the truck, wondering what was going on.

Pretty soon Major Ryker came down the road from the staff house in a jeep. The prisoners were made to form ranks and the major got out and addressed them. We rolled down our windows so we could hear what was going on.

"I have just received word," he began, pausing so your brother could turn his words into German, "that someone has played a little joke on us. A swastika was spotted hanging from a tree near the road over in Pittston Farm. I don't think that is particularly funny. We are still at war, and you men are still prisoners of that war. My prisoners. You must obey rules here just like you would in your own army. I would like those responsible to come forward and admit their guilt."

Major Ryker was a small man with a worm-thin mustache and glasses. He stood with his hands behind his back, like a teacher waiting for a student who had misbehaved to come forward. However, none of them did. They all remained silent, standing in formation.

"I have already placed some of you in the guardhouse on reduced rations. So you know I mean business. This is Christmas. I don't want to have to punish all of you for the actions of a few. But so help me, I will," Ryker said, his face turning red. "If you think I'm kidding, you are sorely mistaken. Those who are guilty had better step forward, right now, or you'll wish you'd never been taken prisoner. This is your last chance."

Still nothing.

"All right, that's the way you want it. Sergeant Moore, take these men back out to the work site and have them cut that damn thing down. Then burn it."

"All right," said the sergeant, "let's get back on the truck."

"No!" commanded Major Ryker. "These men have plenty of energy to be climbing trees. They can walk."

"Walk, Major?" asked the sergeant.

"Yes. They could use the exercise."

"But it's eight miles out there, Major. One way."

"A brisk walk on this fine Christmas night will do them good. Besides, it'll give them a chance to think about what they did. And whether it was worth it to keep their mouths shut to protect those responsible."

"But it's—"

"Sergeant. That's an order."

"All right," the sergeant yelled. "You heard the major. Let's get moving. Schnell."

The prisoners, grumbling and exchanging looks with one another, started marching up the road away from camp. The Americans got in their jeeps and followed. It was getting dark already, and we could see the men trudging along in the headlights of the jeeps.

One night in March I remember Ambroise coming home very late from work. My brother had gone with him after school that day, and both came in cold and wet.

"Where have you been?" I asked.

"One of those sons of bitches took off," Ambroise said.

"Took off?" I asked.

"Escaped," my father replied. "We were out looking for him with the soldiers."

There was no work the next day as my father and his crew went out again to help look for the escaped prisoner. I saw jeeps driving up and down the road in the village, and soldiers on transport trucks going out to scour the woods. More soldiers from the base over in Houlton came to help in the search. They even brought in a couple of professional trackers, men who made a living hunting bear in these woods, to look for him. Yet the snow was hard, with a crust on it, and they weren't able to follow his tracks. The dogs supposedly had picked up his scent not far from where he'd run off into the woods, but they soon lost it again. That's what I heard anyway. They searched for days and then gave up. I guess they figured he'd either come in on his own or he'd die out there.

After a while things quieted down. You heard less and less about the escape. By May the war in Europe was over. Then when the ice melted off the lake, somebody found him. A couple of fishermen. From the camp we'd heard the same thing you'd heard: that they were calling it a drowning. The funeral took place on a bright, windy day in May, with the trees just beginning to bud and the smell of lilacs and witch hazel in the air. I stood on the steps of Abbey's store and watched them march by just as they had for the other prisoner, Oswald, nearly a year before. They wore clean uniforms, some with their medals gleaming and their boots polished.

"That's the last thing I remember," I say to Kallick. "Your brother's funeral. The rest is just a blur. Forty-six years is a long time. I'm surprised I remember that much."

When I stop talking, I feel that hot bubble behind my sternum rise into my throat and seem to burst and go out of me. I look across at Wolfgang Kallick. He is holding his brother's diary. He doesn't say anything for a while. His eyes have filled with tears, and suddenly I feel his pain, too.

"You saw my brother's funeral?" he asks finally.

"Yes."

"Did you see where they buried him?"

"I wasn't there at the cemetery when they buried him. But I saw his stone later on."

"Could you show me where it is?"

"It's not there anymore."

"What do you mean?"

"Someone stole it. All the German stones, in fact. Souvenirs, I imagine."

"I see," says Kallick, wiping his eyes with the back of his hand. "You never heard anything else?"

"Like what?"

"Were there any other rumors around the camp? About his death?"

"Nothing you'd place any stock in."

"Do you think he drowned, Frau Pelletier?"

"People drown in Moosehead Lake all the time, Mr. Kallick. People who should know better, too. It's a big lake, and it can be dangerous."

"Did you ever hear anything about the problems with the Nazis?"

"Only what I already told you."

"May I read something to you, Frau Pelletier?"

"We should get going. It's late."

"Just one moment. Please."

"Well, all right. Then we have to go."

Wolfgang Kallick reads with his eyes just inches from the page and his finger trying to follow where his brother's words may lead him.

30 August 44: Bad news today. Oswald Grutzmacher was killed. Had been cutting in a muddy area when struck by a tree. Took fifteen minutes to get the poor devil out, by then it was too late. Carried his body to the truck and then transported him to the clinic, but it was too late. Not much we could do. Bleeding from ears and mouth. Chest crushed. Was coughing up blood. Burial tomorrow.

Though can't say I was fond of Grutzmacher kept thinking about how terrible it would be to die and be buried so far from home. Tragic to think that my end would come here, in these woods, half a world away.

31 August 44: This morning we buried Grutzmacher. Gray skies. Cold rain continues. Guards marched us out of camp on the dirt road to the north. The people stared at us like freaks in a sideshow. Stopped at a small, old cemetery we have passed many times on our way to the woods. It sits beside a narrow, slow-moving river. Quiet and peaceful. Willow tree hangs over the water, and wildflowers and ferns grow alongside the road. Grutzmacher, a farmboy, would like it, I tell myself.

Not all, however, are saddened by the accident. Later on in the woods, R took me aside. "The son of a bitch only got what he deserved, Kallick." R said it wasn't healthy to get too chummy with the Amis. Afterwards heard the Feldwebel and some of his thugs talking as we were being driven back to camp. "So Kallick, are you with us or not?" I turned away and looked out at the woods.

Wolfgang Kallick stops, raises one plump finger to tell me he's not quite finished. He licks his lips, the way a man would who'd come across a desert, then turns many pages ahead in the diary, searching for something.

16 January 45: Camp clearly divided now. There are those who hope for a return to the old order and those busy for the new. And then there are the rest of us—the ones who know the old is lost but have no idea what the new will be like. Fights have broken out and people who have even the slightest doubt about our final victory are called traitors of the Fatherland. K and his bunch of hoodlums bully everyone into believing we can still win. Bad times lie ahead, I fear. Yet with von Rundstedt's defeat reasonable men can no longer hold out any prospect of victory. In a strange way this may be good news. Might hasten the end and bring us home that much sooner.

6 February 45: Have just received news about Belgium today. The Amis responded immediately by cutting our ration of meat to four ounces every third day, and no beer, candy, or cigarettes can be purchased in the canteen until further notice. Big fight broke out over dinner tonight. R got up and gave a toast to the SS responsible for the shootings. Called them heroes who had the courage to defend the Fatherland at any cost. Said we must be prepared to "die in our tracks" as the Führer requested. Words were exchanged. Soon somebody threw a punch and the entire mess hall erupted in violence. Guards came in with clubs. Three men taken to the hospital, and one, Karl Schmidt, may have a fractured skull. Lagerführer Heydt has blamed the Amis and is lodging another formal complaint, though it does little good. The Amis say we started the fight. Can't say where all this will lead. Or whether their side or our own now poses the greatest danger to us.

When Kallick finishes reading this time, he closes the book and puts it back in his briefcase.

"You think it was them? You think the Nazis killed your brother?"

"I think it's a possibility. Anyone who spoke out was in danger. Herr Wattenberg told me they ran the place."

"Did he think it was them?"

"Yes. But I have stopped believing I'll ever know the truth."

On the ride back to Frannie's Cabins, we talk about his having to get up early to drive down to Boston in the morning. He has an afternoon flight and he wonders how long a drive it will be and what sort of condition the roads will be in.

We pull into Frannie's driveway. Before he gets out of the truck, he reaches over and shakes my hand.

"Thank you, Frau Pelletier. For all your help."

"You're welcome," I say. "I only wish I could've helped you more. What are you going to do now?"

"Go to bed."

"I mean, about your brother?"

"Oh," says Kallick. "I will have to see. It has been so long. And as you yourself said, what difference will it make now?"

"But I understand," I say. "How you had to find out. At least try." I glance at the wedding band on his finger. "Do you have a family waiting for you back in Germany, Mr. Kallick?"

"No. My wife died twelve years ago. We had no children."

"And your brother? Was he married?"

"A girlfriend. They had talked about getting married after the war. But she died in the bombing. Good-bye, Frau Pelletier."

"Good-bye," I say. "And good luck."

Then he shuts the door and I pull out of the driveway and head for home. I roll down the window a crack. The sharp night air feels good. It cuts over me, peeling away something like dead skin.

When I get home finally it's close to midnight. I park the truck in the barn and walk up to the house. The packed snow makes a grinding sound under my boots. I pause halfway to the house, glance up at the sky. The single red light of a plane moves slowly from west to east. Probably headed for the airport over in Millinocket. For some reason I think of Frank Cobb. I haven't thought about him in ages, but I can picture his red hair and those pale lashes, his smile that brought down your guard. I wonder what he's doing now, if he settled down out in Arizona, got married. Maybe he takes his wife up in his plane and shows her how small their lives really are.

Then the plane is out of sight, the sky is dark again, and I continue walking to the house. As I get close I see that Mitzi has gotten free from her chain and is curled up at the top of the stairs. In the weak porch light I see her waiting for me on the landing in front of the door. Her head is resting contritely on her paws and I can only guess what mischief she's been up to with Connie's dog.

"Hello, old girl," I say, glad to see her there. She doesn't lift her head though, doesn't so much as whimper. "What's—?" But I stop in midsentence as my head comes level with hers. Her eyes are closed tight and her brownish muzzle is covered with something dark and wet looking. For a moment I try to tell myself it's the blood of a deer. That's all. Then I see it. Between the middle of her closed eyes is a hole I could stick my thumb in. The landing is black with a pool of blood rapidly starting to freeze. In this light it looks the color of liver. I put my fingertips to the spot between Mitzi's eyes. My fingers come away with blood, cool, greasy to the touch.

"Jesus," I say, my own blood turning to ice. "Sweet Jesus."

I sit on the top step, cradle her head on my lap, and begin to cry. I cry for her. For Leon. For Kallick's brother. I cry for them all.

Part 3

Part 3

19

A FEW DAYS later, the first of April. April Fools' Day. Sunny out and warm enough so I just have my down vest on. Winter is slowly, stubbornly giving ground. I thought spring would never come this year, thought maybe they'd forgotten about it. On the tin roof of the barn steam rises from the melting snow, and water drips down, splattering along the foundation. Across the road, along the shore are sections of black ice, water bleeding through the snow. North of here, where the Roach River meets Spencer Bay, they already had a jeep go through. Some kids screwing around—lucky nobody was hurt. And Harve Michaud is telling fishermen not to build fires on the lake when they're ice fishing. The ground in back of the barn, where the sun strikes directly all day, is softer. It's still frozen deeper down, but at least now the backhoe can cut through it.

I'm up in the seat of the Case, working the levers. The tractor is old. I've had to have the hydraulic system worked on, but it still runs pretty good. I raise the backhoe and then ram its teeth into the ground. The work is slow going. I chip away at the earth, breaking off piece by stubborn piece. Sometimes a chunk as large as a cinder block comes free from the solid ground and tumbles into the hole I've made. Other times I shiver as the steel runs head-on into a large rock. Each time the teeth take a bite out of the earth I can feel the impact up in my shoulders. Like somebody grabbing you and shaking you roughly out of a sound sleep.

When the hole is deep enough—a couple feet, I figure, ought to be plenty—I lift the supports, put the tractor in gear and drive around to the front of the barn. I lower the bucket and climb down. Over near a pair of rusting engine heads sits the fifty-gallon drum. I grab ahold of it and lower it gently on its side, and begin to roll it toward the bucket. It's heavy, much heavier than I'd have thought. With each revolution I hear a dull thud resounding inside the drum—*pluff . . . pluff*—as if your heart had torn itself loose and was flopping around inside your chest. It reminds me of the other day, sitting in the Spruce Goose, listening to that guy fill the drum up with sand. I roll the drum into the bucket, then get back up in the seat of the tractor. I tip the bucket so the drum won't roll out and raise it off the ground. I back the tractor up, then drive around to the hole.

Only after I try it do I realize the drum won't fit, it's too high by a good six inches. I consider taking Mitzi out and burying her without it. When I put her in the drum the other day I didn't know what else to do. But I think of coyotes and wild dogs getting at her. I don't like the idea of seeing her now, though, hard and stiff as a board. That hole in the middle of her head, too. I don't think I could take that. I decide to dig deeper so the drum will fit. I raise the bucket and then slam the teeth deeper into the earth. I do it again and again and again, making room for one more. *You must have room for one more?* I pull the throttle way back and the old Case strains, coughing black diesel smoke, sputtering. I pound away at the earth. *Bang . . . bang . . . bang.* It's like I'm trying to break the earth, crack it open to see what's hidden inside. If somebody pulled into the parking lot now and saw this wild old lady working a backhoe like this, he'd probably think he was watching someone who'd lost her marbles. And maybe I have, I don't know. Funny, but I feel almost that it's not me doing this, acting this way, but somebody else. This other woman I don't even know, this stranger, and I'm just watching her. That's the way it feels.

Finally the hole looks deep enough. With the bucket I nudge

the drum sideways. There's hardly a sound, the fit is so snug. I don't even hear the thud inside. Then I cover it with the frozen blocks of dirt, blocks that will melt and become earth again in just a few more weeks. For now, however, the break in the ground looks ragged, ugly. With the backhoe curled into itself like a mighty fist, I punch the blocks down, crushing them, pulverizing them, trying to make it look as if nothing's happened here. I don't say anything, no prayers, because dogs, I know, are lucky enough not to be burdened with souls. They owe nothing, rest peacefully in the ground like stones.

Once finished, I go inside and wash my hands. I make myself some tea and try to calm down. Take it easy, I say. I've spent the past few days trying to figure out what I should do. Like a fool I even tried to tell myself Mitzi's death might have had nothing to do with it. Maybe it was just some kids screwing around with a gun. Maybe some hunter who didn't like her running deer. Maybe . . . But who was I trying to kid? I was afraid, that's what it was. Afraid for my own neck. Afraid to end up in the ground, too. It wasn't any accident, I know. Not Mitzi, not that German boy either. And not Leon. It's all mixed up together, all connected somehow. And that man who's been calling, he's in the middle of it. Now I'm in it, too. In up to my neck, whether I like it or not.

I go over and look up the number, call the police station. When a woman dispatcher answers, I ask to speak to Chief Chambers. She puts me on hold. I find myself listening to somebody singing about a power lineman.

"Hello, Libby," Chief Chambers says after a while. "What can I do for you?"

I take a deep breath. "Somebody shot my dog."

"Jesus. Was it an accident?"

"Wasn't an accident," I explain. "He shot her right between the eyes and left her on my doorstep."

"You said *he*. Do you know who did it?"

"No. Well, I don't know his name. But I think I might've talked to him on the phone."

"You spoke to him?"

"Yes. He called me a couple of times."

"Did he threaten to kill your dog?"

Through the window, I can see the patch of broken ground behind the barn. The edges are ragged and the snow around it is dirty. It looks like a badly stitched rip in a white tablecloth.

"No," I say. "Not in so many words."

"What makes you think he was the one, then?"

"He . . . he threatened me."

"He threatened *you*?" Chief Chambers asks.

"Yes."

"How?"

I pause for a moment, wondering how to explain it, where I should start. "Remember I told you the night my brother went into town somebody called him. It was him. It was the same man."

"How do you know?"

"I recognized his voice," I say. "I'd recognize that voice anywhere."

"Why'd he threaten you?"

"I don't know."

"You don't have any idea? What did he say to you?"

"That I should keep my nose out of it."

"Out of what?"

"That's just it. I'm not real sure. Something to do with my brother, I think. Something that happened a long time ago."

"And you don't know what that was?"

I consider telling him how the man had told me to stay away from Wolfgang Kallick. But if I tell him that I'll have to tell him the rest of it, too. About the German and that night and the thing I've never really wanted to admit to myself, let alone anybody else: that perhaps the German's death *wasn't* accidental, and perhaps those men standing outside that night knew something about it. That Ambroise and Leon knew something, too, something they never wanted to talk about and something I was too afraid to want to know. I'd have to tell him that, too. So I say only, "Leon never told me anything about it." Which is the truth.

"This man, he thought you knew, though? Whatever it was?"

"I guess so. That's the only thing I can think of."

"And you think that's why he killed your dog? To threaten you?"

"I imagine so."

"You don't have any idea who it could be?"

"No." I pause before saying, "Chief Chambers?"

"Yeah?"

"How would we go about having an autopsy done on my brother?"

"That's a big step, Libby. We'd have to get a court order. Have the body exhumed, then shipped down to the medical examiner's. We'd have to have a pretty good reason. Doc Proulx signed the death certificate as being accidental. We have no evidence of it being anything else."

"What about the fact I was threatened? And how about my dog? Isn't that evidence?"

"We'd need more of a reason than somebody shooting your dog to go exhuming a body. The people down in Augusta will want some hard evidence. Is there anything else you can tell me?"

"No," I say. Then, "Wait, there is one thing. Leon took a gun with him to meet that man in town."

"He took a gun?"

"Yes. I had a gun upstairs in the strongbox. A Luger. And after Leon left here it was gone. He had to have taken it."

"We didn't find anything on him."

"I don't know about that. I just know he took it."

"Why do you think he took a gun with him, Libby?"

"I guess because he thought he needed one."

"Why didn't you tell me about the gun before?"

"I didn't find it missing until after the funeral."

"He could've hocked it for money. He could've sold it to this man he was meeting. Maybe that's why we didn't find it on him."

"Chief, the gun was sitting in the box where I keep the store's receipts. If he wanted money there was a couple hundred dollars there. He just took the gun."

"Tell you what, Libby. Whyn't you come in and fill out a complaint about the dog. And we can talk about the rest of it. We don't want to go off half-cocked. In the meantime, if you're worried about this guy, maybe you can have somebody stay with you for a few days."

"I'll be all right."

"I can have one of my men take a ride out there. Check up on you."

"I'd appreciate that."

I'm heading into town to see Chief Chambers when the truck makes a funny noise. There's a cloud of blue-gray smoke in the rearview, then the truck just dies on me. I coast to the side of the road, near Beaver Cove, and get out. The radiator is belching steam and the engine smells of burnt oil. *Damnit!* I get back in the truck and wait. After about twenty minutes who comes by in his Bronco but Harve Michaud.

"What's the matter, Lib?"

"Something's wrong with the engine."

"I'm heading into town. Hop in."

He drops me off at Hanson's garage. Billy Hanson goes out with his wrecker and tows my truck in.

"Hear that?" he says, as we stand in one of the bays of his garage and listen to the truck make this awful banging noise. It sounds like a bunch of marbles flopping around inside a dryer. In the other bay his son Ronny is working under the hood of a car. He's swearing bloody murder. Billy says, "You thrown a rod, Lib."

"Can you fix it?"

"Christ, you got over a hundred and fifty thousand on this thing. Don't you think it's time for a newer truck? I still got that Dodge. Give you a good deal."

"Can you fix this one?"

"Sure I can. But what do you want to sink that kind of money into a twenty-five-year-old truck for?"

"How much will it cost?"

"For a complete rebuilt? You oughta have a valve job while we're at it. I'd recommend it."

"Sure."

"Let's see. I'll need to send the heads out to be milled at Larson's, down in Monson. Parts and gaskets'll probably run you about five hundred. Figure that much, maybe more for labor. Whole shooting match you're looking at a grand. Give or take."

"That's a lot of money," I tell him.

"It's up to you, Libby."

"How long will it take?"

Billy wipes his nose with a greasy rag. "Depends if I can get the parts. If I can, a week. Ten days maybe. If not, who knows? I can give Crabtree's a call. They stock for these old small-block Fords."

"All right. Why don't you."

While Billy heads into the office to call on the parts, I watch his son Ronny as he works on the car. I can see the front—the bumper and grill—is smashed in, and the windshield on the driver's side has a head-sized crack in it. It looks like a spiderweb, with long fingers of broken glass fanning out from a solid center. Ronny, who's only nineteen or twenty, but already balding like his old man, is struggling to get the radiator free from where the grill has been caved in.

"Dirty son of a bitch," he curses.

"Somebody must have a headache," I say.

"Hey, Miss Pelletier," Ronny says, looking up. "Didn't see you standing there. Oh, yeah. A headache, all right."

"Somebody from town?"

"I don't know. It's a rental car."

"What happened?"

"Pop towed it in a couple of days ago. Guy ran off the road down near Caratunk. Near the river."

"Know who it was?"

"Naw. Ask Pop." Then Ronny goes back to work, swearing at the radiator.

I glance in the driver's window. There are shards of greenish glass on the dash and sprinkled over the seat like rock candy. I put my fingertips to the jagged glass of the windshield. I don't see any blood, though just touching it makes me wince. Then, while I'm waiting for Billy to return, I walk around to the back of the car. A Buick, I see. I look at the plates: Massachusetts. I tell myself there could be other red Buicks with Mass plates in town.

"Okay," says Billy, finally coming out of the office with a paper in his hand. "Looks like we're in business. They have the parts in stock. I'll have Ronny take a run down tomorrow and pick 'em up. Your lucky day, Lib."

"Yeah, my lucky day," I say.

"You gonna need a loaner?"

"I guess so."

"I got an Escort out back. Rent it to you cheap. Forty bucks, the whole week. Good on gas."

"What about that car?" I ask, pointing at the one his son is cursing.

"That's not mine to let you have." Then to his son he says, "For crissakes, Ronny. Don't fart around. Use the goddamn torch and cut the sonofabitch out."

"I can get it out," replies his son.

"I meant whose car is that?" I ask.

"Oh. It's a rental. Got a call on the radio the other morning. Some guy had run off 201. Would've ended up in the Kennebec 'cept a tree stopped him."

"Was he all right?"

"By the time I got out there, the ambulance had already taken him down to the hospital in Skowhegan. That's all I know."

"Somebody from town?" I ask.

"*Ronny*—use the goddamn torch," Billy yells at his son. "We got the water pump on Mrs. Shay's wagon. I promised her we'd have it today."

Ronny grumbles but walks over to the acetylene tank.

"Somebody from town?" I repeat.

"I don't know," Billy says. "You gonna want that Escort? I'll throw in a tank of gas."

"Sure. All right."

"Let me go get it, Lib."

As I wait, I look over at the red car again. Could it be his? Kallick's? I mean, what are the chances?

After I sign the papers and pay Billy for the week, I drive over to the police station. It takes some getting used to driving such a small car, and an automatic at that. I haven't driven an automatic in years. At the station I ask for the chief. The dispatcher, a young woman with frosted hair and plum-colored lipstick, says he got called out on an emergency. I tell her about Mitzi, and she has me fill out a complaint form.

"That's odd. We had another dog killed out near Little Squaw Mountain," the young woman says. She's reading a magazine. She doesn't look up. On the cover is a picture of Saddam Hussein. His dark eyes glower. He looks stern and forbidding. "Somebody poisoned it. You ask me that's really sick. What's wrong with people they got to go killing dogs."

I shrug. As I'm filling out the form I ask casually about the accident down in Caratunk.

"Oh, that. Some guy ran off the road," she says.

"Somebody local?" I ask.

"Naw."

"You wouldn't remember his name, would you?"

She shakes her head.

"It's kind of important," I say. "I might've known him."

"Just a minute." She puts down her magazine and goes over to a file cabinet. She comes back in a minute.

"Somebody named Wolfgang Kallick."

"Kallick," I say, feeling my stomach tighten with the news.

"Yeah. He was from Germany."

"You know how he's doing?"

She picks up the magazine again. "They had him listed in critical condition. That was yesterday."

"He gonna pull through?"

"I don't know."

"You know what happened?"

"Looks like he hit a patch of ice and went off the road. I don't know if I should be telling you all this."

I turn and leave the police station without finishing the complaint form.

She calls after me, "What about your dog?"

I hurry out to my Escort, get in, and head south for Skowhegan.

20

"Is HE GOING to be all right?" I ask a tall blond nurse with thick calves. We're in the intensive care unit of the Fairview Hospital in Skowhegan, and the nurse is checking Kallick's blood pressure. He lies in a narrow bed at one end of the ICU. A bandage covers the top half of his head, and he has several tubes sticking out of him. One, coming out of his mouth, is hooked to a respirator. With each pump his chest rises fitfully, hesitates for a moment, then collapses toward the bed again. Another tube sticks out of his nose while a third comes from somewhere under the covers, draining away this bloody yellowish fluid into a bag hanging over the bedside. His eyes are closed. One is black and blue, and badly swollen. I recall the smashed windshield in Hanson's garage.

"He's a little better," the nurse replies, without looking up from what she's doing. "Are you a relative?"

"No. Just a friend," I reply. "What's the matter with him?"

"You name it," she says, shaking her head. "He has a fractured skull. Plus a ruptured spleen, a lacerated liver, a compound fracture of his forearm. The big thing we're concerned with now, though, is the liver."

"Is he conscious?"

"He's in and out. He came out of the coma last night. But he's still a very sick man. Do you know if he has any family in Germany?"

"I don't think so."

"Any relatives or friends? Anybody we should contact?"

"No, I'm sorry, I wouldn't know. You see, I only met him a couple of weeks ago."

"I thought you said you were a friend?"

"More of an acquaintance really. Can I stay here?"

"For a little while."

"Is he conscious?"

"He's out of the coma. He's just sleeping now."

"Can he talk?"

"He uses a pad to write down what he wants. When he wakes up just don't tire him out."

After she finishes taking Kallick's blood pressure, she says, "I'll be back later."

I pull up a chair and sit next to his bed. I wait. I watch his chest rise and fall. For a long time I just sit there watching him. I'm not even sure why I came. Except that somebody ought to be here. He shouldn't be alone. I think how terrible it is that he came all the way over here looking for answers about his brother and he ends up like this. I think how one brother dying over here ought to be enough. We don't need another. I don't know why but I put my hand over his. It still feels warm. At my touch he slowly opens his one good eye, looks over at me.

"How are you?" I say.

He nods his head slightly. The effort seems to pain him. Then, with a glance, he indicates the bedside table. I see a small pad and a pencil.

"You want this?"

He nods again. I hand it to him. With his right hand—his left arm is in a cast—he opens the pad, lays it on the bed, writes something. When he taps the pencil point against the paper I know that he wants me to read what he's written.

I pick the pad up. There's only one word: *"Danke."*

"That's all right," I tell him. "Can I get you anything?"

He picks up the pencil again and writes something else. It says in shaky, almost illegible letters, "Ice." *Ice*, I think, wondering what he could mean by that. But then I see him run his tongue over his cracked lips.

"Is your mouth dry? You want some ice?" I ask.

He nods.

I go out to the main desk and ask for some ice. The tall blond nurse gets me some, plus a facecloth. I wet the cloth and wrap the ice with it. When I return, I begin to dab Kallick's parched lips. He sucks on the cloth. His one good eye follows me.

"How's that?"

I see him mouth the word *danke*.

"Is there anybody you want me to call? Back in Germany?"

He shakes his head.

"You sure? Any friends. People you work with. Anybody at all?"

His lips form the word *nein*.

"Is there anything else I can do for you? How about your flight? Should I call the airline?"

Kallick closes his eye. I take that to mean no. He seems to drift off someplace for a time. For a few seconds I think he's fallen back to sleep. His chest is lifted up and down without any effort on his part, as if he were a puppet and someone were pulling a string attached to his sternum.

"Well, I just wanted to see how you were," I offer. "I should get going so you can get some rest."

Yet as I make a move to leave, I feel his hand on my wrist, grabbing me. It makes me think of the way Leon grabbed, surprising me with his strength.

"Stay," he says, though no sound comes from his mouth. "Please."

"All right. For a little while then."

I dab his lips some more with the cloth. From my pocketbook I get out a tube of Chap Stick and coat his dry lips.

"Is that better?" I ask.

He nods.

"You're gonna be all right," I say.

He doesn't answer. He just stares at me.

"Do you remember the accident?" He stares at me blankly. "Do you remember that?"

He lifts his hand to his forehead, touches the bandage. He picks up his pencil again and writes something in German this time. It's hard to make it out but finally I decide it says, "*Was ist passiert?*"

"'What happened?' Don't you remember? You were driving on 201. You skidded off the road down near Caratunk. I guess you hit a tree. That's what I heard anyway."

He shakes his head.

"You don't remember? You must've been on your way to Boston. You were going to catch a flight home, back to Germany. Remember that?"

This time he nods.

"Well, you had an accident. Your car skidded off the road. I saw it in the garage and, believe me, you're lucky you're alive."

He shakes his head no. I can't tell whether he means he doesn't feel lucky or that he doesn't remember the accident.

"It'll come back to you, don't worry."

But he shakes his head again, this time so violently I'm afraid he's going to pull the tube out that connects him to the respirator, that he'll stop breathing.

"Take it easy," I say. "Don't get yourself all worked up."

He looks up at me, his eyes frantic. His hand finds my wrist again and he clings to me.

"What's the matter? Should I get the nurse?"

With a great deal of effort his lips come together, trying to form some words. But I don't understand what he's saying.

"What? What are you trying to tell me?"

He picks up the pencil. He hastily scribbles something down on the pad. I read it, but it's in German and I don't know what it says.

"What? I don't understand."

He makes another attempt. This time he writes the words in

English. He prints slowly, painstakingly, so I'll understand. When I pick up the pad, though, the writing is still unsteady, that of a boy in kindergarten. I can make out two words distinctly now: *no accident*.

"No accident?" I say.

He nods.

What is that supposed to mean? For a moment I wonder if he's confused. If, like Leon, he can't tell the difference between now and forty-six years ago. Does he mean that what happened to *him* wasn't an accident? Or what happened to *his brother* wasn't?

"What wasn't an accident?" I ask. "You mean what happened to you? Or your brother?"

But I look into his one eye and see that he's not confused at all, that he knows exactly what he's saying. And what he's saying is this: that *neither* was an accident. Not what happened to his brother, nor what happened to him. With his finger he calls me closer. I lean over, place my ear close to his mouth. I hear his lungs wheezing, hear him struggling to speak. I can smell his sour breath on me. Finally he says, "*Nein*," and I know what he's trying to tell me.

He closes his eye, exhausted, and his head sinks into the pillow. The blond nurse, now accompanied by a slender doctor wearing faded jeans and running shoes, comes into the room then.

"I'm sorry but you'll have to leave now," says the nurse.

"Okay." Then to Kallick I say, "I have to go now. But I'll be back. I promise." Without opening his eye, he nods. Before I leave, though, I lean over him once more, whisper in his ear, "I understand. I do. It's my business now, too." He doesn't move, and I'm not sure he's heard me.

It's midafternoon as I'm driving north on 201. The sun glints off the fast-moving Kennebec, swollen with spring thaws and sending huge ice floes crashing into one another. If you went in there you wouldn't have much of a chance. Wouldn't last five minutes. I feel this anger rising in me, pushing up from my belly. Enough is enough, I think. No more. It's gone on too long.

As I drive, I hear something faint, something way in the back of my mind. It starts out like the whisper of a lover. Like the wind blowing through the trees in autumn. Or like the faint sounds the mice make in the attic. But then it grows, it gets louder and louder until there's no denying it any longer: *Socatean Bay*, it says. And suddenly I remember what it was I had heard about Socatean Bay, and why that dream about the men standing out in the driveway has been coming to me lately.

I remember: Every few minutes going to the kitchen window and looking out, waiting for them to come home. It was already pretty late, past nine o'clock. It'd been dark for a couple of hours, winter darkness, the sort that drops down like a black wall right after supper. Ambroise sometimes would get home late, especially when he'd stop with some of the men for a few after work. Sometimes he wouldn't get home till midnight. I was used to that. But Leon was with him that night, a school night. And besides, it was a special night: Leon's birthday. I told Ambroise to get home early so we could celebrate. I'd made Leon a cake, chocolate with coconut frosting, with twelve candles waiting to be lit. I'd put on the top of the cake, *Happy Birthday, Leon.* For supper I'd made him all his favorites, too: I'd used some of our ration points to buy a canned ham at Abbey's, and some scalloped potatoes and creamed corn, canned pineapples. But with them being so late, the ham had gotten hard and dry in the oven and the potatoes had gathered a brown crust on them. So I finally had to take them out and set them on the counter, figuring I'd warm them up as soon as I saw them coming down the cove road.

In a box in my bedroom was the present I was going to give Leon—that sweater I'd knitted him. I was worried that it wouldn't fit him. Leon had gotten bigger that winter. He was still small for his age, but he'd grown three or four inches overnight, it seemed, and now I wondered if maybe the thing would be too small.

When it got to be nine-thirty and there was still no sign of them, I really started to get worried. It was very cold out and I thought maybe something had happened. An accident. A tractor slipping on the ice or a power saw ricocheting off a frozen tree and into a man's leg. Maybe a pile of logs breaking free. Or a limb snapping off and falling on somebody—the men called them widow makers. Things like that happened. Logging was a dangerous job, and when Ambroise would be late sometimes I couldn't help but worry. Where were they? I wondered. What was the matter?

I decided to put my hat and coat and boots on and head down to Abbey's to see if he'd heard anything. He had a phone. If anything was the matter, he might have heard about it. The night was bitter cold. As I passed Asa Shaw's place I could see across the cove all these spotlights on over at the POW camp. Something was the matter.

"Ambroise hasn't come home yet," I said to Charlie. "You heard anything?"

"No," replied the old man, his pitch black glass eye looking out the store's front window. "But something's up."

"What do you mean?"

"Christ, those soldier boys are going up and down this road like a bat out of hell. Something's going on."

"If you hear anything about Ambroise or my brother, you let me know, okay?"

"I sure will, Libby."

I went home and waited. Looking out the window, across the cove, I could now see the headlights of jeeps and army trucks. What was going on? I wondered. Where were they?

And I remember this: Close to eleven o'clock I heard the trucks pull up in the driveway. I'd dozed off in the parlor. I went to the kitchen window and looked out. I saw four or five trucks, their headlights piercing the darkness, men standing around. At first I thought they were soldiers, but then I saw the trucks were those of the men who worked for the paper company. There was Ambroise's Ford with its crumpled front fender. I felt relieved, though I still couldn't pick out Ambroise or Leon or any of the others, for that matter.

They stood out there for a long while in the dark. I could see their cigarettes glowing, their smoky breaths mingling with the exhaust of the trucks. Eight or ten men in all, huddled in a loose group, the way players huddled in a football game to plan out their next play. From the background light of the headlights I could make out that some of the men carried things. Axes and peaveys, and what looked like guns, too. And I could hear a howling, and then make out the pair of dogs in the bed of one of the trucks. They were baying, snapping at the air, sending out puffs of smoke. The men just stood there, huddled, smoking, waiting for something. From where I was I couldn't tell if they were talking or not. They might have been. I thought about opening the door and calling to them, but for some reason I didn't.

After a long while, two figures broke apart—Ambroise and Leon, I could tell—and walked up to the house, their boots making a grinding sound in the snow, a sound like a file being pulled through a saw's teeth. Then the other men got in their trucks and took off, heading around the cove toward Abbey's.

It was Leon who entered first, bringing a gust of cold air with him that froze my ankles. I remember feeling two emotions, one right on the heels of the other. Relieved that they were both all right, I called out, "Happy birthday, Leon." But right after that I caught the look on his face. He wasn't crying but it looked as if he had been, or still might. His eyes were red and watery, and the color was drained from his face.

"What's the matter?" I asked. "Where were you?"

"My feet hurt, Lib," Leon said, fighting back tears.

"What happened?"

"My feet are wet. I think I got frostbite."

"Go get those wet things off," I told him. "I'll heat some water."

I looked over at Ambroise then, who had his back to me and was stamping the snow off his feet in the mudroom off the kitchen.

"What's going on?" I asked. "How come you're so late? I was worried sick."

Ambroise was slow to turn around. Even before he said anything I could see that something had happened, something terrible. As with Leon, his face had paled and his gaze was tired and blunted with what I took at first to be anger. But the more I looked at him the more I realized it wasn't anger, at least not *just* anger. It took me a few minutes to decide what his look spoke of. Then it came to me: Ambroise, a man as hard as nails, now looked so vulnerable. The only time I'd seen him look like that was right after Ma had left.

"What happened?" I asked again. "Did somebody get hurt?"

Ambroise took his hat off, unzipped his jacket. He stared at me for a moment. He looked suddenly smaller and older too. He reminded me of Pepé Pelletier, right before he died of cancer in the hospital. The brittle look of his jaw and cheeks.

"One of those krauts took off," he said. "We were out looking for him."

"That's all?" I remember saying, relieved. "Nobody was hurt?"

Ambroise headed over to the cabinet over the icebox and got the fifth of whiskey down. He got a cup from the sink and sat at the kitchen table and started to drink. He stared at the birthday cake on the table as if it were something he'd never seen before— a piece of the moon or a dinosaur egg.

"You hungry?" I asked. "I made a ham."

"I ain't hungry," replied Ambroise. "I don't know about Leon."

I heated some water on the stove and filled up a pan. I put some Epsom salts in it and then went over to where Leon was sitting in the parlor in the dark.

"They hurt, Lib," he cried.

His naked toes were pink and raw looking, like small carrots.

"Here," I said. I kneeled on the floor and rubbed his feet.

Then I lifted up my shirt and put his toes against my belly to warm them. They were the coldest thing I'd ever felt. Colder than the coldest winter day up here. Colder even than when, years later, I would kiss Ambroise on the cheek as he lay in his coffin. Leon said he had lost the sensation of the toes of one foot, and I was afraid they were frostbitten.

Through the doorway, I could see Ambroise sitting at the table in the kitchen, facing away from us, toward the window, his suspenders cutting into his broad back. He was smoking a cigarette and drinking whiskey. The light from the kitchen fell through the doorway and spilled in a rectangle across the parlor floor.

"Where'd he escape?" I asked.

Neither of them said anything.

"My feet hurt, Lib," Leon said.

"Where?" I asked. For a moment I guess he thought I was asking where the German had escaped. He looked over at Ambroise. So I said, "Where do they hurt, Leon?"

"Both little toes. I can't feel them."

I took his feet from under my shirt, put them between my hands, and began to blow on them, rubbing them gently. Leon started to cry.

"It'll be all right," I said, but he kept on crying.

"Why on earth did you keep him out this long, Ambroise?" I called to him.

"He didn't say anything," my father replied. "How was I to know his feet hurt?"

"He's half frozen, for heaven's sakes. If he gets frostbite it'll be on your head."

"He'll be all right," Ambroise said. "Won't you, Leon?"

Leon looked down at his toes.

"You didn't need to bring him out on a night like this. And you didn't need to keep him so long."

"One of those bastards took off and I didn't have time to bring him back. We had to go looking for him. Didn't we, Leon?"

My brother continued looking down.

"Where'd he take off?" I asked again. Neither said anything. So I asked Leon.

My brother hesitated, looked over toward Ambroise.

"The bay," Leon whispered.

"Socatean Bay?" I said.

He nodded, looking over my shoulder toward Ambroise.

Then I heard Ambroise behind me, getting up from the table.

"What the hell you talking about, Leon?" he said. When I turned I saw him in the doorway, filling the parlor with darkness. He was looking down at Leon. "We weren't cutting nowhere near the bay. The sonofabitch took off along the North Branch. That's where we were cutting. My bet he's halfway to the border by now."

Leon kept staring at his toes. Then my father turned and headed down the hall to his bedroom. I heard him shut the door.

I said to my brother, "They'll be all right. And we'll have your birthday party tomorrow. All right, Leon?"

My brother didn't say another word about that night—not then, not the next day, not ever. Whatever had happened out in the woods that night, I was never to learn of it. Oh, I might have had my suspicions, my doubts. A lot of people around here did. But I was only a girl, and like a lot of people it seemed easier— *safer*—just to put the whole thing behind me. To forget about it, to say it had just been an escape and leave it at that. And why not? What was the point in dredging up the past?

21

IN TOWN I STOP at the library. Roberta Pike is sitting on the floor behind the main desk. All these catalog cards are spread out on the floor around her. She doesn't notice me right away, and when I look down on her I notice that her red hair is thinning. I can actually see her shiny white skull beneath. She's so tall normally I never see the top of her head.

"Hey, Libby," she says on seeing me. She quickly stands, fluffs up her hair.

"You owe me any books, Lib?" she asks.

"Not that I know of."

"I thought you owed me a quilting book."

"I brought that back a long time ago," I reply. "Listen, remember you said you had some old copies of the *Herald*."

"Yes. Down in the basement. Why?"

"Could I look at them?"

"You want to look at them *now*?"

"Sure, why not?"

"We close at four, Lib. It's almost three now."

"So I have an hour."

"It's a mess down there. I don't know that you'll have time to find what you're looking for."

"Would you show me where they are?"

Annoyed, she snorts through her nose, then says, "Suit yourself."

I follow Roberta's narrow hips and scratchy opaque nylons toward the back of the library, where she opens a door.

"Be careful," she says. "The stairs are pretty steep."

She turns on a light and we go down into the basement, which, not surprisingly, smells of moldy paper. We walk past old grade-school desks heavily carved with graffiti, maybe some I myself had once sat at, past metal bookshelves that hold cheap paperbacks and stacks of dusty 78s. Roberta turns on a forty-watt lightbulb hanging from the middle of the ceiling and then we continue on over to the wall. Against the wall is a large stack of newspapers. Some of the papers have spilled down onto the damp floor.

"Here they are. I warned you it's a mess."

"I don't mind."

"Any particular issues you looking for? Oh, that's right. You were interested in the POW camp."

"Yes," I say. "Around May 1945."

"Lord knows where that is. I keep saying I'm gonna get down here and straighten up."

Roberta doesn't make a move to head back upstairs, though.

"I'm not that busy right now," she says. "If you tell me what it is you're looking for maybe I could help."

"That's all right. Tell you the truth I'm not sure myself."

Her nose out of joint, Roberta says, "Well, just pick up after yourself. And remember we close at four." She turns and leaves me to the smell of rotting paper.

The light here isn't very good, so I scoop up an armful of newspapers and bring them over to one of the school desks nearer the light. I pick up the first issue and see a headline that says something about Eisenhower deciding to run in 1952 and the school board voting on a bond for a new roof for the high school. The next issue down has a front-page article about Henry Robotaille expanding his Ford dealership in town. The date is January 1951. Deeper in the pile I come across some 1950 issues—December, November, October—as if a pattern is forming. However, just as I'm getting close to September 1950, I run into an issue dated October 1964. On the front page is a picture of Police Chief Elton Bishop, a heavy, bulldog-faced man, receiving some award from the Maine Association of Police Chiefs.

I finish the pile, lug it back over to the wall, and pick up another. And when I finish that, another, and then another after that. All without any luck. The dates will sometimes get closer to 1945, but suddenly they veer off without warning and I find myself reading something about how the Piscataquis Lumberjacks basketball team beat the team from Millinocket for the 1961 state semifinals. There's no rhyme or reason to the piles. It seems as if somebody just dumped them here.

I take a cigarette out of my pocketbook and light it. In the corner, behind a metal shelf, I hear a faint scratching noise. A mouse? But then something dark scurries across the floor, something more substantial than a mouse, and hides beneath some boxes. I shiver. When I finish the cigarette, I crush it out on the floor and shove it beneath the desk with my toe so Roberta won't see it and give me hell.

I pick up another pile and begin hunting through it, occasionally recognizing a face or a name or recalling an event. There's Larry Bidwell standing in front of Bidwell's Furniture on Main Street after the big storm in 1949 damaged his place. Or the fire that burned down the Sheshuncook Inn up on the north side of the lake. They suspected arson. There's Tom Bevins smiling as he shakes the hand of Ed Desauliers, who he beat for the first select-man job in 1948. Ed Desauliers. The old man I spoke to in the nursing home. The man in the photo must be in his thirties, with a wide mouth and thin lips like a toad. I keep digging.

At last, near the bottom, I reach a pile whose top issue is dated September 1945. It says, "Japs Surrender Unconditionally!" I riffle through the first few issues and see that they go back in time, to August, then July. And when I lift the pile, trying to grab as much time as my arms can hold, I see the next issue down has a date of August 1944. *Here*, I think. *Whatever I'm looking for it has to be here.* I pick up the pile and bring it over to the desk. When I look at my hands, I find they are covered with this chalky white stuff. Its damp, sweetish odor makes me think of my mother's brand of talcum powder.

I start skimming through the pile of papers. Like that photo of Leon's, these pages are also brittle. Some crumble into fragments at my touch. And the chalky white dust, fine as bonemeal, makes the back of my throat burn. I see stories about the war, about men who were wounded and recovering in hospitals in the Philippines or England. Or about others coming home, or in some cases, not coming home: Charlie Tohay, killed in France, and Moxie Phipps, who died in the Pacific, and Harry Klatka's brother Will, who died in Italy. I keep turning the pages, hurriedly, knowing my time is running out, and still not sure what it is I'm looking for, what I hope to find here. In a June issue there's a story about the POW camp, about several prisoners taking extension classes from UMaine. There's a photo of some prisoners sitting at benches watching as a teacher writes something on a small blackboard. As I look at the picture I think I recognize one of them, a heavy man with baggy pouches under his eyes: Jurgen, the cook? It could be him.

I look at more issues. A picture on the bottom of the front page of the June 14th issue shows the dedication for a memorial for two East Forks boys who'd been killed in the war. The caption below the picture says, "A memorial was dedicated this week in East Forks for two young men killed in action, Cpl. Daniel Ross, 22, of Dug Hill Road, part of the 28th Field Artillery, and Pfc. Jacques 'Toots' Bellevance, 19, of Rt. 201, a radio operator for the 169th Infantry." I don't recognize the first name, but the last I know must be related to all those Bellevances over in East Forks. I glance at the picture. In it several people are standing around the stone slab. But I don't have much time, so I turn the page and keep reading, finding more stories about local soldier boys, about the war and death and people coming home.

I come finally to May. I try to recall if it was May that they found him. I think it was but I can't be certain. Late April or early May—that's usually when it's ice-out on the lake. I'm skimming along, trying to read in the poor light of the basement, when, at the bottom of the second page, *there it is.* It's a small article, only a few paragraphs. But I feel something metallic snap in the back of my head, like a trap clamping down on a leg, biting into flesh. The headline reads, "Autopsy Reveals Prisoner's Death a Drowning."

> After performing an autopsy on a body recovered from Moosehead Lake this past week, medical authorities have determined that the cause of death was drowning. The person, identified as Dieter Kallick, the German POW who escaped from the Sheshuncook camp this past March, is believed to have fallen through the ice after his escape attempt. According to authorities, Kallick died shortly after fleeing into the woods. This finding was based on the condition of the body. While the death is being labeled accidental, suicide could certainly figure as a motive, so said the army's medical spokesman, Captain Joseph Grantland. "He could have been lonely for family or distraught over the imminent defeat of his country. I've seen it happen before with POWs." A positive identification was supplied by . . .

I'm about to read on when I hear Roberta coming down the stairs. She stops halfway down and calls over to me, "Yoohoo. I need to have you come up now, Lib. I'm closing up shop."

"All right. Let me just put these back."

When she heads up, I tear out the article about the autopsy and stuff it into my pocketbook. I pick up the pile of papers and bring them over to the stack. I don't bother trying to straighten them out. Several papers spill onto the floor. As I'm picking them up, my eye falls on the photo I noticed before. The one where they were dedicating the memorial to the East Forks boys. As I glance at the people standing around the memorial, one face, a man's, catches my attention. He looks vaguely familiar, someone

I'd seen before, though I can't say where. I decide to rip it out, too, and slip it into my pocketbook. My hands are covered with that fine white powder.

Upstairs, I ask Roberta, "Has that man been back?"

"What man?"

"The one you said was interested in the POW camp."

"No," Roberta replies. "Just you."

"What did his voice sound like?"

"I told you already. He didn't have any accent."

"No, I mean, was his voice real rough. Like sandpaper."

"I don't know. I don't really remember. It was just a regular sort of voice. Did you find what you wanted?"

"No," I say. "I didn't."

When I leave the library I drive over to the nursing home. Inside, I ask the receptionist, a young girl with big front teeth, where I can find Ed Desauliers.

"Is he expecting you?" asks the girl, beginning to pick up the phone.

"That's all right," I say. "I want to surprise him."

"If he's not in physical therapy he should be in room thirteen. Halfway down on your left."

I walk the down the hall until I find room 13. There are two beds in the room. In one an old man is sleeping, snoring, his mouth open. Seated in a wheelchair looking out the window is another man. He has long white hair turning to yellow and he's staring out the window, out at the lake. A book is open and face-down on his lap. The only thing about him that tells me it's him is the wide, lipless mouth. He still looks like a toad, an old one, with liver spots all over his face.

"Mr. Desauliers," I say.

He looks away from the window. He stares up at me for a moment before saying, "They already had me up. I wanna just stay put for now."

"No, I don't work here, Mr. Desauliers. I'm Libby Pelletier."

His eyes, dull gray, the color of solder, narrow on me. His wide mouth parts but no words come out.

"I called you, remember? I asked you about—"

"I know what you were asking about. You were asking about the camp."

"That's right."

"I told you I don't remember anything," he says, turning and looking out the window again.

"I know," I say.

"I told you not to come here, too."

"I just want to ask you something, Mr. Desauliers."

"You listen to me, young lady. I don't know nothing about what went on up there."

"How about your brother?"

"I told you already, Beany didn't know nothing either."

"Who *would* know then?"

"I can't help you."

"Would Tom Weston?"

"I said, I can't help you." He picks up his book and pretends to read.

"How about somebody named Alf Mitchell? Would he know? Is he still alive?"

"I *told* you, I don't know what you're talking about. You can't come in here and start pestering people with your damn questions. I got a bad heart, you understand. Now if you don't get the hell out of here I'm gonna call somebody and have 'em throw you out."

"All right," I say. "I'm going."

At home I make myself a cup of tea and sit at the kitchen table upstairs. From my pocketbook I take out my cigarettes. As I do, I catch sight of the yellowed corner of one of the newspaper articles I ripped out of the *Herald*. I remove the one about the autopsy and lay it flat on the table. I smooth out the wrinkles, careful that I don't rip the fragile paper. I think how maybe, just maybe, this might be paper from wood that Ambroise cut. That those Germans cut, too. Wouldn't that be something? I start reading where I left off:

A positive identification was supplied by fellow inmates. The body was found by two out-of-state fishermen who were trolling off Hardscrabble Point in the Mt. Kineo section of the lake. Pete Davis of Manchester, New Hampshire, and Benny Russo, also of Manchester, found the body and reported it to the local authorities. They will share the $100 reward offered for information leading to the capture of the escaped prisoner.

Major Denton Ryker, commander of the Sheshuncook camp, said, "We regret this unfortunate accident, especially so close to the end of hostilities. But these men are still prisoners of war—a war, I might add, which they're responsible for starting." Major Ryker said the POW's family in Germany would be notified through official channels. The remains were interred with full military honors in the Sheshuncook cemetery. The case has been officially closed.

I think about what Spotty said. How Pop Flynn told him they'd found the body in Socatean Bay. And what Leon had said that night—that the logging crew had searched for the escaped German in the bay. I recall, too, how Ambroise had snapped at him when he said that. Leon was just a kid then, he could've been mistaken, I guess. But I know he wasn't. We used to fish the bay, and he knew where it was as well as anyone. Just a few miles from the camp. I think there are too many things that don't fit together, that don't make sense. How it was too cold that March to go through the ice. How the only way anybody would have known the German had gone through up in the bay would be if he was *there* when it had happened.

I go over to the counter, get the phone book, and look up Tom Weston's number. I dial, let it ring.

When he answers I say, "Hello, Tom. It's Libby Pelletier."

"Why, Libby, how are you?"

"I'm all right." In the background I can hear his dog yipping, as if, even through the phone lines, he can smell a stranger. "I wonder if you could help me with something, Tom?"

"Just name it."

"Alf Mitchell," I say.

"What about him?"

"Is he still alive?"

"I believe so."

"You know where I could find him?"

"Now what would you want with him?"

"Remember that picture I showed you the other day? The one with the paper-company men and the Germans?"

Tom coughs, clears his voice. "What about it?" he asks, a cool note of suspicion slipping into his voice.

"You said one of the men in the picture was a Mitchell."

"I wouldn't know about that."

"But you told me it was, Tom. You said it was Goose Mitchell."

"Did I? I forget. Christ, Lib, that was a long time ago."

"You said you recognized him."

"I might've been mistaken. My memory of those days ain't so hot anymore."

"Let me ask you this, then. Did his brother work up there, too? Alf Mitchell?"

"I don't remember."

"You don't remember, Tom? Or you don't *want* to remember?"

Tom coughs, but doesn't say anything.

"You know where I could find him?"

"Let me give you some advice, Lib. You stay away from Alf Mitchell. He's a mean son of a bitch. And crazy, too. All them Mitchells were a little touched."

"Is he still over in Jackman, Tom?"

"No."

"Do you know where I *could* find him?"

"If I tell you, you didn't hear it from me. You understand?"

"Sure."

"Last I heard he was over in Milan. Doing some trapping near Seboeis Lake. What do you want with him?"

"I think Leon and him might've been mixed up with something. Something that happened the night the German escaped."

"That's ancient history, Lib. Forget about it."

"I can't forget about it."

"Ain't gonna do nobody any good to go messing with that now."

"I don't think Leon died by accident, Tom."

Tom falls silent. I can hear the dog barking. I picture him scratching at that spot on the floor. Finally Tom says, "You don't?"

"No, I don't. I think he was killed. Maybe because of what he knew. Tom . . . do you know what happened? That night?"

"Nope."

"You don't have any idea?"

"I don't know what you're talking about."

"I think you do, Tom. I think you know something and you don't want to tell me."

"I did my job, Lib, and I kept my nose out of the other business."

"Tom . . . please."

"I gotta go."

"Wait . . . please . . . talk to me . . ."

"I was back at the maintenance shop that night. One of the tractors was having some problems. Whatever happened out there wasn't my concern."

"But something happened. Something *did* happen to that German boy, right?"

"I wouldn't know. Like I said, I wasn't there that night."

"But you know something, Tom. You do, don't you?"

Tom is quiet on the other end for three . . . four . . . five seconds. And it's in that silence that I know he *is* holding something back. I don't know if he was part of it or not, but I know he knows something.

"Please, Tom. It's been too long."

"There was a war going on. Things happened. I'm not saying they were right. They happened on both sides. But you can't change the past, Lib. The best you can do is just leave it alone."

"I tried, Tom. All these years I left it alone."

"Who do you think your nosing around's going to help?"

"My brother was killed for what he knew."

"I gotta go."

"Tom—"

"Take care of yourself," he says and hangs up.

When I get off the phone I go over to the table, sit down, and finish my tea. Outside, somewhere in the night I can hear the frenzied baying of a pack of dogs, the sort of noise they make when they're running deer. I think of Mitzi lying stiff in that barrel in the ground. And I think of Leon, too.

As I go to light another cigarette, I remember the other piece I tore out of the newspaper. I take it out of my pocketbook and look at it. It's a picture about a war memorial being dedicated over in East Forks, a town thirty miles southwest of here, over on the Kennebec. Not far from Caratunk, where Kallick ran off—was *run* off—the road. In the picture several people are standing around a squat granite slab with a plaque set in its middle. Two of the men have those VFW or American Legion caps on. I glance at the faces of the people. I never knew many folks from East Forks. Yet one face, a man's, makes me stop. Where have I seen him before?

I pick up the phone and call the operator. I ask if there's a listing for an Alf Mitchell, over in Milan. I know it's a long shot. But what do I have to lose?

"I have a listing for an Alford Mitchell," the woman says.

"Where is that?" I ask.

"On Brownville Road."

"That might be him."

She gives me the number. I go over and get the bottle of Fleishmann's and pour myself a strong drink before dialing the number. I need it. As the phone rings, I feel myself being pushed along by that powerful current, something as strong, as unstoppable as a spring flood. I couldn't stop now even if I wanted to. The phone's ring pierces my ear like a drill bit, sinking right into my brain.

"Yeah," says a man's voice on the other end.

I don't say anything. I just listen.

"Who's there?" he snaps. "Who is this?" The voice is scratchy, dry as that white newspaper dust.

"Is somebody there, for crissakes?"

I wait on the other end for a few more seconds, my heart pounding wildly inside my chest. Then I quietly replace the receiver.

22

TEN MILES SOUTH of town I take a left and drive east on Route 6. The sun's directly in my eyes. I see trucks filled with logs heading for the chip plant over in Milan, and just past Guilford, I get behind a farmer on a John Deere, hauling a cart filled with manure. The sour ammonia smell cleans out my sinuses.

In Milan I stop at a diner to buy a pack of cigarettes. While I'm there, I ask directions for Brownville Road. A pretty blond girl with a purple birthmark on her cheek tells me how to find it.

"What you want to do is head up this road about three miles," she explains. "You'll cross the railroad tracks, then start looking on your right for a sign. You gotta be real careful or you'll miss it."

I take out a cigarette, then realize I'm out of matches, that Roland probably borrowed my lighter.

"Here you go," the blond girl says, handing me a book of matches.

I head north, keeping the Pleasant River to my right. Just past the railroad crossing, just as the girl said I would, I spot a sign nailed to a spruce tree: BROWNVILLE RD. I turn right down this road, which is muddy and rutted from the spring thaws, hardly more than a tote road. I worry about getting the Escort stuck out here. I drive down this road, trying to avoid the deepest ruts, for about a mile.

I have no idea where it leads, or what I'll find at the end of it.

I just keep looking at the mailboxes or at signs tacked to trees, with names painted on them: Borrup, Hobbs, Bryant, LeCroix, Leadbetter, Roncourt. Pretty soon the road switches back, and right at the bend I see a hand-painted sign nailed to a tree: "A. MITCHELL." I turn down this drive, which is little more than an old tote road, overgrown with hemlocks and paper birch whose naked branches scrape against the side of the car. When the road forks I follow the power lines to the left, the only sign that someone lives down here. About a quarter mile down this road, the woods open up, "let in the daylight," as the loggers used to say. Sitting in the middle of a cleared area is an old yellow school bus that's been converted into someone's home. The windows have curtains over them and a stovepipe juts out of the back with smoke curling skyward. A blue Chevy pickup with a gun rack in the rear window sits in the driveway. Junk is scattered around the place: a car without any doors, a large console TV set with the picture tube smashed out, a mattress with its gray guts spilling out. Out in back of the bus is one of those satellite dishes, angled toward the light like the head of a sunflower plant.

I pull up and shut the car off. I wait there for a moment, resting my hands on the steering wheel to keep them still. Over near the bus is a wooden rack with animal skins hanging out to dry. One's a red fox, its bushy tail blowing in the wind. The others could be muskrat or otter. *What are you doing?* I ask myself. Why don't you just go to the police? Let them handle it. But it's on account of Ambroise and Leon, my wanting to protect them at all costs. That whatever part they played in the German's death, I don't want anyone to know. I feel I owe them that, feel that I need to protect them even in death. But I also owe it to Leon to find out the truth. To find out what happened to him.

When I glance up, the curtains move aside and I see a hawk-like face peek out momentarily. Then they close again. I get out and walk up to the bus.

I knock on the glass door, which is covered from the inside by a green army blanket so I can't see in. I can hear a TV on inside, loud, some sort of game show. My heart contracts, as if it were trying to get smaller and smaller, take up less room in my chest. After a while someone pulls back the blanket and works the handle that opens the door: It's as if I were a child waiting for the bus, and this man is the driver going to take me to school.

Though he's standing two steps above me, I can tell he's no taller than I am, but solid, with thick legs. Built like a badger. Maybe seventy, seventy-five years old, yet it's hard to tell because his skin is very windburned and deeply furrowed. He has several days' growth of gray beard. His eyes are black and greasy looking, like olives, and separated by a long, sharp nose. He's wearing a down vest stained with oil and something dark that could be blood, while an orange hunting cap sits on top of his head. He stares at me for a moment, his head cocked a little to one side so he has to look at me out of the corners of his black eyes. He appears surprised to see me, but he also has something I take to be a smile playing around the edges of his mouth, as if he's only half surprised. Maybe he's been expecting me.

"You Alford Mitchell?" I ask.

"Eyah."

"I'm—"

"I know who you are," he says. The same dry, hoarse voice, raspy, as if he'd gotten a fish bone stuck down there. "You're Ambroise Pelletier's kid. What you want?"

"To talk."

"What about?" he asks.

"Some things."

"I'm busy right now," he says. He coughs up some phlegm and spits it on the muddy ground beside my feet.

"I could go to the police," I threaten.

He turns his head momentarily to look at me directly, then tilts his head again and cups his hand behind his ear. "Come again?" he says.

"You want me to go to the police?"

Mitchell scratches his unshaven face. He stares at me for several long seconds. As I turn and make like I'm going to leave, he says, "Wait a second. Let's talk." I pause, glance up into the bus. Behind him I see wash hanging from a rope and I can smell something oily, like fish frying. I think of the dark hole in Mitzi's forehead, Kallick lying in the hospital bed, the gash over Leon's eye—do I really want to go into this man's home? Get back in the car and head out of here while I still have the chance, I think. But it's too late—I can't run. I've come here to find out about my brother and I won't leave until I do.

It's dark inside, even with all the windows. Most of the seats have been taken out and replaced by a bed, some crates, a compact refrigerator, a small black-and-white TV. *Jeopardy!* is on. A man who looks like he's wearing a toupee gets an answer wrong and a loud buzz sounds. In the back of the bus there's a small stove made out of an oil drum, with a pot simmering on it. Steam wafts upwards and with it a musky smell. Along one wall hang several skins curing on metal stretchers, and lying on a table is a half-skinned animal. It's too big for a muskrat, maybe an otter or a marten. The head and upper body are slick and naked—dull yellowish fat and pale flesh exposed. A spike's been driven through its lower jaw to hold its narrow head down to a wooden board beneath it. Beside the head lies a bloody straight razor.

"Sit there if you want," he says, pointing to an unmade bed.

"I'll stand," I reply.

"Suit yourself," says Mitchell.

He picks up the razor and begins to carefully cut away the skin from the flesh and peel it back, the way you would an orange. His hands move quickly, skillfully. There's no wasted motion. I look at his fingers, recalling what Roberta said about the man who was in the library. But his fingers are all there.

"Now what is it you wanted?" he asks.

I wonder where to begin, where to start. Finally I say, "It was you, wasn't it?"

"It was me, what?"

"That called those times?"

He doesn't answer, doesn't even look over at me. He just keeps methodically working the skin back.

"Why did you threaten me?"

"Threaten you? Now why would I want to do that?" he says, his scratchy voice as irritating on my nerves as a rusty nail being pulled out of a piece of wet wood.

"Was it on account of what my brother knew?"

"And what is it he knew?"

I don't say anything right away. I watch his hands. When he reaches the animal's hind paws he makes circular cuts just above the dewclaws. Then he pulls the pelt, inside out, completely away from the animal, which doesn't even look like an animal anymore. More like a piece of painted clay, something somebody had made to sell to tourists. Only the lusterless black-blue eyes and the pointy little teeth let you know that it once was alive.

"He knew about the German," I say.

"German?"

"You know what I'm talking about. The one from the camp." My heart is now as small and tight and cool as a clamshell in my chest. My knees feel rubbery. But I try not to let him see I'm afraid. "I know what happened." I try to bluff him.

"Is that a fact?"

"Yes," I say. "It is. So don't try to act like you don't know what I'm talking about. I know about everything. About the German prisoner, and how you ran Kallick off the road. And about my dog, too."

"Dog?" he says.

"I know you shot him, you son of a bitch."

"Don't know what you're talking about, lady."

"You're lying," I say.

Mitchell looks over at me. "You got a lot of piss and vinegar in you, I'll say that. Come in a man's home and call him a liar."

I pause for a moment, wondering how far I *can* go—how far I *should* go. It's the feeling you have when you go out onto ice and hear it begin to crack.

"Leon told me everything," I say, another lie. "What happened that night."

"He did, eh?" Mitchell says, seemingly without much interest. He inspects the hide, rubbing his greasy fingers over it. There are pieces of yellow fat and rubbery globs of congealed blood sticking to it. He scratches them off with his fingernail, then drops the pelt into a crate on the floor, full of other pelts. He picks up the razor from the table, holds the animal's body down with one hand, and, with the other, in one smooth motion cuts off its head. He pries the head free from the nail and tosses it into a garbage can. Then he scoops up the body and brings it over to the stove, where he drops it into the pot. Steam rises. With his back to me, he picks up a wooden spoon and begins stirring what's in the pot.

"He told me what they did to the German," I say.

"*They?*" Mitchell says.

"The ones with you. Leon told me right before he went into town that night. Right before . . . you killed him." As soon as I say it I realize exactly why I came: that I had to know for sure it was this man who killed my brother.

Mitchell turns toward me, the spoon in one hand, the razor poised lightly in the other. He sights me out of the corners of his eyes. "Before I what?"

"Before you killed him. I never believed it was an accident. You could fool everybody else but not me."

"I didn't kill nobody, lady."

"You denying you called? I recognize your voice. How'd you kill him anyway?"

"I told you I didn't kill nobody."

"What did you do? Did you hit him over the head so it looked like he fell?"

He stares at me for a moment. "I think you better leave."

"Or did you get him so drunk he passed out and froze to death?"

"You don't know a goddamn thing, lady. You're just jabbering."

"I know enough to go to the police."

"Huh!" he says, smiling so his lips part and I see these small too-white dentures.

"You think I won't?"

"Go ahead. Nobody stopping you."

"I will."

"And what the fuck you gonna say?"

"I'll say you killed my brother."

"You ain't got no proof I did a goddamn thing."

"I'll ask for an autopsy. They'll find out he didn't die by accident. They'll start poking around, and who knows what they'll find?"

"Still don't prove I had anything to do with it."

"No? I'll say you're the one who called. The one who threatened me. I can say I recognize your voice."

"If you know so much, how come you're here? How come you ain't talking to the police already?"

"Why'd you kill him?"

"I told you—I didn't kill your brother."

"I didn't mean him. I *know* why you killed him. I was talking about the German. What did he do to you?"

"Get the hell out of here."

"He was a prisoner."

"Get out! Now."

"I'll go.to the police. I will."

"Go ahead. You ain't got no proof. You ain't got shit. You're just blowing smoke out your ass."

"Maybe. But then again, maybe the police would still like to hear about it. About what Leon told me. And I can tell them how you threatened me. There's laws against threatening people."

"Get outta here."

"I bet the police would like to hear that."

He takes a couple of steps toward me, the razor held out in front of him. I back up, bump into the bed, and fall down onto it. The metal bedsprings creak.

"You gonna kill me, too?" I cry.

He stops, though, looks down at me.

"Go ahead. Kill somebody else. Spill some more blood, you bastard. You're good at that."

He points the razor at me and says, "You know what's good for you, you'll keep your goddamn mouth shut, lady."

"Tell me why you killed that boy."

"Just like I thought. You don't know nothing. You're just bluffing."

"I know. Leon told me. He just didn't tell me why."

"Fuck you," he says, shutting the blade and putting the razor into his pocket. "Get out."

"He didn't hurt anybody."

"You heard me. Get out while you still got the chance."

I stand up from the bed and hurry toward the door. When I'm outside, my heart pounding crazily, the sunlight glaring off the melting snow so I'm momentarily blinded, he calls after me: "You think you goddamn Pelletiers ain't got blood on your hands."

23

ALL THE WAY home I drive too fast, pushing the little car. For miles I don't even remember turning the wheel or shifting or stopping. Everything just flies by me, a greenish blur. I can hear what Mitchell said: *You think you goddamn Pelletiers ain't got blood on your hands.* Coming through the center of town I nearly run a red light and have to slam on the brakes. A guy in a white Land Rover, coming the other way, honks his horn and throws his hands up as if to say, "What the hell's the matter with you, lady?" Then he shakes his head and takes off. My hands are trembling, and my chest is tight with the close call. In Bidwell's Furniture store I notice a sign that says, "Everything Drastically Reduced." When the light turns I look both ways before heading carefully toward home.

There I get out the photo from my pocketbook, the one that shows the group of people standing around a memorial for the two East Forks boys. It's been in the back of my mind since last night. I look at the one face I feel I've seen before. A middle-aged man with a mustache, square jawed, good-looking. The father of one of the dead boys, I imagine. Next to him are two teenaged boys—other sons?

I spend the next couple of days wondering what I should do, if I should go to Chief Chambers and tell him what I know, insist on an autopsy. I can tell him I recognize Mitchell's voice as the man who called. That I think he was the one who killed my dog. That I think maybe Leon had something on Mitchell, that he knew something connecting him to the death of that German POW, and that was why he'd killed my brother. But none of this is what you could call *proof*. And would anybody buy such a story anyway? It sounds farfetched even to me. And what about Ambroise? What if he's involved? I think again about what Mitchell said, how the Pelletiers have blood on their hands, too.

I try to go about my business but find myself haunted by that face, the one in the memorial picture. Where have I seen it? Day and night I think about it, see it in my dreams. Every once in a while, as I'm doing something, scrambling eggs for a customer or taking the garbage out back, I'll feel myself on the edge of knowing. Sort of the way you feel when you can't think of some actor's name and yet it's almost on the tip of your tongue.

I ask around. Connie West, I recall, used to have relatives in East Forks. But he just looks at the photo and says he hasn't been over there in years. I show it to Hoppy McCray and Al Royce, but they don't have any idea who the man in the picture is either.

Roland pulls in one afternoon with his rig and dumps off a pile of fresh-cut saw logs. The red oak smells bitter, like vinegar.

"That should do you the rest of the year," he says. "And give you a pretty good start on next."

"Thanks."

"I'll cut and split it for you when I get a chance."

"You eat supper yet?"

"No."

"Come on in and get washed up."

That evening, after I clear the supper dishes, we play a couple of hands of setback at the kitchen table upstairs. Roland is a crazy bidder. He takes chances. He'll go three on a jack and a sawbuck. I play more cautiously. I like to wait with a fistful of cards and set people back. But tonight I can't concentrate. My mind's on other things.

"Your truck still in the shop?" he asks.

"Yeah. Billy's having a hard time getting some parts."

"You need a ride anywhere, you let me know."

"I got a rental car," I explain. "Let me ask you something, Roland. You know anybody named Ross? From over in East Forks."

"Can't say I do," he says.

"How about Bellevance?"

"There's a shitload of Bellevances over there. Which one you looking for?"

I show him the picture of the men.

"That one," I say.

"How come you're so interested in all these old pictures?"

"Do you recognize him or not?"

"I used to know an old guy named August Bellevance, over in East Forks. This's from back during the war. You figure this guy'd have to be, what, eighty-five, ninety now?"

"About that, I imagine."

"August would be pushing ninety."

"Is it him?"

"It's hard to say," he replies, leading off with the queen of hearts. "I haven't seen August in years."

"Did he have a son named Toots?"

"You got me. You oughta ask Spotty Haines," Roland offers. "He might know. Christ, he knows everybody and his brother. It's getting late, Lib," he says, looking over at me. "Maybe I should get going."

"You don't have to drive all the way home tonight," I say, throwing down a king to his queen.

"Jesus Christ," he says. "How come you never bid?"

"I'm not like you. I want to be sure I got the cards before I make a move."

The next afternoon I call the hospital in Skowhegan. I'm told that Wolfgang Kallick is doing better, that he's off the respirator, though still in critical condition.

"Please let him know that Libby Pelletier called," I say.

I turn the Closed sign face out and take a ride over to Spotty's place in North East Carry, about fifteen miles away. I take the Golden Road, a private road owned by the paper company. Suzie West, Connie's daughter, works the tollbooth. When she sees me she lifts the gate and waves me on through. It's a bright, windy spring day. The sky is clear, a soft flat blue, the color of veins. The earth is softening, giving out its secret smells: the scent of wild-flowers, of forsythia and wild onion, Labrador tea and fiddle-heads, and the trapped odor of dirt coming to life.

Beyond Shack Pond I take a left and head west, toward North East Carry. When I reach the lake I drive south, along its north-easternmost rim. The water is a gray-green, almost free of ice, except for out in the middle of the cove where a few football-field-sized ice floes hang like huge whales. At the sign for Spotty's place—HAINES' CAMPGROUND AND GUIDE SERVICE—I turn toward Norcross Mountain. I stop at the front office, get out, and go inside. Alice is on the phone behind the front desk. She holds up one finger to me as she says into the phone, "Oh, yeah. Fishing's been great." Then she winks and rolls her eyes at me. Little white lies—everybody's got to make a living.

After she gets off the phone she says, "Hello, Libby."

"Hi, Alice. How's business?"

"Terrible. We've had half a dozen cancellations already."

"Everything's slow up here."

"The last group canceled were in the reserves. They don't know if they're going over to the Gulf. What brings you over here?"

"Where's Spotty?"

"Busy. Can I help you with something?"

"I need to see him."

"Cabin number two. But if you're thinking of going out fish-ing with him, he can't. He's got work to do."

"I'll only be a minute."

I walk down to cabin two. When I open the screen door of the cabin, I see that Spotty's covered with white paint. He's work-ing a roller, whitewashing the tongue-and-groove pine walls.

"You do good work, Spot," I say.

"Huh," he replies, without smiling. "Nice day like this I oughta be fishing. What're you doing here, Lib?" he asks, putting down his roller in the paint tray and wiping his hands on a rag.

"Got a question for you."

From my pocketbook I get out the picture of the memorial. I hold it up in front of him.

"Who's that?" I ask, pointing at the face I feel I've seen before.

"Drove all the way over here just to ask me that?" he says. "Business must be slow over there, too."

"It's kind of important. I think I've seen him before. I just can't say where."

He wipes his hands on his trousers and then takes the photo. He brings it over to a window. "These fellows ain't from town. Says East Forks here."

"Right. But I've seen that one before. Pretty sure anyway. I just can't place him."

"Can't really say, Lib. It's been a long time."

"Figure his name has to be Bellevance or Ross, or relatives at least. You know some of those Bellevances from over East Forks way?"

"Hell, there's a tribe of Bellevances over there. Never heard of any Toots Bellevance though." He pauses, stares at the picture for several seconds. "I used to know an August Bellevance. Would probably be about this fellow's age."

"Think he might be related to this one?"

"They're all related." Spotty picks at a paint scab on his chin. "Humph. Wait a minute. I betcha I know who this one is now."

"August Bellevance?"

"No. But seems to me I recall there was a couple of Rosses used to work for Great Northern. I don't know if any were killed in the war but they lived over in East Forks, as I recall."

"You sure?"

"No, I'm not sure. But it could be."

Ross, I think. Suddenly that tightened spring in my head

snaps. "Was one of them named Freddie?" I ask, recalling the
man in the back row of the logging picture. The good-looking
one with the mustache and square jaw. The one Tom Weston said
was Freddie Ross. Is that where I'd seen him before?

"Come to think of it there was a Freddie Ross worked with
your old man. Way back."

"During the war?"

"Could've been."

"Thanks, Spotty."

"You ain't busy you could pick up a brush and help me."

"I gotta go. Thanks."

I get in my car and take off.

As I'm driving toward East Forks, I find myself not a mile from
the Sheshuncook cemetery, where the German is buried. At the
fork that turns south into the village I see the old Texaco sign
rusting away in the bushes, the one that used to advertise Abbey's
store. I'd ridden this same road to bring Oswald to the infirmary.
As if it hadn't been nearly half a century ago but only yesterday, I
recall the wild look in his gray, chalky eyes as he was trying to
die. And I recall, too, the interpreter—Dieter Kallick—sitting
next to me in the truck. I recall his dark slender hands as he gave
me a cigarette. The scar across his palm. The silky ring of his
voice when he said, "*Das Vergnügen ist ganz meinerseits, Fräulein.*"
The half-smile on his face. Did my father help to put him in that
grave?

A logging truck comes right up on my tail and lays on the
horn, making me jump. At first I think it might be Roland's
Peterbilt, but I see in the mirror it's not Roland. It's some young
kid with a smile on his face, thinks it's funny he almost scared me
half to death.

In the small village of East Forks, right on the Kennebec, I
stop in a bait shop and ask a short balding man where the memorial in town is.

"Memorial?" he says, scratching his head. "Humph. Let me

ask my wife." He calls into a back room, "Dottie, you know where they got a memorial in town?" After about a minute a woman with salt-and-pepper hair pulled into a bun comes out.

"A what?" she asks. When she opens her mouth I see that one of her front teeth is missing.

"This lady's looking for some memorial in town," the husband says.

"A memorial?"

"Yes. For some boys who died in World War Two," I explain.

They stare at each other for a moment. Then the wife says, "Oh, you know what. I betcha she's talking about the center green. You know, in front of the church. Don't they have a little stone or something there? That's the only place we got like that."

"Never noticed it," says the husband.

"Sure. It's where they shoot the guns on Memorial Day."

"Thanks," I say.

It only takes me a few minutes before I find the Congregational church and the center green. I park the car and get out. I walk up to the memorial, which sits under a big beech tree carved with graffiti and still clinging to last year's yellowish leaves. It's a rough granite stone, about four feet high, inlaid with a bronze plaque covered with green patina. I read the inscription: "To those brave East Forks youths who unselfishly laid down their lives in the line of duty." And below that it says, "Pfc. Jacques 'Toots' Bellevance—Born Oct. 14, 1924–Died June 15, 1944, South Pacific." And then: "Cpl. Daniel George Ross—Born April 12, 1922–Died Dec. 17, 1944, Malmédy, Belgium."

Malmédy. The place where the Germans had slaughtered American prisoners. I think about how feelings changed after we heard about that place. And I think about Freddie Ross. A man who'd had a son killed—murdered—by Germans. Who'd have every reason to hate them, to want to get revenge. Who'd worked with Germans every day, rubbed shoulders with them, broke bread with them. I wonder if it could mean anything or is it just another coincidence? I get in the car and head home.

*   *   *

When I get back, I go into my bedroom and sit at my desk. I take out the logging picture I found among Leon's things. I place it side by side on the desk with the one of the memorial. Although I'm not positive, the pictures being too fuzzy, I see that it *could* be the same man, Freddie Ross, in both. The man who worked for my father and the man who'd lost a son at Malmédy could be the same. Yet it's as I'm staring at the logging photo that something else occurs to me. In the back row, standing between Goose Mitchell and Freddie Ross, is that young kid. The only one nobody recognized. The one Tom had said was probably a day laborer passing through town. Just a drifter. As I stare at the picture, though, I find that he, too, looks suddenly familiar now. And when I look at the other photo I see that one of the teenaged boys standing next to Freddie Ross looks a little like the young kid—and *both* resemble Freddie Ross. It's hard to say if it is the same person or not. Just that it's possible. Could it be Daniel Ross's brother? Freddie Ross's son? And if so, could it be the Freddie Ross—Dr. Ross—that I'd spoken to? The one who said he didn't know anybody else who worked up at the POW camp? But why would he lie to me?

I give Tom Weston another ring.

"Tom, it's Libby again."

"Can't talk now. I'm just on my way out."

"Just one question. Remember you said Freddie Ross worked up at the camp."

"Lib, I don't want to talk anymore about that business."

"Please, Tom. Just tell me one thing—did his son work up there, too? Freddie Ross Junior."

I can hear Tom inhaling. "Yes," he says finally. "Now don't call me anymore."

I dial the operator and ask for the number of Dr. Frederick Ross of Augusta. The phone rings several times before a woman picks it up. At first I think it's a recording, the voice is so perfect, so flawless.

"This is the Ross residence."

"Is Dr. Ross in?" I ask.

"No, he's not. May I help you?"

"Do you expect him back soon?"

"It's hard to say. He was called in to the hospital. To whom am I speaking?"

I hesitate for a moment, wondering if I ought to tell the truth. Then I say, "This is Libby Pelletier."

"Are you a patient of his?"

"No, nothing like that. I just need to talk to him."

"Why don't you leave your number and I'll have him call you as soon as he returns."

I give her my number. Then I ask, "Are you Mrs. Ross?"

"Yes."

"Did your husband have a brother named Daniel?"

"Yes, as a matter of fact, he did. He died in the war. Why do you ask?"

"I think I used to know him. When he was a boy."

"Did you know my husband, too?"

"I don't think so. But I'd like to talk to him about his brother."

"I'll have him call you."

Around ten that night I call back. I get the wife again, who tells me her husband still isn't home. Yet her tone has changed. There's an edge to it, as if he's told her something about me.

"It's very late," she says.

"What time do you expect him?" I ask.

"I really couldn't say."

"I need to talk to him. It's very important."

"Would you like to leave a message?"

"No. I need to talk to him. It's personal."

"I'll tell him you called," she says, the smooth flatness of her voice breaking for a moment and annoyance seeping in like water in a cellar. "Now good-bye."

24

I TRY TO REACH Dr. Ross several times over the next few days. But each time his wife answers and tells me he's not home.

"Did he get my message, Mrs. Ross?"

"I gave it to him, Mrs. Pelletier. You have to understand, my husband is a very busy man. I'm sure he'll call just as soon as he has a free moment."

He doesn't call, though. So I dial information again and get his office number.

"Dr. Ross's office," a woman says when I call.

"I need to speak to Dr. Ross."

"He's with a patient right now. Is this an emergency?"

"Yes."

"All right. Whom may I say is calling?"

"Mrs. St. James," I say, using the first name that comes into my head.

After about a minute a man comes on the line.

"Hello," he says. "This is Dr. Ross."

"Dr. Ross."

"Yes."

"I need to talk to you."

"Oh," he replies, caught off balance for a moment. "I'm afraid I can't talk right now. I'm seeing a patient."

"Dr. Ross."

"I really have to go."

"Dr. Ross, wait. Why did you lie about your father working at the camp?"

"What?"

"When I asked you if he worked up at the POW camp you said you weren't sure."

"I said he might have."

"But you *knew* he worked up there."

"I wasn't sure. It was a long time ago."

"You had to know he worked up there . . . because *you* did."

"I afraid you're mistaken."

"No, I'm not. I have a picture. It's of my father's logging crew. You *and* your father are in it."

He's quiet for a moment. Then he says, "Listen, I worked up there for a little while. A couple of months right after high school, while I was waiting to get drafted. So what?"

"Then why didn't you tell me?"

"It was just a couple of months. It slipped my mind. It was a long time ago. Now if you'll excuse me, I really must go now."

"Did what happened up there slip your mind, too?"

A glassy emptiness fills the silence on the other end. It gets so quiet, in fact, I can hear those little insect noises in the lines somewhere. Like tiny jaws chewing on the wires. Finally he says, "What are you talking about?"

"About the German. The one they found dead."

"I've had enough of this."

"I think—"

He hangs up.

In the evening I try calling his home again, but now I don't even get his wife. I get the answering machine.

After a couple of days of waiting, I decide to drive down to Augusta. The day is sunny but windy. Gusts of wind from the north sweep across the turnpike and slam into the small car, shoving me sideways.

I have this picture in my mind. I see Leon, twelve, thirteen years old, carrying that terrible secret—whatever it was—around with him every day after his twelfth birthday for the rest of his life, having it eat away at his insides like battery acid, making him suffer for what had happened, for what he'd been a witness to, having it ruin the rest of his life. For that reason—even more than for what happened to him out on the ice—I have to know, or at least try to know, the truth.

I get off the turnpike at Augusta and drive east until I reach State Street, where I turn south. Off to my left is the Kennebec River, while on the right I pass the Capitol. I turn off of State and onto another road and then another, keeping my eyes open for Millbrook Terrace. Several times I have to pull over and look at the map I have spread out on the seat. When I find Millbrook, I turn right and drive up into a development of impressive older homes. Many have circular drives and some have columns in front and swimming pools out back. One or two have these little jockeys holding lanterns near the driveway. At last I find 93 Millbrook Terrace, which turns out to be this big white plaster house with Spanish tiles on the roof. A sign in front says, "Dr. Frederick Ross, Orthopedist." Someone who sets bones.

I park the car in the street and get out. I head up the brick walk and ring the doorbell. After a while a woman opens the door. She's my age, but thin and frail as a cornstalk, with bright red lipstick the color of a rooster's comb set against his pale skin. And a string of pearls around her skinny neck.

"Yes?" The same flat, edgeless voice as on the phone. I picture her having gone to Wellesley or Smith, where she'd learned how to be a doctor's wife, to give flawless dinner parties for other doctors and to talk this way.

"I came to see Dr. Ross. I'm Libby Pelletier."

"Oh," the woman replies. "Well, I'm afraid that's quite impossible. He's making rounds at the hospital right now."

"When do you expect him back?"

"I'm not sure. It could be quite some time."

"I have to see him. It's very important."

"If you want I can tell him you stopped by. He'll call you as soon—"

"I'll be out in my car," I interrupt.

"But it might be hours."

"That's okay. I got plenty of time."

"You can't just wait out in the street," she calls after me.

I go out to the car and sit there. After about ten minutes the woman comes out, knocks on the glass.

"Excuse me. You can't just wait here."

"Why not?"

"Because you can't," she says, glancing up and down the street.

"I need to see your husband."

"Is there anything I can do?"

"No."

She sighs, shakes her head, but then goes back up into the house. I wait another twenty, thirty minutes maybe. Up the street are parked several trucks of men who make a living cutting the lawns and trimming the hedges of these homes. Then there's another knock on the window. When I turn, I see Mrs. Ross there again.

"I just called the hospital," she says. "My husband is going to be very late."

"I can wait."

"What do you want with my husband?"

"He knows."

"If you don't stop pestering us I'll have to call the police," the woman threatens.

I think about that for a moment, then decide I'd better leave for now. "All right," I say. "I'll go."

I drive up the street but then pull over and park, far enough away so she can't see me but from where I can still watch their house in the rearview. I wait. I turn the radio on and listen to a C and W station out of Portland.

Hours pass. It begins to get dark. The cold starts creeping

into the car, so I pull my down vest tighter around me. From my shirt pocket I take out a book of matches and light a cigarette. Around nine I see a pair of headlights come up the street and pull into Ross's driveway. I quickly start the car, turn around, and drive up to his house and park. I get out and catch someone just as he's getting out of a yellow Mercedes.

"Are you Dr. Ross?" I ask.

"Yes," he replies. "Who *are* you anyway?"

"I'm Libby Pelletier."

"What do you want?"

"You ought to know."

"I don't."

"You were there, weren't you? Please, Dr. Ross. I need to know—that's why you lied about working at the camp. You were there that night."

"I don't know what you're talking about. Now I'm very tired and you'll have to excuse me," he says, turning and heading up to the house.

"I know about your brother," I call after him. "I know about Malmédy. I understand."

With this he stops and turns around. He stares at me. The light from the porch shows a tall, slender man in his mid-sixties. He has a full head of soft silver hair and a long straight nose. His eyes are dark, maybe brown, though in the light it's hard to say. When he puts his hand to his face I see that he's missing the tip of his index finger.

"What about Malmédy?" he asks.

"Leon told me," I say.

"What did he tell you?"

"He told me about your brother."

Ross glances down at his shoes, then says, "I don't know what you're talking about."

"I suppose it wasn't you in the library, looking up the camp."

"And what if I was? No law against that."

"Dr. Ross, you were what—eighteen, nineteen?—when they

killed that boy. I can understand that. There was a war on and people hated the Germans. But what about now? What about my brother, Dr. Ross?"

"Now wait a minute."

"My brother didn't do anything to you. Why was he killed?"

"I . . . I didn't."

"What kind of man are you, Dr. Ross?"

He takes a big swallow of air, rolls it around in his mouth as if he doesn't like the taste. He looks quickly over his shoulder toward the house. Then he breathes out slowly.

"I didn't. You have to believe me."

"Why should I?"

"I swear. I didn't have anything to do with your brother."

"All right, maybe you didn't. But I bet you know who did."

"What do you want?" he says.

"I want to know what happened."

"I don't know, I told you. I had nothing to do with your brother."

"No, not just that. I mean that night. With the German POW."

Dr. Ross glances nervously up and down the street. Then he says, "Okay. I might be able to help you. But not now. Not here."

"When?"

"Listen. There's a Burger King down the road. On State."

"Yes."

"I'll meet you in the parking lot tonight." Dr. Ross glances at his watch. "I have some things to do first. Let's say eleven o'clock."

"How do I know you'll show up?"

"I'll be there."

"I could go to the police."

"I give you my word."

I have no choice.

"Eleven," I say.

I'm sitting in the parking lot of the Burger King sipping a coffee. I glance around, scanning the lot. It's eleven-fifteen. He's late. I'm wondering if maybe he's changed his mind when a yellow Mercedes pulls into the space next to mine. I recognize Dr. Ross behind the wheel. His window slides down and he says, "You didn't tell anybody else about tonight, did you?"

"No."

"Follow me."

He pulls out and I follow him up State Street, past the Capitol. We cross over the Kennebec, which glistens in the moonlight. He drives fast and I have to push the Escort just to keep up. He pulls onto Route 202 and heads north. We're driving for about ten miles when I see signs for Elephant Lake. Just past a boarded-up gas station, the Mercedes makes a sharp left-hand turn onto a narrow dirt road. In the rearview mirror I catch a pair of headlights slowing down behind me. But as I turn to follow Dr. Ross, they speed up and disappear into the darkness. We drive down this road and soon come to a fork, where we take another left. After about a half-mile or so the road comes to an abrupt stop beside a body of water. A stand of white pines comes right down to the water's edge. I can make out in the moonlit water, a dock, a small fishing boat moored beside it.

Dr. Ross gets out of his car and comes walking up in my headlights toward me. He's wearing tan trousers and a red plaid hunting jacket. His skin looks gray in the light. As he approaches, I feel this jagged piece of glass twisting in the pit of my stomach. *Don't, Libby*, a voice warns. *Don't get out.* But I don't pay it any mind, I'm in too deep already. I shut the car off and get out.

The ground is spongy with needles and it smells of pine and swamp. Across the lake you can see a few lights, but where we are it's deserted and, except for the sound of the wind cutting through the branches, quiet. Dr. Ross takes out a pack of cigarettes and lights one. He offers me a cigarette and I accept. Up close, as we share a match, I can see his face is drained of color and his eyes look haggard and old. He takes a drag on the cigarette, and for a moment we just wait there in the night.

Finally he asks, "So what do you want to know?"

"Leon never told me a thing," I say.

"He didn't?"

"No. Not a word."

"Then how do you know about any of it?"

"I don't *know*. I never really *knew*. What got me started was when this German fellow came to town asking questions about his brother."

"Kallick, you mean?" he asks.

"You knew about him, then?"

"Yes."

"After Leon died I started to get these phone calls. Somebody warning me to stay away from Kallick. To keep my nose out of it. That's when I suspected the German's death hadn't been an accident, and that it was connected to Leon's somehow. Help me fill in the holes—please."

"If I tell you anything, what are you going to do with it?"

"I'm not sure. My brother's killer, I want him punished. The rest, it doesn't matter."

"I had nothing to do with your brother—it's Libby, right?"

"Yes."

"Nothing at all to do with that, Libby. You have to believe me. That was Mitchell."

"I thought so. I recognized his voice as being the one who'd been calling. I went to see him."

"You did?"

"Yes," I reply. "To ask him some questions."

"What did he tell you?"

"He said he didn't kill my brother."

"He's lying," Dr. Ross says. "Did he say anything else?"

"He threatened me."

"Mitchell's a very dangerous man, Libby. He threatened me, too. Said if I told Kallick anything I'd end up like your brother. If he knew I was talking to you he'd kill us both."

The doctor pauses for a moment, looking out across the lake. "I'm not such a bad man, Libby. I'm not really. I can't count the times I've thought about going to the police and telling them what happened. Just to have it be over with."

"I'm not here to judge you, Dr. Ross. I just want to know what happened."

The night is cool and I lean against the warm hood of the car and listen as he begins to talk.

"When we got the news about Danny—that was my older brother," Dr. Ross begins, the words seeming to rise up out of the darkness around us, as if oozing from the damp ground itself, like the smell of swamp and pine needles, "my father took it pretty bad. Yet it wasn't so much that he died but the way he died—taken out and slaughtered like you'd slaughter a pig. Then the bastards tried to cover it up by burying him and the others in the snow. It was a month or more before we learned exactly how he'd died. I remember Pop sitting at the table with the letter from the government, sobbing, swearing he'd pay them back. He wanted revenge. And he wasn't the only one, either. Everybody around here was looking for revenge.

"That day we'd finished cutting. We were pretty far from camp, logging way out past Pittston Farm. The Germans had been loaded in their truck and sent back. All except for one. The one who interpreted for the Germans. I don't know why it was him. I think they were just looking for a German, any German, and he just happened to be it. Somehow they got him away from his group of prisoners, got him all alone way out in the woods. They figured by the time the army truck got back to camp and took a head count, they'd have been finished . . . finished with whatever it was they were planning.

"I'd heard some things. Rumors that day. Some of the older guys—Pop Flynn and Willard Walker and the Mitchells—talking about how they were going to make one of those bastards pay. On account of my brother. I can't say I was against it. After all, he was my brother. I hated the Germans for it. But I thought we'd just rough him up a little bit, get it out of our system, and let it go at that. A lesson for them that they couldn't do that to one of ours and get away with it.

"Anyway, after the army truck left, we met at a place out in the woods. It was dark except for the lanterns. There were eight of us there, plus the German. The two Mitchells. Willard Walker. Pop Flynn. Beany Desauliers. My father and me arrived a few minutes after the others. Your brother Leon was there, too, though your father wasn't. Some of the boys were drinking, passing a bottle around. When we got there I saw that the German was surrounded by the others. He was naked. They'd stripped him of his clothes and he stood there in the snow in his bare feet shivering. He kept shifting from one foot to the other. I could hear his teeth chattering. Somebody had already hit him because his mouth and nose were bleeding.

"They were swearing at him and he stood silently, looking down at the ground. He tried to cover himself with his hands. A couple of the men had pine switches and they'd jab him in the sides, or strike him across the buttocks or legs. When he cried out or jumped trying to avoid a blow, everybody would laugh. 'Look at the goddamn Nazi dance,' someone would joke. 'Hitler's jig.' I laughed, too. For a while I just watched, but then I picked up a stick and started to hit him too. Something told me it was wrong but I hit him anyway, just like the others. Each time I hit him I thought about Danny. How they'd taken him out into the snow and just shot him like a dog. The German, you could see, was afraid. But he never cried and he never begged them to stop.

"We kept this up for a while—hitting him with the switches and laughing. Then two men—it was the Mitchells—grabbed the German's arms and tied them behind his back with a piece of baling twine. One held him while the other beat him. I remember seeing blood on the snow. All this blood. After they'd beat him up pretty good, they let him go. He fell down on his knees, and then over onto his face. With his hands tied behind his back he couldn't get up. We were in a circle around him. For a long time no one did or said anything. I thought that was it. I thought we'd put him in the truck and bring him back now. We could've said he'd tried to escape and there'd been a fight. A little blood, no one would've cared. But then Goose Mitchell stepped forward out of our circle.

"He had an ax handle in his hand—I don't even know where he'd got it. He touched the German on the head with it. The German didn't look up at him. Mitchell said something to him, something I didn't catch at first. The prisoner remained quiet. Then Mitchell smiled and repeated what he'd said. This time I heard him clearly: He asked the kid if he was ready to die. Mitchell looked over at us and laughed and we laughed, too, but nervously, because we weren't sure what he had in mind. Goose Mitchell was like that. You never knew what he was thinking. He told the German to pray. The kid still didn't move. Mitchell told him once more and this time the German turned his head a little and looked up at him. His face was a mess. He put his lips together like he was going to say something but no words came out. Instead—and I still remember it now—he smiled. At least that's what it looked like. I think that's what decided it for Mitchell. 'Sonofabitch thinks I'm kidding,' Mitchell said. He then raised the ax handle over the German and brought it down across his shoulder. You could hear the bone crack and the German slumped heavily over onto his side. I cried out 'Jesus Christ Almighty.'

"All of us watched for a few seconds, stunned. Everything had changed. Before that moment I felt we hadn't done anything that we couldn't undo, couldn't change back to the way it had been. Now, though, there was no going back. And before anyone could say or do anything, the other Mitchell took the ax handle and hit him once more, too, this time across his chest. I'll never forget the sound. Like a paper bag popping, this rush of air coming from the kid's mouth. The German lay curled up on the ground, his arms twisted behind him, moaning. Then the Mitchells turned to the rest of us. 'Who's next?' one of them asked. Nobody moved at first. So one of them—Alf, I think it was—said, 'C'mon, you gutless bastards. Freddie. It was your Danny these sons a bitches killed,' he said to my father. I remember my father hesitating at first. 'You owe it to Danny,' Mitchell said. My father took the ax handle. He raised it up and hit the German. Then somebody else took a swing and somebody after that. No one said anything, no one tried to stop it. When it was my turn, I took the ax handle and struck him, just like everybody else. I only hit him once but it was enough. I can still remember the feeling of his bones cracking under the blow, and, in the lantern light, the hollowness of his eyes. *Jesus*, I kept thinking. *Jesus Jesus Jesus*. Because I knew I would never forget that look in his eyes—not then, not ever.

"The German was lying there on the snow, curled up into a ball but not even trying to defend himself anymore. He wasn't dead yet, though. I could hear a noise deep in his throat, a rattling sound as he tried to suck in air. That's when Goose Mitchell gave the ax handle to your brother. I guess he didn't want anybody to be left out, to be clean of this, anyone who could tell on the others. He wanted everybody to be soaked in blood. I remember your brother, just this little kid, taking the handle from Goose. And Goose saying, 'Go ahead, Leon. It's all right. Hit the son of a bitch. He's just a lousy kraut.' And Leon hesitating for just a moment before picking up the handle and striking the German. 'Hit him again,' Mitchell cried. 'Attaboy.' And your brother did. Everybody was laughing and cheering him on, like it was a game. He struck him again and again. Your brother getting his hands bloody just like the rest of us. But he was only a kid. He didn't know any better.

"The rattling noise in the German's throat stopped. Shortly after that your father arrived. I don't know if he'd known about what they had planned to do or not. I don't think so, though. I remember when he got there he looked around at us, slowly, and then at the German. He said, 'What in the hell are you doing?'

"'Just paying 'em back for what they done to Danny,' Goose Mitchell said.

"'Christ Almighty,' your father said, kneeling down beside the German. 'He didn't do nothing.'

"Then Alf said, 'Maybe he didn't pull the goddamn trigger, Ambroise. But he's guilty just the same. All them kraut sons a bitches are guilty. Everybody here lost somebody to them bastards.'

"We stood around while your father and the Mitchells argued about what we were going to do next. Your father kept saying it was wrong what we'd done. That the German hadn't hurt anybody. He said maybe the boy wasn't dead yet and they could still bring him back to the infirmary. He said maybe it wasn't too late yet.

"'It's plenty late, Ambroise,' said Goose Mitchell. 'What's done is done.'

"'And what if I tell 'em who did this?' your father threatened.

"Goose and his brother looked right at your father. Goose said, 'I wouldn't do that, Ambroise.'

"'You son of a bitch, you gonna kill me, too?' your father said. I remember. Your father was the only one to stand up to them.

"The three of them stood there staring at each other for a long time. I wasn't sure what would happen. I remember somebody— Willard Walker, I think—saying, 'Come on, Goose. Ambroise ain't gonna turn his own in for a goddamn kraut. Right, Ambroise?' Your father looked around at the men, taking us in one at a time, like he was still deciding what he was going to do and who he could count on. That's when Goose Mitchell told him about Leon—his being part of it. Ambroise looked over at your brother, and when Leon looked down at the ground, your father knew it was true. After that Ambroise didn't say anything. He didn't like it but we knew he'd go along, keep his mouth shut because of your brother.

"They untied the German's hands and then they put his clothes back on him. I didn't know it at the time but they'd already planned on making it look like an accident. They carried him and put him in the back of one of the trucks. We got in and headed in the direction of the camp. A few miles before we got there we drove out to Socatean Bay. We parked the trucks and took along some axes and a crowbar. We picked up the German and carried him out onto the lake. I don't know whose idea it was, to make it look like an accident. But we started chopping a hole in the ice—all of us except for Ambroise and your brother. They stayed back in one of the trucks. I remember the ice was thick and it took a long time to cut through it. It was freezing out and our boots got wet from the water. When the hole was big enough, we took the German and shoved him down into the water. I think he was dead—I like to think he was anyway. But he must've still had air in his lungs for his head kept bobbing up. We had to push him down under with the crowbar until he was beneath the ice.

"Afterwards we drove back to the camp and by that time they knew a prisoner was missing. They assumed, like we knew they would, that he'd escaped. So we went out and pretended to help the soldiers look for him. We told them he must have taken off out near Pittston Farm, so as to lead them away from where we'd dumped the body. Late that night we stopped at your place, where the Mitchells made everybody swear an oath. Your father didn't want to go along with it but he had no choice. On account of Leon. We swore that we'd never utter a word of what went on. That no matter what happened we wouldn't say anything. And if anybody broke the oath he was a dead man.

"A couple of months later when the body was found, we worried that they'd know it wasn't an accident, that they'd see how badly beaten he was and start to ask questions. But the war in Europe was over by then and I guess the army figured it was easier to say it was an accident than to stir up trouble. Yet that's why I went to the library. To see if there was anything in the paper about an autopsy, anything else that might connect us to the murder.

"I was drafted right before the end of the war. When I got back I went to college and then med school. I moved down here,

I guess trying to put some distance between me and what had happened up there. I lost contact with the people from that night. Except for my father. Yet he and I never mentioned what happened that night, not once before he died. Over the years death silenced the others."

Dr. Ross pauses then, drags on his cigarette so it momentarily illuminates his face. His eyes shine with a strange glow.

"That's what happened," he says. "I'm not proud of what we did. I've had to live with that for forty-six years. In my dreams I've seen that German's face so many times, the hollowness in his eyes. How many times did I think about turning myself in. But there wasn't just me to consider, I told myself. There was my father. The others. The memory of my brother. But mostly it was fear that kept me from doing anything. I was afraid of what the Mitchells would do. And as time went by, it just seemed easier to bury the past and forget about it. Until now."

25

I DON'T KNOW what to say. Don't know what to think either. To be afraid all those years that your father had taken part in a murder and then to find out he hadn't, that he'd actually tried to prevent it. And that it was your twelve-year-old brother who'd had a hand in it. Dear God in heaven. I think about poor Leon carrying that with him all those years, that terrible secret. That was the closed place inside him he'd never let anybody see, the poison that had eaten away at him. That was it.

Dr. Ross tosses his cigarette on the ground and crushes it with his heel.

"When Kallick came and started snooping around, Mitchell got scared," he says. "He called me, warned me about the dead German's brother. I told him just to sit tight. That Kallick wouldn't find anything. That we weren't in any danger. He was afraid of your brother, though."

"Why?"

"I guess he wasn't sure Leon could be trusted to keep his mouth shut."

"So he killed him?"

"Yes. He told me he'd kill me, too, if I opened my mouth. He's crazy."

"And it was Mitchell who ran Kallick off the road?"

"It must have been," the doctor replies. "Libby, who else knows about this?"

"Nobody."

"You sure?"

"Yes."

"And you didn't tell anybody you were meeting me tonight?"

"No. Not a soul. What are we going to do now?"

The doctor shoves his hands into his coat pockets and glances toward the dock. "I'm not sure. We have to be careful."

"We should go to the police."

"Yes. Of course. The police. Maybe we—"

Dr. Ross stops in midsentence, looks off to my left, up the road we came in on. When I turn, I see the outline of someone walking toward us. The figure is squat and walks heavily, his knees bent, his body slightly forward. From the moonlight that filters through the pines, I see that he carries something in one hand. When he gets within a few feet of us he stops. It's Alf Mitchell and the thing he's carrying is a gun.

"It wasn't your business," Mitchell says to me. His raspy voice vibrates in the darkness.

"You made it my business," I say.

"I warned her," he says to Dr. Ross. "The damn bitch wouldn't listen."

"What are you doing here?" Dr. Ross asks.

"You know, Doc, I was gonna ask you the same thing."

"You going to kill us like you killed Leon?" I say to Mitchell.

He glances at Dr. Ross, then at me. "I told you I didn't kill your brother."

"Am I supposed to believe that?"

"You believe what you want, lady."

"You're the one who called the night he was killed. He was meeting you in town."

"Yeah, I called," Mitchell says.

"And it was you who killed my dog."

"That was a warning," he says, waving the gun around. "But I didn't—"

"Just be careful with that," Dr. Ross interrupts.

"Don't you worry, Doc. I'm real careful with this," Mitchell says. "I'm still curious, though, what you two was doing out here."

"I just wanted to find out what she knew," replies Dr. Ross.

"You tell her anything?"

"No."

"He didn't have to tell me. I already knew," I say. It's so close to the end it doesn't matter what I say. If I'm going to die I ought to know the truth at least. "You killed him because he knew what happened that night. That's why, isn't it?"

"We swore an oath," Mitchell says. "All of us there that night. He was gonna tell Kallick what happened."

"Why?" I ask.

"How the hell do I know? I guess he had some crazy idea of getting it off his chest before he died. Maybe he worried about going to hell. I warned him. He wouldn't listen."

"So you killed him?"

Mitchell smiles, looks over at the doctor.

"What'd you tell her, anyway?" he asks Dr. Ross.

"Nothing."

"You tell her I killed him? Is that what you told her, Doc?"

"I didn't tell her anything."

I ask, "You get him drunk and then hit him to make it look like he fell on the ice?"

Mitchell turns to me. I hear a click and realize that he's just flipped off the safety. "You oughta ask—"

Mitchell never finishes his sentence though. A sudden blast and then another—*peooong, peooong,* so close together you almost can't tell them apart—shatter the night. I flinch from the explosions, but I can still see Mitchell, surprise freezing his expression in place. He pivots toward the doctor right before he stumbles backwards and then collapses.

"Son of a bitch," Mitchell curses from the ground. He's still holding the rifle with one hand. His knees jerk up and down, and his boots kick at the dirt.

The doctor walks over to him, a pistol dangling from his hand. He stands over him for a moment and Mitchell tries to lift the gun. Dr. Ross fires again, from point-blank range, and Mitchell falls silent. The doctor squats beside the body. The smell of gunpowder is heavy in the air.

It's all happened so suddenly I haven't had a chance to be frightened. Only now do I feel my heart fluttering inside my chest. I take a breath, let it out slowly. *It's finally over.*

"Is he dead?" I ask.

"Yes," replies the doctor.

"He would've killed us."

"Yes, he would have."

"Thank you," I say. "Thank you, Dr. Ross."

With his back to me, the doctor strikes a match. He begins to go through Mitchell's pockets. I reach into my own coat pocket, find my cigarettes and matches. My hands are shaking, and it takes a moment to light one. *Over.* As I watch Dr. Ross, my gaze falls on Mitchell's chest, where the doctor has rested his gun. I stare at it for several seconds. Maybe as long as ten.

It's a Luger.

I take a step toward him, but he senses my movement and picks up the gun and aims it up at me.

"Hold it," he says.

"You took that off Leon, didn't you?"

He doesn't say anything, doesn't have to.

"It was you. It wasn't Mitchell. He was telling the truth. You killed my brother."

"He wouldn't listen. I offered him money. I told him, what difference will it make to anybody now. What about *my* brother? What about all the others who died?"

"If it was so unimportant, why'd you have to kill him?"

Dr. Ross shakes his head.

"I have a good life and I wasn't going to ruin it for something I'd done half a century ago. If it got out it could have made things, well, unpleasant."

"So you killed him because it would have made things *unpleasant*? You bastard."

"I didn't go there that night with the intention of killing him. But he just wouldn't listen. Then *he* pulled the gun."

"And what happened?"

"There was a struggle. Mitchell and I were able to take it away from him. I hit him with the barrel and he fell and hit his head. That's the truth."

"Was he dead when you left him?"

"Yes."

"And you had Mitchell calling me afterwards? Or was that his idea?"

"That was mine. I paid him to do that. I didn't know what Leon had told you. I wanted to make sure you didn't tell Kallick anything. I just wanted it to be over with."

"But then you ran him off the road?"

"I just meant to scare him. I didn't mean to hurt him." The doctor looks down at Mitchell. "I'm not a bad man."

I laugh out loud, a harsh sound, like that made by a screech owl in the middle of the night.

Just before he turns, I lunge at him. But Ross is too quick for me. He swings around and I feel the gun butt slamming down into the bones of my cheek. There's a ringing sound in the back of my head, then this explosion of bright, multicolored lights. Then darkness as pure and cold as the bottom of a lake.

I am riding a dark wave. Floating, but on something more solid, more tangible than air. I feel this gentle rocking sensation, which is only broken now and then by a sudden jerk, my head bumping up against something hard in the darkness, and then everything is smooth again. I have the feeling, too, that wherever it is I'm going I'm going feetfirst, but not exactly falling, not going downward, but moving vertically. Somewhere in the distance is a noise: this high-pitched whining sound that occasionally seems to come closer, turn into a throaty growl before receding again.

There's a bitter smell in the darkness, too, like smoke from a green-wood fire, and across my face passes something cool and soft, like a silk scarf. The only thing that hurts is my feet, which isn't so much a real pain as it is a discomfort. They're cold. In fact, I can't even feel them. The numbness extends upwards from my feet, up to my knee, toward my thighs. After a while I feel something cool and solid around me, pressing against my back, the back of my head, holding me in its rigid grasp. *I'm dead. That's it.* And this rigid thing that holds me must be my coffin. For a moment panic seizes me and I feel my chest tighten. But then that gentle rocking sensation eases the fear, and it slides away as I speed feetfirst into this darkness.

I ride on like this for some time. After a while I feel myself slowing. I see these figures emerging from the darkness. Two. They walk toward me. Their faces seem to glow, to radiate with this bluish light. They keep getting closer and closer until I can reach out and touch them. When they're right before me I see that it's Ambroise and Leon. They open their arms to receive me. . . .

Suddenly they disappear. The noise stops abruptly and is replaced by another, first a churning, bubbling sound, then a muffled, *chop-chop* sound. It takes me a moment to make out what it is: the lapping of water against the sides of a boat. When I open my eyes I can see stars overhead, and low in the sky, the pale, scarred face of the moon. My head throbs and I can't see much out of one eye. It must be swollen shut. But I'm not dead, I think. I'm in a boat somewhere, out in the night, and I'm still alive.

Soon I hear the slap of an oar in the water. Turning my head slightly, cautiously, I can see, out of the corner of my good eye, a figure seated in the stern. It's Dr. Ross. He's sitting there working an oar. Pretty soon I hear the scrape of gravel on the bottom of what I know is an aluminum boat. Then he stands, heads up to the bow, and, using the oar, guides us in. When the boat stops, I can hear him jump out into the water and pull it in.

I close my eyes, pretend that I'm still unconscious. Yet I can feel him standing there looking down into the boat. He doesn't make a move for a few seconds and I try to hold my breath, try to remain perfectly still. Finally I hear him reaching down into the boat, grabbing ahold of something next to me, and struggling to drag it out onto shore. I can hear him straining with the effort. I can hear the thud of a shoe as it whacks the gunwale of the boat, then splashes into the water. Mitchell's body, I think. I hear him pulling the body through the water, then up onto the shore. I hear leaves stirring and twigs snapping, hear Ross curse once. Then the noise dying down as he gets further into the woods. Then I don't hear anything, just the water lapping against the hull and that pounding inside my head.

When I'm sure he's gone, I touch my hand to my left cheek. It aches. I feel the gash in the skin, the bone soft beneath it, pliable. In the moonlight, I can see my fingers are covered with blood.

Ross is gone for a while. Maybe a minute. Maybe five. What should I do? Get up and try to make a run for it in the woods? Or try to start the motor and take off? But when I lift my head off the bottom of the boat, I feel suddenly dizzy. My head spins, so I lie back down.

After a while I can hear footsteps coming back through the undergrowth. I hold my breath and try to lie perfectly still. I can sense the doctor nearby, smell his cologne and the odor of cigarettes on his breath. He reaches into the boat and grabs me roughly under the arms as he struggles to lift me over the side of the boat. I feel something in my shoulder pop as he yanks on my arm. My head echoes with pain and I have to fight the urge to cry out. He drags me through the freezing water, and up into the woods. Finally he stops, lets me drop like a sack of grain onto the ground. I hear him wheezing from the effort. Then he leaves.

I open my eyes. Above me in the darkness are the thin upward-curving arms of spruce trees. To my right is a large boulder. When I turn to my left I can make out Mitchell lying a few feet from me. I reach out and touch his neck. His skin is already cool. I look behind him. Through the trees, maybe a hundred feet away, I can see water in the moonlight. I don't hear Ross. Maybe he'll take off. Maybe that's his plan. Just drop us here where no one can find our bodies.

But soon I hear him coming through the woods. In the faint light I can make out that he's carrying something. When he gets close I shut my eyes again and try to keep my heart from jumping out of my chest. Squinting, I see him kneel down beside Mitchell. I hear him working something, turning something. The metal top of a can. Then I smell it: *gas!* It's a gas can, and he's going to set us on fire.

The gas spills out of the can. With my eyes shut tight I can hear the liquid splashing over Mitchell's body, can feel an occasional ice-cold drop splatter on my own. A little grazes my face, sending a shiver through me and burning at the corner of my eye. The smell is terrible, overpowering. I try to hold my breath. I try not to cough or gag with those sickening fumes in my nose. I await my turn to be doused, telling myself it'll only hurt for a second, then it won't hurt anymore, and I'll be with Leon and we won't ever be separated again. Please, God, just make it quick. Don't let me suffer. I begin to pray silently, repeating the prayer over and over again: *Holy Mary, Mother of God, pray for us sinners now and at the hour of our death. Amen.*

The sound of spilling gas ends abruptly, and I hear Ross turn and head off into the woods. Only as his footsteps begin to fade do I dare to open my eyes, just in time to see his outline disappear in the direction of the boat. I figure he must be going back for some more gas. As I lie there waiting for the end, I see the one named Oswald, the one killed by a falling tree. I see the desperate look in his eyes as he waited for death to take him, and suddenly I don't want to die.

Then *do* something, I tell myself. I push myself up so I'm on one elbow. My head reels and the gas fumes send a wave of nausea rolling through me. I turn over, fight the urge to retch. I pull my knees up and begin to crawl toward the boulder. I just reach it when I hear Ross coming back through the woods. I press myself against the base of the rock, which is covered with moss and holds that secret smell of the great age of all things. In the weak moonlight that filters through the trees I can see that he is carrying another gas can.

He stops no more than five feet from me and unscrews the top. Yet as he's about to pour, he must realize I'm not there. He wheels quickly around.

"Libby," he says.

He searches the darkness. He seems to look right at me for a second, but then turns toward the lake.

"Where do you think you're going? You can't get away."

He takes a couple of steps away from me. He's standing right next to Mitchell's body. His head is cocked forward, looking into the darkness, straining to see.

I reach into my shirt pocket for my matches, praying that they're still dry. I pull them out, lift the cover, and rip off a single match as quietly as I can. I'll have only one chance before he hears me. Please, I think. Please light.

"I won't hurt you, Libby," he says. "I promise."

I strike the match and it catches. I touch it to the others and they burst into flame. Ross spins around. He drops the gas can at his feet, which sends a spray of liquid over the ground. From his jacket he pulls the Luger. In the split second it takes him to fumble with the safety, I'm able to toss the flaming matchbook at Mitchell's gas-soaked body. There's a sudden rush of air, followed by a *whoooosh*. Mitchell goes up in flames and then, before he has a chance to fire the gun or to move, Dr. Ross, too, is bathed in fire. Flames leap from his fingertips and for a moment he just seems to stare at them as if he can't understand what's happened. He appears to look at me for just a moment, all emotion drained from his eyes save one: surprise. He drops the Luger, slaps at his body, and staggers for several steps in the direction of the lake. But he slows down and collapses on the ground. Right before the flames completely engulf him, I hear him cry once: "Holy Mother of God."

I feel only cold. Freezing cold. I push myself far enough away from the inferno, and then curl up in a ball at the base of a spruce tree, its knobby roots pressing against my back, and wait for first light.

Part 4

26

IT'S A MUGGY, summer afternoon as I drive south into Piscataquis. The sky is a cloudless blue-gray, heavy and low, the sun as flat as an egg in a frying pan. I can feel the sweat trickling down my back wetting my blouse. Heading past Lily Bay I see fishing boats out on the lake, with trolling poles angled backwards. It's a month past peak fishing, and Spotty tells me nobody's catching much of anything. The fish are deep, in cold water. The summer tourist ferry, *Mt. Katahdin,* is cruising for points north, for Kineo and the new resort they just opened up there. In town I see red-white-and-blue banners hanging across the street and wrapped around the stop signs. Flags fly in front of every store. In the window of Bidwell's Furniture there's a big sign that says, "We Support Our Operation Desert Storm Troops." And yellow ribbons circle the trees on Main Street.

I stop at the A&P to pick up some supplies for the Boston lawyer, who's arriving tomorrow for a long Fourth of July weekend. The store has a sale on geraniums, most of which look pretty pathetic, but I buy three anyway. I pick the register where Trudy McCray is working. She's been working full-time ever since Hoppy got laid off at the mill a month ago.

"Hi, Trudy," I say as she runs my groceries over the electronic scanner. "How's Hop doing?"

"Oh, that one," she says, blowing a strand of loose gray hair out of her face. "Fishing. That's all he does now. Like he was on vacation."

"Maybe he needs a break."

"I'm the one needs a break. Fifty-seven years old and here I am with these eighteen-year-olds talking about lipstick and who's picking them up after work."

"Maybe you ought to dump Hop and get yourself a young one, too."

"You know, I've got a good mind to," she says, laughing. "Couldn't you see me necking out on Corbins Point?" Trudy then looks over my shoulder even though there's nobody behind me in line. She says under her breath, which smells of Juicy Fruit and tobacco, "And how's everything with you?"

"I'm all right."

"I mean, really?"

"I am, *really*," I reply, though I know exactly what she means.

"You guys coming over to the cookout tomorrow?"

"Sure."

After I leave the A&P I head over to the post office and have Bert Osgood mail a package for me. It's Missy's baby quilt, only a year late but, like they say, better late than never.

"You want that insured, Lib?" asks Bert.

"You'd better," I say.

He tells me how much it is and as he gives me back my change he asks, "That downstate business all cleared up?"

"All cleared up," I reply.

Bert wants to ask more but I don't give him the chance. I turn and leave the post office. Outside I hear the premature explosions of firecrackers. Adolescent boys over in Brewster Park, lighting them with cigarettes and tossing them at the feet of their buddies. Cursing and laughing. The recklessness of youth.

As I pass the center of town Billy Hanson waves and I wave back. I think about stopping to fill up the truck with gas, but the last thing I want is someone else asking me if I'm all right, asking about that "downstate" business." I take a right and head for the cemetery on Ridge Road. A plane is just lifting off the lake from Souter's Fly-in Service.

*　　　*　　　*

I'd driven down to the hospital in Skowhegan. Kallick had been doing a lot better. He was out of intensive care. With crutches he was able to get up and walk down to the lounge. We looked like the walking wounded, the two of us. His head was still bandaged up and I had stitches, a black eye, one arm in a sling from where Ross had dragged me. But we were alive. After everything we were still alive. The sun was streaming through the hospital windows. Outside I could see a red maple just beginning to push out buds. I told him the whole story, too. About Leon's part, about my father knowing but covering it up all these years. I didn't hold anything back. I just let it all come out.

When I finished, he said, "I am so sorry, Frau Pelletier."

"Sorry?" I said. "For what?"

"For getting you involved in this."

"I was already involved. I just didn't want to know it."

"My only reason for coming here was to find out what happened to my brother. I only wanted to find out the truth."

"Me, too."

"Let the dead bury the dead, Frau Pelletier," he said.

"Oh," I said. "I have something for you." From my pocketbook I took out the photo of the loggers. I handed it to him and said, "I think that's your brother."

He looked at it for a while, but he said he wasn't sure. He said it might be. I told him he could have it. I had other pictures of Leon and Ambroise. We talked for a while. He said he was going to go back to Germany in a couple of days. What had brought us together was a war that had happened a long time ago and half a world away, but it had only just ended for both of us.

When I get to the cemetery I park the truck and pick up two of the plants I bought. I carry them over to the big cedar tree near the back. As I approach I see that Leon's grave has a new wooden basket filled with yellow and red tulips, their big heads swaying in the breeze. Who? I wonder. Some woman friend of Leon's?

Stephanie maybe? I get down on my hands and knees and begin pulling up weeds around the stones. The soil is poor here, sandy and dry, and weeds have the upper hand. Plus the cedar is always shedding its rust-brown needles. But it's private and I like the fragrant cedar smell. I say a prayer for Ambroise, then one for Leon.

I get back in the truck and drive Route 15 north. Past Rockwood I take a right and cross over the Moose River, heading for Brassua Lake. The logging roads are in pretty good shape now, but dusty. A taste like milk of magnesia fills my mouth. Even with the window rolled up, the dust still comes flooding into the truck. When I reach the lawyer's cabin I stop and begin to haul the bags of groceries inside. I haven't been here in months. Not since that time with Wolfgang Kallick. I go around cleaning and straightening up the place, opening the windows to let the trapped air of winter out. I put new sheets on the bed, which I know on Monday when I come back to change will smell of lovemaking.

When I finish it's only three o'clock. Roland's not expecting me till six. He's making dinner—breaded pork chops and corn on the cob—and then we're going out to see a movie. Something with Bruce Willis. I'm staying at his place in town tonight, and tomorrow we're going over to Hop and Trudy's for a Fourth cookout. Then tomorrow night we'll drive up to Rockwood for the fireworks on the lake.

When I finish getting the cabin ready, instead of heading south, back toward town, I drive northeast, toward Sheshuncook. Reaching the old Texaco sign, I take a right onto the road that heads down into Sheshuncook. I drive south until the woods thin out and I'm at the northern edge of the village. Just off the road to the right sits the old cemetery. I haven't been here in years. I pull to the side of the road and shut the truck off. Ahead of me is a parked car. A man waits behind the wheel. In the cemetery I see a woman kneeling by one of the gravestones. I get out and walk toward the back, which is bounded by the river, slow moving and quiet now that the spring thaws are well past.

When I get close to the woman, I see that she's wearing a yellow bandanna and sunglasses, a bulky green sweater though the day is warm. She's old, much older than I am. Yet her skin is smooth and her gray hair sweeps attractively down over one eye. In profile her features seem familiar to me, particularly the fullness of her old mouth, the haughty angle at which she holds her head. While I know it's impossible, a crazy thought, my heart nonetheless flutters like a sparrow with a broken wing, and one word jumps into my mind: *Her?* Could it be her? After all these years? I stop and stare at the old woman for a moment.

"Oh," she says, her hand flying to her chest when she senses me standing behind her. As soon as she turns around, though, the feeling that it could be my mother vanishes. She's just some old lady putting flowers on a grave for the Fourth of July.

"No one ever comes here," she adds, recovering. Staring up into the sunlight the skin on her face is almost transparent, like a thin layer of gauze.

"I imagine it's pretty quiet," I say. "Always was."

"You have people here?" she asks.

"Sort of."

"I know most of them here. Shaws and Klatkas and Tohays. There's a bunch of Gagnons right over there. You wouldn't be a Gagnon, would you?"

"No," I reply. "I'm a Pelletier."

"Pelletier. Some Pelletiers used to live across the cove. You any relation to them?"

"I'm Ambroise Pelletier's daughter."

"I remember an Ambroise," she says, struggling to her feet. "Tall fellow, with a dark complexion. Worked for the paper company, didn't he?"

"Yes. That was my father."

"I'm Martha Abbey."

"Abbey," I say. "Any relation to Charlie Abbey?"

"That was my uncle. He used to run a store down the road."

"I remember him. He had a glass eye."

"Yes. He's right there." She points to a stone. Most of the stones here are very old, white granite or brownstone or slate. But this one is newer. It says, "Charles Fenton Abbey, 1883–1972."

"My goodness," I say. "We used to buy bread and fishing line at his store. I don't recall you."

"I grew up right down the road. But when I got married I moved down to Portland. I come back now and then to visit. Hasn't changed much."

"No," I reply.

"Where are yours?" she asks, glancing around the cemetery.

I hesitate for a moment, then, pointing toward the river, say, "Over there."

"Didn't know there were any stones over there."

"It's kinda overgrown," I reply.

"Well, I hope this weather holds for tomorrow." The man in the car honks the horn, and the old woman says, "Wes's giving me hell. I got to go."

"Good-bye," I say.

"Good-bye." She pauses for a moment, however. Then says, "Your father used to drive a Ford Coupe. I remember now. Married a girl name of Denise, if I'm not mistaken."

"Yes," I say. "That was my mother."

"What a small world," she says.

The old woman moves over to the car, walking briskly for her age, gets in, and the car pulls off down the road toward the village.

The grass down by the water is green, and it smells of wild onions and lilacs, and something else too. The rank odor of a dead animal rotting away in secrecy. Over near the big willow tree I stop, look around. *Right here*, I think. This is where the grave markers used to be. Three of them. Plain white stone markers, with their names, and dates of birth and death, and the word *Soldat* written at the bottom. Now it's just grass.

I sit on the ground, feeling the dampness of the earth soaking through my jeans. I start a prayer, but then give it up and just sit quietly. Prayers seem out of place here. The sun's warmth bathes my shoulders, the back of my head. It feels good after the long cold winter and I'm in no rush to move, to get on with whatever's next. The water in the river moves slowly, small eddies unfolding into larger and still larger ones as they move on toward the lake. A fish, a good-sized squaretail, hits the surface. There's a flash of white underbelly and then green tail and then nothing. A tree moans softly against another, as if making love, and somewhere not too far away a loon's sad cry floats in the air like that of a lost child. I lay down, my head resting right on the moist earth, and close my eyes. I see bright red spots moving like spiders behind my eyelids. I can almost eat the warmth. I could stay like this for a long while.

Except that something comes suddenly between me and the light. A momentary shadow cutting slantwise across my face, bringing with it the faintest chill. I open my eyes to see, way up, a plane inching across the deep blue bowl of sky. It's so far up I can hardly hear its engine. I imagine whoever it is up there being able to see for miles, see all the way to New Hampshire and beyond. I picture whoever it is looking down at the earth. But if he did look down, at this small green place set beside a river, would he wonder what it was he saw on the ground? Would he think it was a rock maybe? A headstone that had fallen over? Certainly not an old woman sleeping on the grass of a graveyard on the day before the Fourth of July?

READ MORE IN PENGUIN

In every corner of the world, on every subject under the sun, Penguin represents quality and variety – the very best in publishing today.

For complete information about books available from Penguin – including Puffins, Penguin Classics and Arkana – and how to order them, write to us at the appropriate address below. Please note that for copyright reasons the selection of books varies from country to country.

In the United Kingdom: Please write to *Dept. EP, Penguin Books Ltd, Bath Road, Harmondsworth, West Drayton, Middlesex UB7 0DA*

In the United States: Please write to *Consumer Sales, Penguin USA, P.O. Box 999, Dept. 17109, Bergenfield, New Jersey 07621-0120.* VISA and MasterCard holders call 1-800-253-6476 to order Penguin titles

In Canada: Please write to *Penguin Books Canada Ltd, 10 Alcorn Avenue, Suite 300, Toronto, Ontario M4V 3B2*

In Australia: Please write to *Penguin Books Australia Ltd, P.O. Box 257, Ringwood, Victoria 3134*

In New Zealand: Please write to *Penguin Books (NZ) Ltd, Private Bag 102902, North Shore Mail Centre, Auckland 10*

In India: Please write to *Penguin Books India Pvt Ltd, 706 Eros Apartments, 56 Nehru Place, New Delhi 110 019*

In the Netherlands: Please write to *Penguin Books Netherlands bv, Postbus 3507, NL-1001 AH Amsterdam*

In Germany: Please write to *Penguin Books Deutschland GmbH, Metzlerstrasse 26, 60594 Frankfurt am Main*

In Spain: Please write to *Penguin Books S. A., Bravo Murillo 19, 1° B, 28015 Madrid*

In Italy: Please write to *Penguin Italia s.r.l., Via Felice Casati 20, I–20124 Milano*

In France: Please write to *Penguin France S. A., 17 rue Lejeune, F–31000 Toulouse*

In Japan: Please write to *Penguin Books Japan, Ishikiribashi Building, 2–5–4, Suido, Bunkyo-ku, Tokyo 112*

In South Africa: Please write to *Longman Penguin Southern Africa (Pty) Ltd, Private Bag X08, Bertsham 2013*

READ MORE IN PENGUIN

A CHOICE OF FICTION

The Ghost Road Pat Barker
Winner of the 1995 Booker Prize

'One of the richest and most rewarding works of fiction of recent times. Intricately plotted, beautifully written, skilfully assembled, tender, horrifying and funny, it lives on in the imagination, like the war it so imaginatively and so intelligently explores' – *The Times Literary Supplement*

None to Accompany Me Nadine Gordimer

In an extraordinary period before the first non-racial elections in South Africa, Vera Stark, a lawyer representing blacks' struggle to reclaim the land, weaves an interpretation of her own past into her participation in the present. 'With great dexterity and force Gordimer combines all these stories – career, colleagues, political struggles, sexual love, identity, family – into a compelling narrative' – *Daily Telegraph*

Of Love and Other Demons Gabriel García Márquez

'García Márquez tells a story of forbidden love, but he demonstrates once again the vigor of his own passion: the daring and irresistible coupling of history and imagination' – *Time*. 'A further marvellous manifestation of the enchantment and the disenchantment that his native Colombia always stirs in García Márquez' – *Sunday Times*

Millroy the Magician Paul Theroux

A magician of baffling talents, a vegetarian and a health fanatic with a mission to change the food habits of America, Millroy has the power to heal, and to hypnotize. 'Fresh and unexpected . . . this very accomplished, confident book is among his best' – *Guardian*

English Music Peter Ackroyd

'Each dream-sequence is a virtuoso performance on Ackroyd's part. In his fiction he has made a speciality of leap-frogging time, so that the past occupies the same plane as the present. Never before, however, has he been so chronologically acrobatic, nor so confident' – *The Times*